two gentlemen
sharing

two gentlemen
sharing

william
corlett

alyson books
los angeles | new york

MANUFACTURED IN THE UNITED STATES OF AMERICA.
COVER DESIGN BY CHRISTOPHER HARRITY.

THIS TRADE PAPERBACK IS PUBLISHED BY ALYSON PUBLICATIONS,
P.O. BOX 4371, LOS ANGELES, CALIFORNIA 90078-4371.

FIRST EDITION PUBLISHED BY LITTLE, BROWN AND COMPANY (UK): 1997
FIRST ALYSON BOOKS EDITION: OCTOBER 1999

99 00 01 02 03 **a** 10 9 8 7 6 5 4 3 2 1

ISBN 1-55583-527-9
(PREVIOUSLY PUBLISHED WITH ISBN 0-316-88170-8 BY LITTLE, BROWN
AND COMPANY.)

LIBRARY OF CONGRESS CATALOGING-IN-PUBLICATION DATA
 CORLETT, WILLIAM.
  TWO GENTLEMEN SHARING / WILLIAM CORLETT.—1ST ALYSON
 BOOKS EDITION.
  ISBN 1-55583-527-9
  I. TITLE.
 PR6053.07T86 1999
 823'.914—DC21   99-39914 CIP

COVER ILLUSTRATION BY JULIANNA PARR.

For
SIÂN
who read this first,
in Florence

Contents

1

At Mrs Sugar's

'Have you heard, my dears? The Hall House is sold at last.' Mrs Sugar was slicing ham with studied concentration as she made this announcement. The recipient of the meat, a woman with a distant, distracted expression and clothes to match, was more intent on the carving than on the speaker but the other customers crowded into the little shop all responded with satisfying interest.

'Really, Mrs Sugar?' exclaimed a woman in jodhpurs and tweed hacking jacket. 'Do we know who?'

'I'm sorry, Mrs Daltry, that I have so far not been able to ascertain,' Mrs Sugar replied with the carefully assumed vowels she saved for her favoured customers. 'My informant, Miss Briggs at Lashams,' the local estate agent, 'seemed to think that the purchaser was a gentleman from London.'

'Oh Lor! Not another commuter?' Heather Daltry groaned. 'The village is becoming nothing more than a dormitory. One can scarcely breathe for exhaust fumes between six thirty and eight, morning and evening.'

Meanwhile the woman at the counter was trying to catch the carver's attention.

'That's more than enough,' she said in an agitated voice.

'I'll just give you this one delicious slice, my dear,' Mrs Sugar told her, cutting it extra thick. 'The Brigadier will come back for more tonight, Mrs Jerrold, I'll be bound. Like Oliver Twist he'll be. And no wonder! My ham is the talk of the county on account of the secret ingredient I put in the water.' As she spoke she was now wrapping the meat in greaseproof paper. Then laying the little parcel on the scales she gave them a sharp rap with her clenched fist. 'Drat these scales! They stick, you know.'

Heather Daltry turned and raised her eyes in a way loaded with meaning. The slender woman in a flowing cloak standing behind her frowned.

'You should have them checked, Mrs Sugar,' she announced, making a statement, rather than a suggestion.

'I've had them checked, Mrs Simpson,' Mrs Sugar replied indignantly. 'A man from the ministry came himself.'

'It's Ms,' Diana Simpson said, impatiently. 'I've told you that before.'

'Yes,' Mrs Sugar agreed, wiping her hands on her overall skirt, 'I dare say as it is, but not round here, dear. That's all a bit too newfangled for us locals. We're simple folk with simple ways. There's Miss and Mrs and sin in between. And that's all we know about it.' Then, without pausing for breath or any rejoinder, she continued: 'And would that be all, Mrs Jerrold, or can I interest you in a nice tart? There's my Bramley apple or a sweet plum jam. Made this morning. Fresh and full of goodness.'

'Oh, no thank you. The Brigadier is a slave to indigestion. Pastry is particularly fatal for him.'

'But not my pastry,' Mrs Sugar said in a peeved tone, and producing a stub of pencil from behind her ear she started to add up a column of figures on a pad in front of her.

'She should get a proper till,' the woman at the back of the queue observed to no one in particular as she glanced at her watch.

'You newcomers from town are always in too much of an 'urry,' the old man in front of her muttered.

'Really, Tom. We have lived at Pinchings for twelve years, which scarcely makes us newcomers, and I personally have not lived in a town since I was up at Oxford . . . which is more years ago than I care to consider,' the woman added, pulling at the collar of her gabardine and glaring at the man.

'Be that as it may, Miss Hopkirk. But I well remember my old dad saying: "Town and country they never should mix. Town's full of vermin and land's full of ticks."'

The other customers looked suitably bemused by this and the woman to whom the remark was addressed shook her head as if in despair.

'I am Miss Fallon, Tom. How many times must I tell you?'

'Proves my point,' the old man muttered. 'You newcomers all look alike to me.'

Miss Fallon shrugged irritably. 'It is really quite easy to distinguish us. Miss Hopkirk is the short one. Miss Bridey has the fuller figure. And I am the tall one with glasses.'

Tom, whom it would seem was not to be dignified by any other name, glowered up at her from under furrowed brows. 'There's tall and tall,' he told her in the voice of a seer. 'I'd have to set you all next each other to know what was and what wasn't.' Then turning once more to face the counter, he raised his voice petulantly. 'Oh, get a move on, Bessie Sugar, you great besom. I could have sired a football team while I've been stood here.'

'Not with my help!' Heather Daltry whispered, making Diana Simpson look away, for fear of betraying her feminist principles.

Meanwhile Mrs Sugar had completed her sum and now slipped the paper across the counter for the Brigadier's wife to check.

'If you give me a ten-pound note, dear, I'll put the change towards the Christmas club for you.'

'Oh, no. I don't think so,' Rosemary Jerrold said, staring short-sightedly at the sum and then rooting in her purse for the correct money. 'The Brigadier would find that most odd when doing the accounts.'

'Odd, dear?'

'He would think March a little early in the year to be saving for Christmas.'

'Soonest started, soonest mended,' Mrs Sugar opined, as if her words had some dark meaning beyond the understanding of mere mortals.

'Yes,' Mrs Jerrold said doubtfully. 'I dare say you're right. But is there any guarantee that we will be here next Christmas? And what will become of the money if we are not?' As she spoke she was putting her purchases into her basket. Then nodding and smiling she edged her way past the queue, murmuring, 'Thank you so much. Excuse me. Goodbye. Thank you. I'm so sorry. Thank you.' Until, reaching the door, she called out one last 'Goodbye!' as she escaped with relief to the street.

It was a raw day with a keen little wind blowing in from the coast that felt as if it had started its journey somewhere just north of the Russian steppes. Mrs Jerrold pulled her coat closer round her and turned down the hill towards the green.

The village of Bellingford had begun as a cluster of cottages where three lanes met and had prospered and grown from the latter days of the first Elizabeth until some time during the reign of the third George, when the gentry had abandoned it for the comforts of the expanding town of Fairlow, five miles away. The dwellings round the green were for the most part thatched, half-timbered cottages, with a few more imposing houses built in a mellow red brick. A scattering of later Victorian and Edwardian villas had been introduced when a new rich sought once more the fresher air and quieter ways of country life.

Out of sight of the green a small council estate had been added during the sixties, and later still a garage and filling station had arrived. The property boom of the eighties had also paid a visit, and at the other end of the village, beyond the shop, on land that had once been a gentle meadow with a view for miles across open farmland, there was now a group of doubtful mock-timbered residences, with bright-red roofs and leaded windows. At the entrance to this suburban ghetto stood

a seemingly permanent billboard which read: 'Tudor Drive –
Executive homes for the discerning buyer'. To which an
unknown graffiti artist had later added in red paint, the letters
now fading with time: 'Ban cruel sports' – as though the writer
was acquainted with some special nefarious pastime indulged in
by the executive residents.

The village also boasted a part-Norman church – St Michael
and all the Angels; a pub – the Hart at Rest; a village hall – with
a stage for dramatics and enough space for flower shows, art
exhibitions and occasional village meetings; Sugar's General
Store – 'cooked ham to a secret recipe always in stock'; and an
antiques shop – which was invariably closed.

Undoubtedly the finest building in Bellingford was the Hall
House. This small Queen Anne gem stood to one side of the
green with a narrow garden in front just wide enough to permit
a semicircle of drive from the pair of imposing gates that
pierced its iron railings bordering the road. This drive swept up
to a hooded portico and then continued round the side of the
house to end with a flourish in a yard surrounded by stables
and outhouses.

Behind the property a broad terrace gave access by a flight of
shallow steps to several acres of cultivated grounds and wood-
land. These woods eventually petered out at a perimeter fence
beyond which farmland rolled, dotted with trees and the occasional dilapidated barn. Nearer to the house the grounds were
laid out with lawns and borders, a walled vegetable garden and
many fine specimen trees, including willow and magnolia and
dipping cedars where rooks nested in the spring. There was also
the added delight of a splashing stream that cut through the
woods, skirted the lawns and wound through a shrubby wilderness before disappearing from sight into a tunnel. It then briefly
emerged in the next-door garden, where it formed a small and
dreary pond before passing on to dissect the village green and
ford a narrow lane – the eponymous Belling Ford.

Mrs Jerrold's way home passed in front of the Hall House.
Cockpits, the house she had occupied with her husband the

Brigadier since he had retired from the regiment fifteen years before, lay just beyond it, where the land began to rise towards the church. (It was here that the stream surfaced before crossing the green.) Indeed the gardens of Cockpits shared a communal brick wall with the grounds of the Hall. Thus the Jerrolds would be the immediate neighbours of the newcomers at the Hall – although neighbourliness was sadly not a human attribute which the Brigadier had been blessed with at birth. Nor was it one that he had encouraged his good wife to nurture since she had joined him in the state of matrimony – if not of love – forty years before.

So it happened that on this raw March day it was the Brigadier's wife who became the first person in the village to see one of the future occupants of that lovely house. She was passing the gates when what appeared to be a slim youth in jeans and a leather jerkin came out of the front door and ran down the steps to the BMW parked on the drive. As he did so he looked over his shoulder and shouted:

'Rich! We're going to live here, you know! It's meant to be a home. Not a set for the end of Act Two, for fuck's sake!'

Then, as he opened the boot of the car and produced a bulging briefcase, he caught sight of the elderly woman in her beige coat staring at him through the railings, her mouth slightly open with surprise and an expression of dismay.

'Oops!' he exclaimed. 'Pardonez-moi!' and dropping her a deep curtsy he slammed the boot and retreated once more into the seclusion of the house.

'Oh dear!' Mrs Jerrold gasped. Then she frowned and shook her head. 'Oh dear me,' she whispered. 'The Brigadier won't like this one little bit.'

2

'Fresh Woods . . .'

Two men observed this scene on the drive from one of the front windows on the ground floor of the Hall House. The first was aged above sixty and was probably closer to seventy – though he never spoke of the matter even to himself. He was tall, slim and distinguished. The only obvious concession to vanity was his silver hair, which was carefully combed across a balding patch on the crown. His rather conservative dress – a dark overcoat covering a pinstripe suit – gave him the appearance of an MP or a Harley Street doctor.

His companion in contrast looked younger than his years. He was in fact in his mid forties but could have passed, lit from below and with a smudge on the lens, for early thirties. His was an infinitely more glamorous wardrobe – casual but expensive. The thick multicoloured sweater had been designed in Italy, the pale cream T-shirt in France, the well-cut jeans and high boots in America – and if there were any doubts about the authenticity of these garments, each had a label to prove it. His dark hair was cut fashionably short and his face, with a surprisingly tanned complexion for so early in an English spring, was unmarked apart from smile lines round the mouth and the hint of a frown.

The older man was holding a clipboard on which he had been entering notes before the distraction outside had brought them both to the window. 'Oh dear!' he winced, as the curtsy was dropped and the beige woman's reaction was witnessed. 'That sort of behaviour isn't going to endear you to the natives.'

'Oh, please! Bless!' his companion groaned.

'The child must be told.'

'Yes. But not by you, Laurence. So just keep out of it, will you?'

'I shan't say a word!'

The front door slammed again and a voice was heard calling: 'Rich?'

'We're in here.'

The boy entered, carrying the briefcase.

'The first native has been sighted. I think she heard me say "fuck" but they probably don't speak the language. So what's been decided?'

'This will be my study,' Rich replied.

'Study? And what are you going to study in your study?'

'All right then – office.'

'You mean you're going to bring work home? I thought you said that the weekends would be for us.'

'Perhaps Richard means a place for him to escape to.'

'From whom?'

'Life! We all need somewhere that we can call our own. You after all are having the entire attic.'

'As a studio and workroom, Laurence. I will be running a business here. Rich is going to be in London all week.'

'What else are we going to use this room for?' Rich asked, irritably. 'We've so many fucking rooms we'll get lost if we don't at least give them a name.'

'You don't like it here,' Bless sighed, making a statement.

'I love it. But there are nine bedrooms!'

'So?'

'What are we going to do with nine bedrooms?'

'Make them into five and four bathrooms. I thought we'd

covered that. You should have looked at the place properly before you bought.'

'I don't have the time, Bless. I am in the middle of two productions . . .'

'Oh, God! Here comes ulcer number three.'

'I'm serious . . .'

'I know. So am I.' Bless dropped the briefcase on the floor and walked across to the fireplace with his hands in his pockets. He stared at the floor, sighed and then said all on one breath: 'I knew it. It's all a ghastly mistake. We shouldn't have bought this place. It's my fault. I got carried away.'

Rich took one look at his crestfallen face, then crossed and put an arm round him.

'You love it?'

Bless nodded, then looked at him with his head on one side. 'Actually it's you that I love,' he said. 'This is more somewhere to live . . . To live with you.'

'I'll go upstairs and do some measuring,' Laurence said, walking towards the door with exaggerated stealth.

'It's all right, Laurence. You're quite safe. I'm not going to rip his clothes off.'

Laurence stared coldly at the boy.

'And this room . . .?' he asked in a haughty, obviously disapproving tone.

Bless grinned and kissed Rich on the cheek. 'This is his study!'

'Yes, oh lord and master,' Laurence said sourly, and he made a note on his clipboard before going out of the room.

'Oh shit! Is he going to disapprove of me for ever?'

'He takes his time getting to know people,' Rich said, holding him from behind and snuggling into his body.

'But – he doesn't have to, does he? Get to know me, I mean.'

'Laurence is my oldest friend, Bless.'

'Yes, yes! You told me! But you have a live-in lover now.'

'Let's go and look at the drawing room again.' Taking his hand, Rich pulled him out of the room and across the hall towards the back of the house.

'I am, aren't I?' the boy said, following him.

'What?'

'Your lover now.' He said the words with exaggerated deliberation.

'What do you think?'

'I think you're quite difficult to get to know yourself,' Bless replied gravely. Then he grinned. 'But I'm prepared to give it my best shot.'

They looked at each other from across the room. Then Rich smiled. 'He's actually a very good architect. We're lucky to have him.'

'Don't – please!' Bless exclaimed.

'What?'

'Treat me like a retarded child. Laurence is not here because he's a good architect. We don't even need an architect. I could do a plan of what's required on the back of an envelope while cooking a risotto. He's only here because you don't want to hurt his feelings . . .'

'Keep your voice down.'

'And the reason his feelings could be hurt is he thinks he owns you.'

'Bless – shut up!'

'Where are you going to be living Monday through Thursday?'

This was now turning into an ancient argument.

'At my flat,' Rich replied. '*My* flat, Bless. Mine.'

'Your flat that I have never once set foot in the whole one year, two months and seventeen days that we have . . . what is the politically correct description for what we've been doing?'

'Fucking,' Rich replied crossly.

'Oh, really? And I actually thought we meant more than that.'

'Oh! For shit's sake!'

'Well – why did we never fuck, Rich dear – as you so sweetly call it – in your luxury penthouse apartment? Will you tell me that.'

'Because it is also Laurence's home. And we have always had an agreement . . .'

'Not to drag home your little bits of stuff. I know, I know.'

There was an awkward silence. Upstairs they could hear Laurence pacing out measurements and moving from room to room. Rich took a deep breath, maybe to steady himself or more likely to control his temper. Bless walked away, ashamed of his behaviour and annoyed with himself for allowing Laurence's presence to affect him so.

'Sorry,' he said at last, staring out of one of the long windows at the terrace and the gardens beyond.

'I *am* buying a house for you,' Rich exclaimed, his voice a mixture of irritation and pleading.

'I thought it was for us.'

'Bless!' his friend pleaded. 'You know what I mean.'

'Yes.' Bless nodded. 'It's just . . . Why do I feel like a kept woman?'

'Because that's what you are!' Rich said, crossing and giving him a hug. Then he groaned. 'What'll we do with all that land?' he said, looking out at the rolling acres.

'Do we need to do anything?'

'Yes!'

'What?'

'I don't know. All those things Percy Thrower used to tell us on *Blue Peter*. Digging and pruning and . . . I don't know, that's what I'm saying. I've never dug a trench in my life.'

'You make it sound like the Somme.'

'It might just as well be. It has to be controlled – nature. You have to show it who's boss. Otherwise it . . . takes over.'

He shuddered and walked away, but Bless stared at the view with renewed interest. 'It actually looks surprisingly neat – considering the place has been empty. Maybe it does itself?'

'You mean it's all astroturf and polystyrene trees? Sorry! That there is the real thing – not panto time at the Grand, Wolverhampton.' And then he couldn't resist adding, 'Any more than my study is a set for the end of Act Two.'

'Touché.'

'Which play, by the way?'

'*The Murder of Roger Ackroyd*!' Bless said with a shudder. Then he shrugged. 'It was Laurence, he was winding me up.'

'You shouldn't let him. Oh – and . . . the curtsy . . .'

Bless groaned. 'Mistake?'

Rich nodded. 'Big!' He grinned. 'You have to be butch in the country.'

'Oh, dearie, dearie me! That means both of us, heart. You don't actually look a son of the soil yourself.'

'I don't? Why?'

'The Missoni and Saint Laurent? They'll have to go. Plus fours and a Barbour, I think, don't you?'

'Mmmh!' Rich purred. 'I might quite like that.' And crossing to him he put his hands on Bless's waist.

'Richard, behave yourself! Laurence is upstairs. What were we talking about?'

'The garden.'

'Oh, yes!' Bless said, turning once more to look out of the window. 'Seriously, it does seem surprisingly neat.'

'Only because the family kept on a gardener while they haggled over the will. The agent persuaded them that the grounds were a big selling point.'

'Mmmh.' Bless nodded, now deep in thought.

'Do you actually know anything about gardens?'

'God, yes! Flowers grow in them. The smell of new-mown grass . . . and wheelbarrows and watering cans and . . . Roses. And . . . well, I'm not good on names – but I expect I can learn. Then there's . . . weeding and . . . You have to do a lot of planting as well. You put the dirty end in the soil. I know loads about gardens.'

'We'd better keep on the gardener.'

'Only until I have mastered the art,' Bless said, moving away, still staring thoughtfully out at the grey and dismal day. 'If I am coming to live here, then that means really live. I don't intend to behave like a refugee. I shall become part of the community.'

'How?'

'I don't know.' Bless shrugged. 'How does one . . . integrate? Is that the right word?'

'Sounds good to me!' Rich said with a grin.

'You wait. I'll show you. I'm going to get to know the entire village. I shall organise things and we'll give garden parties and . . . What does one do in the country?'

'Country pleasures.'

'Don't be crude, Rich. We are the lords of the manor now. We must act accordingly.'

'Won't there be any country pleasures?' Rich sounded disappointed.

'Of course there will. Are you mad? We'll probably do it out in the street where we can be sure of frightening the horses. I may be going to integrate – but I'm certainly not giving up being me.'

'Thank God for that,' Rich sighed.

'God, honey, has very little to do with it!' Bless reassured him, with a Mae West bump and a hand on his zip. And the Hall House, Bellingford, would have been christened there and then in the drawing room if Laurence hadn't come in brandishing a tape measure and a look of reproof.

'I'm cold,' he said. 'Let's get back to London and civilisation.'

3

'. . . And Pastures Green'

Maggie Heston poured wine into two glasses as Bless came into the room, towelling his hair. 'Drink,' she said.

'Yes, ma'am!' He bowed obediently. Then, shivering, he crouched down in front of the gas fire and held his hands towards it, burning his bare knees where they protruded from his dressing gown.

'Are you naked under there?' Maggie asked, opening a bag of Kettle Chips and taking a handful into her mouth.

'Keep your distance, Heston. One false move and I'll have you for sexual harassment.'

'You're kidding. If I set my mind to it you wouldn't stand a chance.' She chopped the air with the side of her hand. 'Kerpow! And you're flat on your back, pleading for mercy.' Then she sighed and took another scoop of crisps. 'Don't worry – you're quite safe. I've given up sex. It does my head in.'

'That's because you fall for nerds and psychopaths.'

She nodded emphatically. 'True! Whereas you . . .?'

'Whatever you may think of Rich, he's not a nerd.'

'And as for being a psychopath – you have to know someone for ages before you find out the real person.'

'I have known him for ages.'

'A year!'

'*And* a bit.'

'Oh, a lifetime!'

'Listen! The longest I spent with a lover prior to this was eighteen days.' He shuddered. 'And that was horrendous.'

'He *was* a psychopath.'

'You could say!'

Maggie crunched energetically. 'I'm telling you. I was the one who had to pick up your poor wounded body, remember.'

'Well – what are friends for?' He shook his head, letting his long straight hair fan out behind him.

Maggie looked at him over the rim of her glass and decided to say nothing more on the subject of Richard Charteris – for the time being at least. Then putting the glass down she ran her hands through her own thin, short hair, as if checking to see that it was still on her head. 'It isn't fair.'

'Now what?' Bless asked, stretching.

'Your hair.'

'The one thing it is is fair.'

'No! I mean it isn't fair that you've a luxuriant thatch of honey blond while my hair is mousy – and goddamn thin . . .'

'This is not honey – it's a natural auburn. Which is bad news, actually. I read somewhere that the lighter the follicles the shorter their life. I'll be lucky if I'm not bald by the time I'm thirty.' He winced, realising he'd strayed on to dangerous ground. Maggie's hair was not her best feature. It was thin and nondescript and she, quite rightly in his opinion, had a terrible complex about it. He therefore quickly and deftly changed the subject. 'Shit!' he groaned. 'I will one day be thirty!'

'Excuse me! Not for another three years,' Maggie exclaimed, brushing aside his unreasonable angst. 'Go on then,' she continued, slipping off her shoes, 'tell me about the day.'

'What about it?'

'How did it go?'

There was a pause as Bless hitched himself up, leaning on one elbow, and stared into the fire.

'Laurence came with us.'

While Maggie digested this piece of information she leaned forward and took another handful of crisps. Then when it became clear that he wasn't going to add anything to this apparently loaded statement, she threw the packet across to him.

'Do you know how many calories there are . . .?'

'Oh, please! You need your strength. You're a growing boy.'

'That's the problem,' he said, filling his mouth and crunching.

Maggie stared at him, then she shrugged. She was now considering the 'What the hell? I'm his best friend. What are best friends for' scenario, and said: 'Why are you doing this, Bless?'

'Sorry. Am I hogging the fire?'

'No! I mean – why are you leaving London? Why are you going to bury yourself in the middle of the country? Why?'

'Love.'

'Shit!' Then she shrugged and nodded. 'I know you love him. But wouldn't it be wiser, safer even, to start off somewhere semi-rural, like Barnes or – oh God, I don't know – Hampstead is disgustingly bosky.'

'Hampstead? Are you crazy?'

'I agree it isn't exactly the heartbeat of the metropolis but people do live there, you know.'

'That is precisely the point. Rich's flat is in Hampstead. Laurence is in Hampstead.'

'Then tell him to give bloody Laurence the flat. He can afford it, can't he? He's Rich by name, Rich by nature.'

'He says if we were living somewhere down the road . . . Laurence would feel rejected.'

'But he is rejected.' A new and awful thought. 'He is, isn't he? I mean, they're not still screwing?'

'I don't think they ever screwed. Anyway, not for years.'

'Says who?'

'Please! You've never even seen Laurence. I promise you they're not sleeping together. No one could be screwing Laurence. They could never get close enough. He wears gloves when he shakes hands.'

Maggie shrugged. 'An extreme form of safe sex?' Getting no response, she reached across and grabbed the bag of crisps off the floor. Then hooking a leg over the arm of the sofa she swung her foot backwards and forwards and munched moodily.

'You'll get fat . . .'

'Don't you dare say that. Not now . . .'

'Why? What's so special about now?'

'I am in a state of shock.'

Bless frowned. There were times when conversation with Maggie was like the mating of the spiny porcupine – all spikes and no respite. This new state of shock had him nonplussed.

'Why are you in a state of shock, Maggie?' he asked, deciding to try the reasonable approach.

She looked at him for a moment longer, then got up from the sofa, crumpling the packet and dropping it in a waste-paper basket as she crossed to the window. She sighed, and stared down into the street.

'Mags?' Bless said, watching with mounting concern. 'What is it? You're not ill, are you?'

'No,' she answered, keeping her back to him. 'I'm not ill.'

'What then?'

'I don't want you to go away.'

'Oh, for heaven's sake! We'll be fifty miles down a motorway. We're not going to Siberia.'

'You say "we" all the time now.' As she spoke, she turned slowly and looked at him. Then she smiled. Bless supported his head on his hand and returned the look. She was wearing tight black pants and a sloppy T-shirt that billowed over her big, firm breasts. The problem hair was ringed by light from the window, her face was in semi-darkness.

'You're missing your nerds and psychopaths, that's your trouble,' he said.

'No. I'm facing up to the fact that I'm going to be missing you.'

'Mags . . .'

'So – OK. If you want to bury yourself . . .'

'I love him, Mags.'

She walked over to the coffee table, picked up the bottle of wine and replenished her glass. She didn't offer to fill his.

'Besides, it'll be months before we can actually move down to Bellingford. You know what builders are like.'

'Then why the hell did you give up your flat?'

'I had to give a month's notice. I'm in the way here?'

'Of course not. You can stay as long as you like. If I suddenly and unexpectedly become involved with a fabulous Italian count – then you'll have to go. I don't think I'd trust you with a fabulous Italian count!'

'Fear not,' Bless assured her, stretching out again and sighing with contentment, 'my count has come.'

'Not an easy line for a school matinée.' They giggled, and Maggie returned to the sofa. 'What are you going to live on in the depths of the country?'

'Not Rich – if that's what you're suggesting.'

'I'm not suggesting anything. I'm merely enquiring.'

'Bharnhoff Knitwear.'

'Bless – please!'

'What?'

'You've so far had a commission for one sweater design. It's brought you in – how much?'

'They paid me three hundred pounds. And,' he raised his hands, stopping her in mid breath, 'before you point out that that isn't exactly going to keep me, admit it is a start, Mags.'

'It may also be an end.'

'I have an agent.'

'Terrific. So you give away money in commission as well!'

'If she gets me the jobs, I'll gladly pay the commission.'

'If!'

'I'm still in good nick. I could get modelling work.'

'The neighbours are really going to love seeing the young squire plastered all over their colour supplements advertising slimline tonic.'

'Slimline tonic! I wish! Have you any idea how much I'd earn if I was contracted to Schweppes? Jesus! I could keep Rich.'

'Hardly, darling. He's worth millions.'

'Which is *not* why I am going to live with him.'

'I know. It's his dick you're going to live with. But who is going to pay for your Y-fronts and toothpaste?'

'*I am.*'

'*How?*'

'By the sweat of my fucking brow!'

Maggie nodded. 'That's what I said. He's just paying you for sex. He's going to keep you.'

'You're determined to be against this, aren't you?' Bless asked glumly. And then he got angry. 'You're just like everyone else, Mags. Because we're two men you make it all improbable and impossible.'

'Bullshit.'

'Yes, you do. In your mind, you do. If we were a man and a woman – would you ask me all these probing questions? Of course you wouldn't. But I am a man – and so is Rich. And we have decided to live together. Not in anonymity in Barons Court but in a beautiful house in a beautiful village in the beautiful English countryside. Now – what we are doing is legal. It isn't even novel . . . So what is it that you're objecting to?'

Maggie lifted her hand in a dramatic gesture of anguish. 'The sky is filled with flames, Bless.'

'Oh, God! We've got to the trance stage!'

Maggie gasped and gagged. 'I'm choking on the smoke,' she hammed. But this sudden exhibition of Grand Guignol had little effect on Bless, who merely combed his hair with his fingers and took another swig of wine.

'Maggie, sweetheart,' he murmured, getting suddenly interested in a scratch on his arm, 'just try to hold on to reality, will you? Tell yourself your hair will grow . . . You will meet an Italian count . . . You will go to the ball.' He looked up at her and smiled sweetly. 'And finally believe that all your babies will come out head first, laughing and smelling of grass . . .'

'You think I want them arrested? And don't change the

subject. You know where the smoke is coming from, Bless? You know what the flames are? You know what the ash is that flutters down around us . . .' She mimed the fluttering and was really warming to the performance.

'The sooner you get another job the better,' Bless groaned. 'You're dramatically deprived.'

'All your burning bridges . . .'

'I'm going to put some clothes on,' he said, getting up and crossing to the door. Then he added: 'I may be gone some time,' with Oatesian significance.

'All your burning bridges, Bless.' Maggie jabbed a finger at him. 'You've done it this time. There's no turning back.'

'Fresh woods, Mags!' he said, going out of the room. 'And pastures green,' he called as he crossed the hall to her spare bedroom, which had become temporarily his room in town. At least until the Hall House was ready. After that, who knew what would happen? He might never see London again . . . And catching sight of his reflection in the mirror over the chest of drawers, he frowned. She's right, he thought. No turning back now. Then, holding his hair at the nape of his neck, he slipped on an elastic band to secure the ponytail and grinned. 'Poor bald bitch!' he called. 'You're the one who's jealous.'

'Go plant potatoes!' came the answering cry.

'I might just do that. We do have an enormous garden.' Then, lowering his voice, he whispered to his reflection in the glass: 'Fresh woods and pastures green!'

4

News From Doris Day

Contrary to the poet's observation, April was not the cruellest month that year. It was in fact extremely well behaved. The showers came at night and the days were sun-dappled with enough warmth to persuade all but the most pessimistic to leave off their coats and loosen their collars.

In Bellingford the gardens responded in a symphony of stippled greens, yellows and creams, and the muddy yard at Martin's Farm could truly be said to be busy, in a regular tizzy. Meanwhile . . .

'How I tried to pick a daffodil . . .' Doris Day warbled as she cleaned the inside of the drawing-room windows at Cockpits. Her grasp of the words was minimal, though the tune was usually recognisable. Doris had made her famous namesake's repertoire her own over the years and she was never without a song to suit the occasion. Today she was in a good mood – due more to the fact that the Brigadier was out than to the sun on the garden. Mrs Day – few now called her Doris – had been cleaning at Cockpits since the Jerrolds had arrived there, and in all that time she had scarcely exchanged more than a few brief platitudes with the Brigadier: a curt 'Good morning' as he passed her in the hall, a hurried 'Excuse me!' if she happened to find him unexpectedly in a room. It was not that Mrs Day was particularly afraid of him, nor could it be said that the Brigadier had the slightest regard for her. They were simply people from totally different backgrounds who had never been intended to mix and were not going to start now, so late in both their lives.

Mrs Day was local, born and bred. Her husband Stan had driven a team of carthorses at Martin's Farm before the advent of the tractor. He'd been taken by the flu not long after VE night and committed to permanent rest near a yew tree in the graveyard of St Michael and all the Angels where it was intended that his wife would one day join him. She, meanwhile, left with a brood of children to support in a changing world, had managed as best she could working on the land and seeing each of her offspring out of the house and into employment as soon as they reached fifteen. All but one of them had long since left the village. They and their families were now scattered the length and breadth of the globe, from Adelaide to Alberta.

The exception was Alec, Doris's youngest, the baby of the family. He was now in his fifties and worked for Partridge, the local builder, doing odd jobs. He was not what one would call skilled. But he could knock down a wall or do a bit of plastering so long as it wasn't in too prominent a position. His work was slow and his finish rough – which might explain why his wife, Jeannie, had run off with a window cleaner more than twenty years before, taking the twins and all the savings with her.

At the time Alec had feigned surprise and even a sort of distress. He had naturally gone home to his mother for succour, and once under her roof he'd heaved a sigh of relief and remained there ever since. Mrs Day was by then living in one of the council houses up on the estate, and really from the moment Alec arrived his quality of life improved dramatically. His food was cooked for him, his clothes were washed and ironed for him, even his shoes were polished for him. But although the provision of such creature comforts made a pleasant change from the chaotic home life that his wife had offered, it was the peace of mind that he now experienced that really appealed to him. Alec had never been cut out to be a husband and father, and from the moment of their departure he hadn't given another thought to any of his renegade family.

As for Doris, the arrangement suited her well. Alec brought in a small wage, he paid half the rent and housekeeping, and she was saved from having to spend much time with him by the simple expedient of his going out each evening to the public bar of the Hart at Rest, where he played darts and dominoes with his few cronies, while drinking innumerable pints of gut-rotting cider from the barrel. He would then weave his way home and fall into bed sozzled and satisfied to prepare himself for another day spent in an identical manner to the one just past. He and his mother rarely conversed, and when they did it was in short, monosyllabic sentences delivered without any eye contact and very often from separate rooms.

But once in a while Alec got hold of a piece of gossip, and when he did, his mother was the first to know.

'. . . And my special friend's not special any more . . .' Mrs Day trilled, spitting on a window pane and rubbing hard to remove a stubborn streak. Then she stood back, admiring her handiwork, and watched the Brigadier's wife walk across the lawn towards the house, carrying a few twigs of flowering blossom. As she saw her, the older woman – for Doris must have been well into her seventies even if she had started producing her brood when scarcely herself out of nappies – smiled. It was a surprisingly malevolent expression; the look of someone who has bad news to impart and is biding her time in order to choose the most effective moment to do so. Picking up her cleaning things, she hurried out of the room and headed for the kitchen.

Rosemary Jerrold was filling a bucket at the sink.

'Lovely blossom,' Mrs Day opined, darting into the room. She was a thin, wiry woman and her movements were quick and darting – like a mouse or an insect. In fact it was an insect that she most resembled. She had the angular, lop-sided gait of a praying mantis. Her arrival now made Mrs Jerrold jump, splashing water from the bucket.

'Oh! Mrs Day! I didn't hear you enter.'

'Your nerves, dear! You need a tonic.'

'This sunshine is tonic enough.'

'Yes, dear. You've been in the garden.' Mrs Day had a habit of stating the obvious. 'Lovely blossom!' she cooed. 'Lovely, lovely blossom. I love lovely blossom.'

'Yes. It's for the church, of course. The Brigadier does not care for cut flowers in the house.'

'And why is that, dear?' Mrs Day enquired, putting a light under the kettle on the gas stove.

'I think because he was so often on manoeuvres. There was no opportunity for the niceties of decoration in the close confines of a tent. Consequently the Brigadier does not now care for anything too decorated. He takes it as a sign of weakness. We have always lived a plain, simple life. You are boiling a kettle, Mrs Day?'

'I am, my dear. That's right. Time for elevenses. A nice cup of tea.'

'Good gracious, I feel you have only just arrived.'

'Imagine my surprise, my dear,' Doris continued, ignoring this dig. 'My Alec – he's been doing wonderful work at the Hall House, by the by . . .'

'Yes, that is certainly surprising,' Rosemary Jerrold murmured, lifting the bucket from the sink to the draining board. Mrs Day glanced at her, frowning and clearly wondering if this was intended to be a criticism of her son. But the Brigadier's wife seemed oblivious of any tension and continued: 'I understand that there are extensive refurbishments going on at the Hall . . .'

'Four bathrooms, dear!' Mrs Day announced, with the scandalised tones of one who started life washing at the yard pump. 'Imagine that! Four bathrooms . . .'

'A large family?' Mrs Jerrold suggested, twisting the ends of the sprays of blossom and putting them into the bucket.

Mrs Day licked her lips and smiled. Then she poured milk into two cups and crossed to put tea into the pot and to wait for the kettle.

'You'll be glad I expect to have neighbours again,' she said.

'I fear not. We have grown accustomed to the quiet. The young gentleman I saw – I suppose one of the sons – seemed rather . . .' She searched for an adequate word. '. . . rather outlandish. One must hope that he doesn't play loud music or shout in the garden. The Brigadier does not care for other people's noise.'

'I think you will find, dear, that the young gentleman in question is no one's son.' Mrs Day poured boiling water into the pot. 'Lovely tea. Lovely, lovely tea. You'll have a cup, my dear?'

Mrs Jerrold was vaguely irritated that she was being invited to tea in her own kitchen, but was too well bred to register more than a slight frown. Mrs Day meanwhile had seated herself at the table and was pouring out two cups without waiting for an answer. She then scooped sugar into one of them and stirred it with the spoon from the sugar bowl.

'Oh yes, dear!' she said, blowing on the cup. 'I rather think you've got hold of the wrong end of the stick there.'

'Stick?' Mrs Jerrold asked, her irritation now showing in her voice. 'What stick?'

'The young gentleman, dear. He's nobody's son. Oh, no.'

'I only saw him once. I thought . . .'

'Wrong, dear. You thought wrong. That is if my Alec is anything to go by. He's met him, you see. Met them both . . . They came down to see how work was progressing and my Alec was there – plastering a ceiling . . .' She sucked her tea noisily. 'I could do with a biscuit.'

'I am afraid we have none,' Mrs Jerrold said, her irritation increasing.

Mrs Day stared at her thoughtfully.

'I just thought I should tell you, Mrs Jerrold, that the two gentlemen who have bought the Hall House are looking for someone to do their work, and I have been highly recommended.'

There was an ominous silence. Rosemary Jerrold had grown accustomed to her cleaner. It would be hard breaking in someone new. The Brigadier liked things done in a certain way, and he liked them done invisibly. Mrs Day was old, but she was quick and neat. Although she concentrated only on surfaces that showed, she left the house after each visit with a semblance of polished order. She was as near to being like the Brigadier's beloved batman, Jonesy, as one could hope for in civvy street. Jonesy had lived and died by two maxims: 'Quick in and out' and 'What the eye don't see there's no need to polish.' To both of these rules Doris Day also subscribed. To lose her now would therefore be a disaster.

'There is perhaps some gingerbread in a tin,' Mrs Jerrold offered diffidently.

'That would do, though a Viennese shortcake would be more to my liking,' the employee accepted grudgingly.

'I haven't got any,' her employer snapped, rising from the table and crossing to the pantry. There had grown between them, she acknowledged, a regrettable role reversal of which the Brigadier would not approve. Mrs Day ruled the roost while she was at work at Cockpits. Indeed all the heavy cleaning was done by her mistress and was usually timed to coincide with the infrequent visits of the Brigadier's sister, Phyllis, who seemed to take disproportionate delight out of executing household duties. But Mrs Day's weekly visits were none the less essential to the smooth running of the home, and now was not the time to bother about the trivial matter of hierarchy. Not if she were, as appeared, leading up to the giving in of her notice. For Mrs Jerrold also had an adage by which she lived. It was 'Better the devil you know than someone new in your life' – which could perhaps explain why she had remained wedded to the Brigadier for more years than seemed credible. Now, faced with the possibility of losing her inadequate but familiar cleaner, she decided on humouring her, on even going so far as to engage her in conversation. 'Two gentlemen, you say, Mrs Day?' she called as she went into the pantry and reached for the cake tin, making her voice animated and even friendly. 'Are there two of them, then?'

'That is correct, dear. Two gentlemen sharing.'

'They are father and son, perhaps? Or brothers?'

'No, dear. Oh dear me, no, dear. Two gentlemen sharing, I tell you. Well, we know what that means, don't we?'

Mrs Jerrold was now genuinely puzzled. 'Do we?' she called.

Doris Day adjusted her thin buttocks on the hard wooden seat and grimaced. 'Two gentlemen sharing,' she repeated, with a note of bitter distaste. 'That's what's to become of the dear old Hall. Miss Price, God rest her soul, would die at the news – if she weren't already dead, that is.'

'I'm sorry. I don't follow this at all,' Mrs Jerrold said, coming back into the room carrying the cake tin.

'Two gentlemen, dear. You know . . .'

'Do I?'

'Homos.'

'They are both home owners?'

'That I could not say.' Now Mrs Day was growing irritable. Her news was not being received with the required gravity.

'But I am not quite clear what it is that you *are* saying.'

'The Hall House is bought by two men,' Mrs Day said with slow irritated precision. 'Two men, Mrs Jerrold.' She was now spelling it out to the best of her ability. 'Unmarried men.'

'They are possibly good friends.'

'That I do not doubt.'

'Perhaps they have suffered some tragedy and have moved to the country to make a new start in life. A disaster in the City, perhaps? Or a family matter? One hears such awful stories . . .'

'Mrs Jerrold! Do concentrate, woman! I can't put it no plainer.' Her accent slid dramatically into the local patois as her indignation grew. 'You will have, living next door to you, men who share everything together. Men – like that.'

'Like what?' Rosemary Jerrold blinked, trying to understand.

'The kind as get up to unnat'ral practice,' Doris Day whispered.

'Unnatural?'

'Ah! It's getting home to you now, is it?'

'And how does this . . . unnatural practice manifest? They do not belong to a cult, do they? Or the Labour Party? The Brigadier would not care for that.'

'Oh, God help us all, woman!' Doris Day slammed down her cup and leapt up from the table. 'You's a great gob of spit, that's what you's. Talking to you's like talking to a blocked drainpipe. Nothing gets through.'

'Where are you going?' the Brigadier's wife gasped.

'To finish my cleaning of the sitting-down room. And it may as be the last bloody work I do in this house. You've wrung me dry with your everlasting dumbness.'

'You are offensive!'

'And you're bloody daft! I'd rather work for the buggers next door than put up with the likes of you's!' And with a toss of her head, she slammed out of the kitchen.

'Well, really!' Rosemary Jerrold exclaimed. And then she started to shake. She did so hate unpleasantness. But more than that, she could not abide mystery. What was it that the dreadful woman was trying to tell her? What did it matter if the Hall House had been taken by two gentlemen sharing? What was unnatural about it? Good heavens! She and the Brigadier had spent most of their lives surrounded by hundreds of men sharing. The backbone of the Empire depended on men sharing. The public school system was founded on men sharing. One must hope that Mrs Day had not become a women's libber. That would not do at all . . .

So her mind raced and revolved as she sat at the kitchen table with the unopened cake tin in front of her. Life could be so confusing for an innocent abroad . . . And Rosemary Jerrold suited the role almost too well.

Two gentlemen sharing? she reasoned, trying to calm herself. Actually I think the Brigadier will rather like that. He's a man's man. He wouldn't at all have liked some flibberty woman moving in next door. No! I think I have good news for him for once. I shall tell him that our new neighbours are to be . . .

5

'Two Gentlemen
Sharing . . .'

Bessie Sugar heard the news later that same morning. She got it off Tom who'd heard it from Ned who'd been told it by Charlie who played darts with Alec. Like Indian whispers it was a mangled version of a doubtful truth by the time it arrived at the shop.

'Yes, my dear. I hear as 'ow one of them is a pop star and the other is his sugar daddy. I expect it'll be in all the papers. We'll have 'tographers camping out in the lane and charabancs coming down from London, full of gawping schoolgirls . . .'

The recipient of this diatribe was a mild, plump woman who had only come in to buy some mint humbugs and a loaf of bread. 'Oh dear!' she exclaimed, fidgeting with her purse.

'I know. That's precisely how I feel myself, Miss Bridey. You've said it all, dear! Oh dear, indeed! But there! That's progress, isn't it? That's modern life. Nothing stays the same. We're to have that sort living in our midst now.'

'And you have heard all this from . . .?'

'My sister Doris's boy, Alec. He was there in the house when they called to check on progress.' Mrs Sugar tutted and shook her head. ''Course, I dare say it takes all sorts and I'm not one to judge a book by its cover . . .'

'But will it be so bad, Mrs Sugar?' Miss Bridey enquired, with a tremble in her voice. Although in many ways a timorous person, she was not one to allow injustice to pass unchallenged, nor was she comfortable in the presence of obvious gossip – perhaps because, in her younger days, she had suffered from being the subject of it herself.

'Bad?' Mrs Sugar exclaimed. 'It will be disastrous.'

'But to have artistic people in the village could be . . . stimulating.'

'Stim'lating?' Mrs Sugar gave a derisive snort. 'You don't know what these people get up to.'

'Do you?'

'I read the newspapers, Miss Bridey. I keep 'breast with the times. I have to, being in a position in the village. People look to me to keep 'em informed. You mark my words – and remember you heard it first from Bessie Sugar – with pop stars it's all boom! boom! boom! and staying out all hours.'

'But not here! There would be nowhere for them to go. There are no nightclubs . . . nor . . . low places. They will do all that in London and come back to Bellingford for a rest.'

'You can't tell, can you?'

'Presumably even pop stars have home lives. They cannot be performing all the time. Any more than say . . . that nice Mr Daltry from the Woods is a solicitor outside office hours.'

Mrs Sugar glared at her sourly. She did not like to be crossed. 'I could not speak about Mr Daltry and his habits,' she announced, passing the packet of mints over the counter. 'Though one has heard certain things . . .' she added, with a sinister stare as she took the proffered money into a greedy hand.

'Thank you,' Miss Bridey said, with pointed politeness.

''Course, you're newcomers, you lot at Pinchings. It's maybe not the same for you as it is for us as 'as lived in the village all our lives and our parents before us. We locals hate to see change. But there it is. Nothing we can do. I'll put your little bit of change towards the Christmas club, shall I?' And without waiting for an answer, she entered a note to that effect in a ledger and dropped the money into a large jar. 'Poor old Bellingford,' she hurried on, brooking no argument. 'In the limelight without so much as a by your leave. We'll not be able to call our homes our own. It won't be our lovely sleepy village any more . . .'

'My change . . .?'

'Gone in the Christmas club, my dear. Miss Hopkirk asked me to open the book for you. Or was it Miss Fallon? I get all you folk from Pinchings that muddled up . . .'

'I can't imagine why.'

'It's having so many women under one roof . . .'

'We are to save for Christmas already?' Miss Bridey protested, then she shook her head in resignation, raised her hands in surrender and made her way to the door. Mrs Sugar had a smile that masked a closed mind, and to try to penetrate it would, she knew, be a waste of time.

Once outside she turned her steps in the direction of her shared home with a feeling of nagging discontent. Not only did she sense she had just been subjected to a gross example of legerdemain, but there was an uncomfortable air of prejudice about the conversation which she knew she should have combated but was fully aware that she had failed so to do.

Miss Bridey, still shaken by the event, mentioned her conversation to Miss Hopkirk that same lunchtime. And that afternoon Miss Hopkirk, out walking in Belling Wood with Rag, Tag and Bobtail, her adored corgis, happened to meet Heather Daltry out for a ride on her equally adored chestnut gelding, Belter. It seemed only natural to Miss Hopkirk that she should pass on this titbit of local gossip.

By the time Heather got off the phone that evening the story that had spread round a sizeable portion of the county had grown from simple proportions to an outlandish concoction about the Hall House having been bought by a drug-addicted paedophile and his male lover who had himself until recently been selling his body on the streets of Soho – or was it King's Cross? There is a nice distinction about a grossly inaccurate rumour; it depends for its credibility on fine points of detail.

'But,' gasped Melanie Barlow, who lived in one of the executive villas on Tudor Drive and was married to Barry in computers, 'what about the children?'

Sandra Green, her informant and neighbour, married to Simon in insurance, hesitated. She had only just heard the story herself – from Olive Snelling, who ran the creative writing course at Fairlow Leisure Centre – and had therefore not had the time required to consider it in depth. 'I don't think they have any children, Melanie,' she said, straining every brain cell. 'You see, they wouldn't be the type . . .'

'No, Sandra! Not theirs. Ours.'

Sandra sucked a finger thoughtfully and considered this new dimension. 'Well,' she said at last, 'Simon works with a man who he's sure is that way and Simon says you wouldn't even know it if you saw him walking down the street.'

'That's hardly the point, is it?'

'What I'm saying is – Simon quite likes him . . . And there's nothing in the least funny about Simon.'

'Quite. What I meant was drugs, Sandra – what about the drugs?'

'Simon says cannabis ought to be legalised and that it would be a good thing for the insurance world if it was . . .'

'Why?'

'I don't remember, but I think it's got something to do with the premium . . . something like that. The world of insurance is a closed book to me.' She used the simile with an airy confidence which stemmed from her two years in creative writing.

A silence fell over the executive fitted kitchen as Sandra contemplated either the mysterious world of her husband's career or more probably the infinite problems she was encountering with the second chapter of the great English novel which she had started as part of a resolution on New Year's Day.

Eventually, with a depressed sigh, Melanie rose from the table and collected gin, tonic and two glasses from the corner fitment. 'Drink, Sand?' she asked, and poured without waiting for an answer.

'Well, I shouldn't,' her friend replied, glancing at her watch. 'But go on then. Simon's taken Gary to judo.' She rose and crossed to the door. 'I'll just nip to your smallest – won't be a jiff. A drink'll help me relax,' she added, skipping from the room. 'I'm having real trouble with my creative writing at the moment.'

'Well, I did warn you!' Melanie called. Then she sighed again. It had been another boring day on the executive estate. Now, although the evening was half over, Barry was still not home. He seemed to spend longer and longer hours at the office and she half hoped he was having an affair, if only to bring some interest into their lives. Nor had the children returned. Wayne, aged twelve, was at target practice, and Karla, aged nine, was at modern movement. She might just as well spend the time with Sandra as on her own.

'Actually, I had an affair with a chap who was,' she remarked, lighting a cigarette, when Sandra came back in, straightening her skirt.

'Was what?' Sandra asked, sitting again at the table and rubbing her hands.

'You know – gay. Though I didn't know at the time, of course.'

'Cor! That's a strong gin, Mel. You want to make me tight?'

'Have some more tonic then.'

'Grazie!' Sandra and Simon had spent three holidays in la bella Italia and she was getting the hang of the lingo – though it wasn't easy.

'It really upset me, if you must know.'

'What did, Mel?' Sandra asked, her voice instantly filled with concern.

'Finding out the guy I was having this affair with was gay,' Melanie snapped, losing some of her cool in the face of Sandra's constant incomprehension.

There was a long pause as this information sank in, then Sandra shook her head and smiled. 'But – how could you have an affair with him if he was gay, Mel? I mean . . . They're not built that way.'

'Oh, they are. Believe me, they are.'

'Well, I know they are . . . But they're not, are they? At the same time, they're not.'

'Well, like I say – we seemed to manage. Until . . .'

'What?'

'He went off with an air steward.'

'No! It's so public – an aeroplane.'

'It wasn't on the plane, Sandra!'

'Oh! Good! But it can happen. It's called the Mile-High Club and you have to do it in the toilet. I read about it in a book – or was it a film? I can't imagine how you'd ever fit two people in one of those little loos. And the folding door would make it . . .'

'It wasn't on the plane, Sandra,' Melanie hissed, her irritation coming to the boil.

'Sorry. Was I bunnying? Where then?'

'I'm trying to tell you.'

'You've been on your own all day, haven't you? I can always tell. You've got the moody blues.'

'*Sandra!*'

Sandra put her hands over her mouth and shut her eyes.

'Thank you!'

'Go on then. I'm listening.'

'It was pretty ghastly, if you must know. It upset me a lot.'

'Oh, Mel! I'm sorry.' And Sandra leant across the table, giving her friend all her attention.

'You see – I was the one who made it happen. It was me who met the air steward – coming back from Ibiza with a girl-friend . . .'

'He had a girlfriend? The air steward? I thought he was gay.'

'No. I had a girlfriend. We'd been to Ibiza together.'

'You mean . . .'

'No, Sand. Don't even say it.'

'But . . .'

'I was not a lesbian at the time, Sandra. I was simply on holiday in Ibiza with a girlfriend – like you and me are friends – and on the way back I got chatting to this air steward. He was called Glenn. I asked him out – make up a foursome, you know? Bring a friend, that sort of style . . .'

'What happened?' Sandra asked, now totally caught up in the story.

'He and my boyfriend took one look at each other and they ended up under my double duvet.'

'No! What did you do?'

'I can't remember. It was ages ago. Had a cup of tea, probably. We didn't drink so much in those days . . .'

'Well, that's life, isn't it, Mel?'

'Yeah! That's life, Sand,' Melanie agreed morosely. 'Finish your glass and have another . . .'

Of course not everyone in Bellingford was attached to the grapevine, nor read the smoke signals at dusk, and there were many who remained unaware of the imminent arrival of Rich and Bless at the Hall House.

Lavinia Sparton – erstwhile prima ballerina of the Ballet Romantique, acquaintance of Galena Ulanova and rival autumnal leaf to the great Markova herself – rarely mixed with any people from the village. Having once been a leading light in a dazzlingly bright milieu she saw no reason to shine in the wilderness. So it would be some time before she would discover that two of 'the boys' had joined the little society in which she now found herself. Which was a pity. Because Lavinia was in the twilight of her life, and having spent much of it in the company of her husband Henry, now departed – a man not obviously given to excesses, either emotional or material – she was starved of sympathetic conversation and yearned for a little colourful attention in which to blossom and perhaps even, dare one hope for it . . . dance?

Diana Simpson did not hear the story until it was already yesterday's news. She had recently left the village to join an all-female commune in southern France, which she had seen advertised in a feminist journal. Unfortunately for her, and later for many other people, she had while she was there attracted the attentions and desires of one of the more unusual members of the group – a free spirit with a huge capacity for drinking the cheap local wine and smoking loose roll-your-own cigarettes with a peculiarly sweet scent. This woman, an Italian called Carlotta da Braganizio, had fallen madly in love with her and pursued her with a tenacity that would have been commendable in a bloodhound or a secret homing missile. The situation had become impossible and Diana was that very evening packing her case prior to a night flight in her Citroën Deux Chevaux. (Which she sometimes called 'Pinky', but not in the politically correct circles to which she now aspired.) Her escape from Arles would cause innumerable problems when she finally managed to make it back to the village – problems that would have far-reaching and in some cases life-changing effects.

And, of course the rector, Andrew Skrimshaw, and his wife, Margaret, would remain totally in the dark until several weeks after the new inhabitants of the Hall House were installed. No gossip ever filtered through the screen of ivy that covered the rectory, any more than the light of day managed to penetrate those heavily curtained windows. It was not chance that made Andrew's most fervent prayer 'Lighten our darkness we beseech thee, Oh Lord . . .' Nor was it accident that made him – one of the few truly good people in the community – so singularly incapable of making friends with any of his flock. Andrew and Margaret harboured their own secret doubts which made them emotionally reclusive. Even their children – David, aged thirty and Julia, aged twenty-eight – seldom willingly visited them, and when they did they each made sure that their sibling would not be present. It was the greatest mystery to Margaret, who had herself come from a happy, though limited, home on the North Yorkshire coast, how her present circumstances had evolved. If she had had any of her husband's faith, which sadly for her she had not, then her prayer would probably have been more in the style of the question 'Why, oh Lord? Why?' But as she was firmly of the opinion that the Lord had gone away many years ago – if indeed he had ever been there in the first place, which she doubted – she didn't indulge in any praying and spent her time instead in a state of deep depression, brought on by the perplexity of living next to a man with a faith that she couldn't share, couldn't understand and found, if she was honest with herself, rather silly. While Andrew prayed, Margaret pondered – and often wept.

Meanwhile perhaps one of the last people to be told the news that evening was the one who would most suffer and change with the arrival of his new – and oh so very close – neighbours.

Brigadier Selwyn Jerrold, OBE, was seated at the table in Cockpits, toying with a plate of cottage pie, when his wife Rosemary broke to him the news that she had been given by her cleaning woman that morning.

'I am to understand, Selwyn . . .' she began, a trifle nervously.

'Speak up,' her husband barked. 'I can't hear you if you mumble.'

'I'm sorry.'

'So am I. I've had a damnably awful day in the Tower.'

'Oh, dear! I'm sorry,' his wife said again, in a weaker voice.

'Well go on. What is it?'

'Nothing important . . .'

'Let me be the judge of that.'

'Yes, dear.'

'Well – get on with it.'

'It is simply . . .'

'Yes?' His voice was growing dangerously weary.

Rosemary, reading the signs, thought it wise to continue the subject that she now regretted having broached. 'Our new neighbours,' she stammered. 'I understand from Mrs Day that it is not a family as such that is to live at the Hall House . . .'

'As such?'

'No.' She felt the last of her courage ebbing away. She watched her husband's small, malevolent eyes glaring at her. She mashed the food on her plate and swallowed air.

'If we are not to have a family "as such" living next to us – then what are we to expect?'

'Unrelated . . . males,' Rosemary murmured, as if hoping her words would pass by without being detected.

The Brigadier had a fork of food midway between plate and mouth. His hand paused in transit. He glared at his wife.

'Say again,' he said, with the chilling tone of the Bloody Assizes.

'I understand that the Hall House has been taken by two gentlemen.'

'Gentlemen?'

'So I am told. Two gentlemen – sharing.'

'No wives?' Judge Jeffreys enquired, his fork still poised.

'Apparently not,' his wife whispered.

'And what is the nature of the relationship of these two gentlemen – sharing?'

'That I cannot say.'

'Cannot? Or will not?'

'My informant, Mrs Day – who is not always to be trusted in matters of information – alluded to them as possibly . . .'

'Possibly?'

'Just – men who . . . share everything together, Selwyn. Men . . . like that.'

Slowly the Brigadier lowered his fork back to his plate. Even more slowly he raised his damask napkin to his lips. Then with a sudden movement he pushed his plate away and rose from the table. 'I am going to the Tower,' he announced.

'Your food,' his wife gasped.

'I am not hungry,' he said, stumbling to the door. Then he turned with a savage snarl. 'Good grief, woman! You can think of food at a time like this?'

'Please don't distress yourself, Selwyn. It surely won't be too uncongenial. They may be keen gardeners . . .'

'Gardeners? Oh . . . Rosemary! I sometimes think I am married to a . . . a . . .' He shook his head. Then, taking a deep breath to steady his nerves, he continued in a voice rigid with discipline. 'I am going to the Tower now. The news you have just delivered could not be worse.' His whole body started to twitch as a spasm of nausea flooded over him. 'It stinks, woman!' he gasped. 'The whole thing . . . stinks.' And turning on his heels he stumbled out of the room, leaving his wife alone at the table.

Rosemary Jerrold also pushed her plate away, her appetite having completely deserted her. Silently she pondered the complexities of life. Was there perhaps something about two gentlemen sharing that she did not understand? Would their presence lower the tone? Would their occupancy affect house prices or increase the council tax? But if so – why? There were three women living together at Pinchings. There was a single woman who was rumoured to be a divorcee at the Hollies. Yet the Brigadier had never particularly objected to these facts – other than to ignore them, as was his wont. Why then should two gentlemen sharing bother him so? Was it the number that mattered? Or the sex? It was all totally beyond her.

Not for the first time Rosemary longed for her husband's sister, Phyllis, to be there. Phyllis had a way of explaining things – particularly those things of an obscure nature that came under the heading of 'life'. Rosemary Jerrold freely admitted, though to no one other than herself, that she and 'life' had parted company many years before – roughly at about the time that she and the Brigadier had plighted their troth. But . . .

'I would have thought,' she murmured in a puzzled voice, 'that there would be distinct advantages to be had from living next to two gentlemen sharing. No babies screaming. No washing on the line. Out at work all day. Probably both members of the golf club. Just two good chums billeted down together. Really!' and now she sounded quite cross. 'Selwyn always has to make such a drama out of everything. Personally I'm delighted at the prospect!' She faltered, conscious of how easy it was to have courage when there was only oneself listening. 'So far as I am concerned,' she continued, beginning to clear the table, 'I look forward to meeting them . . .' Then she hesitated again, remembering the strange, childlike boy who had appeared in the drive. Had he not . . . dropped her a curtsy? Such outlandish behaviour. Then she gasped as her mind's eye focused more clearly on that cold day in March when she had been the first in the village to see one of the future owners of the Hall House. As the boy turned, had she not also noted – noted, but blotted from her memory until now . . . 'He had long hair,' she croaked – her breath strangulated with emotion. 'Oh, heavens!' she whimpered. 'Long hair, like a teenage girl. Caught at the back in a ponytail!' She sank to her seat again, grasping the table for support. 'Not just two gentlemen sharing!' she sobbed. 'Hippies!'

6

The Tower

The Tower in Cockpits' garden had originally been built as one of those architectural follies so beloved of landscape designers. Constructed of mellow brick in the shape of a miniature Tudor turret, it had been put up by an overambitious previous owner after an inspirational visit to Sissinghurst in Kent. Two poky little rooms, one above the other, were connected by a spiral staircase. The ground floor had a door at the side leading out into the garden, and each room had a leaded window. From the upper floor it was just possible, by standing on a judiciously placed chair, to see over the wall into the Hall House grounds.

Over the years rampant climbing plants – the Kiftsgate rose and heady-scented honeysuckles – had been allowed to grow unchecked up the outside walls, which gave an air of contrived prettiness, verging on the picturesque. Originally the place had been used as a potting shed but gradually it had succumbed to neglect, and by the time the Jerrolds arrived it was no more than a ruin.

At first the Brigadier had intended to pull it down, considering its fabric unsafe and its design too pretentious for good taste. But with the dawning of his new career as a man of letters, and the arrival of his word processor, it became clear that he needed an office, and the building fitted the bill perfectly. The Tower – it was he who named it thus – once renovated became his exclusive and hallowed sanctuary. No one, strictly no one, was allowed to enter without his consent, and such consent had never been forthcoming.

His wife had not set foot inside the building since he requisitioned it. What he actually did there wasn't even clear to her. Obviously he used it as an escape – a place to go when a chap wanted to be alone – and as the years went by he passed more and more time within its gloomy interior. She supposed that he must spend a certain amount of the day at his word processor – for he made no secret of the fact that he was the only begetter of *The Bellingford Gazette*, a local magazine produced four times a year and distributed to most of the houses of the village free of charge and regardless of whether the occupants desired a copy or not.

Every part of the *Gazette* was executed by the Brigadier. He was the only contributing journalist, he was the editor, the type-setter, the designer and the delivery boy. The deliveries took place on the last Thursday of each third calendar month. He would start out early in the morning and visit every house in the village and on the executive estate. (He did not, however, bother with the council houses beyond the church – deeming the occupants there to be illiterate and the steep hill upon which they dwelt too exhausting.) He had never been known to miss a delivery date, regardless of the vagaries of the English weather. Even during a force-nine December hurricane he had soldiered (literally) on. He would be seen striding out, a stick in one hand and a canvas bag slung over his shoulder – giving him the jaunty look of a geriatric paper-lad. If accosted he would raise his stick in a gesture of acknowledgement – but never once did he pause to exchange conversation with any of the strangers whom he sometimes encountered.

These sorties round the village were the only time that the Brigadier visited the outside world – apart from driving his wife to Fairlow every Friday morning. There, while Rosemary did the weekly shopping at the supermarket, he dealt with any business that might require attention; usually a visit to the bank or the building society. He would also make small personal purchases and deal with matters of health and hygiene.

The Brigadier was a man of relentless habit. He had his hair cut every second week at the barber's near the market square. He went to the dentist twice a year for a check-up. He bought underclothing once a year and a toothbrush every three months. He liked a roast on Sunday, cold on Monday, Anglo-Indian curry on Tuesday, the last of the scraps in a shepherd's pie on Wednesday, fish from the fish van on Thursday, liver on Friday and either a salad (summer) or eggs and bacon (winter) on Saturday. For lunch he had two ham sandwiches with English mustard. The sandwiches were cut into quarters and the crusts were left on. Breakfast consisted of strong sweet tea (a legacy of his army life), a bowl of bran and two slices of white toast scraped with butter and accompanied by a proprietary brand of marmalade.

There were few if any deviations in the Brigadier's life. There was order. There was discipline. There was a routine. There were also certain standards to be maintained.

The only irregular feature in this totally regulated regime – where even his bowels adhered to the strictest and most admirable timekeeping (thanks probably to the bran each morning) – were the somewhat haphazard and unpredictable visits of his sister, Phyllis.

All that the village knew about Phyllis Jerrold they gathered either from snippets let drop by the Brigadier's wife or from what little Doris Day had managed to glean over the years. It seemed that this good woman devoted her life to looking after an elderly aunt. They lived in a house in Scarborough, not far from the site of the hotel that fell down the cliff. (This fact was commented upon at the time of the hotel's departure by the Brigadier in his 'Home Thoughts From Abroad' column in *The Bellingford Gazette*. After discussing the transitory nature of existence, where even the ramparts of our sceptred isle were not immune to the wastages of time, he alluded to the hotel's sad demise and added: '*It may be of interest to note that the editor's sister lives near to the scene of the disaster and witnessed the descent from a strategic vantage point . . .*')

The demands made upon Phyllis by the aunt were apparently gruelling. But she accepted the work with the patience and forbearance of a saint. Her only escape it seemed was when from time to time her brother, the Brigadier, would travel up to Scarborough to relieve her of her duties. On those occasions Phyllis invariably travelled south and stayed in the house at Bellingford with her sister-in-law, Rosemary.

Mrs Sugar always knew when Phyllis was visiting because the Brigadier's wife bought a bottle of dry sherry and less, if indeed any, cooked ham. Doris Day would be alerted of her arrival by being instructed to prepare the guest room at the back of the house. Although Mrs Day had never met the lady, she was well aware of her presence. She used a distinctive French perfume – Diorissimo – and left surprisingly expensive and exotic lingerie lying about her room. (Surprising, that was, for a sister of the Brigadier – whose own taste in underwear was austere to the point of masochism.)

The reason that Mrs Day had always failed to meet the woman – which needless to say she longed to do – was that Rosemary and Phyllis spent most of their days together outside the house. They passed the time motoring about the countryside visiting country houses and other National Trust sites – an occupation that the Brigadier abhorred, believing as he did that an Englishman's home was his castle and should not be subjected to a lot of nosy parkers. His wife however, who enjoyed these excursions enormously, looked forward to her sister-in-law's visits and once told the queue at Mrs Sugar's that it was as much a holiday for her having Phyllis to stay as it was for Phyllis to be there. Certainly Rosemary's spirits seemed to soar with her arrival and she was always particularly low after her departure.

One thing that could have puzzled people was the question of the car. The elderly Riley in which the two women were sometimes glimpsed whisking off on one of their jaunts was the same car that the Brigadier used when taking his wife shopping in Fairlow each Friday. The explanation, however, was a simple one. Apparently when visiting Scarborough the Brigadier would drive to the mainline station and there meet his sister in the waiting room. They would spend a polite, though brief, time together before he took a train north and she drove back to the village. In this way brother and sister were not forced to spend too long in each other's company – which would not have been advisable. It appeared that they were like the proverbial chalk and cheese, oil and water and the grape and the grain – they didn't go together, couldn't mix together and gave each other the most appalling headaches.

But these visits by Phyllis were the exception to the rule, and for most of the year the Brigadier and his wife lived a solitary and uncommunicative existence under the same roof but not under the same folding star.

Rosemary filled her days gardening, shopping, cooking and generally looking after and running the house for her husband. For recreation there was a baby grand in the drawing room which she liked to play in the afternoons – if the Brigadier was in the Tower – and there was always the church flower roster, which she shared with the rector's wife and the three ladies from Pinchings.

Meanwhile the Brigadier prepared and published the quarterly *Gazette* and occupied himself with manly thoughts and deep deliberation in the Tower. He had hinted at a volume of memoirs and there had once been vague references to 'other works, of a more philosophical nature'. His wife did not press him for clarification of these matters. She simply contented herself with the fact that whatever he got up to in the privacy of his den kept him busy in what would otherwise have been the longueurs of retirement. And of course there was the added bonus that it kept him out of the house.

But if Rosemary had been a fly on the wall of the Tower on this particular evening she would have been more than a little surprised to discover her husband in the upper room, standing in front of a mirror – stark naked apart from a pair of cream long johns. (The Brigadier naturally adhered to the adage of casting no clouts till May be out – and June did not come in until the following week.) After contemplating his sagging frame with impartial eyes, he opened one of a pair of wardrobes that stood facing each other across the little room. Flicking along the clothes hanging on the bar, each in a dust-proof bag, he searched until he found the particular garments he required. Removing the bag, he carefully lifted each of several items off the hanger and placed them over the back of a chair. Then turning to face the mirror on the door of the wardrobe once more, he began slowly to pull on the full dress uniform of his regiment.

He found the trousers were now a trifle nippy at the waist. The top button of the shirt throttled him uncomfortably at the neck. The jacket cut into his armpits. But once fully clothed he eyed himself with a kind of satisfaction. Drawing himself to his full height, he clicked his heels, saluted, and nodded at his reflection in the glass.

'Carry on, Sergeant Major!' he said. Then he turned and walked stiffly to the spiral staircase and descended to the room below.

Once there he lit a lamp on his desk. He took paper and pen from the middle drawer, and reaching to a small cupboard in the top of the secretaire he produced a box of cigars and some matches. Slowly and methodically he prepared the cigar. He struck a match and stared at the orange flame.

'Two gentlemen sharing, eh?' he said, shaking out the match and striking another. 'We'll see about that.'

Lighting the cigar, he took a deep draught of the thick smoke. He choked and spluttered slightly as the nicotine burnt the back of his throat, and gasped for air.

Then, after pausing for a moment, as if in prayer or some other esoteric form of contemplation, he dipped his pen and wrote in his fine, spidery hand across the top of the sheet of paper in front of him: '*Now is the time for our village to unite. Now is the time for our little differences to be shelved. Now is the time for action. Now is the time for a leader to step forward and take up the banner of righteousness, the sword of sanctity and the arrows of salvation . . .*'

As Brigadier Selwyn Jerrold, OBE, continued to write the first draft of the leader column for the June edition of the *Gazette* he felt his patriotic heart leap into life within him. And if he had been more honest with himself than was his wont he would have admitted that the news that the Hall House was shortly to be occupied by 'two raging nancies' – to use the barrack room vernacular – gave him the direction and the inspiration for which he had long searched and that he most ardently desired.

'And did those feet in ancient time,' he hummed, dragging on his cigar, 'walk upon England's mountains green . . .' He felt the blood surge through his manly veins. He had seen the future and it filled him with pride. He saw himself at the head of the column once more. No longer on the scrap heap; no longer a has-been; no longer Brigadier Jerrold – retired. There was work to be done, a fight to be fought, and he was the man for the job.

'I will not cease from mental fight,' he sang, his voice wobbling with emotion. 'Nor shall my sword sleep in my hand,' he trilled. And then, pleased with the sound and moved by the sentiment, he slapped his hand against his thigh and bellowed at the top of this voice: 'Till we have built Jerusalem, In England's green and pleasant land.'

7

At The Limelight Club

'Alan! How are you?' Laurence exclaimed, managing to imbue the question with about as much warmth as the iceberg that sank the *Titanic*.

'Hi, Laurence!' Bless said holding up two glasses of champagne and dodging a passing celebrity. 'Enjoy the show?'

'Isn't that question rather dangerous at a first-night party, dear boy?'

'Not if you're a friend of the producer,' Bless replied, and he started to squeeze his way through the crush.

'Where is Richard? Have you seen him?' Laurence continued, pushing in pursuit.

'Haven't a clue,' Bless called. 'I thought he was with you.' Then, as a large American with an even larger companion blocked off any further conversation, Bless made his escape.

He'd left Maggie in a comparatively secluded corner, guarding two chairs and an edge of table.

'Jesus!' she exclaimed, grabbing the small glass greedily as he slid down beside her. 'What d'you call that? A sip?'

'Thank you, Bless! You really are a treasure, Bless! I risked life and limb for these.'

Maggie blew him a kiss. Then she groaned and took a doleful

swig of the champagne. 'I hate this sort of party. I just saw Max Armstrong and he cut me dead.'

'I didn't know you knew Max Armstrong.'

'I auditioned for him last week.'

'Maggie! Doing a quick burst of "Memories" doesn't guarantee a lifetime relationship.'

'"Memories" Are you crazy? I never do Streisand songs. You do a Streisand song and they put you down for the chorus . . .' She paused and then groaned. 'Oh! I'm so sick of being out of work.'

'So – what are you doing sitting here when the room is thick with casting directors and agents and . . . money?'

'I'm not going to network. Not on my own . . .'

'Well, don't ask me to join you. The dreaded Laurence is circling like a basking shark and I don't feel up to him right now.'

'Where? Show me! I want to see what he's like.'

'You know what he's like. He's a vicious, closeted old queen who makes my life a misery. That's what he's like.'

'Introduce me.'

'No, Maggie,' Bless told her firmly. 'And pull up your left strap before you expose yourself.'

'D'you like it?' she asked, smoothing her hands down her cleavage. 'The dress, I mean – not the boob.'

'I adore the boob. And the dress is sensational – what there is of it.'

'It costs two and a half grand – and it has to go back in the morning.'

'You have it on hire purchase?'

'Please! I have it on loan. Hasn't cost me a cent.'

'You borrowed it? From whom?'

'Stefan in Walton Street.'

'I bet he looks wonderful in it.'

'Probably. But not as good as me. I was walking past the shop and saw it in the window.'

'For sale?'

'Of course for sale. It still has the ticket on it.'

'Knowing Stefan he must have wanted something in exchange.'

'Probably your body. It sure ain't mine.'

'Mine isn't available. I've found my Mr Right – and I'm not going to fuck things up this time.'

'Why do you have all the luck?' Maggie sighed again, teetering towards another decline.

'Because I know when to stop running.'

'Meaning I don't?'

'Meaning just what I said. Don't be so self-obsessed. I was talking about me.' He grabbed her hand and kissed it. 'Some day your prince will come. Trust me!' He grinned. 'I hope Stefan realises that dress'll go back two sizes larger.'

Maggie pulled her hand away. 'Are you saying I'm fat?' she demanded.

'Certainly not. I'm saying you're well endowed. Oh shit. Here he comes.'

At that moment Laurence appeared, squeezing his way through the throng. Arriving in front of them, he lurched against the table, rocking it precariously. 'Bloody awful people, pushing and shoving. Who are they all? Do you know any of them?'

'A few,' Bless replied, rising. 'Laurence, this is my friend, Maggie Heston. Maggie, this is Laurence Fielding, Rich's friend.'

Laurence squeezed past Bless and sat in the chair he had just vacated. As he did so he offered his hand to Maggie, who took it, held it for a moment, and then shook it dubiously.

'I am not "a friend of Richard's", by the way. I have a perfectly adequate identity of my own. Now do be a good boy, Alan, and run and get us some more drinks. Try to use your initiative and secure a bottle. Failing initiative – pull rank!'

'What rank?' Bless asked, looking him in the eye.

'Say you're a friend of the producer,' Laurence suggested with a glare before waving him away.

'Tell them you're his lover,' Maggie called. But Bless had already departed.

There was a moment's awkward silence. Maggie tried surreptitiously to adjust the strap of her dress. Bless, damn him, had been right. The cup size, to put it bluntly, was inadequate. Meanwhile Laurence toyed with his glass and glanced at his nails.

'Have you known Alan long?' he asked at last, avoiding her eyes and watching the milling crowd.

'You mean Bless?'

Laurence frowned. 'I don't care for sobriquets.'

Maggie shrugged and smiled, pleased to be the cause of his irritation. 'But I don't recognise him by any other name,' she explained, using a maddeningly reasonable tone which caused him to turn his questioning, cold eyes on her. Was she being deliberately provocative? he wondered.

'You're an intelligent girl.'

'I beg your pardon?' She allowed a little jab of anger to sound in her voice.

'One does not expect the younger generation to have a vocabulary.'

'Really? Is that why you use long words? To make us feel ignorant?'

'Good heavens no! I don't give a toss how you feel. But I think of myself as a guardian of the English language.'

'Even with a vocabulary borrowed from the French?'

Laurence looked at her again and smiled. 'Good girl!'

'Thanks – boy!' Maggie answered and, raising an eyebrow, she stared at him with what she hoped was withering disdain.

'Oh dear! Was I not being politically correct?'

'That would depend on your politics!'

'You are an actress, Miss . . .?'

'Heston. Yes.'

'Would I have seen you in anything?'

'I don't know. It would depend what you've seen.'

'I never watch the box – so there's no point regaling me with your televisual triumphs.'

'I promise you I wasn't going to.' There was an icy little

silence while they both watched the backs of the people standing in front of them. Maggie took a sip from her fast-dwindling
glass. 'You're an architect, are you, Mr . . .?' She gave a nicely
timed pause before continuing: 'Would I have seen any of your
buildings?'

Laurence smiled, enjoying the cut and thrust. 'Touché! So
what did you make of this bit of trivia to which we have just
been subjected, Miss . . . is it Heston?'

'It is. I thought the bit of trivia fun, rather moving and very
well done. But you I suspect would have preferred to see the
original opera.'

'*Bohème* is not one of my favourites. I think of it as no more
than a bit of trivia itself. But to update it and set it to modern
music – if that appalling din can be called music – seems to be
folly and arrogance.'

'Oh dear! You really didn't enjoy it, did you? Will you be
giving Rich your opinion?'

'Richard? Of course. I already have. He assures me that the
piece was a resounding success off Broadway. I told him that
that is where it should have stayed. But don't let's bother our
heads about it any more. Let's talk about Alan instead.'

'Who?'

'Don't be tiresome, Miss Heston. Your friend – Bless.' He
said the name as though it had a nasty smell. 'What's his game?'

'Game?'

'Now that Richard has inherited a great deal of money it
does seems rather a coincidence that your friend should suddenly take it into his head to want to set up home with him.
Don't you agree?'

'Actually, I think it was Rich who suggested it . . .'

'Yes. Of course. But poor Richard is at an impressionable
age. The middle years, as you will one day discover, are when we
are at our most vulnerable. Besides,' Laurence added, warming
to his subject, 'it was that ghastly little tart who put him up to
it . . .'

At that moment, before Maggie had a chance to defend her

friend's honour and reputation, the tart himself reappeared, triumphantly brandishing a full bottle of champagne.

'Bingo!' he cried, putting it down on the table. 'It's amazing what can be achieved with charm and a tight butt! One flash – and even the waiters are friendly!'

'I rest my case!' Laurence said sourly.

'Darling Bless!' Maggie enthused, rising from her seat and taking the bottle. 'A full one. You clever thing!' And, putting her thumb over the mouth, she gave it a few energetic shakes to work up a good fizz before squirting it in the direction of Laurence.

'For Christ's sake, Maggie!' Bless yelled.

'Oh, Mr Fielding!' she cried, brandishing the bottle dramatically, so that a great stream of liquid spewed over Laurence. 'I'm terribly sorry . . .'

'Are you mad, woman?' Laurence gasped, starting back in his seat and trying to avoid further inundation. 'I am soaking!'

'You'd better take this!' And reaching across, Maggie managed somehow to miss Laurence's outstretched hand and to drop the bottle on to his lap instead. Seeing this new catastrophe she shrieked, dramatically. 'This thing has a will of its own!'

'Maggie!' Bless yelled, retrieving the bottle and putting it down on the table. Then, without thinking, he pulled a handkerchief from his pocket and started dabbing at Laurence's crotch.

'Stop that at once!' Laurence protested, pushing Bless's hand away from this most private of areas. 'Do go away – both of you . . .' he exploded. Then he winced, realising that people were turning to stare. 'Go away!' he hissed, picking up the bottle and pouring champagne as if he hadn't a care in the world.

'With the greatest of pleasure, Mr Fielding,' Maggie said, taking Bless's hand. 'Let's go somewhere more agreeable, shall we? This corner has the peculiar smell of vitriol hanging over it.' And pushing through the crowd, she dragged Bless after her.

'What on earth . . .?' he gasped as they reached the foot of the stairs that led up to the gallery. 'Maggie . . .?'

'He's a fiend – and he asked for it,' she said over her shoulder as she hurried up to the less crowded area near the entrance and cloakrooms.

'He asked for champagne,' Bless said, following her. 'But in a glass – he wasn't seeking total immersion.'

They had now reached the top of the stairs. Here a gallery ran round two sides of the club, with windows overlooking the river and the sparkling lights of the city. Down below in the seething main room they could see Laurence at the table in the corner. He was dabbing his dinner suit and trying not to look flustered.

'Poor Laurence!' Bless giggled. 'What on earth got into you?'

'He was being horrible about you. He called you a tart.'

Bless looked at her and shrugged. 'Is that all? He can do much better than that. Besides – I am. Well, I was . . .'

'Oh, God! I suppose I've ruined everything now,' Maggie sighed. Then she also started to giggle. Putting an arm round Bless's waist, she rested her head on his shoulder and sobbed with laughter. 'I've wanted to do that for years! It felt like winning a grand prix!'

'You can't be drunk . . .'

'I'm in an emotional crisis. I'm going to miss you! Oh – I'm sorry! We were supposed to create a good impression, weren't we?'

'No!' Bless said, laughing again and kissing her cheek. 'I seriously thought you'd lost it! I thought: "She's chosen this moment for her breakdown? Please . . .!"'

'His face! Oh, dear! I can never meet that man again!'

'You're hardly likely to. And as for me – he's determined to loathe me whatever I do! Waste of champagne, though.'

He kissed her again and Maggie pulled his arm closer round her waist and snuggled up to him.

'Let's get away from this awful place,' she whispered.

'Seductress!' Bless murmured, kissing her neck. 'I can't. Not till I've seen Rich . . .'

Maggie turned, putting both her arms round his neck. Then she paused, looking over his shoulder. 'Well, speak of an angel! The light of your life has this minute arrived,' she said, disengaging herself and nodding towards the entrance where Rich had just appeared with his leading lady, Alison Parnell, draped on one arm and his other hand resting on the shoulder of his leading man, Justin Peters. Rich looked excited and a little tight. His black tie was askew and his hair ruffled. They were all laughing and breathless as though they'd been running.

'Hi, Rich!' Bless said, crossing to him and giving him a hug. Justin was already making his way towards the party, passing Bless without a glance as though he were in some strange way invisible. Once at the top of the stairs, Justin paused dramatically, scanning the crowd and making sure that his entrance would be noticed before slowly descending into the clubroom. Meanwhile Alison, after giving Bless an air kiss that didn't even graze his cheek, crossed to deposit her coat with the cloakroom attendant. As she turned back she caught her reflection in one of the mirrors that lined the walls of the foyer, and tweaked at her hair and pouted her lips.

'God! I look gruesome!' she said, eyeing herself with obvious satisfaction. Glimpsing Maggie standing behind her, she turned with outstretched arms. 'Maggie, darling!' she screamed. 'How are you?' and she threw her arms round her, dispensing more kisses that sounded like moths fluttering in a candle's flame.

'Fine, Alison. I'm fine!' Maggie said, fighting herself free of the embrace. 'I *loved* the show.'

'Did you? Did you really?'

'Honestly.'

'Truthfully?'

'Hand on heart.'

'I'm so pleased,' Alison exclaimed, giving her another kiss. 'It is wonderful, isn't it? Really, really wonderful. Oh, not me! I didn't mean me!'

'No, I know. But you are!' Maggie agreed, her voice brimming with generosity. 'You were fabulous. That number in the first act . . .!'

'"Ice in the heart"? Isn't it superb? Not the way I do it . . . But the actual number . . .'

'Fabulous. It'll become a standard.'

'It is wonderful . . .'

'The best number in the show! Sure fire! You can't fail with it.'

'Well,' Alison lowered her voice, sensing far too much attention being paid to the actual song and not enough to her performance of it, 'it's a bit of a bastard to sing . . .'

'That key change! Breathtaking!' Maggie ran on, missing this more ominous change of key in her enthusiasm.

'It's *very* tricky . . .'

'I expect!' Maggie conceded, jamming on the brakes just in time as she glimpsed the warning light. 'But you make it sound effortless. Really you do. It's all you . . .'

'No, no. I didn't mean that!' Alison bubbled gaily, clamping her hands to her heart. 'Honestly, I didn't! You know me – just one of a team . . .'

'They're all fabulous,' Maggie agreed, nodding emphatically and adopting that tone that begs the end of a subject.

But Alison hadn't even started squeezing all the subtle nuances out of Act One yet – and Act Two still waited in the wings for dissection. 'Believe me,' she confided, pulling the conversation back, 'that song is not easy. Not everyone could do it, Maggie . . .'

'Well – you certainly showed you could, Alison,' Maggie told her, gamely going in for another round.

As the two women continued this ritualistic first-night *pas de deux*, Rich and Bless leaned over the balcony, looking down at the party.

'*The Times* and *Telegraph* looked happy,' Rich was saying, 'the *Standard* inscrutable and the *Guardian* and *Mail* were their usual selves . . .' His voice was slurred, his eyes bright.

'You've been drinking.'

'You bet! Since six o'clock. I couldn't watch it. I was so scared.'

'Go on!' Bless pushed his shoulder. 'You're a big grown-up producer!'

Rich looked at him and smiled. 'I want to go home,' he whispered.

'Laurence was looking for you . . .' Bless began, searching the floor for any sign of him. He seemed to have abandoned the table.

'Not with Laurence – with you,' Rich said, putting a hand on his arm.

'Um . . . Laurence is expecting you.'

'OK, I'll come round to Maggie's later, then.'

'Sure. We were just going. She wants something to eat.'

'There's food here.'

Bless shook his head. 'I think she's feeling a bit in the shadows.'

Rich looked across the foyer to where Maggie and Alison were still chattering away. Alison was dressed from head to toe in a froth of pink which set off nicely Maggie's black sheath with the shoelace straps and the fabulous cleavage.

'She doesn't exactly have the look of an anorexic, does she? I mean, she must know that there are certain parts that even her brimming talent couldn't fill.'

'I didn't mean that, Rich. I just mean she feels . . . out of work.'

'So why do I feel guilty?'

'Because you're a good man!' Bless said, squeezing his thigh. 'Mmm!' he purred, liking the feel. 'A very good man!'

'Bless! Not here!'

'You afraid we might shock the glitterati?'

'I'm just naturally shy!' Rich gave him a quick hug.

'You really are, aren't you?' Bless said, melting with love and looking at Rich with a tenderness that he'd hardly even felt before. 'I hope you won't be shy in the country.'

'In the country I'll be far worse!' He placed his hands gently on Bless's cheeks, looking deep into his eyes. Then, pulling his head towards him, he kissed him full on the lips. 'But I won't be shy inside our little house. That I promise.'

'It's not a little house. It's a socking great mansion!' Bless said, laughing happily and putting an arm round his shoulders.

'Size queen!' Rich joked, pushing him away and leaning on the balustrade. 'You are sure, aren't you?'

'About us? Never more sure of anything in my life,' Bless told him, leaning next to him with a hand on his back.

'No. I mean about going to live in Bellingford. You won't feel . . . cut off?'

'I don't know. Not if you're there.'

'But I won't be. Not all the time . . . And you're the gregarious one. You're the one who loves parties . . .'

'So? We'll give masses of parties. We've got four guest bedrooms for a start – and I intend to invite the village to dinner . . .'

'The whole village?' Rich asked, smiling.

Bless shrugged. 'The civilised ones. I shall start with the neighbours and work outwards – like ripples on a pool!'

Rich patted his cheek, then frowned and looked away, back down at the party heaving below them.

'All the same,' he said, 'living in a village is going to be quite a change from all this!'

8

A Baptism Of Flour

'Faggots!'

Bless winced. Had he heard correctly?

'Faggots!' the voice said again.

Scarcely daring to breathe, he raised his eyes and looked across the cold counter at the face of the woman who was staring at him from the other side.

'Sorry?' he said, his voice coming out as a squeak.

'Or would you prefer some of my home-cooked ham, my dear? I think those here present will vouch for it. It's cooked to a special recipe and I put in a secret ingredient.'

Bless glanced behind him and saw several faces – all female – staring at him. They were obviously waiting for him to speak. But he had only come into the shop to see what it had to offer. He had not intended to be numbered as one of the queue.

'Just looking, really,' he explained.

'Then you take your time, my dear. We don't rush about here – not in lovely, sleepy old Bellingford . . .'

'If you want to serve . . .' He gestured behind him where Heather Daltry, next in line, was studying him closely over the top of her shopping list.

'No, no! Let them wait, my dear. Plenty of time!' Mrs Sugar assured him. She leaned heavily on the back of the refrigerated counter and swatted a fly that had managed to get on to the cooked ham. 'Dratted bugs. Just as well I got a freezer counter. The germs don't penetrate through the temperature.' She beamed at Bless and adjusted a strap on her shoulder, probing with her finger and thumb to locate it under her pink nylon overall. 'You'll have moved in, then?'

'Yes. We've been here almost a week,' Bless told her, returning her smile.

'And you've only now found your way into my little shop? Shame on you! I hopes as how you're not going to be supermarket shoppers, my dear. We have to fight to save our lovely old local shops. What you at, Miss Hopkirk?' she said, looking over his shoulder, her voice turning severe.

'I'm trying to reach the flour. You've moved it to a rather high shelf.'

'Is it the shelf that's high or the customer who's short? That's what I ask! Aren't I right, my dear?' And Mrs Sugar grinned conspiratorially at Bless. 'So your mother's sent you out to do the shopping, is that right, dear?'

'Me?' Bless gasped, looking round to see if the remark could possibly have been directed at anyone else. Heather smiled at him, reassuringly. Miss Hopkirk, who had abandoned her quest for the flour, seemed to nod in sympathy, and only the rector's wife, who was near the door and was terribly shy, looked away, as if uncomfortable in his presence.

'Yes, you, child! You don't think these people here have mothers in the village. They're all outsiders. Outsiders don't bring their aged parents with them. They move here to get away from them. Unless they build granny flats, of course – which we try to stop. They build granny flats, put their grannies into homes and let off the flats for extra income. Is your mother happy in the new house?'

'My mother isn't here . . .' Bless whispered.

'Oh dear. Dead, is she?'

'No. She's . . . in Leeds,' he offered, weakly. 'I hardly ever see her. We're . . . not very close.'

'So it isn't . . . your family you're with?'

'No. Not exactly.'

'Mmmh! So – there! You see?' Mrs Sugar said, turning towards the rest of the queue, as though in some way Bless's lack of a live-in mother proved her point precisely. Bless smiled and nodded at the assembly, hoping that the subject was now cleared up and could be left. But Mrs Sugar had some way still to go. 'So . . .' she continued, swivelling her searching eyes back in his direction. 'You've moved into the lovely old Hall House with . . .?'

'My partner,' Bless said, aware that he now sounded rather aggressive. But this third degree was beginning to irritate.

'And it's just the two of you, is it?'

'Yes.'

'It's as we thought,' Mrs Sugar said, making this final pronouncement to those present, as if giving confirmation to a dubious rumour.

Bless, unable to bear any more grilling, quickly changed the subject. 'I think I will have some of those meatballs, thank you,' he said.

'Faggots!' Mrs Sugar snapped.

Bless looked at her in disbelief. He was now sure that she was trying to be offensive – and really, she was succeeding pretty well. But he bit back a spiteful reply, determined to remain pleasant if humanly possible – this ghastly woman had after all the only shop in the village. 'Well . . . if you want to put it like that, it really doesn't bother me. But . . .'

'The meatballs – they're called faggots,' Heather explained, leaning towards him.

'Oh, I see. I thought . . .'

'You thought as how they were meatballs, my dear. Well I dare say as they are. But they're faggots to us.'

'Oh, I see,' Bless said, sounding far from certain. 'Well, whatever they are I'll have four, please.'

'Two for you and two for your partner,' Mrs Sugar said, scooping them out of the dish. 'Is it a business you're running, then?'

'Um . . . Rich puts on plays and . . . shows . . . You know? Musicals and . . . In London.'

'Very nice,' Mrs Sugar murmured, sounding far from impressed or even interested. 'And are you in the pop world too, dear?'

'Me? Oh, no . . . Rich has just had a big hit with his new show. It's called *Manhattan Bohème*. It had really good reviews . . .'

'Isn't that lovely! That'll be one pound sixty – unless I can tempt you to something else? How about a nice cauli to go with them? Or some purple sprouting broccoli – locally grown.'

'No, thank you. That's fine.'

'Not fine for me, dear,' she said, taking his money. 'Hardly worth my opening up! One pound sixty! That won't make ends meet, will it?'

'I'll come in with a proper list . . .' Bless promised, backing away from the counter.

'Mind the lady!' Mrs Sugar screeched.

But she was too late. Bless stepped backwards straight into the diminutive Miss Hopkirk, who was balanced on the tips of her toes, reaching once again for a bag of the elusive flour. She actually had it in her grasp as Bless collided with her, knocking her sideways. With a yelp of surprise she stumbled and fell, tossing the bag in the air as she reached to steady herself. The rector's wife, standing close by and realising the impending disaster, leapt forward like a rugby player, slamming her hands round the falling bag. With a great *whoof!* the paper split and a cloud of white descended on Bless's head, covering him from head to toe in flour.

'Oh, my sainted aunt!' Mrs Sugar screamed.

'Oh, I am so sorry!' Miss Hopkirk wailed.

'Oh, catastrophe!' the rector's wife gasped.

'Oh, shit!' Bless exclaimed.

'Welcome to Bellingford!' Heather Daltry hooted, dusting Bless down and causing the flour to fly in every direction.

'Look at this mess!' Mrs Sugar cried. 'Someone owes me for a two pound bag of flour.'

'I'll pay for it, of course!' Bless exclaimed, returning to the counter surrounded by a cloud of flying white.

'Don't spread it everywhere!' Mrs Sugar wailed. 'You get off out of here. Miss Hopkirk, I'll bring a dustpan and brush and I'll thank you to start sweeping up . . .'

'But I must pay you . . .' Bless insisted.

'No, no! Let me,' Miss Hopkirk cried.

'Nonsense!' Mrs Sugar exclaimed. 'The gentleman will, Miss Hopkirk. I'll open an account for him . . .'

'He doesn't need an account for a bag of flour!' Heather Daltry interrupted her.

'I'll thank you to keep out of this, Mrs Daltry,' Mrs Sugar snapped. 'Off you go then, dear. I'll enter it in the book. Go on . . . make yourself scarce. Look at the mess in here . . .'

Shamefaced and startlingly ashen, Bless escaped out of the shop, clutching his single purchase.

'Young man,' the rector's wife hissed as he was closing the door, 'insist on paying your account weekly. Otherwise it can . . . mount up.' And before Bless could respond, she closed the door in his face and through the glass he saw her turn her back sheepishly, as if afraid of being caught talking to him.

With a racing heart and sweating with nervous shock, Bless hurried down the hill, wanting the safety of his own front door.

It was a warm, sunny day and he would have liked to linger and look round the village. But the flour was caking on his perspiring brow and the slight breeze caused it to corkscrew in the air around him, like a mystical aura. He realised that he must look a bizarre sight – which was not the first impression that he wished to give to his new neighbours.

He had almost reached the bottom of the hill, where the green opened out, and was passing a high holly hedge that protected a small villa – called, according to a wrought-iron sign stuck into the earth, 'The Hollies' – when out of the drive appeared an elderly man with a canvas bag slung over his shoulder and a stick in his hand. The man was intent upon sorting out the contents of his bag – Bless was intent upon getting home. Neither of them was paying enough attention to their surroundings. It was inevitable that they should collide.

'Who the devil are you, sir?' Brigadier Jerrold bellowed, starting back at the ghostly apparition that confronted him.

'I'm so sorry,' Bless exclaimed. 'I wasn't looking where I was . . .'

'Are you sick, man? Look at you. Who are you? And what are you doing here?'

'I'm . . . I'm . . .'

The Brigadier raised his stick – though whether for protection or as an act of aggression was not immediately apparent. 'I asked you a question, young man. We have a neighbourhood watch scheme in operation in this village. And if you don't tell me what the devil you are doing here – disguised I suppose is the nearest definition that I can reach – then I shall be forced to call the police.'

'No, no! You don't understand. I live here,' Bless blurted out.

'Oh, yes?' the Brigadier said, his worst suspicions gradually coming to confirmation.

'In the Hall House. I'm . . . one of the new occupants of . . . the Hall House . . .' His voice dwindled to a whisper as he saw the man in front of him gasp and shudder – giving every appearance of having convulsions or some sort of fit. 'Are you all right?' Bless asked, reaching a hand towards him.

'Don't touch me!' the Brigadier bellowed, bringing his stick slashing down and narrowly missing inflicting a severe injury to Bless's wrist. Then, side-stepping nimbly, he stumped away up the hill. He had only gone a few steps, however, when a new thought occurred to him and he stopped and turned. He discovered Bless, still rooted to the spot, staring after him. 'You'd better have one of these,' the Brigadier brayed, scrabbling with his free hand in the canvas bag while keeping his walking stick raised at the ready. He produced a few pages of A4 paper, stapled together down one side. '*The Bellingford Gazette*. I think you'll find it . . . stimulating!' And thrusting the pages into Bless's hand, he turned again and hurried away.

9

Connubial Bliss

'It's only natural that Laurence should want to come and see the house – now it's completed . . .'

'I'm not talking about Laurence . . . It's you!'

'Me?'

'We've hardly settled in – and you want Laurence here.'

'He is my best friend . . .'

'Not any longer. I'm your best friend now, Rich. Me. Remember?'

'You know what I meant!'

'No, I don't, actually.'

'Yes, you do.'

'Don't!'

'Do!'

'This is ridiculous!'

The sun was setting over the garden and the drawing room windows were open wide. It should have been a perfect evening for a touch of connubial bliss.

'How would you feel if I told you I'd asked Maggie down?'

'Oh, for fuck's sake! I'd be delighted!' Rich yelled, getting up and crossing to pour himself another glass of champagne.

As Rich left his seat, Bless also rose and went quickly out of the French windows on to the terrace. He knew he was behaving badly. He wanted to stop. If he didn't, he'd only make things worse. He put his hands in his jeans pockets and stood staring at the lengthening shadows – and couldn't help noticing the lengthening grass as well. He'd have to learn about gardens, he thought. Then he shook his head and forced his mind to concentrate on the present predicament. Right now he was far too busy learning about living with someone to bother about anything else. 'Go in, Bless!' a voice said in his head. 'Tell him you're sorry. Say it doesn't matter . . .' But it did matter. This was meant to be their first weekend alone together. The first weekend without builders or decorators banging round the house. Their first weekend in their own home. The first weekend of their new life – and they had to share it with Laurence? Laurence! Who would criticise Bless all the time and put him down and bully him and only want to be with Rich and make the fact horribly obvious. Matter? Of course it mattered!

'Bless! Please! Come in and have a drink,' he heard Rich call from inside the room. He somehow managed to make his voice sound both irritated and apologetic at the same time.

'I'm not thirsty,' Bless replied, and he was angry with himself even as he was speaking.

Rich had opened champagne specially – to celebrate. 'Let's have champagne – to celebrate!' he'd said and then, soon after he'd opened the bottle, he told him. 'Oh, I forgot to mention,' he said, sounding dangerously nonchalant, 'Laurence phoned.'

'When?' Bless had felt uneasy at once.

'While you were out at the shop this morning. I forgot all about it when you came back. The flour rather took precedence!'

'What did he want?'

'He's coming down for the weekend.'

He had tried to make it sound like an unimportant statement, but actually he'd dreaded telling Bless and had put it off till the evening, hoping to soften the blow with a well-chosen bottle. He knew Bless would be disappointed. In a way he was disappointed himself. But Laurence was Laurence . . . He'd be feeling lonely in London all on his own. He'd get low and morose. And Laurence on a downer wouldn't be good for any of them. 'When am I going to be allowed to visit?' he'd asked, with that petulant whine that hinted at tantrums. 'This weekend,' Rich had replied. The words were out before he could stop himself. 'I was going to phone you after lunch . . .' The glib lies had flowed effortlessly. But then, to be honest, Laurence making the first approach had simply saved Rich the trouble of doing so himself. It had to be done. He'd always known that. Far better ask him down, make him feel loved and wanted. Get it over and behind them. Then they could all get on with their lives . . .

Some of this Rich had even decided he would say to Bless when he broke the news. But of course if you light the blue touch paper you must remember to stand well clear, otherwise you can get a nasty burn. Now, when Rich wanted to defuse the situation, Bless was out on the terrace smouldering away like a half-spent Roman Candle.

'Please, Bless!' Rich said, going out to him, carrying both their glasses. 'This was an expensive bottle!'

'I'm sure it was – but then, you can afford it!' Bless said. And he walked away on to the lawn, ashamed of himself.

'I couldn't say no,' he heard Rich saying. He was speaking in a low voice and it was quite difficult to hear him.

'What?' Bless asked, irritably.

'I couldn't say no to him,' Rich repeated, the tension in his voice now making him shout.

'Why not? You're finding it perfectly easy to say no to me,' Bless exclaimed, without looking round. As he spoke he could feel his temper rising. He wanted to stop. He knew he should. 'Stop now, Bless,' that voice in his head pleaded. But he was feeling hurt and he couldn't or wouldn't listen to his own sanity. So instead he stared down the long view of the garden and let the words form and flow and disturb the evening silences with their increasingly angry resonance. 'I don't want Laurence to come. But you say he has to. That sounds to me as if you're saying no to me. "No. Bless. I want Laurence here on our first weekend." So – why is it so easy to say no to me when you can't say no to bloody awful Laurence?' He bent over and picked up a small pebble which he tossed away down the lawn towards the shrubby bank of the stream. 'We haven't even had one weekend together since we moved in – not without work to do . . . Oh, what's the use?'

Why didn't the stupid man say something? Why didn't he stop him? Why was he letting him make a fool of himself? Why? Bless swallowed hard and blinked back some tears. 'I'm sorry!' he whispered, and when Rich still didn't respond, he turned slowly back towards the house. Only it wasn't towards anyone that he looked – because the terrace was empty.

'Wonderful! I eat a huge slice of humble pie – and no one is there!' He walked slowly back into the drawing room and picked up his glass from the small table beside one of the sofas where Rich had replaced it. He was about to take a drink when he heard Rich speaking on the phone out in the hall. Which was odd, because he hadn't heard it ring. Unless of course . . .

'Been phoning darling Laurence again, have you?' he said, putting his glass down again as Rich came back into the room. Then he raised his hands, stopping Rich's reply. 'Sorry. I'm sorry,' he blurted out, speaking quickly to avoid the lump in his throat. 'I know I'm behaving like a twelve-year-old. I really am sorry. I'm not usually like this . . .'

'Bless, may I speak?'

'Please, Rich!' And feeling the emotion threatening to engulf him, he flicked open an imaginary fan, fluttered it busily and looked sideways over his shoulder. 'Why fiddle-de-dee, Rhett Butler . . . The canna lilies are all in bloom . . . Last night I dreamt I went to Manderley again . . . Here's looking at you, kid . . .' He stopped and smiled sweetly. 'I warn you – the repertoire can last for hours. I'm sorry, Rich!' And when Richard didn't respond, when he stood there by the door, with one hand still on the handle as if he'd been zapped by Captain Kirk's ray gun (another part of the repertoire), so Bless, losing courage, started all over again. 'Pretty, please . . . Don't make me crawl . . . Don't let's ask for the moon – we have the stars . . . Rich! Stop me, for Chrissake! I'm nervous and – I can't believe my luck. I think if I blink it will all disappear. I'm the happiest bunny in the warren – and I truly don't want to ruin everything. Oh, shit!' He slapped his wrist and then raised both hands in surrender and changed to his best Southern drawl: 'I have always relied on the kindness of strangers.'

The performance over, he threw himself down on the sofa, grabbed his glass and gulped champagne. 'What I am actually trying to say – though you'd be hard pressed to hear it – is . . . Of course Laurence must come. And I shall go out of my way to make him like me. And thank you for the champagne . . .' Then, in a whisper, he added: 'Oh, and I love you. Did I mention that?'

'You really must come and audition for me!' Rich said, sliding down on to the sofa beside him.

'I did. That's how we met. Remember?'

'Like yesterday.'

'Thanks!'

They sat side by side, not looking at each other. Rich had somehow managed to end up holding his lover's hand.

'I feel as though we're on a bus together,' Bless said at last. 'I'm twelve and I'm being taken to the zoo by Daddy.'

'Hey! D'you mind? There isn't that much age difference! Oh, by the way. I just phoned Maggie. She's coming for the weekend too.'

'Are you mad?' Bless yelled, leaping up and moving away.

'I gave her the time of a train. We'll pick her up in Fairlow.'

'She and Laurence loathe each other! She poured champagne all over him.'

'Then we must remember to serve only a cheap vintage.'

'Rich!' Bless could feel his temper rising again.

'What?'

'You should have asked me.'

'I'd hoped you'd be pleased.'

'Oh, God!' Bless groaned, sinking down on to the sofa.

'What does it matter if they loathe each other?' Rich murmured, snuggling up to him. 'Could make for a fun weekend!' And as Bless turned to look at him, they both got the giggles.

10

The House Guests From Hell

But in the end Rich went alone to the station to collect Maggie, because they weren't sure what time Laurence would be arriving and:

'Someone will have to stay in the house. We can't have him waiting on the doorstep.'

Inevitably the someone had to be Bless – because he hadn't taken his driving test yet. That joy was still to come. He'd been having lessons in London ever since they'd found the house. He'd never learnt to drive before because there'd been no call for it. But obviously if he was now going to be living alone in the village during the week it was essential that he should. By the time he had left London he was about halfway there. He was a dab hand at an emergency stop but hopeless at reversing round a corner – he always managed to turn the wheel the wrong way and ended up reversing into the middle of the road. 'Don't worry!' his instructor told him. 'Try doing the opposite to what you think you should!' Which resulted in an interesting little spin along a fairly crowded pavement and wasn't tried again.

Bless was upstairs, putting flowers in Maggie's room, when he saw Laurence's VW come up the drive and park in front of the house.

'He can't leave it there,' he thought. 'Rich won't be able to get to the garage.'

But, of course, telling him so was not a good start to the weekend.

'Where would you like me to park, then?' Laurence asked in a tight voice.

'Round the side of the house, near the stable?'

'Stable?' Laurence snorted, returning to the driving seat. 'My dear! Such delusions of grandeur!'

Bless had written the word 'ignore' on his forehead when he got up that morning, and this was an ideal chance to put the injunction into practice.

'How are you, Laurence?' he asked brightly, joining up again in the yard and insisting on taking the older man's suitcase.

'Hot and sticky. The traffic out of London was appalling. It really isn't a good idea asking people down on a Friday evening. I can't think why you did.'

'I didn't!' Bless said, his voice still bright, leading the way into the house through the side door which opened into the back hall.

'Where is Richard?' Laurence asked, following him.

'Gone to the station.'

'I told him I'd drive down.'

'Not to meet you.' Swallow, breathe, eyes straight ahead; give it an upward inflection. 'Maggie is coming down as well!' They were climbing the stairs and the silence behind him could only be described as ominous. 'We've put you in one of the rooms facing the garden. We thought it'd be quieter – not that Bellingford is exactly noisy . . .'

The room was large and airy. It was decorated in shades of blue and green and the palest of creams. The furniture was good, the double bed extremely comfortable. 'It's never been slept in before!' Bless quipped, still keeping up the bright patter. 'I hope you enjoy breaking in virgins!' Ooops! Mistake! Go for the practical details. 'Here's your bathroom,' he breezed, opening a door and revealing another bright room where even the towels conformed to the colour scheme.

'I am to share the weekend with the Heston woman?' Laurence asked, his voice like shaved ice.

'You remembered her name. She will be pleased!' The sound of a door banging took him out on to the landing. 'I think they're here,' he called, escaping down the stairs.

'Darling!' Maggie screamed, running towards him – a vision in fawn. 'A weekend in the country! I'm so excited!' she gushed. Then she did a complete pirouette, showing off her outfit. A fawn mac, a fawn hat, a muted tartan scarf and brown knee-high boots. Beneath these outer garments was glimpsed a fawn skirt and a darker brown cashmere sweater. 'Burberry,' she announced. 'Every single stitch! What else can one wear to the country? No, wait a minute . . .' She slid her hand up her skirt, lifting the hem as she did so to reveal fawn tights and: 'The knickers are M and S. Sorry!' Then she hugged Bless and swung him round and ended up facing the stairs and landing. Laurence was leaning over the upper balustrade looking down on the scene below with a face of stone and eyes to match – not unlike a gargoyle, really.

'Hi!' Maggie cried, releasing Bless and straightening her shoulder pads. 'How lovely to see you!'

'Hi, Laurence!' Rich called, coming in from the back hall, carrying Maggie's large and heavy suitcase.

'Hi? Have we crossed the Atlantic since leaving the metropolis? Certainly the length and extreme discomfort of the journey would allow one to think so.'

Bless, who had his back to the stairs, caught Rich's eyes and raised his brows.

'Take Maggie's case up,' Rich said, passing it to him, 'and show her her room. I'll open a bottle of champagne to celebrate . . .'

The words were out before he could stop himself. Everyone winced. Memory can play cruel tricks.

'No champagne for me!' Laurence cried. 'And I advise you to avoid it. All this lovely new soft furnishing and acres of fitted carpet. So nouveau! So riche! So clean! Unless of course you want it speedily distressed?' He and Maggie exchanged distant, glittering smiles. 'I shall have an extremely large Scottish when I come down, Richard! My usual mixture!' And he turned and disappeared back into his room, slamming the door.

'Ooops!' Bless exclaimed, unable to retain the sound a second longer.

'Maggie?' Rich asked, sounding fraught and weary.

'Whatever you're serving. But if it *is* champagne – don't let me near the bottle.'

'Come on.' Bless led the way back up the stairs. 'My God! What have you got in this case?'

'My entire wardrobe. I wasn't sure how one should dress.' She paused, then added: 'Sackcloth and ashes?'

'That'll be the day!'

Dinner was served in the dining room at a table that:

'. . . could seat ten at a pinch.'

'Do you know ten people?'

'Of course we do.'

'I know Richard has many friends – but I was asking you, Alan.'

'Well, yes . . . I expect so . . .'

'Bless is extremely popular. He has hundreds of friends. When he gave his twenty-fifth birthday wake he had to borrow a whole house. Mind you, the bedrooms were supposed to be out of bounds – but people ignored that . . .'

'Maggie!'

'Sorry. This is delicious food.'

'M and S. All of it,' Rich said hurriedly. 'We haven't mastered the kitchen yet.'

'M and S! Lovely. Just like my knickers. Why go to Janet Reger for something that regrettably won't be seen by anyone except oneself?'

'You young people talk in code. Do you not cook then, Alan? I'm surprised.'

'I do. Yes. I'm rather good, actually.'

'I didn't know that.'

'He's full of surprises, Rich – I warn you!' Maggie assured him.

'I like that!'

'Oh, yes sir-ee!' she whooped, helping herself to wine. 'There's never a dull moment with Bless in the house!'

'Why do you use that ridiculous name? Where does it come from?'

'Oh, please! It's too embarrassing.'

'We're all friends here,' Laurence said, savouring his wine and sounding about as friendly as a chainsaw.

'I was once in a production of *Christmas Carol* – in rep. I played Tiny Tim.'

'How delicious!' Laurence was now obviously savouring every word quite as much as the wine. 'But they should have called you Tiny!'

'Thank you, Laurence!'

'So? Why Bless?'

'"God bless us everyone." You remember the immortal line, surely? People used to cram into the wings just to hear me utter it. I'm afraid that Bless sort of stuck!'

'He was angelic. Far too tall for the part,' Maggie burbled. 'But *so* sweet. He hopped around on his little crutch . . . We used to say it was a big crotch supported on a little crutch . . .'

'Maggie!'

'What are friends for if they can't brag for you?'

'So you were there as well, Miss Heston?'

'Of course. That's where we met. I played something with a centre parting, I can't remember what now. Nothing very exciting. I was being saved for Viola in *Twelfth Night*. Bless gave us his Orlando! Being a juvenile was a rich experience! You remember when . . .'

'I do not care for too much reminiscence,' Laurence cut in, sternly. 'It kills the art of conversation. Richard, isn't this Beaune a little heavy for the food? The '94 Syrah is drinking quite well and would have been ideal with what is merely a kitchen supper . . .'

'Laurence!' Rich yelped, nervously.

'What?' the older man demanded, raising his eyebrows.

'Don't be so pompous! You're not usually like this.'

'I didn't know that I was being,' Laurence said, lowering his gaze and looking wounded.

'You are lucky – knowing about wines,' Bless said, feeling sorry for him. 'I just drink the stuff without really knowing if its good, bad or indifferent.'

'A palate has to be educated,' Laurence told him, still looking at the table.

'That's what I'm saying. I wish someone like you would educate me.'

'Oh, you don't need me.' Laurence glanced up tragically. 'I'm sure Richard will show you the ropes.'

'Well, it was you who taught me, Laurence,' Rich said, willing the older man to recover his hauteur. Laurence pompous was infinitely preferable to Laurence sulking.

'But that was many moons ago and we live in a society that worships youth. We old has-beens have all been put out to grass now, haven't we?'

There was a moment's awkward silence. The others all desperately tried to think of something to say that would change the subject and save the evening from turning sour and moody.

'What shall we do tomorrow?' Bless enquired, adopting yet again those bright upward inflections.

'Let us see what the day brings,' Laurence advised with ominous prescience.

11

Battle Lines

The day brought rain. Laurence was already in the kitchen when Rich came down.

'Does one have to boil a kettle on this stove?' he demanded.

'Not if you don't want to. We have an electric one as well. But let me do that. You'll have tea?'

'Of course.'

'How did you sleep?'

'I never sleep well in the country. I find all those owls ruin the night and then the birds wake up so ridiculously early.'

'Oh, dear! I thought we'd have breakfast in here . . .'

'Whatever you say. Is your little friend still sleeping?'

'No. He's up in his studio.'

'Heavens! Studio? Do we have a budding RA in our midst?'

'Well – workroom, then! Toast? It's rather good on the Aga.'

'Workroom, indeed! And what work is to take place in this mythical room?'

'It isn't a mythical room, Laurence. It's the loft. I dare say if you could try to be nice for just five minutes Bless might even show you. After all, it was you who drew up the plans for it.'

'I didn't quite believe it was going to be his workroom. I didn't even know the child worked.'

'Laurence, stop it. If you're going to be beastly, I shall send you back to London . . .'

'Good morning!' Bless said, interrupting them as he came into the room. He crossed to Rich who was putting a kettle on the Aga and kissed him on the cheek. 'I hadn't the heart to wake you. You looked so sweet. Don't you think he's sweet when he's asleep, Laurence?'

'I have no idea,' Laurence replied, going to the door. 'I never thought to look. Do you have a paper delivered?'

'Of course.'

'To the front door? Or do you direct *hoi polloi* to some lesser entrance?' He went out into the hall, without waiting for an answer.

'He's cheerful, first thing!' Bless said, grinning.

Rich grimaced and shook his head. 'Never, ever again!'

'What?'

'Will we have him to stay.'

'Want to bet?'

'He's being a monster.'

Bless shrugged. 'He's being how he always is. Maybe you're seeing him in a new light.'

Rich turned so that he was leaning against the Aga and put his arms round Bless's waist, pulling him towards him. 'Thank God you came to my rescue! I could have ended up like him.'

'Over my dead body!'

'Don't die before me, Bless. Promise me that.'

'Of course I won't. I'm half your age!' and he kissed him on the lips.

Maggie didn't surface until just before midday. The rain had stopped and Laurence and Rich were out of sight somewhere in the grounds.

'We don't call it a garden!' Bless told her. 'It's too big.'

They were standing on the terrace and Maggie was clasping a mug of black coffee as though it were a lifebelt on a storm-tossed sea.

'God! I feel dreadful!' she groaned.

'Maybe that's because you finished off a whole bottle of wine after the rest of us stopped drinking.'

'Bless! It isn't kind to remind. I didn't say anything awful, did I?'

'You were so slurred that it wouldn't have been understood anyway . . .'

She shuddered at the memory and stretched her neck, easing out the alcoholic cramp. 'What's that building you can see over the far wall?' she asked.

The building to which she referred was the Tower in Brigadier Jerrold's garden, the upper window of which was partially visible over the dividing wall.

'It's some sort of folly in the next-door garden,' Bless explained.

'They have only a garden, do they?' Maggie teased him.

'Certainly!' Bless grinned. 'They ain't even in the same league!'

'It is gorgeous here, darling. But you will be all right, won't you?'

'All right?' Bless was scarcely attending to her. He was still staring at the window of the Tower.

'It couldn't be more of a change from Belsize Park . . .'

'Follow me!' Bless suddenly said, darting back into the house. 'But come quickly . . .'

By the time Maggie caught him up they were upstairs on the first floor and had entered the master bedroom.

'You're going to seduce me – with your man likely to come in at any moment?' Maggie squeaked dramatically.

But Bless had crossed to the big bay window that occupied the centre of the wall. There, on a circular table, were some binoculars. He lifted them and standing well back from the window trained them on the point where the Tower appeared, shrouded in greenery, beyond the wall.

'Look!' he whispered, handing the binoculars to Maggie and pulling her into position.

Maggie peered through the glasses. For a moment she couldn't find what it was that she was supposed to be looking at – then she gasped. 'There's someone in there. With bins. He's watching the garden!'

'I see him all the time. So far he hasn't seen me seeing him. At least – I don't think so. If he has, it doesn't seem to deter him.'

'Who is he?' Maggie asked, outraged.

'The house is owned by a Brigadier Jerrold . . .'

'The room he's in is so dark you can't really get a good look at him,' Maggie said, stepping forward until she was by the sill.

'Maggie! He'll see you,' Bless cried, dashing forward to stop her.

'So? Two can play at his game . . .'

Bless pulled her away from the window then took the binoculars and lifted them to his eyes. Through the lens he saw the sleek features of a man he recognised but couldn't at once place. Then, as he watched, he saw the Brigadier slowly turn from surveying the garden and train his own glasses on the house.

'It's the man I met in the street,' he said, talking to himself. Then he gasped as the Brigadier raised his eye line and binoculars met binoculars in open hostility. 'He can see me!' he whispered.

'Good! There is a law against peeping Toms, you know.'

'What should we do?'

'Give him something to watch!' Maggie said, and in a trice her Agnes B T-shirt was off and the straps of her bra slid down her arms as her expert fingers released the fastener.

Bless, mesmerised by the flagrant behaviour of his neighbour, was unaware of this new development. 'What d'you suggest?' he asked. Then he gasped. 'What the . . .?' The man in the tower seemed to be having another fit. He had raised a shaking fist and was gesticulating wildly. 'Maggie, I think he's . . . having a fit!'

'Good!' shouted Maggie, and she cupped both her breasts

and crossed to the window, flaunting them exotically. 'Get a load of these – buster!' she yelled.

'Maggie!' Bless screeched, as she came into his line of vision. 'What are you doing, woman?'

'Playing Lady Godiva to his nasty little . . . Oh, shit!' she gasped turning her back and covering her breasts. 'Guess who's standing down there on the lawn!'

'Oh no!' Bless groaned.

'Mmh-mmh! Got it in one!' Maggie was scrambling back into her bra as she withdrew from the window. 'The architect from Hades has just had an eyeful!'

'Maggie!' Bless sobbed.

'Oh dearie, dearie me! I've done it again, Bless!'

'Dear God!' Laurence exclaimed. 'That ghastly harpy was waving her bosoms at me from your bedroom window!'

'What?' Rich asked, looking up and seeing Bless staring down at them.

'She was there, Richard. She was making obscene gestures . . . You don't think . . .? Oh, dear Lord! Can it be that she fancies me?'

'Of course not!'

'It wouldn't be the first time,' Laurence remonstrated. 'Women do find me attractive. They say I look like Douglas Fairbanks Junior . . . when he was younger, of course.'

'There's no one there but Bless!'

'There was. And I want to know why!'

Finding out why took some explaining. Even Rich seemed a little perplexed by the events. 'But why was she exposing herself?' he asked for the umpteenth time.

'Well – you see . . . The next-door neighbour was watching us through binoculars . . .'

'Yes. You've already said that . . .'

'And Maggie thought . . .'

'Well, I just wanted to teach him a lesson!'

'But why? What had he done? He could be a . . . a bird-watcher.'

'If he is, he won't have seen tits like those before!' Bless giggled.

'It isn't funny, Bless!' Rich was near to losing his temper. 'We have to live here, you know.'

Maggie pulled a face and looked suitably ashamed. 'Sorry!' she said, in a little girl's voice.

'Rich!' Bless cut in, coming to his friend's defence. 'We have every right to take our clothes off in our own bedrooms. We surely don't expect people to be watching us through binoculars?'

'There is, I think, a subtle difference between removing one's garments and flaunting oneself!' Laurence said, sniffing as though at an unpleasant smell and helping himself to a dry sherry from the drinks cupboard as though he were in his own home.

'I wasn't really flaunting myself!' Maggie protested.

'Remember, I saw you, Miss Heston,' Laurence rounded on her severely. 'You were stark naked and . . . being most provoking. That, in my vocabulary, I call flaunting.' He glared at her and then added as an afterthought, 'How you ever managed to play Viola with . . .' There was an awkward pause as he realised the dangers of the path he was taking and withdrew with a shudder.

'It wasn't easy!' Maggie agreed with him cheerfully. 'I had to have a specially cut jerkin. For the trouser scenes I looked like a boy with a very well-developed chest!'

'Yes! I expect you did,' Laurence agreed, sipping his sherry.

But it wasn't until that evening that all the pieces of the jigsaw began to slip into place. Then two things happened in quick succession.

The first was a phone call which Rich took. He returned to the drawing room, where the others were sitting having a pre-supper drink, looking perplexed. 'It was a Miss Fallon,' he said. 'She's invited us to dinner when it's convenient.'

'Oh, God!' Bless groaned. 'I'm not sure if I'm ready to meet the natives yet.'

'Nonsense! I'm sure Miss Fallon will become a great friend,' Laurence murmured. He was reading and only giving them half his attention.

'We haven't made a definite date. I don't honestly think it was the main reason for her call. She said she and her chums wanted to welcome us to the village. She seemed most insistent that we should know it. She said that we'd always receive a welcome at Pinchings.'

'What's Pinchings?'

'It's the name of a house,' Laurence said, drily. Then adjusting his glasses, he proceeded to read from the page in front of him. '"Pinchings will be opening its garden gate to the general public on the second Sunday in July. All proceeds to go to the church cleaning fund." It's mentioned in this funny little rag that I found on the hall table.'

'Oh! I forgot about that!' Bless exclaimed. 'I was given it the other morning. When I was returning from the flour festival, Rich.' He raised his hands to Maggie and Laurence. 'Don't ask! It's too long a story and far too humiliating . . .'

'Actually, it was very funny!' Rich cut in.

'But who gave it to you?'

'The same guy that Maggie frightened off this morning.'

'We don't know that he was frightened. He could be about to sue us for indecent behaviour.'

'No! I saw him. I thought he was having a heart attack. In fact he might have been. He could be lying dead, for all we know . . .'

'What a way to go!' Rich giggled. 'The publicity, Maggie!'

'Who is this man?' Laurence asked.

'Our next-door neighbour. Brigadier Jerrold . . .'

Laurence glanced at the pages he held.

'The editor, no less.'

'Of what? What are you reading?' Rich asked.

'*The Bellingford Gazette*,' Laurence told him. 'And listen to this little gem from its leader column. "Now is the time for our village to unite. Now is the time for our little differences to be shelved. Now is the time for action. Now is the time for a leader to step forward and take up the banner of righteousness, the sword of sanctity and the arrows of salvation . . ."'

'Is there a lot more like that?' Rich asked. 'Only we have supper to cook . . .'

'Patience, dear boy! It gets better,' Laurence assured him, enjoying being the centre of attention.

'It reads rather like Shakespeare. You do it awfully well, Mr Fielding.'

'Thank you . . . Margaret.' He smiled at her – almost warmly. 'Shall I go on? The most interesting part is yet to come!'

'I should hope so,' Rich murmured.

'"A little bird has told the *Gazette* that we in beautiful Bellingford are no longer to be spared the spread of filth that pollutes the outside world. No longer can we pride ourselves on being a little bit of the old England we fought to protect against the barbarians. In a changing world we here in our beloved village have been in touch with the rich past, the happy yesteryears of our heritage. Now all that could change if we do not, each man of us, make a stand. Are we to allow perverts to move into our lovely old houses? . . ."'

'What?' Rich gasped, staring at Laurence with a look of disbelief.

'Oh, shit!' Maggie murmured.

'Let me finish!' Laurence said. 'There isn't much more. ". . . perverts to move into our lovely old houses? Are we to have junkies begging on our leafy lanes next? Should we expect vagrants sleeping in the doorway of the village hall? The danger of a liberal attitude is that it fosters a libertine's world. Decent folk must band together. Do not allow yourselves to be swayed by the artsy-crafty, left-wing *Guardian* wallahs. Listen to your hearts and to your minds and to the English blood in your English veins. This is *our* village. *Our* little corner of this sceptred isle; this realm; this England. Keep Bellingford clean! Watch this space!"' Laurence paused dramatically.

There was silence in the room.

'He then goes on to say that the old roses are particularly good in Cockpits' garden this year and that he congratulates his wife on having cared for them and encouraged them. D'you want any more?'

'Does he mean us?' Bless asked when neither of the others spoke. 'Are we the perverts?'

'Probably. Unless there has been a sudden influx of sexual deviants. But of course in a court of law he would point out that he has named no names.'

'But he knows nothing about us,' Bless protested.

'Except that we're two guys who are living together. It doesn't take a degree in psychology to do the sums, does it?' Rich pointed out.

'So? Why shouldn't we live together. It isn't illegal.' Bless's voice was showing tension. 'What difference will our being here make to him? We're not asking him to watch us in bed. In fact, as neighbours we'll probably turn out to be depressingly dull.'

'I'm not so sure about that!' Laurence said, sounding pompous again. 'He's probably got photographs of Margaret's bosom now – to add to his dossier!'

'It might help,' Maggie suggested, cheerfully. 'You could use it as proof that you screw women. Well . . . I was at a bedroom window at the time . . .'

'I don't screw women. I don't even want to. What the fuck has it got to do with him who I screw?'

'Oh – ignore it, Bless!' Rich said. 'He's obviously a nutter.'

'He's a nutter who happens to live next door to us,' Bless said, frowning. 'I'm going to pay Brigadier Jerrold a call.'

'No, Bless! You'll only make things worse.'

'This happens to be our home now. This is where we've chosen to be together. I'm not going to live here under sufferance or by pretence. I'm proud to be your lover. And if people don't like it – that's their problem. Not mine.'

Laurence gave a round of applause. But Rich raised his

hands. 'I agree,' he said. 'And thank you! The best thing is just to ignore it . . .'

'And hope it'll go away, Rich? Well – what if it doesn't? What does he mean, "Watch this space"? Is he going to bring in the heavies in their jack boots – while we sit around, ignoring? No way. I'm going to confront him.'

'I say, how splendid!' Laurence clapped his hands gleefully. 'Do go while we're here, won't you?'

'Too right. I will. I'm going first thing tomorrow morning,' Bless said, still shaking with anger.

'It's Sunday. Better wait until after church parade,' Laurence advised. 'Will we all be going? To church, I mean. Not to the confrontation.'

'I don't want anyone with me. I shall do this on my own,' Bless said, and he hurried out of the room.

'That was rather impressive,' Laurence said, staring after him.

'It's best just to ignore it,' Rich muttered.

Laurence looked at his friend thoughtfully for a moment, seemed as if he was going to say something, but then decided to remain silent.

'I can't go to church,' Maggie said mournfully. 'Though I sometimes long to.'

'What prevents you?' Laurence asked her.

'I'm a lapsed Catholic. The confession would last a lifetime!' As she spoke she reached across in front of Laurence and helped herself to an open bottle of wine.

'I'm not at all surprised!' Laurence agreed, watching her. Then he sighed. 'I should open another bottle, Richard. Miss Heston seems to be having most of that one.'

'Good idea!' Maggie exclaimed, emptying more wine into her glass. 'Really, Mr Fielding! You would drive a saint to drink!'

'Your Catholic upbringing has, if I may say so, a lot to answer for.'

'Really?' Maggie asked, looking puzzled.

'I have often observed that the possibility of forgiveness through confession allows for unbridled indulgence.'

'Whereas you lot simply wallow in guilt!' Maggie observed with a dazzlingly cold smile.

'Ah yes, Richard. Do open another bottle. If we are to have an evening of theology we may as well all get thoroughly plastered.'

12

Just Another Sunday Morning

The bells of St Michael and all the Angels rang out erratically. One of the ringers seemed relentlessly out of synch. On the downward roll his or her bell leapt in uncomfortably close to the previous one; on the upward sweep there would be an agonising pause before it and the bell above rang out in unison. The resultant noise had an unsettling effect. It created a nervous anticipation which interfered with the Sunday papers and would have kept Jimmy Porter looking back in anger for all of eternity.

Up on the executive estate, however, the call to worship fell on deaf ears. Radio Two and the sound of lawnmowers almost drowned out the peals. The squeal of the young at play and car engines being tuned added to the drowsy languor of suburban rest.

The bedroom curtains of Melanie and Barry in computers were still closed. Their children were old enough to get their own cornflakes and Sunday morning was for Mummy and Daddy. 'Our one chance in the week, Sand – so long as he isn't in a stupor from the night before or I haven't put my back out at aerobics. I mean, it's like we've become middle-aged. We used to be a three-nights-a-week couple – now we're lucky to fit one in on a Sunday morning. Pathetic! How about you, Sand? You and

Simon still passion's playthings? Or has having little Gary cramped your style?'

'No. He's as good as gold, Mel. We gave him a TV in his room, didn't we?'

'Well, Wayne and Karla surf the net – but they still need attention every night of the bleeding week.'

'Actually, Mel, Simon can be quite romantic.'

'Really?'

'Oh, yes. He's a beast when he's roused. You'd be surprised.'

'I would, really. I mean, he seems so quiet . . .'

'Yes. But you know what they say – the quiet ones can be deceptive.'

'And then – being in insurance doesn't exactly reek of sex, does it?'

'I think that's what does it, Mel. Simon works so close to the life-and-death situation that when he gets into bed he feels he has to make the most of it. I mean – you never know when your call may come, do you? The grim reaper rapping on the window pane.' She shuddered with creative energy. 'Time's hurrying footsteps . . .'

'Oh, do shut up, Sandra. I sometimes regret you ever started creative writing. It's like living next door to Barbara Cartland.'

'I wish!' Sandra exclaimed ruefully. 'She's proved herself as a writer, Mel. That you can't deny.'

'But all that pink, Sand.'

'I quite like pink . . .'

On this particular Sunday Sandra and her Simon were taking Gary to the coast. 'Not a picnic,' Simon had explained to Barry in computers when they were both mowing their lawns the previous morning. 'We prefer a pub lunch. Half of lager and a ploughman's, that sort of style.'

'He would be a lager and ploughman's guy, wouldn't he?' Barry later confided to Melanie, with crushing condescension. Barry was more of a gin and tonic and scampi in a basket man himself. So while Sandra, Simon and little Gary headed for sea, sand and strong cheddar, Melanie and Barry were sleeping off cardiac arrest. They had been to a dinner party at the Potters' over the road the evening before. Doreen had cooked entirely from Delia Smith – but 'added extra cream, as it's a special occasion' – and Stan had served several bottles of Châteauneuf-du-Pape which they'd brought back on the ferry when they'd taken the camper van over and done a serious shopping spree in Calais. Delia's pork chops à la Normande, as interpreted by Doreen, had been as rich as Croesus, and the Châteauneuf, as poured by Stan, had been heavy as hell. Melanie and Barry in computers had been up most of the night in intimate communication with the en suite toilet and the Alka Seltzer tablets.

At Pinchings Miss Hopkirk, Miss Bridey and Miss Fallon were putting on their coats. Although it was a warm day the church was always like a morgue – which in a way was suitable.

As Miss Bridey, the plump one, came down into the hall, she was attempting to fasten the buttons of her summer coat. She found Miss Fallon, the tall one, adjusting her hat at the mirror set into the hall stand. 'I wonder if the gentlemen from the Hall House will be at church?' she said, glancing over her shoulder.

'If they are we must make a point of introducing ourselves,' Miss Bridey observed. 'It's time we were off. Where is Ethel?'

'Seeing to the dogs,' Miss Fallon replied, crossing to the front door.

'We must hurry, Ethel!' Miss Bridey called, giving up on the buttons. 'This cotton coat seems to have shrunk over the winter,' she observed, going out of the door. Miss Fallon glanced at her ample frame and generously said nothing.

'Here I am!' Miss Hopkirk, the short one, burbled, hurrying out to join them. 'Rag wanted to go. That set Bobtail off – and then I thought I'd better let Tag out as well.'

'Those dogs are taking you over,' Miss Fallon said severely as she closed the door and checked that it was locked.

'Yes, dear! I expect they are!' Miss Hopkirk beamed at the suggestion.

Miss Bridey tugged again at her coat, but to no avail. 'I was saying to Marjorie,' she said, taking her attention away from the depressing thought of her expanding waistline, 'if the gentlemen from the Hall House are in church, we must make them welcome.'

'Of course we shall.'

'God made all creatures in his name, after all.'

'Even spiders?' Miss Fallon asked pointedly, knowing Miss Bridey's horror of all arachnids.

Anthony Daltry checked that he had small change for the collection and then bent to dust his shoes with a tea towel.

'Tony! That's for dishes!' his wife Heather said coming in from the garden.

'You've got mud all over yours,' Anthony said, looking at her brogues. 'What have you been doing?'

'I went to see Belter.'

'I don't know why you don't sleep with that horse.'

'At least if I did I would be sure of his fidelity.'

'Please!'

'What?'

'Don't start that again.'

'I'm not starting anything,' his wife said, sourly, as she glanced in the mirror and pulled at the collar of her blouse.

'You never used to want sexual reassurance all the time.'

'I do not want reassurance. I would just like to know what you get up to during the week.'

'I commute. I work to keep us. I endure privation and hardship . . .'

'I phoned the office. Miss Harkness said you were out to lunch.'

'I do have to eat.'

'It was after four, Anthony!'

'I was with a client.'

'I have only your word for that.'

'Heather, look at me! I am balding. I am bulging. I am probably also boring. Do you really see me in the role of a Lothario?'

'Looks can be deceptive.'

'Oh, for heaven's sake! I am about as likely to be having an extramarital affair as is . . . our vicar,' Tony exclaimed, groping for a suitably preposterous example of sexual impropriety as he switched on the alarm system and pushed Heather ahead of him out of the kitchen door.

Meanwhile the vicar, so recently instanced as an improbable adulterer, was robing in the vestry of the parish church of St Michael and all the Angels. As he did so, he was staring at a postcard that was propped up on the table in front of him. It had arrived earlier in the week and had occupied his mind considerably ever since. The picture was of the gigantic statue of the Virgin and Christ child, situated on a hill overlooking the town of Le Puy on the western edge of France's Massif Central. The detail was first rate and it was possible to discern human faces peering out from the viewing platform within the Virgin's crown. There was a small boy with his hand raised, clear for all to see as he emulated the infant Jesus's cheery wave. The iconography was perhaps a little too Roman for delivery to an Anglican vicarage. But the feat of engineering undoubtedly had a universal appeal and the statue could be appreciated as a curiosity as well as a religious object. However, it wasn't the picture but the message scrawled on its back that had so puzzled and perturbed the recipient and continued now to hold his attention. 'Dear Vicar,' it read, 'I'll be returning to Bellingford before the end of the month and will require your assistance. I'll contact you on arrival and hope you'll be available to do an exorcism with all possible haste. Yours, D. Simpson (Ms).'

An exorcism? It was a long time since the Revd Andrew Skrimshaw had been called upon to conduct that most pagan of Christian ceremonies. But the memory was still vivid for him and the implications as terrible as before. Was the postcard genuine? Or had D. Simpson (Ms) discovered something that the vicar had hoped would be for ever buried? Had, in fact, D. Simpson (Ms) unearthed a certain skeleton and was she even now preparing to use it against him and his family? If so, he wondered, was there a prayer in the Anglican liturgy that could evoke protection against . . . blackmail?

'I particularly enjoy the Sabbath in an English village,' Laurence announced as he and Rich strode out of the Hall House gates and turned their steps towards the parish church. 'People would say that an English village is a dull place. But it is its very conformity, yes! its dullness even, that appeals to me. I actually enjoy the sense of boredom that accompanies the day. I find it stimulating. In many ways I am absolutely on the side of our friend the Brigadier. If I lived next door to you I wouldn't have wanted you to move in either.'

'Laurence! You're the one who's been encouraging Bless to confront the beastly man with all guns blasting.'

'And I hope he does. Because I do not belong here. But if I did – I would want to maintain the status quo. Look around you, Richard. What do you see? Peace, tranquillity . . .'

'And you think Bless and I will change all that?'

'Of course not. If you had let me finish I was about to add the word normality to the list.'

'By normal you mean . . .?'

'It's perfectly obvious. I wouldn't want perverts living next door.'

'Perverts? You can call us that?'

'I may be queer,' the older man remarked in a severe voice, 'but at least I know how to behave. Good morning,' he said, bowing to the woman who had just that moment emerged from the drive of the house they were passing.

'Oh, dear!' Rosemary Jerrold exclaimed, and she immediately turned tail and disappeared back through the gates.

'Extraordinary behaviour!' Laurence observed, watching her retreating figure. Then, glancing at the sign on the gate, he smiled grimly. 'Interesting! This house is Cockpits.' As he spoke he poked at the name plate with his walking stick. 'The editorial address for that amusing little rag we were reading. One can only assume therefore that that poor creature must have been the Brigadier's wife.'

'Do hurry, Laurence! If you insist on playing Miss Marple we shall be late for the off.'

'Richard! We are going to a service of worship. Not the St Leger.'

'It might just as well be. Why on earth did I let you talk me into this?'

'Because you are the new squire and because you do know how to behave.'

'Implying that Bless doesn't?'

'Precisely. One's private life should not be allowed to inconvenience other people. The horses should be allowed to go unfrightened in the streets.'

'You're outrageously closeted, Laurence.'

'Thank you!' Laurence beamed, as though he'd just been paid an enormous compliment. Then, raising his hat again, he called, 'Good morning!' to the three elderly women of assorted sizes who were about to pass through the lych gate that he and Rich had now reached.

'Oh! Good morning!' Miss Bridey said, with a brimming smile.

'Good morning!' Miss Hopkirk echoed.

'Good morning!' Miss Fallon added. She was ahead of the other two and had to look back over her shoulder. 'You're the gentlemen from the Hall House, I believe?'

'Well . . .' Laurence hesitated.

'You are most welcome!' Miss Bridey enthused. 'Really, most welcome.' And the three women all nodded their heads emphatically as they hurried into the church.

'Thank you so much!' Laurence called after them.

'They now assume that you're the owner of the Hall House!' Rich observed.

'No. Surely . . .'

'Well, they certainly think you're one of the new occupiers.'

'Am I not?' Laurence asked, looking squarely at Rich and taking him by surprise.

'Well, no. Of course you're not . . .' Rich said, the words out before he had time to consider and possibly soften them.

'I see,' the older man said, his voice grim. 'I had somehow

thought that Bellingford was to be my home from home in the country in the same way that the flat has become your *pied-à-terre* in town.'

'Well – it goes without saying that you'll always be welcome . . .'

'As a guest? I'm not sure how I shall fit in – as a guest. There is an impermanence about such a role that I could find agitating.'

'Nevertheless – you'll always be welcome . . .'

The older man cleared his throat. 'Thank you,' he said.

There was now an awkward pause. Neither of them had left space for any further discussion without things being said that could be hurtful and regretted later.

'We'd better go in,' Rich said at last. 'We shall be late.'

Laurence stalked ahead of him, his straight back and raised head a picture of reprimand and wounded sensitivity. Rich sighed and followed more slowly. Not for the first time he wondered if the move to Bellingford wasn't proving to be a terrible mistake.

13

The Brigadier Arranges A Visit

Rosemary Jerrold sat at the drawing room window in Cockpits. She was still wearing her coat and clasped her handbag and gloves in her hands. A warm sun was streaming in through the open windows and a blackbird was singing out in the garden. But Rosemary felt none of the sun's warmth, nor did she notice the bird's sweet music. She sat in a state of suspended animation, her attention hovering in a gloaming world of half thoughts and nagging fears. She should be in church – but really, if she were, her state of mind would not have been very different nor her sense of worship greatly increased.

Later her husband came in to her. He had been crossing the lawn from the Tower and was surprised to see her through the window.

'I thought you were at morning service,' he said.

'As you can see, I am not,' she replied after a moment. She did not turn to look at him as she spoke, but continued to stare with unseeing eyes out of the window.

'Not feeling up to snuff?' her husband asked, confused by her manner. He was accustomed to his wife being quiet in his presence, but he expected a degree of nervous respect, of eagerness to please, which now seemed to be missing.

'I met . . . one of our new neighbours. The younger one was not present. But . . . the other one. The more . . . conventional one. Well, at least his hair is somewhat shorter and he wears a jacket . . . He was outside the gate as I was leaving. I could not avoid seeing him. He was in the company of an older gentleman . . .'

The Brigadier grimaced. 'The older ones are very often the worst of the lot. As a breed, poofters do not improve with age,' he muttered.

'They were on their way to the church, I think,' his wife continued. 'Certainly they were not dressed for a walk in the countryside, and where else would they have been going at such an hour of a Sunday morning?' She pondered this thought, then shook her head, as if dismissing any other possible explanation for their unexpected appearance at her gate. 'I would have had to walk beside them. I turned back. I did not feel . . . confident to be in their company.'

'Quite right too! One mustn't have anything to do with that type. We are all judged by the company we keep.'

Rosemary turned her head quickly, now for the first time looking at her husband. Was there a gleam of accusation in her eyes? The Brigadier cleared his throat and rubbed his palms together.

'I have just spoken on the telephone to Phyllis,' he said, seeming almost flustered by his wife's expression. She meanwhile raised her eyebrows, blinked, then looked away.

'How was Phyllis?' she asked, her tone conversational.

'Not so good. Aunt Maud is being very demanding.'

'I am sorry to hear that.'

'Yes. I shall have to go up, I'm afraid. If you could pack my things. I shall be away for several days.'

'You cannot go until tomorrow.'

'I beg your pardon?'

'There are no trains to Scarborough on a Sunday, Selwyn.'

'No. Quite so. Well then – tomorrow it must be. But as soon as is possible. The matter is urgent. Phyllis seemed most distressed.

As usual it will be left to me to sort things out. I will telephone her again and make arrangements.'

'Why did you not arrange things at the time?'

'I naturally wanted to consult with you first.'

'Thank you, Selwyn,' his wife said, twisting her gloves in her hands.

'You will not mind if my sister pays a visit for a few days?'

'I should welcome it,' Rosemary Jerrold assured him.

The Brigadier turned abruptly and left the room. But once in the hall he hesitated and looked back. 'If there are any callers today, I do not wish to be disturbed. Tell them that I am not at home . . . will you?'

'Naturally,' his wife replied, without looking at him.

14

Recalled To Life

The light of dawn had somewhat cleared Bless's brain. One of his virtues was an ability to go back on his words if it seemed appropriate, and as he washed up the breakfast things it became more than obvious that to go storming round to the Brigadier's in a state of high dudgeon – was there, he wondered, a low version? – wouldn't achieve anything and would probably make matters worse. The gentle approach was the obvious answer.

He would woo his new neighbours. He would charm them into submission. He would be so irresistible that they'd plead for his friendship. And he would start not with the galloping major but with his faded wife. He cheered up enormously at the thought. Taking the kitchen scissors, he went out into the garden. He would pick the Brigadier's wife a posy. A posy seemed suitably rustic. It would be his first neighbourly gesture. Later he would take in home-made jam and, once he had mastered the art, crisp new loaves and sponge cakes brimming with cream. He was quite carried away with the possibilities. Mrs Jerrold would soon bless the day that he arrived to live beside her, and she would in time persuade her husband. They would all become the best of friends and the Brigadier would look upon him as a son.

When Maggie woke she knew at once she was dead. There

was no pain. Her body pressed down against the mattress, inert and lifeless. Even the silence that surrounded her was thick and leaden. She had died in the night. It had been bound to happen sooner or later. Almost certainly the cause would turn out to be acute alcoholic poisoning. It no doubt served her right. Though Laurence could not escape a certain responsibility. He made her nervous, and when she was nervous she didn't notice how often she emptied and filled her glass. Last night she had drunk as though there was to be no tomorrow, and now here she was being proved right. She was dead and this was Limbo. She vaguely remembered about Limbo from her days in the convent. It was a sort of waiting room where you were put until the station master decided which was your correct train. Hers she felt sure would be a stopping diesel on a commuter line with clouded windows and grimy seats, progressing with shuddering slowness through an endlessly dreary industrial landscape.

Thought of a view forced her up into a sitting position. She stared round glumly at the room she was in. She'd never seen it before in her life. It was like the set for the final few moments of *2001: A Space Odyssey* – pale green, pristine and completely incomprehensible. Getting out of bed, she stumbled towards the curtained window, through which chinks of light beckoned. Steadying herself for a moment as if preparing for a herculean task, she took a deep breath. Then, with a dramatic gesture, she threw the material aside. The bright light beyond corkscrewed into her brain. Raising her hands for protection, she peered between the fingers. As she did so the silence was transformed to a cacophony of piercing whistles and trills as a million demonic birds shrieked at her. She clamped her hands over her ears, risking blindness in favour of this new torture.

Bless, down below in the garden, looked up in surprise. He was greeted by a view of the Heston breasts with their owner just behind them doing a gesture suitable for the Scottish play or a Munch painting. He raised his hand in greeting. It held a mass of white and pink roses, surrounded by sprigs of rosemary and other twiggy herbs.

'How dear of him,' Maggie whimpered. 'For my grave, I suppose.' Then her knees buckled under her and she sank into a praying position with her elbows on the sill and her chin propped up on her hands.

Bless seemed to be calling to her from the other world. Perhaps he was at some kind of séance. 'How sweet! He's trying to reach me!' she murmured. But it was useless. She couldn't hear him. And now he was also pointing towards a wall that skirted the garden. Was he perhaps in Paradise? she wondered. That had always been described as a garden . . . But no, she was getting confused. Bless was one of the living – it was she who had passed away. Turning her gaze in the direction he was pointing, she could just make out, beyond the wall, the roof of a small tower. It reminded her of something . . . something from her past . . . Then, with another wave, Bless disappeared from sight.

She was terribly thirsty. Somehow she managed to pull on the shroud that she found lying across the end of the bed. It covered her nakedness and closely resembled a dressing gown she had once owned – in the land of the living. 'I'll just have a drink of water,' she whispered, 'before I get on the train.' And straightening up in an attempt at dignity, she stumbled towards the door.

When she reached the top of the stairs she could hear a bell ringing. When she reached the hall she realised it was a telephone. When she reached the telephone she rose again from the dead. The voice at the other end was American and reassuringly animated. 'Hi!' it said. 'Is that Richard Charteris?'

'Certainly not!' she croaked. 'I am far more butch.'

'This is Sol Fienstein,' the voice explained.

Maggie made an instant recovery. Sol Fienstein was one of Broadway's biggest producers. She had once been presented by him. Well – the RSC had been presented and she had been part of the RSC. She'd played Doll Tearsheet with a cleavage that diminished the Grand Canyon, according to the *New York Times*.

'Hello, Mr Fienstein. It's Maggie Heston . . .'

'Maggie! Baby . . .' the voice said, clearly not knowing who the hell she was. 'Is Rich there?'

'I don't think so. I'm a house guest. I was in one of your productions – with the RSC . . .'

'A wonderful company, doll . . .'

'That's right. I played Doll . . .' Even if Mr Fienstein didn't remember, he sure was going to.

15

First Contact

Bless pressed the bell. An electronic peal echoed through the house. Then he waited. Eventually, after what seemed a long time, the door opened. The woman who stood before him was wearing a coat and hat. Perhaps she was on her way out, he thought. 'Yes?' she asked, her voice nervous.

'Mrs Jerrold?'

'Yes?' she whispered.

'I'm Bless Maynard.'

'Pardon?'

'Your new next-door neighbour.'

'Yes.'

'I've . . . brought some flowers.'

'Very nice,' she murmured. But she didn't reach out to take them.

'They're for you,' Bless explained, pushing the bunch towards her.

'My husband does not like flowers in the house,' Rosemary Jerrold stammered.

'Why not?'

'They remind him of death.'

Bless was disappointed. 'I picked them specially,' he said.

'So kind.' The boy looked dejected. So she relented and took the flowers. 'They're . . . lovely.'

'I don't know the names of all of them. These are roses here and . . . there are other things.'

'Yes.'

'Is your husband at home?'

'He has to go away.'

'I hoped . . . we might meet.'

'He will be gone some time.' As she spoke she was edging the door closed again.

'Perhaps, when he returns?' Bless suggested, putting his foot in the opening and leaning against the smooth wood, anxious not to lose contact.

'What did you want?' Rosemary asked, her voice tense as she exerted pressure on the door.

'I hoped we might be friends,' Bless said after a moment.

'Friends?' she gasped.

They were now struggling, one either side of the door, creating an impasse. Rosemary, in her agitation, was using both hands to give herself added power, and as she did so she poked the flowers she was holding round the side of the door. Inadvertently they went into Bless's face. A twig grazed his eye. In surprise he moved his body away. As his weight was taken from the door it slammed shut, trapping the bouquet. The roses, caught as under a guillotine, fell in a shower of petals and the smell of crushed herbs. Bless pulled away, his eye stinging and watering badly.

'The flowers! I picked them specially! As a gift for you!' he shouted through the closed door. But no answer came back. Nor did the door open again.

Bless backed away down the drive, still staring with his good eye and wiping the wounded one with a handkerchief. Looking up, he glimpsed a figure watching from an upstairs window. It was the Brigadier. He seemed strangely lifeless, like a statue.

Bless raised a hand. It was a gesture reminiscent of a messenger in a Greek tragedy. 'All hail!' he called. But the Brigadier remained motionless and staring. 'Oh well – fuck you!' Bless yelled, overwhelmed with sudden anger, and he held up a single finger to emphasise the sentiment. The Brigadier didn't flinch. Bless stabbed his finger in the air again – a futile gesture, producing no reaction whatsoever. Then, feeling rather foolish, he turned and hurried away down the drive.

That was a hopeless beginning, he thought, as he returned to the house. He was now not only bad-tempered but thoroughly depressed.

Maggie was sitting on the stairs in the hall, eating cold potatoes from a tureen. 'Oh, terrific! You finally got up!' Bless snapped, venting his ill humour on her.

'I feel dreadful.'

'So you should.'

'Why?'

'Because you drank crates of wine last night and ended up doing all the songs from *A Chorus Line* – with movements.'

'With movements?' she groaned.

'With movements.' Then he sighed and sat down beside her on the stairs and took a potato from the dish. They both munched, glumly.

'Sol Fienstein phoned,' Maggie said at last, speaking with her mouth full.

'Sorry?'

'From America. He's sending a fax. Something about Rich going over tomorrow . . . He seemed quite excited.'

'Going over where tomorrow?' Bless asked.

'New York.'

'Well, he can't, can he? He has another week of holiday. He promised me.' Maggie shrugged and crammed in another potato. 'He's surely not going to swan off to New York and leave me here?'

'Why not?'

'Because . . . well . . . we're not even settled in yet. I can't drive. I don't know anyone in the village. That creep next door loathes me. I don't know how the Aga works. We have to engage a cleaner and a gardener and . . . Rich has all the money. What will I live on if he . . .? Oh, shit!' he said, getting up and stumping off towards the kitchen.

'That's show biz, darling!' Maggie called, running her fingers round the bottom of the tureen and then licking off the buttery juices. 'Ugh!' she groaned. 'I feel sick now . . .'

Rich and Laurence returned from morning service with the self-righteousness that the C of E dispenses to its flock in place of Catholic absolution or eastern nirvana. They had done what they ought to do and been seen to do it. It was a highly agreeable state of mind.

As soon as Rich heard that Sol had phoned he dived into the study and there followed a lot of animated muttering from behind closed doors. Later he emerged exuberant and flushed.

'I'm off to the States,' he announced.

'Now? Or will you stay for lunch?' Bless asked, wishing he didn't sound so beady.

'I'll go up to town tonight and fly out first thing in the morning. I must get on to Steve to fix a ticket . . .'

'Excuse me,' Bless cut in, lowering his voice, aware that both Maggie and Laurence were hanging on to their every word. 'I thought you were still on holiday.'

'Holiday? Are you kidding? The moguls call! We've got a serious bite for the film rights on *Manhattan B . . .*' and he hurried back into the study to make yet more phone calls.

'Well!' Laurence murmured, replenishing his sherry glass with a smug smile, 'it seems the little wife is to be left to fend for herself.'

'Pardon me while I powder my thighs,' Bless snapped and he hurried out of the room.

'You are such a bitch, Mr Fielding,' Maggie remarked.

'I know! I just can't help it!'

Later in the afternoon Laurence set off for London wanting to avoid the post-weekend traffic and soon after Rich and Maggie left also, in Rich's BMW.

As Bless closed the back door after them the house seemed suddenly very big and Bellingford as isolated as Outer Mongolia. He went from room to room, clearing up in a desultory way. There were beds to strip and lunch to be cleared.

'I hope it isn't going to be boring here,' he said to the empty kitchen.

16

Things That Go Bump In The Night

Meadow Lane was not the most direct route from Fairlow, nor had it been built for speed. But it was little used and all its twists and turns with its high hedges and its looped overhead branches gave a sense of secrecy and of cover. In the dead of night along this rural byway a Deux Chevaux sped as if driven by a maniac. The little car bucked and swerved round the corners, mounted the steep verges and narrowly avoided catastrophe with an awkwardly positioned wayside sign as it careered to a junction and screeched into a new direction.

Reaching the top of the hill where the ground fell away towards the Belling Brook and the bowl of hills that contained the village, the car abruptly slowed and pulled into the deep shade of a spreading chestnut tree. The headlights were snapped off and the engine silenced. After a moment's pause the driving door swung open and a figure climbed out into the dark and breathing night.

The view down into the village was palely lit by a half-moon. Not a light glimmered in any of the houses. Nor was a sound heard from all the sleeping homesteads. Even the dogs were silent, leaving the night to the hooting owls in the churchyard trees and the screeching hunters of the dark. The lone figure watched intently as the seconds turned into minutes. Whoever it was who had just driven with such urgency towards Bellingford and was now skulking in the shadows like a fugitive or a felon appeared to be the only living human abroad at that ungodly hour.

When satisfied that this was so, this same person returned to the car. Opening once more the driver's door he or she leaned inside and released the brake. Then, with hands on the steering wheel and exerting all their strength, they pushed the little car towards the brow of the hill. As the steep gradient started to take effect and the car began at first to coast and then to glide with gathering speed downwards towards the village, the driver leapt inside and pulled the door closed, taking care not to slam it noisily.

When the car had almost reached the ford the sound of an engine broke the silence. Lights could be seen flashing amongst the trees up near the church. Another vehicle was approaching the village along the main Fairlow road.

The driver of the Deux Chevaux looked across the village green round which the lane curved. Then, after glancing once more in the direction of the approaching lights and making a hasty calculation, they engaged gear. The motor at once roared into life. With a surge of energy and a loud popping of exhaust the little car leapt forward, wheels screaming. It cleaved the water of the ford like a speedboat on a lake, spewing a bow wave to right and left. Then, as the driver pulled on the steering wheel, the car swerved off the lane and started a mad dash straight across the grass of the green, heading for the houses on the other side. The headlights flicked off again and the way ahead disappeared into black as the car bucked and bounced over the rough ground.

At the same time, up on the road by the church a powerful Audi screeched round a corner, its lights illuminating the heavy summer trees and sending brilliant rays leaping amongst the branches. The driver changed gear like a champion as the car started the descent to the village.

The Deux Chevaux had now reached the far side of the green. Its wheels hit the kerbstones, making it shudder and lurch, then it crunched down on to the road and swung round, heading in the direction of the main part of the village. As the car straightened up, the driver was dazzled by the lights of the other vehicle reflected in the rearview mirror. It would be only a matter of moments before it overtook them. On an impulse, prompted by fear, panic and a desperate need for somewhere to hide, the Deux Chevaux swung in through the gates of the Hall House.

Once inside the comparative security of the grounds, and shrouded a little from the outer world by the shrubs of the front border, the car sped up the short drive and swerved round the side of the house, squealing to a halt in the stable yard.

Bless woke with a start. The by now familiar silence of Bellingford was shattered by the sound of a car speeding past the front of the house. Then, after a screech of brakes and a crunch of metal, a horn started to blare and a dog barked somewhere up in the village.

Bless leapt out of bed and hurried to the landing. From the window at the head of the stairs he could see the drive and a partial view of the green beyond. The lights of a car were shining into the side shrubbery beside the wrought-iron gates. The car itself was propped against one of the gateposts. As Bless watched, a figure emerged from the driving seat and opened the bonnet. A moment later the sound of the horn was quelled. Then the figure turned and stared up the drive, towards the house.

Bless was standing stark naked at the window. Fearing he might be seen, he pulled back into the shadows. The stranger started to walk slowly towards the house. His movements were furtive, as though he wished for secrecy – though how he could hope for it after such a dramatic arrival seemed absurd. Bless turned and ran back to his bedroom. If investigation was called for, he decided, it would probably be best not to conduct it in the nude. Grabbing a pair of jeans he hopped and pulled as he hurried down the stairs. He managed to get the jeans on as he reached the hall. Once there and with time to secure only the top button, he wrenched open the front door and switched on the porch light at the same time. Immediately in front of him, with his fist raised in a threatening gesture, stood a tall, well-built young man with dark, curling hair and lean, sharp features.

The two men stared as they weighed each other up. The stranger's eyes moved slowly down the length of Bless's body and then up to his face once more.

'Hello!' he said at last, smiling and lowering his fist. His voice was warm, like a friendly massage. Bless gasped involuntarily and became acutely aware that the flies of his jeans were open. 'I'm looking for . . . a friend,' the stranger continued, raising his eyebrows in a knowing way. His words were somewhat obscured by a heavy foreign accent.

'A friend?' Bless gasped. It was only a few hours ago that he'd been pleading with Rich not to go off and leave him amid the alien corn, and now . . . Was he really being propositioned on his own doorstep? And in the middle of the night? Was this what life in an English village had to offer? He felt quite flustered and only remembered just in time that he was no longer a single person. Isn't that typical? he thought. You get a good relationship going for the first time in your entire life and only *then* does a drop-dead-gorgeous Adonis come knocking on your door.

'You seem startled,' the man said, leaning in towards him with his arm nonchalantly resting on the door frame. His deep, sexy voice sent shock waves down Bless's spine.

'Startled?' he gasped. 'Well, it's the middle of the night. I was in bed . . .'

'I can tell!' the stranger said, glancing again at his bare chest and unbuttoned jeans.

'What is it you want?' Bless asked, trying to control his agitation and managing to sound aggressive.

'I told you. I am looking for a friend. Have you seen anyone?'

'Seen anyone? How could I have? I was in bed . . .' Bless repeated, then wished he hadn't.

'Lucky bed!' the stranger grinned. 'Were you alone?'

'That's none of your business,' Bless replied, now sounding prim.

The stranger smiled at him again, his dark eyes flashing. Then he nodded. 'I will search about. Yes?'

'No!' Bless said quickly.

'Why?'

'Because this is a private house.'

The stranger looked him up and down. Then he smiled. 'You going to stop me, yes?' And he reached out and chucked Bless under the chin.

'Don't you threaten me!' Bless warned him. 'I have a black belt in karate.' And he raised both his hands and crouched, ready for the chop. As he did so he could feel the cool night air blowing into his gaping flies. The other man pulled back in mock alarm and held up his hands in surrender. Which was probably just as well. The black belt Bless referred to had been given to him by an ex-lover and was only ever intended as a fashion accessory.

'Please! You must help me,' the man said. 'I have to speak with her.'

'Who?'

'Diana. I know she is here somewhere. I have followed her for many days . . .'

'I don't know who you're talking about,' Bless protested. beginning to feel irritated.

'I am her friend. Only I can help her . . .'

'I say. Is everything all right?' This was a new voice that cut in, taking both Bless and the stranger by surprise. As they turned they saw a figure coming up the drive. Footsteps crunched on the gravel and as they drew closer the light from the porch revealed a man wearing a thick dressing gown and carrying a garden rake.

'Yes. We're fine, thank you,' Bless called, turning away from the amused and unswerving gaze of the foreigner and hurriedly doing up his flies.

'I'm Tony Daltry. From the Woods,' the new man explained, as he drew near. 'I heard a noise – and thought you might need assistance . . .'

Then another voice was heard shouting from the lane beyond the railings. 'What the devil's going on there?'

'Oh, Lord!' Tony grimaced. 'We've roused the Brigadier! Nothing to worry about, Brigadier!' he called.

'That, sir is a matter of opinion!' the Brigadier snorted, appearing on the drive behind them. He was dressed in pyjamas and an army trench coat and was carrying a rifle at the ready.

'Do take care, old chap!' Tony admonished, crossing towards him and pushing the barrel to one side. 'That thing might go off!'

'No point having a gun if you're not prepared to use it,' the Brigadier bellowed. Then he swung round, pointing the rifle at Bless. 'Go on then. Explain. Not that I'm in the least surprised by any of this. Now you people have arrived in the village we'll be lucky if we get a decent night's sleep ever again. Well, I won't stand for it sir. You understand? I won't damn well put up with it.' And as he spoke he took several more steps towards the door, elbowing the foreigner out of the way and sticking the rifle into the pit of Bless's naked stomach.

'I say! Steady on!' Tony Daltry exclaimed.

'You keep out of this!' the Brigadier snarled. 'You may have a lily for a liver. Well, I don't.'

'If you shoot me,' Bless said quietly, 'I shall die here on the doorstep in a sea of blood and entrails and you'll go to prison for the rest of your life. Now put that beastly thing away and go back to bed.'

'Listen to me, laddie!' the Brigadier snarled. 'There are laws in this land that still apply to your sort – even if you have managed to pervert justice and common sense and decency. And one of them pertains to public affray. You can't go banging about in the middle of the night . . .'

'Banging about?'

'Disturbing the peace . . .'

'I was not disturbing the peace. I was tucked up in bed fast asleep. I've been as much disturbed as you . . .' Bless interrupted him, his temper rising. Then he in his turn was interrupted by the sound of a car engine revving. The three men at the door turned to look down the drive in the direction of the noise. They saw the Audi reverse at speed out of the gates – its front end crunching down on to the ground as it was pulled away from the gatepost. A moment later, with a screech of tyres, the car roared up the road towards the village.

'There! You see! Now are you satisfied?' Bless demanded. 'The whole thing had nothing to do with me.'

'We are judged by the company we keep,' the Brigadier said. spitting venom.

'Oh – fuck off!' Bless retorted, losing his patience.

'Oh, very pleasant!' the Brigadier crowed. 'Barrack room talk!'

'That should make you feel at home then, shouldn't it?'

'You horrible little poofter – you'll be hearing from me,' the Brigadier barked, and he strode away down the drive, brandishing his rifle above his head.

'Sorry about that,' Tony Daltry said quietly, watching the Brigadier's departure. 'Bit of an old reactionary. Keeps himself to himself – but fights his corner. Best if you just ignore him . . .'

'What is it that I've done to him?'

'Oh . . . you know,' Tony said, waving his hand vaguely. 'Not much live and let live in that type. Doesn't go in for . . . you know . . . the alternative lifestyle . . .' He was obviously floundering now and getting into deeper and deeper water. 'Well – if there's nothing more I can do . . .' he continued. Then he brandished the rake. 'Grabbed the nearest weapon that came to hand.' He laughed, nervously. 'You and your . . . your pal and you . . . Whatever . . . Anyway . . . You must come and have dinner sometime – both of you . . . together . . . As it were . . . Meet the wife. That sort of thing . . .' And still muttering, he hurried away to safety.

'Thank you!' Bless called. Then he went back into the house and closed the door and leaned his back against it for support. 'Honestly,' he said to the dark hall, 'it's like being on an alien planet.'

17

The Staff Of Life

Dawn on the alien planet was heralded by the trilling of phones and the ringing of bells. Bless lay in a heap at his side of the bed, staring at the ceiling and trying to gather his wits. Nothing seemed familiar. The line, 'The isle is full of noises, sounds and sweet airs . . .' was his first recognisable thought.

'Oh, no!' he whimpered. 'Please not *The Tempest*!' Bless had once played Ariel. It had not been a happy experience. The local critic had referred to his 'rather effete performance', which had rankled considerably, seeing that the bard himself described this tiresome character as an 'airy spirit' – which didn't exactly smack of Rambo or Schwarzenegger – *and* the critic was a known closet case who had tried to corner Bless in the car park after a performance of *You Never Can Tell*. Hell hath no fury like an old poof scorned . . .

But the noises continued and the nightmare evaporated. The irritating warble he distinguished as the sound of the telephone ringing on the table at Rich's side of the bed. He slid across the king-size space and grabbed the receiver.

'Yes?' he growled.

'It's me.'

'Who?'

'Me!'

'Me? Who – me?'

'Me – me!'

Bless yawned, scratching his shoulder. 'I suppose you called to tell me your tiny hand is frozen.'

'No. That's your line,' the voice said.

'Who is this?' Another bell was still ringing somewhere in the house.

'Bless? Are you still in bed?'

'Rich?' Bless cried, sitting up and recognising the voice. 'Where are you?'

'At the airport.'

'I think there's somebody at the front door.'

'Are you still in bed?'

'I had a disturbed night. I've got to go . . . the door.'

'I wanted to say I'm sorry.'

'So you should be!' As he spoke Bless was once again struggling into his jeans, the receiver wedged between his shoulder and his ear.

'If I can pull off this Sol Fienstein deal it'll be worth millions.'

'You're already worth millions.'

'Don't exaggerate.'

'Me? Not exaggerate? You kidding? Reality makes me nervous.'

'I love you . . .'

'Got to go, Rich. Call me from New York.'

'I meant to tell you, after church yesterday I arranged . . .'

'The door, Rich . . . Love you!' Bless blew a kiss down the phone as he replaced the receiver. Then he raced to the landing, this time pulling on a T-shirt. As he did so the thought crossed his mind that the visitor might be the hunk from the previous night. He checked his flies as he ran down the stairs.

'My name is Doris Day,' announced the ancient woman standing in front of him on the doorstep.

'Hi! I'm Rock Hudson,' Bless quipped.

'Good morning, Mr 'Udson. I have come as arranged. As I

did not as yet have a key and as I could not raise you round the back passage I took the liberty of coming to the front.'

Bless blinked. 'Say again?'

'I am engaged, Mr 'Udson.'

'Congratulations.'

'My time starts from the moment I arrive. I have been ringing for twenty minutes.'

As Bless struggled to fathom what was happening, an old man in plus fours and sports coat and with a battered trilby hat pulled down over his ears appeared from the stable yard.

'There be a tiddy little tin can of a car parked across my premises,' he announced with a hostile glare.

'Your premises? Who are you?' Bless asked, sinking deeper into the mire of incomprehensibility.

'That there, Mr 'Udson, is Old Tom,' the diva from Hollywood announced.

'But why is he here?'

'I be your gardener. But I'll be buggered if I know how I can garden with a car parked up my tool house.'

'What car?' Bless moaned.

'The car as is stuck in the back yard.'

'I shall make some tea,' Doris Day announced, pushing past Bless and entering the hall.

'Oh, please!' Bless sighed, sighting a sort of oasis at the suggestion.

Doris Day surveyed the hall. 'A nice and airy place!' she announced. 'Now don't you worry about me. I'm quite used to finding my way about in strange places. Nothing I like better than a good snoop round. This room is an office, is it?' she asked, pushing open a door.

'Are you goin' to move this car or do you expect me to mow with my dentures?' Old Tom demanded.

Weak with confusion, Bless went down the front steps on to the gravel and winced his way towards the back yard, his bare feet protesting at the sharp stones.

'You should wear boots, you know,' Tom observed. 'You

could get a nasty cut if you 'appened on some broken glass or a rusty tin can. I had an old mate cut his toe off, 'ay-making. He was wearing sand shoes at the time – on account his bunions were playing up. There she is . . .'

She was the Deux Chevaux. Bless stared at the car and then walked slowly round it as if hoping for a clue. 'I don't know who it belongs to,' he said at last.

'Well, I can't get my mower out if I can't get in my tool house, can I?'

Bless opened the driving door and leaning inside released the brake. 'I'm learning to drive,' he called out. 'So far I have discovered where the brake is situated, and that's taken me fourteen lessons. Perhaps,' he added, emerging once more and facing Tom, 'we could now push the car to one side?'

'I don't push. It's bad for my 'ernia,' Old Tom advised him. So Bless did the pushing and found it quite easy, the car being so light. 'I shall now mow – as I intended,' Tom announced, sweeping past him with a petulant air.

'Did Mr Charteris engage you?' Bless asked timidly.

'I always garden here. I did for Miss Price and she were a real lady.'

'Well, I'm giving it my best shot!' Bless told him with a cheerful shrug. 'But I'm finding the wardrobe tricky at the moment. It's not really dirndl weather but it's too warm for tweeds.'

'You're another bloody daft incomer, you are,' Tom said, turning his back and going into the stable.

'Yes, I expect you're right,' Bless agreed with a nod. Then he crossed to the back door and rang the bell. After several minutes he heard singing as the other member of his newly acquired staff approached along the back corridor.

Though the words were unfamiliar the tune was recognisable and Doris Day trilled cheerfully as she drew the bolts and the Yale was turned.

'Darling Doris!' Bless exclaimed, going in. 'That was always one of my favourites.'

'I'll thank you not to be familiar, Mr 'Udson,' she told him as she led the way back to the kitchen. 'I've put on a kettle. You can bring the tea in the parlour.'

Bless waited for the kettle to boil, then put cups and saucers, milk and sugar and, as an afterthought, a barrel of biscuits on a tray. Finally filling the teapot, he carried the whole lot through to the drawing room, where he found Doris sitting in an arm-chair with her feet on a footstool, looking at a copy of *Hello!*

'That Fergie!' she exclaimed, as he entered. 'Look at the sight of her! Showing off her bathroom and toilet, I don't think. Time was our royal family didn't have bowel movements – now it's all over the papers. Thank you, dear,' she added as Bless handed her a cup of tea, placing it on a small table beside her chair. 'Three sugars. I need it for the energy.'

'Did Mr Charteris . . .? Um . . . I'm not sure why you're here.'

'Caught him after church, dear. Saw him from my window. I don't go myself. Never saw the need. I live so near the blessed place I feels as if it rubs off anyway. 'Cept funerals, 'course. And my own wedding . . .'

'So . . . he engaged you?'

'I told you, dear. Him and the nice elderly gentleman. And what a gentleman! Doffed his hat – you know the style. I told him I was available three days a week: Monday, Thursday and Friday. On Tuesday and Wednesday I do her next door.'

'Sorry?'

'Mrs Jerrold at Cockpits. Terrible state that place is in. Hasn't seen a paintbrush since the Armistice. Pass us another of the biscuits, dear, and you'd be advised to purchase chocolate shortcakes another time. Something with a bit more to bite on. So I said to him – Yes, I can fit you in. But only three days a week, mind.' She glanced up at the ceiling. 'My son did a lot of your plastering.'

'Really?'

'I don't think he did the fancy work, though,' she added in a disapproving voice. 'Fiddly bits gather dust. And you, dear? What's your line of business?'

'I used to be an actor.'

'There. I thought I'd heard the name! But you're not acting no more?'

'Not at the moment.'

'Never could see the point of it. Grown people pretending. It got me hot and bothered just to watch them. Not that I went often – pictures and the like. I did see *The Pyjama Game*. But it was too poli'cal for me. We country folk don't like pol'tics, thank you very much. Those MPs getting up to all sorts. Coming out of their cabinets and the like.' She shuddered and shook her head. Then, picking up her cup of tea, she blew on it noisily. 'I'll just make myself at home today, dear. Then on Thursday I can make a proper start.'

'Start?'

'Cleaning. Though I doubt you'll be very dirty. You people clear up after you, don't you? There used to be two gentlemen sharing up at Britannia House. Oh, this was years ago! They were as neat as neat. You scarcely knew they were there . . . I remember once they had an 'ouse party. A whole chara of men arrived in bright colours. You never did see the like . . .'

'Oi!' Old Tom called, appearing outside one of the French windows. 'I needs you.'

'No peace for the wicked, dear!' Doris said, settling back in her chair and flicking through the magazine on her lap. 'You put some shoes on before you go out.'

'There's a person asleep in your summerhouse,' Tom announced as soon as Bless joined him.

'A person? What sort of person?' Bless gasped.

'A human person – unless of course they be dead. Yes. That's more like it. 'Appen there's a body in your summerhouse.'

18

The Vanishing

The summerhouse was situated at the end of the main lawn. It stood in a glade beside the stream and was screened from the house by the heavy branches of weeping willows and banks of rhododendron.

'Miss Price used to come here for a bit of peace and quiet,' Tom remarked as he led the way slowly across the grass, 'away from the 'urly-burly of the village.'

Bless looked around, listening to the twittering birds, the soughing breeze and the miles and miles of silence. He'd been living in Bellingford for only two weeks, but already the thought of a bit of 'urly-burly seemed rather appealing.

'She never did get used to the pace of modern life,' Tom continued. 'So she used to totter over 'ere on 'er frame and she'd just sit and think.'

'You were fond of her?' Bless asked.

'Fond? I wouldn't go s'far as t'say that. She can be a right vixen.' He stood still for a moment, shaking his head and staring into space. 'I don't know what she'll make of having a body in her summer'ouse. I doubt she'll be too pleased. She likes the place to 'erself.'

'Well, maybe that doesn't matter now – seeing she's dead?'

'That's as I say – I don't know that for certain as I didn't go in . . .'

'No, not this present body . . . I meant Miss Price being dead.'

''Appen!' Tom said, giving Bless a dark look. 'But then again with that one you never can be sure. She wasn't a woman to give in easy.'

'All the same – she was very old, wasn't she?'

'Not for these parts. She'd be ninety-seven come August . . .'

'That's . . . a good age!' Bless mumbled.

'You'll have to speak up, I'm 'ard of 'earing,' Tom complained.

'It wasn't important!' Bless sighed.

'I didn't get that either.'

Bless just shook his head, ending the conversation, and they walked on until they reached the trees, where a grass path lead off the lawn into the clearing.

'You'd best go on alone,' Tom said. 'Shock isn't good for my 'eart.'

'You have a heart condition as well as a hernia and being hard of hearing?' Bless remarked. 'You seem to cover most of the aitches! Let's hope you avoid halitosis and hives.'

'Bloody daft you are! Well – don't dither. See what's what.'

So Bless went alone into the glade and crossed to the summerhouse. The door stood wide open and the interior, once he entered, was clearly empty.

'There's no one here,' he called. 'I say, Tom! There's no one here.'

'That is very rum,' Tom announced, entering the glade. 'For I saw with my own eyes.'

'Come in and look.'

The old man joined him in the small room. Together they solemnly looked round. There was a pile of decaying deckchairs, a rolled sun umbrella, a folded garden table, plant pots of various sizes – but no corpse.

'Ah!' Tom said, after a moment. 'That's as 'ow it is, is it? I thought it might be.'

Bless stared at him, trying to make some sense of this mysterious observation.

'You can smell it?' Tom asked him his voice no more than a whisper.

Bless sniffed obediently. The air was musty and damp, a mixture of old soil and rotting canvas. 'What? Smell what?' he asked.

'Tuberose,' Tom murmured. 'She had it sent down to her in bottles from Lunnun. Tuberose. No doubt about it!' He removed his trilby and held it clamped to his chest. 'It be the old lady I saw. As clear as the day is. There now! It be Miss Price.'

'Where? Where did you see her?' Bless demanded. Although he'd always hankered after a supernatural experience, now didn't seem either the time or the place. Nor was the company exactly conducive.

'She's as sitting in that chair. Just there. Slumped sideways – just how she always was when she was having a bit of peace and quiet. She had on an 'at and she was covered with a rug. I seed her with my eyes.'

'Can you see her now?' Bless asked, searching if not for apparitions then at least for a glimmer of sanity in the old man beside him.

'Oi smell her,' Tom said, playing his trump card. 'Oi smell 'er all around me.' And he started to back slowly out of the summerhouse, as if he'd just laid a wreath on a memorial. Once outside he turned and ran with faltering steps away across the glade and out of sight through the branches of willow. 'Oi smell 'er!' he called. 'Oi smell 'er for certain. She be 'ere. Oi knows it . . .' and his voice faded into the distance.

Bless sighed and cast his eyes heavenwards. The roof of the summerhouse was sagging and rotten. In one corner there was a trapdoor. From it a frayed piece of blanket dangled, caught in the wooden trap, hanging listlessly in the stale air. The whole place was mouldy and depressing. We'll probably pull it down and build a disco, Bless thought as he turned and walked out into the fresh air, then I can escape here for a bit of 'urly-burly.

Tom was standing in the middle of the lawn, with his back to the willows. As Bless approached him he saw the old man take a handkerchief out of his pocket and wipe his brow. 'Can you smell it now?' he whispered.

Humouring him, Bless sniffed again. This time he did notice that the air was heavy with scent. He looked round. Old roses tumbled and entwined along the borders at the edge of the lawn. He lifted a hand, pointing. 'It's not surprising, Tom. There are roses everywhere,' he said gently.

But Tom shook his head. 'No! It's the other world,' he gasped. 'The scent of Paradise. You weren't 'ere. I was and I seed 'er – with my own eyes.' He wiped his brow again and then blew his nose violently.

Bless thought of pointing out that he'd have difficulty seeing with anyone else's eyes. But the old man was obviously shaken and so, instead, he took pity on him. 'Look,' he said. 'would you like to come into the house and . . . I could make you a cup of tea?'

'Lord save us – no! I must work. No time for tea and the like. She be watching me. I must work . . .' and he staggered away towards the motor mower without looking back.

As Bless returned to the house, Mrs Day appeared at one of the French windows. 'There was a telephone ringing,' she called.

'Did you answer it?'

'It stopped.'

'Oh dear!'

'If you want me to answer the telephone that'll be extra. I never do at Cockpits. The Brigadier don't like it. If you want me to, I shall of course – but it'll be extra.'

'I'll . . . ask Mr Charteris,' Bless said weakly, following her back into the drawing room.

'So – he 'olds the purse strings, does he?' Mrs Day asked, set-tling once more into the comfort of her armchair. 'You tell him if he wants a secretary that comes as extra.' And picking up her handbag from the floor beside the chair, she rummaged in it, found a comb and small mirror and rearranged her hair.

'You won't be doing any work today?' Bless asked, tentatively.

'I am familiarising myself,' the old woman replied, popping the comb and mirror back into her bag and picking up another magazine. '*Country Life*, they call it!' she muttered with a sneer, glancing at the cover. 'Not the country life I've been used to. Country life's all mud and rutting in my book. A gabardine coat and a plastic rain 'at – that's what we locals call country life. Not these fancy 'ead scarves and twin sets and pearls . . .'

19

Came The Dawn . . .

The warbling of a phone once again woke Bless from dreamless sleep. As he switched on the lamp and slid across the bed, it occurred to him that perhaps he should sleep either in the middle or on Rich's side if he was to be constantly woken in this way. The alarm clock was also on Rich's bedside table. He has every convenience, Bless thought irritably. Why does he take it for granted that he should have total control?

The clock hands showed five minutes after four.

'D'you have any idea what time this is?' he demanded, lifting the receiver.

'I love you too!' Rich said.

'What time is it there?'

'I dunno! 'Levenish.'

'Are you drunk?'

'Utterly!'

'How long have you been in?'

'I haven't been in . . .'

'I mean in New York, Rich!' Bless said, his voice sounding dangerous as the obtuse replies started to irritate. There was a long silence over the Atlantic. 'Well?' Bless snapped when he could wait no longer.

'I had to go out to dinner,' Rich mumbled, slurring his words.

'Oh, really? And there was no time to call me?'

'Sol met me at the airport.'

'And there was no time to call me?'

'He'd arranged meetings and . . . dinner and . . .' Rich started to whimper. 'I've had three vodka martinis. Each one of them was served in a small bucket.'

'And during this orgy of alcohol you could find no opportunity to call me?'

'I feel awful, Bless,' the voice at the other end of the line moaned. 'I think maybe I'm going to die!'

'Good! Why didn't you call me?'

'I am calling you – aren't I?' He now sounded like a teenager caught on the hop.

'Oh – go away. You really piss me off when you're like this. Just . . . go away.' Another long silence ensued. So long that Bless thought he'd been taken too literally. 'Are you there?' he asked eventually, rather spoiling his position of wounded indignation.

'Yes,' the voice whimpered.

'Well, you shouldn't be! Piss off! I'll speak to you tomorrow.'

'I have to go to LA.'

'When?'

'Tomorrow.'

'What for?'

'We're wooing a studio boss. I have to go on a yacht or something. Oh God! I feel sick at the thought . . .'

'Do me a favour, Rich. Be sick in your own time.'

'I miss you!'

'Terrific! Have a nice day!' Bless snapped, and he slammed down the phone. 'Shit!' he shouted, and getting up he walked over to the window. 'I just sounded like a nagging wife!' He stamped his foot and yelled, 'SHIT!' at the night. Then, walking back to the bedside table, he switched off the lamp and sat on the side of the bed. But the dark made his mood worse. It closed in around him and stifled him like a warm blanket. 'SHIT!

SHIT! SHIT!' he repeated, switching the lamp on again.

He rose quickly and crossed back to the window. The black night pressed against the house and the silence was broken by the screeching of owls and a murmuring wind. He turned slowly, surveying the room behind him. The big bed glowered at him, its covers hardly disturbed by his solitary occupation. Even his pile of yesterday's clothes looked forlorn and lonely on the end sofa without Rich's pile beside them.

'I'm getting maudlin,' Bless sighed as a tear trickled down his cheek, 'and I haven't even had the pleasure of a vodka martini.' Now the light in the room was contributing to his mood. It showed up the emptiness. 'What a very large room for a very small child!' he said, using the clipped vowels of a Noël Coward. And crossing yet again to the bed, he switched the lamp back off and lay down.

But he couldn't sleep. He tossed and turned and punched his pillows into small, unforgiving lumps. The grandfather clock in the hall chimed away the quarters. He got to the point where he was waiting for the next one as an actor waits for a cue.

Gradually the dark started to thin as a new day inched up over the eastern horizon. And with the dawn came the bloody birds . . .

'Good morning!' they whistled. 'Boy! Was that a night!' they cheeped. Some of the naughty ones started the quick flight back to their own nests. Do birds have one-night stands? Bless wondered. Do they practise safe sex? 'And where have you been?' a blackbird screeched to her mate, knowing full well he'd stopped over with the blackbird next door. Or maybe he'd been to a friendly pigeon? Do birds deviate? he wondered. Is that what they're doing when they flap backwards and forwards, circling and spying? Are they actually on an endless cruise? Looking for a bit on the side? Do wrens lust after larks? Is the raven a mean dude in leather, with tattoos in all the most improbable places? Is the yellowhammer a peroxide blond? Is the male pheasant a drag queen?

Eventually as the chorus turned into a full-blown opera, he

gave up the unequal struggle for sleep and instead got up, put on his clothes and went downstairs.

But if the bedroom had seemed big, the house seemed enormous. He stood in the dark hall filled with moonlight and shadows and looked at all the closed doors and the darker entrance to the back passage. We really must find a new name for it, he thought. Eventually he let himself into the drawing room. He crossed dejectedly to the windows and stared out at the early dawn light as it seeped into the mass of black trees and gradually defined shapes and distances. He missed the mighty roar of the metropolis. He felt like Gloria Swanson peering out through the blinds in *Sunset Boulevard*. He tilted his head into the right angle for his close-up and he spat once for Andrew Lloyd-Webber.

One of the shapes – a trailing, shrouded thing – emerged from the hanging willows near the glade and started to creep stealthily across the lawn towards the house. At first Bless watched without being certain what it was he was seeing. Then, with a shiver, he realised that what it was was a human figure. And yet perhaps not entirely human? Grey stuff flapped around it and there was no definite sign of head, shoulders, face or any other recognisable attributes of the human form . . .

'A ghost?' he whispered. And as he spoke he noticed that the air in the room was heavy with scent. 'Tuberose!' he said, adopting Old Tom's country twang. 'It be 'er!' And opening the French window, he stepped out on to the terrace. 'Angels and ministers of grace defend us!' he called, raising his arms in the *mode dramatique*. He'd always fancied himself as Hamlet – but nobody else had and the nearest he'd got to the role was in a camp revue when he'd strolled across the stage, wearing black tights and lighting a cigar to the strains of 'A Whiter Shade of Pale'.

'Oh . . . cripes!' a very human voice gasped somewhere in the gloaming, and with a flutter of grey, the spectre turned and ran.

But not fast enough. Bless caught up with it as it disappeared into the summerhouse. As he entered he was in time to see it scrambling on to a chair and reaching for the open trapdoor.

'Stay where you are!' he shouted in his best mid-Atlantic. 'One move and you're dead!' And, as an afterthought, he picked up a folded wooden chair and brandished it in a threatening fashion.

The figure froze, arms raised. The grey stuff, an old blanket, slid slowly to the ground, revealing cropped hair and the back of a rather ethnic ensemble (one of those dresses with little bits of mirror sewn round the hem and a scooped neckline and voluminous sleeves) in a vivid shade of red.

'Don't shoot me!' a female voice cried.

'Shoot yer?' Bless snarled, warming to the part. 'I ain't goin' to shoot yer. I'm goin' to club yer to death!'

'Yes! You would! You . . . fiend!' the woman sobbed. And turning, she toppled off the chair and fell to the ground in a trembling, heaving heap.

'I'm not really going to!' Bless reassured, putting down the chair and crossing towards her.

'Stay away from me!' the woman gasped, wriggling away from him and finding herself hemmed in by a corner of the room.

The light was growing stronger now, and as Bless leaned in towards her he saw a look of fear on the woman's face.

'I say,' he said, 'don't be scared. I won't hurt you. I use a humane mousetrap and release spiders from the bath wrapped in quantities of loo roll.'

'Who are you? What are you doing here?' the woman asked, still cowering away from him.

'I'm Bless Maynard and this is my summerhouse.'

'Your . . .? Yes, of course. The house has been bought, hasn't it? How stupid of me. I thought . . . Help me! Please, you must . . . help me!' And, as she spoke, she scrambled across the floor and grabbed at Bless's leg in an imploring manner.

'Don't!' Bless said, getting embarrassed. 'Someone might see us! I have a very dodgy neighbour with binoculars. This sort of behaviour could give him a heart attack, and much as I despise him I've decided to rise above it and view him with compassion. Oh, do let go of my leg,' he pleaded tugging at her constricting hands. 'You're stopping the circulation! Come on. Come in the house . . .' And leaning down, he pulled the woman to her feet and supported her as he led her away from the summerhouse and across the lawn.

20

Diana's Story

They sat in the kitchen and drank quantities of tea. The woman was distracted and any little sound made her jump and turn as if she were expecting some disaster to strike.

'You're safe here,' Bless reassured her. 'This is an English village, not downtown Chicago.'

'Chicago!' she snorted. 'What would you know? You don't need to leave home for danger, believe me. It's far closer than you could possibly imagine.' And she shook her head and cradled her mug between clenched hands and rocked backwards and forwards, making little sobbing noises.

'Are you in pain?' Bless asked. 'Where does it hurt?' He leaned towards her again, thinking that perhaps he should examine her for wounds. But as he moved, so the woman started back, slamming her mug down on the table and dodging round behind her chair with her hands raised in a protective manner.

'Oh, for God's sake!' Bless exclaimed irritably. Her behaviour smacked of the am drams. If there was one thing guaranteed to make him twitchy it was overacting – unless, of course, it was terribly well done. The difference between Olivier in the film of

Othello and the Gay Cavaliers Strolling Players' production of *Orpheus Descending* could not be too strongly emphasised.

'You think I have the devil in me, don't you?' the woman gasped.

'Sorry?'

'You can see him.'

'See . . . who?'

'The devil. That's why you reacted as you did.'

'When?'

'I heard. I'm not a fool. I heard. When you first saw me in the garden – you called out to God for protection.'

'I did?'

'You are so lucky. I have . . . forfeited such protection.' She slumped down again in the corner, going back into a spiritual decline. Then another thought occurred to her, seizing hold of her and making her leap up. 'Get the vicar,' she demanded. 'You must go at once and . . . get the vicar.' As she spoke, she rushed towards him, trying to drag him up out of his chair and push him towards the door. 'Quick! Now! No delay!' she pleaded. 'Go! Please! You *must*. It's almost too late.' And she started to sob once more.

'On the contrary, it's far too early,' Bless declared extricating himself from her clutches and feeling his embarrassment level reaching an all-time high. 'Look – do please calm down. I'm not used to all this. If you don't I shall have to ask you to leave.'

'Leave? I can't leave, you . . . stupid man!'

'Right! That's it,' Bless said, trying a more manly approach. 'Go on! Out! Or I'll phone the police and . . . have you arrested for . . . trespassing or something . . .'

'But you don't understand – if I go now they'll catch me.'

'Who will? What is it that you're afraid of?'

The woman stared at him with bleary eyes. Then she shook her head again and sniffed, wiping her nose on the back of her hand. 'I can't explain to you. I need the vicar. If you won't fetch him then at least let me phone him.' And as she spoke she made a beeline for the telephone, conveniently positioned on a corner of the dresser.

But Bless was quicker and reached it first. He placed both hands firmly over the receiver. 'Vicars are like doctors,' he told her. 'They no longer do night calls.'

'It's broad daylight,' the woman wailed, 'and vicars are known to be early risers. Besides, it's at night that the powers of darkness are released.'

'This isn't *Candid Camera*, is it?'

'You live such an ordered life. You have no idea what goes on out there.' As she spoke she gestured towards the window. Beyond it was a view of the stables with their walls smothered in pale-pink roses. It seemed a remarkably peaceful scene.

'What exactly is it that you require a vicar for?' Bless asked, his attention momentarily distracted by what he thought was a movement out in the yard. He crossed quickly to the window but saw nothing untoward and decided he must have been mistaken. 'Mmmh?' he queried, turning back towards his visitor. 'How can a vicar help you?'

The woman sank back down on to the chair on which she had originally been sitting, and sighed. 'I need absolution,' she whispered.

'I don't think they go in for that sort of thing nowadays. They're too busy paying for roofs and central heating . . .'

'You're not listening to me. I am possessed! I need . . . exorcism . . .'

'Shit!' Bless exclaimed, feeling a rush of blood to his cheeks. Extreme embarrassment made him blush. 'Why on earth would you need something as . . . extreme . . . as that?' he asked, now using voice 7e from the technique book – light, bright and with a hint of humour.

'That is a very long story,' the woman replied.

'Yes! I thought it might be.' Bless sighed. 'Look – don't feel you must explain. I don't really want to know. It was simply an idle query. I wouldn't dream of prying . . .'

But the woman took a deep breath and prepared to tell him,

whether he wanted to hear it or not. 'All my adult life,' she began, 'I have been messed about by men. You wouldn't understand that of course – being a man yourself . . .'

'Oh, please! Men? Tell me about it! I've known some mega-shits.'

'You have?' She looked at him with bemused eyes. He smiled, shrugged and poured more tea into her mug.

'You're sure you wouldn't like some toast?' he asked, suddenly feeling peckish himself.

But she shook her head. 'I couldn't eat now,' she gasped. 'The very thought of food makes my gorge rise.'

'Oh, well – we don't want that,' Bless murmured, and realising there was to be no escape, he sat once more and adopted the listening mode – legs folded, hands resting in his lap, head on one side, mouth slightly open and attention stamped across his face. 'Tell me all about it,' he said, adjusting his voice to the new role.

'Earlier this year,' the woman began, 'I saw an advertisement in a feminist journal . . .'

'Are there such things?'

'Please don't interrupt.'

'Sorry!'

'I am finding this very difficult.'

'I shan't say another word.'

'Where was I?'

'The advert in the feminist journal . . .'

'Oh, yes! It was for a commune in the South of France. A commune for women. The Sisters of Lysistrata. You haven't heard of them, have you?'

'Good God – no!'

'Neither had I. They were looking for new members. In the first instance one was invited – should one pass certain stringent tests – to visit for a month. The tests were obviously a safeguard on both sides to be sure that one would fit in and that one would be acceptable to the other members of the group. Each applicant had to write a series of letters, send a number of photographs of themselves, answer a lengthy questionnaire, give extensive details of their financial state, their sexual experience and status . . . In short one was being examined in depth as to one's political and feminist principles. The whole thing was gruelling. But, in the light of my own marital disaster – I went through a very unhappy experience with a social worker called Arnold, the details of which need not concern you . . . Anyway, I found the process of applying – the letters I had to write, the questions I had to answer, the intimate particulars I was asked to divulge – strangely releasing. I decided there and then – or rather here and then, for it was here in this village that I made all the original contacts – and using my home address, a foolish mistake, as it has turned out . . . But I'm ahead of myself.' She gasped and Bless thought for a moment that she was going to cry again. But she regained her composure and shook her head deliberately. 'No. At the time I decided that I liked the sound of The Sisters of Lysistrata a whole lot. I have a classical background and also I warmed to the idea of an exclusively female society. So much less hassle, I thought, without any men, and then there would be the added pleasure of the exchanging of experiences. I was at a boarding school as a girl – and really those early years were the happiest in my life. So you see, the idea of a sisterhood greatly appealed to me and I became quite desperate to be accepted as a member of the commune. But of course, self-worth not being my strong point, I was certain that my postal submission would be totally inadequate and that I would be turned down. Imagine my surprise therefore when I received a letter from France saying that I had been accepted for the trial period.'

There was a long silence as the woman went into what seemed to Bless like a trance. Then she turned and looked at him again. 'My name is Diana. Did I say that?'

'I don't think you did,' Bless whispered, nervous about disturbing her train of thought.

'And you are . . .?'

'My friends call me Bless.'

'I hope I may be considered a friend in time . . . And I hope I will get your blessing.' She paused again, staring at him hard. Then she nodded her head. 'I can see that I must tell you . . . that I must tell somebody what has happened to me.' And swallowing cold tea from her mug, she resumed her story.

21

Enter The Devil

Oh dear! It wasn't at all what she had been led to expect.

The Sisters of Lysistrata lived in a converted farmhouse surrounded by a few hectares of scrubby arable land on a hillside overlooking a rocky, parched landscape. The house had been converted into a school by the previous owners and it still retained its institutional atmosphere. 'I had imagined somewhere intensely pretty, with flowers growing in profusion and the scent of wild thyme heavy on the air. Nightingales singing in the dark woods and a flowing river . . .'

There were twenty members of the commune, and Diana was the only new applicant to arrive that spring. She had to share a room with two other women. The next-door room was occupied by a motor mechanic with a shaved head who came from Bologna and was called Carlotta: 'Which at first I found confusing, as I was convinced that she was a man and had no right to be there . . .'

Carlotta took an instant liking to Diana, and towards the end of her second week at the commune she went to her room one evening and discovered that her bed had been moved into Carlotta's room and that Carlotta was telling everyone they were shacking up together. 'None of this had been discussed with me. I mean, it came as a most terrible shock. I had no idea . . . I'd tried to be friendly with the woman, of course – I wanted to get on with everyone – but . . . Look, I have absolutely nothing against lesbians and think that all people should express their true sexuality fearlessly. Of course I do! But . . . Although I happen to be moving away from the bastard sex – I'm sorry, but that is how I think of men . . .'

'Don't worry about it,' Bless assured her. He was actually beginning to enjoy the story and was wondering if there were any similar communes for men.

'But I am leaning towards celibacy,' she continued, 'and not – well . . . quite frankly Carlotta was far more masculine than Arnold or any other man with whom I have associated. I have never been entirely at ease with testosterone – it gives me violent palpitations and affects my blood pressure. The two girls in my room seemed sympathetic to my predicament. One of them was a German horticulturist called Marlene. She advised me to ask for a new billet. The other, a rather dim Canadian called Gloria Sweatling, thought I should confront Carlotta and appeal to her feminine psyche. Weighing up the two possibilities I decided on the former. Although Carlotta's English was good I didn't feel confident that I would be able to express my understanding of and at the same time my negative reaction to her obvious lustful intentions.

'I should explain that the commune is run by three women, known to us as "the Family". They are the founder members and they are the owners of the house and farm. There is "Mother", who is in her sixties and was once an air stewardess, I believe. She has long blonde hair – though the colour comes from a bottle, I suspect, and not from nature – and she has kept her figure remarkably well. She was at one time married to a writer of science fiction and receives an alimony cheque every month. She has several children who visit her from time to time. The other two members of the Family are a former nun, known to the commune as "Auntie", who spends a great deal of each day in spiritual contemplation, and a rather pretty younger woman, called "Daughter", who is a *cordon bleu* cook and was briefly in prison, I believe, for possession of marijuana.

'So, on the advice of my friend Marlene and with the support of Gloria, I decided to approach Mother. I saw her after breakfast on the following day, having spent the previous night avoiding Carlotta's advances by getting her drunk on brandy, a bottle of which I had brought with me to the commune for medicinal purposes. Eventually she fell into a deep sleep and we managed to pull her on to her bed. Once there, she lay on her back and snored. It was so horrible . . .' The woman shuddered and put her hands nervously to her cheeks.

'Don't go on if it's too upsetting,' Bless told her.

'No! I've started, so I must,' the woman said. 'Mother listened to what I had to say and then, to my surprise, said that she would call a meeting to discuss the matter. The entire commune were summoned before lunch. We gathered in the big living room. People were seated on chairs facing a raised platform. I was invited to sit on the platform with Mother on one side of me and Carlotta on the other.

'The whole thing was ghastly. I didn't know what was going on. I faced all my sisters, who stared at me as though I were in some way on trial. To my horror Mother told them about our conversation of that morning. I mean, Carlotta was actually sitting next to me as my accusations were revealed. I was appallingly embarrassed.

'When she had finished speaking Mother explained that the Sisters of Lysistrata had no secrets from each other and that therefore she would open the meeting to the company so that they could all express their reactions to what had been said. At first the sisters seemed tongue-tied. Carlotta ranted a lot in Italian and French – I am no linguist, unfortunately, and had hoped to improve my French while at the commune – so I was unclear what was being said. But gradually the others seemed to abandon any support they might have had for me in favour of Carlotta. I was stunned. I was the innocent party, and yet their sympathy was obviously with her. The general consensus of

opinion seemed to be that I should learn to let go of my bour-
geois prejudices and that Carlotta was a mainstay of the
commune and invaluable to the running of the place. She was
the only person who knew how to operate the electric generator
and she was the only one who enjoyed driving the farm tractor.
In short, she was too useful to them, and although I suspect that
others of the sisterhood may themselves have had to avoid her
advances at one time or another, not one of them was going to
come to my assistance now . . .

'In fact I would go so far as to say that what had happened to
me – the bed-moving, the advances, the whole sordid thing –
was intended and even expected. My selection as a potential
member of the sisterhood was based solely on a need to satisfy
Carlotta's cravings . . .'

'You mean . . .?'

'Yes. I mean precisely what you are thinking. I was recruited
for Carlotta. That's why they had advertised for a new member.
That is what a new member was required for . . . Someone to
keep Carlotta happy.'

'Oh, surely not!' Bless exclaimed. 'You mean, like the white
slave trade?'

'Why not?' Diana demanded. 'Carlotta was too useful to
them all. She was willing to do all the hard work for the commune – she actually enjoys physical strain so it was really no
hardship to her. But to lose her would have been disastrous for
them. And to keep her, they had to reward her. Her reward was
to be a female companion of her choosing. They must all have
been so relieved when that companion turned up.' She gasped
and blinked incredulously. 'When, in short, I turned up.'

'I can't believe any of this!'

'But, yes! It all fits! Carlotta as good as told me so herself. I
think she hoped she was flattering me. She explained that it was
she who had selected me from the applicants' letters. She particularly liked my pictures – she has a penchant for redheads,
apparently – this was before I dyed my hair, of course. It is really
the most glorious Titian red and one of my chief features.' She

ran a hand through the shorn tresses. 'I had to sacrifice it in a desperate bid for freedom,' she sighed. Then she shook her head and continued with determined bravery: 'She was also intrigued by a certain detail of my CV.'

'What was that?' Bless asked, breathless with anticipation.

'Although I have been married, Arnold and I were not physically attracted. And as Arnold was the only man with whom I have ever actually cohabited, and as I am not given to promiscuous behaviour . . . You understand?'

'I'm not sure that I do,' Bless whispered, nervously.

'I have never known a man, Blessing . . .'

'It's just Bless.'

'I do beg your pardon.'

'It doesn't matter. You mean . . .?'

'Biblically. I have never known a man . . . biblically.'

'You're . . . a virgin?' Bless gasped. 'I didn't know they still existed.'

'Was!' the woman wailed. 'I was a virgin . . .' and she dissolved into a flood of noisy tears.

'But not any more?'

'Not any more,' she choked.

'Probably just as well,' Bless tried to reassure her. 'Virginity is one of those things that's best got rid of as quickly as possible. It only makes you tense and stops you enjoying yourself . . . At least – that's what I found. But, I don't quite understand. You were at an all-female commune. I mean . . . How could . . .? What exactly happened?'

'I happened!' a man's voice interrupted them. And as they both turned, they saw the mysterious hunk, the midnight caller. Mr Sex-on-legs himself, step into the kitchen from the back passage.

Diana screamed. Bless gasped. The Hunk smiled.

'It's him!' Diana shrieked.

'Who?' Bless yelled – he had to in order to be heard above the din.

'The devil! The devil! I am possessed by . . . the devil!' and with a final croak of anguish she toppled forward, slid off her chair and landed on the floor.

'Cara mia!' the devil murmured, hurrying to kneel beside her. 'The poor child. She has fainted. You will bring some water, Mr Bless? We must revive her.'

22

Oh, What A Tangled Web . . .

That same evening, as Bless was loading the dishwasher with the supper things, he was wondering how it had come about that he had two unpaying guests ensconced in the house, both of whom were total strangers to him. The only explanation was that events had simply overtaken him. He had been powerless to stop them.

That morning he and the Hunk had managed to get Diana up to one of the guest bedrooms. Once there she had revived quickly and insisted on both the men going to collect her belongings – two suitcases and a large carrier bag – from the Deux Chevaux still parked in the yard. While they were there, they decided it might be prudent to push the car into a spare stable, and by the time they returned to the bedroom she was already undressed, apart from a voluminous petticoat, and in bed. She actually looked thoroughly at home and had piled up the pillows in a comfortable way, but as soon as she saw the Hunk she cringed back, pulling the covers up round her shoulders, and going back into the Grand Guignol performance of earlier – gasping uncontrollably and pointing a shaking finger, while firmly clamping the bed covers across her chest. Bless, wearying of yet more histrionics, decided that Bette Davis was called for. A touch of the Baby Janes, perhaps? A sharp slap across the cheek to induce sanity? If nothing else it would make him feel better. But as he raised his hand he was thwarted by Diana, who instantly grabbed it and held it in a trembling but vice-like grip.

'Get him out of here!' she croaked. 'I beseech you to . . . get him out of here!'

'I don't know who writes your script, dear!' Bless said, pulling his hand free. 'But dump them – or you'll never win an Oscar.'

'Diana!' the Hunk pleaded with her. 'You are confused . . .'

'Seducer!' she hissed.

The Hunk raised his hands in a gesture of defeat. 'She is impossible!' he cried, his Latin temperament bubbling to the surface. 'I did not even touch her.'

'Guard me, you must guard me!' the woman whimpered, still clawing at Bless.

'Yes, all right!' he told her, brushing her hands away. 'Honestly! It's worse than *Cell Block H*. Just pull yourself together, have some sleep, and I'll come back later.' Then, turning, he pushed the Hunk towards the door. 'As for you – out!' he said. 'You're obviously not welcome here. So come on . . .'

'All right! No problem! Why would I want to stay?' The man shrugged. 'She's not really my type at all.'

'Devil!' Diana shouted as they both left the room and Bless closed the door behind them. 'You devil!' the muffled voice continued, and they heard the sound of the key being turned.

'She's locked herself in!' Bless muttered. 'Bloody woman. Using the place as if she owns it!'

'She is a stupid bloody woman!' the Hunk snorted.

'Yes! I have to say I agree with you.'

'So much fuss over a penis!'

At the time Bless decided not to pursue this intriguing statement. But by the evening he was still wondering quite where the penis had come from, to whom it belonged and what it had to do with Diana.

All this had taken place before seven that morning, and

Diana did not reappear downstairs until six thirty in the evening, hair washed, clothes changed and ravenously hungry.

Nor had the Hunk been in evidence for most of the day either. As soon as they had deposited Diana in the guest room he'd also expressed the need for immediate sleep.

'I have been driving for three days. Not stopping except on the ferry and then I was searching, searching . . . It was imperative I find her. When she was not there, I realised she must be on another boat. It was terrible. I waited at the port – and only knew she had arrived when I saw her little car speeding away . . .' As he spoke he was walking along the landing. 'She runs from me. All the time she runs! She will not stop and let me tell her what has happened.' Passing Bless's open bedroom door he turned and went inside. 'This is fine,' he said, looking round and sounding like a prospective buyer or a hotel guest.

'Would you mind not barging into other people's rooms!' Bless exclaimed, hurrying in after him.

'Of course!' the Hunk said with a shrug and a dazzling smile. 'Later, when I have slept, we will make things better together. Yes?'

'No!' Bless fumed. 'I don't want you to make things better. I want you to go!'

'Ciao, baby! But first I sleep,' the Hunk announced, crossing to the unmade king-size bed. 'This is your bed? Yes?'

'Yes – as it happens.'

'That is good!' the Hunk announced, undoing his belt and peeling off his jeans. 'You will not mind my using it?'

'Yes, I do bloody mind!' Bless snapped.

'But why?' the Hunk asked.

'Because . . . Because . . . Well, I don't live alone, for one thing . . .'

'But if you did? Then it would be different?'

'Maybe.' Bless could feel his resolve weaken.

'That is good,' the Hunk said, taking off his T-shirt and standing before him naked except for Calvin Klein briefs and a pair of socks. 'I like you also . . .'

'I didn't say I liked you. And I'll thank you not to strip – without being invited,' Bless blustered. He knew he was blustering. He was ashamed he was blustering. But really, the nerve of the man!

'You look wonderful when you're cross!' the Hunk said with a yawn. And falling backwards on to the bed, he went immediately into a deep and blissful sleep.

Bless stared down at the perfect specimen of manhood lying in front of him. At least with Rich in America he wasn't likely to suddenly turn up out of the blue if the worst – or, depending on one's viewpoint, the best – were to happen . . . Not that anything was going to happen. But supposing it did? If, by some terrible stroke of misfortune (or luck, ditto the viewpoint), Bless was lured off the straight and narrow . . . Well, at least no one need know. Mind you, if nothing at all happened, the presence of the Hunk would still be difficult to explain. Oh, Lordy! Sometimes life played cruel tricks . . . Didn't it just!

As Bless was acknowledging the possibility of a quick infidelity while no one was looking – an 'Oh, God! Was I drunk last night! What did we do?', a 'You must understand, I'm only doing this to get it out of the way and then no more', a 'This doesn't really mean anything; it's just a habit that's taking a bit of breaking' – the telephone beside the bed started to ring.

The sound made him jump as if he'd been caught going down on the prostrate body instead of just staring at it with his mouth open. He was instantly guilty. Here he was standing by his own matrimonial bed with a near-naked, drop-dead dish lying flat across it, whose name he didn't even know. It was quite like old times. Except that it wasn't old times. He was now a responsible, faithful, one-man man, and there was no way he could speak to anyone under these circumstances – and particularly not Rich, whom it was more than likely to be.

So instead Bless hurried down the stairs and answered the phone in the study. But the caller wasn't Rich. It was Maggie, ringing to see how he was settling in and how he was and that he wasn't too lonely on his own . . .

Lonely! If she only knew.

'I really miss you, Bless. It's silly, I know, but I'm lonely without you. And I'm blue . . . Oh, God! I want a man in my life . . .'

'So, what's new?'

'I thought maybe I should come down,' she added brightly.

'When?'

'Today.'

'No! You can't!' Now he was shouting down the phone, but he couldn't help himself. If Maggie arrived now – with the house full of strangers – the word would be round London before anyone could say Giorgio Armani. Besides, he was still shaken by the Hunk. Shaken and stirred. He was by no means certain how the next few hours would pan out. The last thing he wanted was his best friend muscling in – and Maggie could muscle like a stevedore for the right man.

'Bambino! What is the matter with you?' he heard her say.

'Bambino?' he gulped. 'Why did you say that?'

'Bless, are you all right? You haven't been . . . glue sniffing or whatever it is you children get up to now?'

But he wasn't listening to her. He was remembering a deep velvet voice whispering, 'Cara mia!' Weren't those the words he'd heard the Hunk use when Diana had fainted?

Italian! The man is an Italian? a voice screamed in his head.

If Maggie got one look at the Boy David and discovered he was Italian, there would be no holding her. She would claw her way to hell and back for an Italian. Her passion was to be laid by an Italian. Her dream was to be whisked away on a yacht, in a Mercedes, or even, if pushed, on a Vespa by an Italian – preferably an Italian count with a palace in Tuscany, but she was ever a realist and any old Italian would do – so long as the old Italian was a young Italian and looked even half as tasty as the *plat du jour* now snoring on the king-sized at the top of the stairs . . .

'Oh, Christ!' he gasped as all these thoughts flashed through his mind, like the entire life of a drowning man. Then: 'No!' he cried, realising he had some fast inventing to do. 'It isn't possible for you to come down today.'

'Why not?' she demanded.

'Because . . . Laurence insists on coming.'

'Oh, God! You can't be serious?'

'Deadly.'

'Why? What does he want?'

'Something to do with drawing up plans for the stable block. He'll be here for several days. It's going to be hell . . .'

He was appalled how easily the lie leapt into his mouth. It wasn't like him at all. Bless was the good friend who tried to tell the truth and wanted only to please people. But then, he thought – as he closed the dishwasher and checked with the handbook to see that he'd done it right (Bless hated machines) – he was living in the strangest of times . . .

23

Supping With The Devil

Dinner had been a subdued affair. At first Diana had refused to eat at the same table as the Hunk. But Bless had already laid places for three in the kitchen and he absolutely refused to open up the dining room – which was only ever intended to be used for smart soirées. Eventually Diana's hunger got the better of her, so she settled down as far away from the Hunk as she could and commenced hogging most of the macaroni cheese that Bless had rustled up as if the whole bowl was intended for her.

'I have eaten practically nothing but bread and olives for weeks,' she announced.

'It is the truth.' The Hunk nodded enthusiastically. 'When I found her she was near starvation.'

Bless glanced across the table and thought that really she looked quite well padded, but didn't want to spoil a good story.

'Where was that then?' he asked, reaching and dragging the bowl away from Diana so that he and his intended – if that was how it was to be – could have a few mouthfuls.

'In Le Puy!' the Hunk answered. 'I had a summons from my sister. She sounded desperate. She needed my help. She used our family motto: 'Torni un po' piú tardi'. I knew at once she was in desperate trouble . . .'

'Don't listen to him,' Diana said, speaking with her mouth full.

'Look, d'you mind? You're a guest – and this is my table. I can do what I want here.'

'Huh!' she snorted, cutting herself a large hunk of bread. 'I warn you – he who sups with the devil should use a long spoon.'

Bless blinked, then waved a dismissive hand. He'd never got on with Aesop.

'What is this . . . what is her meaning?' the Hunk asked, sounding particularly confused as he battled with: 'Zee long spoon . . .?'

'Don't ask!' Bless advised him.

'You see?' the woman raved. 'He'll talk to you – and then he'll have his way with you.'

'We don't need to talk if you don't like,' the Hunk said, smiling at Bless divinely.

His sleep has obviously refreshed him and, being Italian, he can't help being flirtatious, Bless decided. But when the Hunk reached across the table and pinched his arm, saying: 'I like you!' Bless immediately panicked. 'Just keep talking,' he told him, pushing the hand away.

The Hunk shrugged and forked food into his mouth. 'My sister is a good girl – but she is impetuous,' he continued with his mouth full. 'I was worried. So I drove across Europe to reach her. We are a very close family. The parents not so much – but the children. I have a brother who has black hair all the way down to his navel. You would like him, I think. He looks like a Michelangelo and fucks like a rabbit.'

'Well, really!' Diana gasped, mopping her plate with a wedge of bread and chewing strenuously.

The Hunk shrugged and smiled at Bless. 'It runs in the family. Our parents were very strict with us and . . . we rebelled. My brother, he likes boys. My sister, she likes girls. And me, I like

you very much! Serves them right! Huh? So, I get to my sister
where she is living – and she is distraught . . .'

'This is the first I've heard about a sister,' Diana cut in, filling
her glass with more red wine and slurring her words from the
several glasses she'd already imbibed.

'But she loves you, Diana. That is all I hear – how she loves
you and how you spurn her.'

'Spurn her? Me? I don't know what you're saying.'

'She is demented. I have seen her like this before. It is dangerous. It is best with my sister to give her what she wants.
Otherwise . . . She is very strong, you know. It is not wise to
thwart her.'

'Who is your sister?' Diana gasped, as a glimmer of light
dawned in her fuddled brain.

Meanwhile Bless had risen from the table and was collecting a
bottle of red wine from the dresser. Diana obviously considered
the other bottle was meant entirely for her.

'You do not know?' the Hunk asked, staring at her incredulously.

'Know? I know nothing. I was working at the bar in Le Puy.
It was there that I had gone into hiding.' She turned and
addressed herself to Bless. 'I left the commune with scarcely
any money. It was deposited in Mother's safe and obviously I
couldn't go and ask . . . I was making an escape. I took only my
clothes and a few personal belongings. Also some food from the
larder to help me on my way. I don't consider this as stealing –
I had brought a great deal of cash with me.' She hiccuped and
blinked. When next she spoke, her words were more slurred
and more desperate. 'By the time I reached Le Puy I was utterly
lost. I had been driving like a woman possessed . . .'

'Diana!' the Hunk pleaded.

'Stay away from me!' she spat.

'Just go on with your story,' Bless told her, pouring wine
into his own and the Hunk's glasses.

'Ciao, bambino!' the Hunk murmured, patting Bless's
thigh.

'I had to find somewhere to hide. I had no money for petrol.'

'You should have contacted the British consul,' Bless suggested, escaping from the Hunk's probing hand and hurriedly returning to his seat.

'In Le Puy?'

'I suppose not.'

'I managed to find work in a bar. Me! A graduate! Clearing tables! But there was worse to come, wasn't there? I had no idea what was in store for me.'

The Hunk looked suitably chastened and hung his head. Then he seemed to revive. He took a gulp of wine and shrugged and grinned at Bless in a friendly way.

'I knew I must swallow what little pride was left and buckle to,' Diana continued, now speaking as if unaware that anyone else were present. 'I needed money to buy petrol and to feed myself. Besides, I was certain I was being followed and thought if I lay low for a while it would be to my advantage. Then, when I was ready, I could make a dash for the Channel and home. But of course I little knew what powers of darkness had been unleashed.' She glared at the Hunk, who gave her a sweet, encouraging smile. 'One night, in the bar, I saw this . . . this . . . fiend staring at me. He seemed friendly at first. He smiled at me . . . I smiled back . . . I was lonely. I wanted company. He accompanied me home to the hovel in which I was staying and he . . . he . . . he ravished me.'

'What? Just like that?' Bless exclaimed.

'No! No! It is not true!' the Hunk cried. 'We sat in your room and gorged on cheap wine and biscuits . . . I am a red-blooded Italian. I admit I have a problem. I admit it. There. But I thought you were keen . . .'

'You made me drunk – you brute!'

'I didn't fuck you, Diana. By the time I'd got your clothes off, you had passed out.'

'You exposed yourself to me,' Diana sobbed, downing more wine. 'It is the last thing I remember. I have never seen anything so grotesquely *large* in my entire life . . .'

The Hunk looked across at Bless, simpered and shrugged. 'It's true,' he said. 'I have to admit it.'

'There isn't any dessert,' Bless said hurriedly. 'Perhaps – a little cheese?'

'You're cute!' the Hunk whispered.

'What is the name of your sister?' Diana interrupted them.

'You still don't know? You silly girl. She is Carlotta da Braganizio, of course.'

'Carlotta?' Diana whimpered.

'Yes. Carlotta is my big sister.'

'My God! Oh, merciful heaven! She's sent you here to catch me!' Diana screamed and tried to rise. But too much red wine made her stagger back and fall in a heap on her chair.

'Not at all! I knew straight away you weren't for her. I have come to protect you. Only I know how to cope with my sister when her blood is up. She has inherited the masculine side of the family personality. She can be stubborn, cruel and hugely strong. I love her. She makes me laugh.'

'I'm going to die,' Diana whimpered. 'Fetch a priest!'

'You are Catholic?' the Hunk asked. 'Carlotta will be crazy for you.'

'She already is. And I am certainly *not* a Catholic. I'm naturally an Anglican! Get the vicar, Mr Bless. Please – you must! Can't you see now what a terrible thing has happened to me?'

'It wasn't so awful, Diana . . .'

'Let me be the judge of that,' Diana raged at him. 'I am the abused party.'

'Oh, dear! I am sorry. Yes? See – I have followed you all this way, just to make it up to you.'

'Stay away from me! Get the vicar. I'm . . . besmirched!' And heaving herself up with both her hands, she staggered drunkenly across the kitchen. 'I won't come out of my room until he has gone and I have been given . . . exorcism.' And she went out, slamming the door after her.

There was a long, awkward pause. The Hunk looked suitably shamefaced and shrugged a lot. Bless folded his arms and then unfolded them. As an actor he'd never known what to do with his arms.

'Did you?' he said at last.

'I told you – no. Nothing happened. She passed out.'

'And if she hadn't? What then?'

The Hunk shrugged and looked shifty.

'Maybe – a bit.'

'What? You'd have raped her . . . a bit?'

'No! No! Not rape. She wanted me. It was as if we were drugged. Perhaps the wine she had bought . . . I like to fuck. Is such a bad thing? Huh?'

'You disgust me,' Bless said, rising and moving away from the table.

'No more hysterics – please!'

'Go away!'

'I like you. I want to stay.'

'Well, I don't like you – so go.'

'Really?' He sounded quite amazed. 'You don't fancy me?'

'I have a great capacity for fancying shits!'

The Hunk grinned. 'You do fancy me!' He sounded relieved.

'I actually can't stand the sight of you. Now go.'

'Really?' He sounded wounded again.

'Yes! Now! At once! Fuck off!'

And so the beautiful, the desirable, the hunkable Hunk rose slowly from the table and walked sadly to the door. Then he hesitated. 'You and me – maybe we could start over again?' he suggested. 'I'm sure we'd get it going . . .'

'No,' Bless replied. And he turned his back and didn't look round until he heard the front door slam out in the hall.

So, later, Bless stacked the supper things into the dishwasher and then checked the manual to be sure he'd done it correctly before switching on. And after that he sat alone in the kitchen as the light outside the window faded to dark, and he felt grubby and ashamed; depressed and not a little deflated.

'I always fall for shits!' he told the empty room – thereby acknowledging that he had fallen for the Hunk. I shouldn't have told him to go, he thought as the gloom of a lost opportunity set in. 'I always fall for shits!' he said again. Then he remembered Rich and knew that he was the only really nice man in the entire world, and he suddenly wished like mad that his lover was at home. 'Miss you Rich,' he said in a small voice.

24

An Evening At
The Hart At Rest

Sometimes, on a Tuesday evening, Melanie and Barry in computers would slip down to the local, late in the evening.

'I think it's a good idea for Barry to mingle with the poor people. Otherwise we can seem too stuck up. Just because we've got savings in a building society and live on an executive estate, it doesn't mean we can't be friendly. After all, the bottom might fall out of computers – then where would we be? Look what happened to estate agents. One day they were rich and then – bang! – they were poor. I read in the *Mail* where one ended up living in a cardboard box just next to the National Theatre, as poor as a church mouse. Lost everything: his wife, his family, even his dog. Still, if he had to be down and out, it wasn't a bad place to choose, was it? Nice and handy for the tube, with the river on your doorstep, lashings of culture and very central for shopping and sightseeing . . .'

Tuesday happened to be the evening that Sandra Green attended her creative writing class in Fairlow, and sometimes if Simon was at a loose end, and if he could persuade Doreen Potter to baby-sit little Gary, he would join Melanie and Barry for a swift half or two.

Barry was not all that keen on this arrangement. He

thought Simon 'a bit of a wanker, if the truth be told, Mel'. But surprisingly Melanie seemed recently to have taken a bit of a shine to him. 'Well, not a shine exactly, Barry. But I do feel a touch sorry for him. He doesn't have any interests – and with Sandra writing the great English novel – I don't think – and going on about 'narrative thrust' and 'character development' all the time . . . Well, it can't be much fun for him, can it? And you must admit, he's very good about buying his round, considering he's only in insurance and not very high up at that.'

So what had started as an occasional occurrence was turning into a regular date, and on this particular Tuesday evening the three of them strolled down to the Hart together.

'Sandra will drop in when she gets back from class,' Simon explained – though he needn't have bothered because Sandra always dropped in on her way back from class if she knew Simon would be there. But it was something that Simon always said and he was a meticulously predictable man. Now, as he spoke, he moved to the outside of the pavement, to protect Melanie from any marauding highwaymen – another of his nice, polite little ways.

'She still doing her stories, is she?' Barry asked as he strode ahead of them – there only being room for two on the narrow pavement.

'Oh, gosh, yes! She's really got the bug.'

'D'you get to read what she writes then, Si?' Melanie asked, glancing at him sideways and deciding that his profile was a lot better than she used to think, and that although to be fair his hair was a nondescript beige, she hadn't noticed before how sweetly it curled round the back of his ears.

'No. Not really,' Simon replied in a rather doleful way – his usual tone. 'I did used to read some of her bits and pieces. But since she's gone into it in a big way she says she doesn't like me to. I think maybe it puts her off. It's very private being a writer – that's what she says. It's like a bodily function, apparently – intimate and almost sacred.'

'Fancy!' Melanie said after a brief pause, feeling that some comment was called for.

'What is it then that she's writing, Simon? Sort of novel, is it?' Barry asked.

'That's the ticket, Barry. A novel about life on an executive estate.'

'Oh dear! I hope we won't have to take her to court . . . defamation of character, anything like that.'

'Oh, Lord, no! It isn't our executive estate. That I do know.'

'Oh, really?'

'No, Barry. She's setting the whole thing down in Devon. She says the air's more romantic down there.'

'Well, there's certainly not much romance in the air round here!' Melanie exclaimed, and, catching Simon's eyes as he glanced towards her, she smiled and winked.

Reaching the High Street, Barry, who was still ahead of them, had just stepped off the pavement to cross the road to the pub when round the corner from the lower village roared a high-powered motorbike, driven by a burly figure in leathers and helmet. Barry leapt back, narrowly avoiding being run over, and the bike sped away up the narrow lane towards the next village, emitting a long raspberry of exhaust, followed by the stench of fumes.

'Cor, Barry! That was a near thing!' Melanie exclaimed.

'Idiot!' Barry yelled, shaking his fist and getting quite worked up.

'Steady, old son!' Simon told him. 'You'll give yourself a heart attack. Road rage is the number-one killer these days, you know.'

'Pedestrians don't get road rage, you pillock!' Barry rejoined, striding across the road in a fury that belied his statement.

'Excuse me, Barry, but Simon should know, seeing he's in insurance,' Melanie told him, tucking her arm into Simon's and walking at a more leisurely pace. 'You should listen to him,' and she gave Simon's arm a squeeze and flashed a glossy, secretive smile that made him distinctly nervous. So much so that, as they neared the door of the saloon bar, he disengaged himself from her clutches almost too quickly, as if he were guilty of some indiscretion, and hurried forward, catching up with Barry.

'Let me get the first round,' he said. 'What'll it be Melanie? Your usual?'

'No,' she replied, looking sulky. 'I think I'll go for something exotic. A rum and blackcurrant, maybe. Or – I know – I'll have a snowball, thank you, Simon. If Stan can remember how to make one!'

The saloon bar was always fairly quiet during the week. The village locals all congregated in the public – where Alec, Doris Day's son, could usually be found playing dominoes with a few cronies, and some of the younger kids from the council houses played a juke box or occasionally the odd game of darts. So although the Barlows – Melanie and Barry in computers – considered that a trip to the local was their way of integrating with the village people, they were still spared any direct contact by a dividing wall and reassuringly higher prices.

Stan, the landlord, was a dour man who had once been in the RAF. He and his wife, Patsy, had taken over the Hart soon after he was demobbed, and any sparkle that they may have brought with them had over the years dwindled and died, leaving only a raffish moustache – on Stan – and a diamond wings brooch – on Patsy – as evidence of their former selves. Patsy now rarely appeared in the bar and it was rumoured that more gin went up to the flat above than was ever served across the counter down below, and Stan spent all his days sitting on a stool near the saloon bar till, reading fantasy novels with lurid covers and titles like *Zong, Dreamer of Zigogg*, *The Vipers of Tippee* and, a much-loved favourite, *The Goddess of Inner Splott*. Sandra Green had on occasions tried to lure him towards what she considered more literary works, but to no avail. She was herself quite keen on some of the more modern women writers – or so she claimed after a session with Olive Snelling and her creative writing group. But actually Sandra didn't do much reading herself. The reason for this was, she explained, that she couldn't risk reading while she was engaged in her own writings for fear of being influenced by another author's style.

On this particular Tuesday, Anthony Daltry was sitting at a table in the window, nursing a pint of bitter and doing the *Times* crossword in a desultory way. He was on his way home, having taken a late train from town, and was bracing himself for a barrage of questions from Heather – blasted woman! – about his late arrival. He nodded to 'the execs' as they entered, but didn't feel it necessary to make conversation.

At another table a group from one of the outlying villages were enjoying a noisy get-together with friends from Fairlow. And there were three younger men at the bar talking cricket, while their women sat at a table and talked high finance.

'Oh, this is nice!' Melanie said settling at a table in the middle of the room.

'I'll just . . .' Barry in computers murmured, heading for the Gents.

'I hope you're not getting old men's problems, Barry.'

'I happen to need a pee, for Christ's sake!'

'Temper!'

'A snowball, please, Stan,' Simon said, placing himself in front of mine host.

'An ice cube,' Stan rejoined. 'What is this? Some sort of parlour game?'

'No. It's a cocktail.'

'And I'm the Duke of Windsor,' Stan replied.

'I don't know that one,' Simon quipped. 'Can you make a snowball? It's for Melanie Barlow. She fancies one.'

'She pregnant or something?'

'I don't think so.'

'It's with Pernod, Stan,' Melanie called, helpfully.

'We're out of Pernod,' Stan replied, tragically.

'They're out of Pernod . . .'

'I heard,' Melanie snapped. 'I'll have a gin and tonic.'

'And for Barry?'

'I expect so.'

'Two G and Ts and a pint of special.'

'Your lady wife not coming?' Stan asked as he crossed with two glasses to the optics.

'Bit early yet!'

By the time Simon had returned to the table with the three drinks and a packet of crisps – 'in case anyone feels peckish' – Barry was back, wiping his hands on a handkerchief.

'You're out of paper towel in the Gents, Stan,' he called.

'Oh dear. Throw me in the Tower!'

'No. Not tower – towel . . .'

'He was having a joke, Barry,' Melanie said in a despairing voice as she delved into the crisps. 'Yum! Yum! Salt and vinegar – my favourites.'

'That's why I got them,' Simon said, and then wished he hadn't.

'Oh, you are sweet, Si!' she said, clutching his arm and blowing him a kiss across the table.

'Happy days!' Barry said, lifting his glass. 'Oooh! Bit heavy on the tonic, weren't you, Simon?'

'Take no notice, Si. He's a terrible drunk. So – you and Sandra decided where you're going for your hols yet? La bella Italy wasn't it, last year?'

'Yes. Sandra's partial to Italy.'

'I'm surprised she didn't set her novel there.'

'No. She thinks Devon more suitable.'

'Shame! So, did you find the air in Italy . . . romantic?'

'It was rather close and sultry, actually . . . And I got bitten to pieces. I always do. I'm a slave to mosquitoes.'

'Lucky old mosquitoes! I wouldn't mind giving you a nibble, Si!'

'Take no notice, old son!' Barry in computers reassured him. 'I think she's on the change. It's sex, sex, sex all the time.'

'Oh d-d-dear!' Simon stammered. He did that when he was nervous.

Half an hour later, flushed with intellectual stimulation, Sandra hurried into the bar.

'Here I am!' she cried.

'Here she is!' Simon echoed, his voice brimming with relief. And rising, he gave her a fairly ecstatic peck on the cheek.

'Steady, love!' Sandra exclaimed, blushing shyly.

'Had a good session?'

'Oh, it was wonderful! Wonderful, Simon! We all had to read aloud from our opus and I read first and after I'd finished Olive Snelling said, in front of the entire class . . .'

But poor Sandra was not destined to relate her moment of glory. For just then the mighty roar of a powerful engine shut off all conversation. There was a squeal of brakes and then the saloon bar door burst open and a big figure in bike leathers strode into the room. Everyone stared in silence as the person removed helmet and goggles. A gloved hand scratched a shaven head as the figure slowly sized up the watching clientele.

'You speak Italian – someone? Yes? I am on ze lookout. I need assistance.'

Stunned silence greeted this speech. Then Melanie leaned forward. 'Go on, Sand. You and Si have been studying Italian, haven't you?' she said, pushing her friend forward – like a Christian into the arena.

'Oh, goodness!' Sandra blushed. 'I'm not ready to speak to a real live Italian! Not yet!' Then she smiled shyly and nodded at the stranger. 'Buonasera!' she stammered.

This simple greeting inspired a flood of Italian – like an aria played at double the speed. Sandra gulped, shook her head, smiled several times, and when it seemed that she would never be able to stop the torrent she had unleashed, she raised a hand and waved it like an eager schoolgirl.

'Scusi . . .'

'Well done, Sand!'

Sandra shook her head and looked distraught. 'I couldn't understand a single word . . .'

The stranger beamed at her.

'But you have a toss!'

Sandra gulped and looked desperate. 'Pardon?' she said. And

turning to Simon for help she whispered: '"Have a toss"? What can "have a toss" mean, Simon?'

'We actually say "*give* a toss",' Barry offered, helpfully. 'Not "have a toss" – "give a toss".'

'You!' The stranger pointed at Sandra and smiled conspiratorially. 'You are who, my little chicken?'

'Me? Oh . . . I'm Sandra Green . . . Simon!' Her voice ended in a gasp as she reached out for support.

'I say, old chap!' Simon said, rising and stepping in front of Sandra. 'Please don't call my wife a chicken!'

They faced each other across the room. The rest of the assembly leaned forward, expectantly. The rest of the assembly with the exception of Stan, that is, who never bothered with the real world if he could possibly avoid it. He found the world of Splott, Tippee and Zigogg far more satisfying and had been known to continue reading right through a ram-raid. But for the rest of the people in the bar, the air crackled with potential drama. Until, with a sudden change of mood, the stranger let out a great hoot of laughter and slapped Simon on the back. The blow was so powerful that Simon staggered forward, but was saved from a fall by a strong arm round his shoulders.

'This "chap" you are calling me? Is man chap, yes?'

'Sorry?' Simon squeaked.

'Chap I like. But I am a female chap . . .' And the female chap swung round, roaring with laughter and saluting the entire room. 'Chap! I like it. I like chap!'

'Oh!' Sandra exclaimed, clapping her hands and stepping forward. 'I've got it! You'll be looking for the people down at the Hall House. They're all that way inclined down there . . .' Then she blushed and put her hand over her mouth.

'Say again?' the female chap barked, swinging round towards her and making her jump back.

'Well . . . You know . . .' she whispered. 'They're . . . men who like men . . . Gentlemen . . . Simon . . .'

'Just leave it, Sandra!'

'So?' The female chap nodded thoughtfully. 'This is so? You

have helped me a lot, I think. I look for my brother – my brother is that way sometimes . . .' She shrugged. 'Sometimes not . . . Really, he likes anything that is young and willing. You have met Antonio, yes?'

'I don't think so,' Sandra gasped. 'Melanie, don't you want to say anything?' she mouthed, glancing back over her shoulder. But Melanie shook her head and continued to gobble crisps without once taking her eyes off the stranger.

'Now I am tired. Tomorrow I find Antonio. All will then be bene. You!' She slammed her fist down on the bar in front of Stan.

Stan looked up from his novel.

'How can I help you, squire?'

'You have room?'

Stan scratched his head.

'Can you hum the tune?' he asked.

'I need bed,' the stranger bellowed.

'I don't do bed. I do crisps, pork scratchings, sandwiches to order – but you're too late – or the usual beverages.' He glanced at his watch. 'And we'll be closing in half an hour.'

'Imbecile, I need bed.'

'Bugger off!' Stan said, and returned to his book.

'There isn't a hotel in the village,' Sandra said, trying to be helpful.

'Lavinia Sparton sometimes does B and B,' Tony Daltry suggested. He stepped forward, glancing at his watch. 'But it is a bit late . . .'

'At home everything would be just waking up,' the stranger observed, slapping her hands together.

'They sit up ever so late in Italy,' Sandra confided to Melanie.

'Yes, well . . .' Tony shrugged. 'That's Europe for you. We're still back in the dark ages. It's either a billet down at the Towers – or you'll have to go into Fairlow. There's a Trusthouse Forte there – mini bar in each room, little sachets of milk, that sort of style . . .'

'I need bed. I need bed now. No more talk.'

'I didn't know she did B and B at the Towers. I thought she was dead – at the Towers!' Barry in computers said.

'Lavinia Sparton? She'll do anything for a few bob, poor old thing,' Tony confided.

'Really?' Barry gasped.

'Well, practically. Come on, old son,' Tony said, tapping the stranger on the shoulder with his rolled-up *Times*. 'I'll show you where. It's on my way.' And he headed for the door.

'Arrivederci, my petti di pollo!' the stranger said, tweaking Sandra's cheek between a finger and thumb.

'Oh!' Sandra gasped, massaging her cheek, as the big leather-clad figure gave her a wink and then turned and hurried out of the door.

'What did that mean, Sand?' Melanie asked, scrambling to be beside her friend.

'It's something you get to eat in a restaurant,' Sandra replied in a shaky voice.

'Bloody nerve!' Simon growled, rubbing his shoulder where the stranger had hit him.

'Petti di pollo,' Melanie said thoughtfully. 'Is it something with chips?'

'Oh, do shut up, Mel!' Sandra snapped, and then she burst into tears.

25

B & B At The Towers

When Lavinia Sparton's husband Henry was alive there had been a good deal of money spent on the Towers. He had wanted the house to be a shrine to his wife's great gift. When they met, Lavinia Olganina (her stage name – she had actually been born in Dorking as plain Vera Allgood) had been the première danseuse of the Ballet Romantique, and a huge star. Younger than Markova and Ulanova, she was to her many fans a rival of Fonteyn and the equal of Shearer. But Fonteyn got de Valois as her champion. Shearer got *The Red Shoes* and Lavinia Olganina remained with the Ballet Romantique, dancing her way round the world and with a London season at the Lyceum – that once in a while was known to play to packed houses – every other year. Much later, long after she had officially passed her sell-by date, the company received a visit from the bailiffs and, overnight, her once glittering career went into cardiac arrest. The arrival therefore of rich Henry Sparton seemed like a gift from the gods, and Lavinia determined to hang up her pumps and become an English country lady . . . at least for a while.

The Towers was purchased soon after their marriage, and when Henry handed her the key to the front door, wrapped in a swansdown pouch to remind her of *Le Lac*, he also gave her free rein to create the sort of background and ambience that would make her at ease and comfortable away from the bright lights of her beloved theatre and the – at least to his way of thinking – somewhat peculiar world of the dance.

Lavinia set to with a will. All the rooms were specially designed to capture the spirit of a different ballet. Oliver Messel helped with drawing up the plans, Cecil Beaton added innumerable suggestions and a set painter from the Ballet Romantique – by then sadly out of work and therefore happy to be employed as a house painter instead – was hired to carry out the decorations.

The drawing room was based on *Coq D'Or*, the dining room on *Swan Lake*. The principal bedroom could once have housed the Sleeping Beauty herself. There was a *Spartacus* room for rugged guests, and a *Sylphides* room for the more effete. If there was a full house one might find oneself sleeping with the *Willes*, while brave hearts were put in the workshop of *Dr Coppelius*. The landing was the balcony from *Romeo and Juliet* and one entered a hall straight out of *La Boutique Fantastique*. Originally it had been intended that the appropriate music would play as background in each of these spaces – but the cost of all this excess had been prohibitive and eventually Henry had been forced by his bank manager to put his foot down and insist that enough was enough.

However, one final indulgence had been included before the work was finished, and it was to be Henry's greatest gesture to his adored but demanding wife. A long gallery on the ground floor, originally used as a garden room, was converted into a studio, with mirrored walls, a barre, baby grand piano and the most up-to-the-minute of record players. Here in her private work space his own dear prima ballerina assoluta could practise daily in preparation for a triumphant comeback. It was said that her husband had even considered hiring a theatre – the Garden, Sadler's Wells or, for old time's sake, the Lyceum – for the event and that he intended Margot, Moira and the rest of the girls to form the corps de ballet. (Money, he believed, would talk – even in *le monde de la danse*.)

Then unexpectedly one night, in that way that life can be unexpected, Henry died of a massive heart attack and his own dear prima ballerina assoluta faced a new and bleaker future.

Lavinia discovered that her husband was practically penniless, his banking interests having suddenly collapsed just before the previous Christmas. He of course – considerate to the last – had kept this appalling catastrophe from her. No doubt he hoped to spare her any anxiety that might interfere with her great and God-given gift. Henry had absolute faith in Lavinia's talents. He had fallen in love with her Sleeping Beauty, had wooed her Cinderella and had finally won her Giselle. From the moment of their wedding he had been the happiest of men. Nevertheless, the shock of disaster was too much for him and this sudden reversal of their fortunes almost certainly led to his demise.

With his death Lavinia lost her most ardent admirer. She inherited instead a string of creditors, a broken dream and a lonely old age. Without Henry's constant encouragement and support, her hope of a comeback faded (if indeed she herself had ever seriously contemplated such a thing. She knew only too well the fickle nature of fame and the necessity for constant, punishing hard work – and to practise required a perseverance that was hard to maintain on one's own.) Meanwhile the glorious colours in all her rooms also gradually faded, the drapes frayed and thick layers of dust settled on the plasterwork and the carved wood. Eventually the roof started to leak and the willows in the garden pushed their roots so close to the house that they cracked the paths and threatened the walls, and little by little the whole place took on a veneer of ancient verdigris and crumbling grandeur not unlike the Sleeping Beauty's palace or Miss Haversham's hermitage. And there Lavinia, alone and forgotten, retired into the shadowy interior and dwindled and fell like the last leaf of autumn – a *pas de seul* that her ardent but small body of fans used to

maintain she executed with even more tristesse than the great
Markova herself.

'I do not usually take people without a booking. I think a
booking is most important.'

'I book!'

'No. You must do so in advance.'

'I am desperate.'

'You are not, I think, from this sceptred isle?'

'Say again?'

'You are a foreigner?'

'No! Not foreign! Italian!'

'Ah! Bene! Bene!' Lavinia simpered and fluttered. 'Come sta?'

'Bene, grazie.'

'Qual e lo scopo della sua visita?'

'You speak Italian!' Carlotta exclaimed, continuing in her
native tongue.

'Not so well.' Lavinia smiled, struggling for even the most
simple of phrases.

'But your accent is beautiful.'

Lavinia slowly extended her arms and pointed a toe and
lowered herself into a perfect, though wobbling, curtsy.

'Hey! Baby! You move like a dancer.'

Lavinia slowly rose again, smiling and covering her face with
a caressing hand – her mind meanwhile working overtime. What
was it that the stranger was trying to say?

'Like a . . .?' she asked, hoping for clarification. 'Non
capisco.'

'Like a dancer, baby! You understand? The ballet,' Carlotta
repeated, reverting to her broken English.

'The ballet? Oh! Yes, of course.' Lavinia shrugged. 'I was
Lavinia Olganina.'

Now it so happened that the Ballet Romantique in its heyday
had done several hugely successful tours of the principal cities
of Italy. And it further happened that big, butch Carlotta had,
as a dainty little girl, dreamed of becoming a dancer. And it
inevitably followed that every time the Ballet Romantique hit

Bologna, little Carlotta and her nursemaid were in Box A for every single performance. And so, when she heard the name:

'Lavinia Olganina! It isn't possible!' she gasped, reverting to Italian once more. 'It can't be true? It has to be a dream?'

'I'm afraid my Italian is a little too rusty to catch all the nuances,' Lavinia sighed, lapsing back into English.

'Signorina, I am your slave!' Carlotta sobbed, slapping her chest, dropping to her knees and finally kissing the floor of *La Boutique Fantastique* hall like a supplicant before his goddess.

After that there was no question but that she should stay the night. And so, after a few further pleasantries, Lavinia showed her up the stairs to the bedrooms. At first Carlotta could not decide between the *Sylphides* and the *Spartacus* rooms, but she was guided to the latter by her hostess, who feared that the net curtaining of the *Sylphides* bed would be thick with dust and could seriously damage her lungs if she inhaled too strenuously while sleeping. Carlotta was enraptured with everything she saw and assured Lavinia that the dripping tap in the bathroom, the sagging ceiling in the lavatory and the *Romeo and Juliet* concealed lights that hadn't worked for a decade (necessitating the use of a torch when traversing the landing in the dead of night) were all easy jobs which she'd sort out the following day.

'I would sit now and watch you dance!' Carlotta declared, much to Lavinia's consternation – she hadn't been into the studio since Rudolf Nureyev's death. 'With his passing,' she had told the local radio when they rang for a quote, 'the dance is dead!' What she actually thought was that the Russian leapt about far too much for decency and was a bit of a show-off. In her day the women had been the focal point of a ballet and the men were simply there to act as fork-lift trucks . . . But she knew what the public wanted to hear, and being a consummate artist she believed in giving that public exactly what they desired. Nevertheless, Carlotta's enthusiasm was strangely catching, and she almost went in search of a broom to help her through the *pas de seul* from Act One of *Cinderella*. But stopping herself in time, she merely lowered her face into her crossed and enfolding hands and smiled demurely.

'Tomorrow, huh? Eh, baby? Tomorrow you dance.'

'We shall see,' she murmured.

'Sure! No question! You dance and then I go find my brother.'

'Your brother?'

'Is a long story . . .'

'You have no luggage?' Lavinia enquired, realising how very little she knew about this person who seemed to be taking up residence in her home.

'I wear what I own!' Carlotta exclaimed, and dragging off her boots she started to peel off her leathers.

'Good night, kind sir!' Lavinia exclaimed, making a hasty retreat. And only later did it occur to her that they had not discussed the terms of accommodation, nor had she detailed the breakfast arrangements.

As a precaution that night, Lavinia slept with her door locked. But as she drifted off into sleep she experienced an unaccustomed glow of satisfaction stealing through her tired body. There was someone, here in the house, who remembered her. Someone who had seen her dance. Someone who had knelt at her feet and kissed the ground in gratitude.

God could sometimes be so very kind! To have sent such an unexpected emissary at such an unlooked-for moment.

'Tomorrow,' she murmured sleepily, 'I *must* start a diet and I *must* get back to the barre.'

26

Phyllis

As soon as Doris Day let herself in through the kitchen door at Cockpits she was aware of a subtle change in the house. Twitching her nose, she sniffed the air. Over the lingering smell of burnt toast and the faint odour of damp there hovered a more exotic, more sensual aroma. The kind of perfume that comes in little bottles with tassels and bows.

'Scent?' she said out loud. 'Well, I never! And without so much as a "by your leave, Mrs Day" or a "I do hope you don't mind, Mrs Day"? Well I never!' And unbuttoning her coat, she hung it over one of the kitchen chairs and headed for the hall.

She was halfway up the stairs when Mrs Jerrold appeared at the top of them.

'Oh, Mrs Day!' she exclaimed, seeming flustered.

'Mrs Jerrold?' her cleaning woman responded, continuing to climb.

'I was not expecting you . . .'

'Why ever not? It's Wednesday. I always come on a Wednesday. I've been coming on a Wednesday since . . .'

'No, no! I mean I was not expecting you to do upstairs today,' Mrs Jerrold cut in, sounding irritable.

'No, ma'am. I was not expecting to do so either,' Doris

agreed, reaching the landing and trying to see over her employer's shoulder into the room that she had just vacated.

'Then why are you here?' Rosemary Jerrold enquired.

'I like to see that everything has remained nice and tidy,' the older woman responded, running a finger along the top of the banister and checking for dust. 'I take great pride in my work. Yes,' she added, inspecting her fingertip, 'I gave up here a good going-over yesterday.'

'It all looks lovely,' her employer volunteered.

'It could do with a lick of paint.'

'The Brigadier does not care for a glossy surface.'

'You was in the spare room, ma'am?'

'I suppose I was, yes.'

'Am I to take it you have a visitor?'

'Most unexpectedly – yesterday afternoon.'

'I like to be told these things in advance, so that I can tidy,' Doris said, trying to squeeze past her on the narrow landing.

'It was quite tidy, thank you,' Mrs Jerrold assured her, blocking her way and trying instead to manoeuvre her back towards the stairs.

'I like everything fresh!' Doris said, standing her ground. 'If people are to arrive I like to give the place a good airing . . . Blow the cobwebs away . . .'

'There are no cobwebs, Mrs Day.'

'Get some nice clean air into the frowsty old place . . .'

'Shall we go down to the kitchen?' Rosemary cut in, wearying of her cleaner's well-worn diatribe on the next virtue to godliness. 'We should have a cup of coffee before you start work.'

'As you wish,' Doris said, reluctantly turning and retracing her steps. 'I take it I am not to be told who has come visiting?'

'Oh, didn't I say?' Mrs Jerrold asked, following her.

'No, madam, you didn't.'

'It's the Brigadier's sister, come down from Scarborough for a few days. Isn't that lovely? We intend to turn out all the kitchen cupboards and give the sitting room a proper clean.'

'The sitting room has been scrupulously attended to for more weeks than I care to consider,' Doris said, a sour note in her voice.

'Of course it has. But you know how Miss Phyllis and I love to play houses.'

'Yes, quite. Like Her Majesty with her Wendy house,' Doris said, filling the kettle and then sitting down to be waited on by her employer. Mrs Jerrold hurried to bring cups and milk, saucers and the biscuit barrel, spoons and a jar of instant coffee – everything landing on the table in a horrible muddle as her mind darted from point to point.

'Sugar!' Doris prompted her, watching through sullen eyes.

'Silly of me!'

'Will she be coming down?'

'Who?'

'Who! Well, not Her Majesty, that's for sure!'

'Her Majesty?'

'No! Miss Phyllis?'

'She's unpacking and . . . then I think she intends to have a long soak in a bath.'

'What's the point of that if she's going to be charring for the rest of the day?'

'Not charring, exactly, and I doubt we shall start today. Today we shall take things easy.'

'It's all right for some, isn't it?'

There was silence as Mrs Jerrold waited for the kettle to boil.

'You should get a new one. Something with a bit of oomph to it.'

'A new what?'

'Kettle!'

'I am quite satisfied with the one I have.' Mrs Jerrold frowned, determined not to be brow-beaten by her servant. 'It's your week for doing the inside windows, is it not?'

'Oh, I doubt I'll be able to do them – not on a day like this. Light's that bright I couldn't see to get a good polish.'

'But last time you refused you said it was too dull for you to see the streaks.'

'Well, there you are, you see. I'm that particular. I like my glass to really shine.'

'Oh dear. What will you be doing then?'

'I'm not at all sure. After I've had my coffee I'll just have to nip next door to the Hall House . . .' She gave the name a special tone, denoting a superior dwelling. 'I start there in earnest tomorrow and I want to be sure that that nice young Mr Hudson has all my requirements.'

'Like biscuits and sugar and coffee,' Rosemary Jerrold hissed, as she lifted the kettle and added water to the cups.

'What was that you said, dear?' Doris asked, opening the biscuit barrel and rummaging through the contents in a dissatisfied way.

'I think you should call round to your other employers when you have finished here, Mrs Day. That would be best, don't you agree?'

'I'm not fussy one way or the other,' Doris replied, her mouth full of coconut crunch.

'Good. So what do you intend to be getting on with here?'

'Hall, stairs, sitting room, front porch and the perishing kitchen – like I do every Wednesday,' Doris snapped.

'Splendid! Then we'll do our best to keep out of your way,' Mrs Jerrold said, and she placed the two cups of coffee she had prepared on to a tray. Then, after wresting the biscuit barrel out of her cleaner's hands and placing it on the same receptacle, she held it aloft and headed for the door. 'Make yourself a cup of coffee, won't you? And then make a start!' she said as she went out of the room.

Doris stared at the door and inwardly fumed. She had noticed before that when Miss Phyllis came to stay her employer became more brave and began to answer back and take other liberties. But this time it was worse; this time Mrs Jerrold seemed . . . almost bold in her approach. Doris pursed her lips and drank some milk straight from the bottle thoughtfully. Furthermore, this time there was an entirely new situation. Always in the past the two women were out of the house by the time she arrived for work. But this time the Brigadier's sister was actually upstairs at that very moment. Doris pondered this new development. It was certainly very tempting . . . Doris was slave to a great and insatiable curiosity. Until she knew something that puzzled her she could have no rest. Invariably once the thing was known it proved poor fodder and she would put it aside and forget all about it. But before the forgetting could be allowed to take place, every little item of gossip and local interest had to pass through the fine mesh of her greedy, enquiring mind.

Still cogitating deeply, she went into the larder. There she discovered a bowl of cold rice pudding covered by a plate. She scooped some into her mouth with a crooked finger, savoured it, had another larger scoop with the same finger and then patted the surface of the pudding level once more. Sucking a morsel of the creamy rice from under her nail she walked back into the kitchen.

'We'll see, we'll see . . .' she warbled pensively as she cast around for inspiration. 'Whatever we'll see, we'll see. The outcome's not up to me. So we'll see, we'll see . . .'

Then she nodded to herself, deciding at last on a plan of action, and turning, she darted with one of her sudden, quick spurts of energy out to the scullery. There she collected a bucket and cleaning agents. Returning to the kitchen, she half filled the bucket with steaming water at the sink, and in a matter of moments she was upstairs and on her hands and knees outside the spare room door, washing the paintwork with sloshing, dripping strokes and a great deal of energetic rubbing and wiping.

'When I was still in baby clothes, I asked my Nana, what would befall?' she trilled, warming to her task. 'It might be merry, it might be sad, it might be downright mean . . .' Her voice rose in a quavering crescendo: 'We'll see, we'll see. The outcome's not up to me. It's never been up to me. So we'll see, we'll see . . .'

The spare room door suddenly shot open and Rosemary

Jerrold appeared. Her timing was unfortunate. She received a floor cloth wringing with water and drenched in Vim across her shins.

'What are you doing, woman?' she bellowed.

'The paintwork, madam!' Doris replied, and scrambling forward, still on her knees, she pushed past her employer and entered the room at a fast crawl.

Phyllis Jerrold was seated at the dressing table, with her back to the door. She was running a comb through her wavy blonde hair but stopped as the cleaner appeared. She turned slowly and looked over her shoulder, gazing down at the woman on the floor with an expression of amused and expectant surprise.

'Oh!' Doris Day simpered, grasping on to the end of the bed to help herself to rise. 'Miss Jerrold! Ever so pleased to meet you at last. I'm Mrs Doris Day. It's my task to keep this humble abode shipshape and sparkling.'

There was a fraction of a pause, and then the woman at the dressing table smiled and raised a hand as if in a wave.

'And you do a wonderful job,' she said. Her voice was low and gentle, matching in every way her elegant appearance. Her hair, the colour of bleached corn, fell in a ripple of light down one side of her face. Her lips were the colour of coral and her eye make-up was subtle but alluring. She was wearing a pale cream and pink silk dress with a full skirt that billowed out around the stool on which she sat. The long sleeves ended at tight cuffs and there was a gold bracelet on one wrist and a little gold watch, with a rather loose strap, on the other. Her nails were the same colour as her lips and a simple, but not small, diamond ring glittered on the marriage finger.

She was as much a lady as Doris Day had ever clapped eyes on in all her seventy-odd years, and the sight of her made the old woman feel quite flustered.

'I didn't mean to . . .' she stammered. 'That is to say . . . I just thought I should do the paintwork on the landing . . .'

'Dear Mrs Day,' the lady purred. 'Don't you trouble yourself. Rosemary and I will do it later.'

'Oh, no, madam! I wouldn't like to think of you doing anything of the sort. Good gracious! That's what I'm here for,' Doris burbled, gradually stepping backwards out of this presence of loveliness.

'I am so very pleased to have made your acquaintance,' the lady said, graciously bestowing a smile on the menial. 'I am sure we will see each other often. I intend to be here much more in the future. Dear Rosemary and I are such good friends and I so enjoy the happy times I have in your lovely village.'

'Thank you, ma'am.' Doris blushed, proud to be even a tiny part of a place that had found such commendation from someone who so clearly would know a lovely village when she saw one. 'If there's anything at all I can do to make your stay more comfortable, you be sure to ask, won't you?' And reaching the landing, she stumbled and fell against Rosemary, who was standing in the doorway and about whose presence she had completely forgotten.

'Thank you, Mrs Day!' Rosemary winced, as the old woman stood on her foot. 'Don't do any more cleaning up here, please . . .'

'In fact,' the vision murmured, turning once more towards the mirror and dabbing at her reflection in the glass, as if removing some intrepid speck of dirt from her lovely cheek, 'why don't we give dear Doris the rest of the day off, Rosemary? Then she can go and visit her new employers . . .'

'Oh no, madam! I've only just arrived.'

'No! We insist, don't we, Rosemary? After all, with my brother out of the house, we're all girls together here and should be allowed a little indulgence once in a while.'

'Oh, madam!' Doris Day burbled blithely. 'Girls together! Well, I must say . . .'

'Yes. Do take the rest of the day off, Mrs Day,' Rosemary said, her less effusive tones throwing a cold douche over the proceedings.

'Well, I don't know . . . I really want to clean the kitchen and the sitting room . . .' She really didn't want to leave. If at that moment she could have had her way she would have dedicated herself to a lifetime of waiting on Phyllis Jerrold and serving her in any way the vision of loveliness desired. She was, in short, smitten. Doris Day had met the pinnacle of her wildest dreams. She was, at last, in the presence of – no, more than that – she was working for:

'A real lady,' she muttered to herself as she emptied the bucket into the sink, mopped up the draining board and finally, and with utter reluctance, donned her coat and crossed back to the hall.

'I'm off now, madam!' she called.

'Goodbye, dear Doris!' came back the muffled but unmistakable tones of her heroine. 'I look forward to seeing you again very soon.'

'Yes, thank you, madam!' Doris called, shivering inwardly with exquisite pleasure. 'Well, toodle-oo, then!'

27

D*eus* E*x* M*achina*

To travel incognito in an English village is never easy. For a vicar it is well-nigh impossible. Andrew Skrimshaw decided therefore to brazen it out and to walk down the hill to the Hall House for all the world to see. If anyone accosted him he would greet them cheerily and even pass the time of day with them. Should they ask where he was off to he could reply with utter sincerity that he was going about his pastoral duties. He was visiting the new arrivals in the community – making himself known to two more brave souls, two potential sheep for his flock.

The darker purpose of his visit he would not divulge – even to his wife, Margaret, whom he discovered polishing the brass on the lectern as he passed through the church. He was coming from the vestry, having collected in a briefcase his requirements for the task ahead, and was quite unnerved to find her there, having thought that he had the place to himself.

'You off?' she asked, without looking round.

'Yes. Just a little parish visiting.'

'Good.'

Theirs was a distant, polite relationship.

'I will be back for lunch.'

'Good.'

'Shall I see you?'

'Yes. No. I'm not sure.'

'Good. Well – I shall hope so.'

'Good.'

By now he had reached the door in the south transept, which was used as the business entrance. He thought perhaps some word of encouragement might be required and, looking back, he called: 'The brass looks lovely!'

'Good,' his wife said, continuing to polish.

Then he went out, closing the door, which at the last moment banged – as it always did. The sound echoed through the little church. It forced Margaret to glance over her shoulder. And if the Almighty had been watching – though He was probably far too busy elsewhere – He would have noticed, but not necessarily been surprised to see, that there were tears in her eyes. This fact would not have unduly perturbed Him, however, because Margaret, the rector's wife, cried rather a lot.

Bless was sitting on the hall chair, waiting, as he had been ever since making the phone call to the rectory. So as soon as he heard the bell he opened the door, taking the vicar by surprise.

'Oh!' he gasped, with his finger still on the button.

'Come in!' Bless said, and he almost pulled the man into the house. Once inside he closed the door, first checking furtively to see that there were no strangers lurking on the drive.

'I'm Andrew Skrimshaw,' the vicar said, extending a hand and sounding as if he was about to bless a congregation, or at least bless Bless.

'Yes, yes!' Bless interrupted him, taking the hand impatiently. 'What's more to the point – can you do the job?'

The vicar cleared his throat and looked grave. 'There are a lot of questions I would have to ask first.' When the young man didn't offer any reaction he continued, his voice assuming now the hushed tones of confidentiality, 'Why do you feel in need of this . . . unusual service?'

'Not me! It isn't for me! I've got a raving lunatic locked in one of my guest bedrooms and she won't come out until she's seen a vicar. That's why you're here.'

'I see. And this person is . . .?'

'Diana . . . Simpson, I think she said . . .'

'Simpson.' The vicar said the name slowly. 'Ms Simpson?'

'Well she certainly isn't a mister!'

'What is it . . . that she's hoping for?'

'I can't explain. You'd better ask her,' Bless said, leading the way up the stairs to the landing. Reaching the closed door of the guest bedroom, behind which Diana had taken up refuge against the powers of darkness, he knocked loudly and shouted her name a few times, aware that his voice had acquired a peeved tone that he was in danger of keeping for life.

'Who's there?' Diana called, her voice husky with emotion.

'Me, of course! I've got the vicar.'

'How do I know that?'

'You'll just have to take it on trust won't you?' Bless snarled.

'No. I mean how do I know you are with the vicar?'

'Because he's standing beside me – and that's who he says he is.'

'If he were Beelzebub he would hardly be likely to announce the fact, would he?'

'Look! As I don't happen to be a theologian I have no intention of swapping philosophical debate through one of MY VERY OWN DOORS!' He ended the sentence at megablast.

'Bring me the vicar,' the disembodied voice wailed.

'I've brought you the fucking vicar – sorry, Vicar!'

'Don't worry about it.'

'Thank you. Look, please,' Bless continued, addressing the magnolia panelling once more. 'I'm sure he's who he says he is, he's got his collar on back-to-front and . . . well, he looks like a vicar. Sorry, Vicar.'

Andrew Skrimshaw shrugged understandingly and smiled.

'You have a go,' Bless said wearily. 'I expect you're more used to this sort of thing than I am. You must be trained for it. I only play small parts and do a bit of tap dancing.'

Andrew Skrimshaw frowned, obviously completely losing the drift. But Bless pushed him forward, propelling him towards the barricade.

'Miss Simpson,' the vicar called, his voice gentle and appealing.

'It's Ms,' the voice hissed.

'Yes, of course it is. You know who I am. I'm the Reverend Skrimshaw. I am your vicar – and your friend . . .'

'Oh, really? And how would I know that?'

'Because you sent me a postcard from Le Puy,' the vicar said, enunciating the words as though they were some code or password.

Bless glanced at him apprehensively – but gave him the benefit of any doubts he might be harbouring. Le Puy had after all featured quite heavily in the tale so far. There followed a longish silence. Then a faint *click* was heard.

'The lock!' Bless whispered, relieved. But as he made to open the door, the vicar restrained him, holding up a hand, impelling silence.

Another moment passed, then the door slowly swung inwards and Diana Simpson was revealed to them. Her face was tear-stained, her hair dishevelled. But she was at least still on her feet and at such times one looks for the merest glimmer of reassurance.

'Oh, yes! Now I remember you!' she said, coming out and looking Andrew up and down. 'Well, have you brought your . . . gear?'

'I think you and I need a long talk, my dear,' Andrew Skrimshaw said gently, as he moved her back into the bedroom.

'Well, I'll leave you two to it,' Bless said, relieved. He turned, about to slip away to the sanity of the kitchen.

'No!' Andrew Skrimshaw's hand shot out, catching him by the sleeve. 'A third party must be present.'

'Oh, shit!' Bless groaned, and this time he didn't bother to apologise.

'There is no one else in the house, is there?'

'No,' Bless admitted in a resigned voice.

'Good. Very good. Now, why don't we all sit down?' the vicar suggested, taking a chair and gesturing to the double bed for the other two.

'I can't!' Diana cried, pacing up and down and hyperventilating noisily. 'You must help me. Do I look how you expected?' And when Andrew didn't answer at once, she turned and shouted: 'Well? Do I?'

'I had not invested you in my mind with . . . any particular physical features, Ms Simpson . . .'

'No! I mean – do I look possessed?'

There was a pause as the vicar considered this question. Bless meanwhile decided to surrender to the situation, and sitting on the edge of the bed, he leaned forward, waiting for the next development. It did cross his mind that telling Maggie all about it was going to be enormous fun – though explaining to Rich, without making himself sound a total idiot, might be more difficult.

Still the vicar remained silent. Still Diana stood in front of him, her body tense, her face anguished.

When the silence was turning interminable, Bless was forced to intervene. 'Well? What d'you think? Is she . . .? You know . . . I mean, you'd be more likely to know than anyone . . .'

'Know what?' Andrew snapped, rounding on Bless and using a surprisingly aggressive tone.

'If she's possessed.'

'I am!' the woman shrieked.

'What do you two want?' Andrew asked, rising and using his most commanding tones. 'What have you heard? Why have you got me here? You're reporters, aren't you? Tabloid press!' He spun round, searching the room with his eyes and ducking away from the window. 'You've got some nasty little rat with a camera trained on me, haven't you? Why can't you people leave us alone . . .' And he sank down on to the chair once more, the picture of despair and abject misery.

The effect of this outburst on the other two was significant, to say the least. Bless was gobsmacked and Diana indignant.

'What are you raving about, man?' she demanded. 'We can't have our vicar behaving like this. A vicar has to be a tower of strength in the community. Unless . . .' Now she rounded on Bless. 'Is this true? Do you work for the newspapers? Have you trapped me into telling you my story? You . . . you . . . you despicable . . .'

'LOOK!' Bless exploded, and as he did so he rose and for some reason clapped his hands together. 'I've had enough of this. OUT! Both of you. OUT! This is a private house and . . . you're really pissing me off now. So, go on – O-U-T!' He spelt the last word, jabbing with a finger as he uttered each letter.

Now it was the turn of Andrew and Diana to blink.

'You mean – you know nothing about David, my son?' Andrew asked. 'About his possession – and about the part I played in freeing him?'

'Freeing him?' Diana gasped, latching on to the words.

'Yes. He was possessed – and I sent that demon from him . . .'

'But that's exactly what I want you to do for me . . .'

'Demons have to go somewhere, woman. They can't be left to roam about the village looking for a new home. But I didn't know that, did I? I meddled where I was not allowed . . . and I made matters so much worse . . .'

'Wait a minute, wait a minute, wait a minute . . .' Bless waved his hands impatiently. 'Don't go so fast. You're saying that your son was . . .'

'Possessed. He had got into bad company . . .'

'And you told the . . .' Why did Bless find it embarrassing to talk about it? Sanity, perhaps? 'You told the . . . thing . . .'

'The devil,' Diana snapped. 'You commanded the devil to leave him? So you are able to do what I ask?'

'I will never do such a thing again,' Andrew told her. 'I came here thinking that you might force me – fear of exposure is strong if one is a man of the cloth . . .'

'It's pretty tricky for MPs and show biz as well,' Bless said, he hoped helpfully.

'But why not?' Diana pleaded. 'It's surely an important part of your job?'

'Why not? You ask me why I refuse your request?'

'Certainly I do. I am one of your congregation. I admit I don't actually . . . congregate – but you're not allowed to discriminate, surely? So why won't you exorcise the devil that possesses me? What right have you to refuse me? You're my servant. And if as you say you have done it before – I'm not even asking all that much of you. I mean, you won't need to mug anything up. It should all come quite easily to you . . .'

'You ask me why I will not perform this . . . ceremony for you?' Andrew repeated, his voice shaking. 'Very well then, I see I must tell you.' He cleared his throat and hesitated before continuing in a low, anguished tone: 'When the demon left David . . . it immediately took up residence in my daughter, Julia, who had happened to pop in unexpectedly at precisely the wrong moment, looking for a packet of cigarettes . . .' There was a long silence as the vicar obviously fought with great waves of recollected emotion. Then he shook his head and continued in a more severe tone: 'She has been a wanton ever since. Lewd and lascivious . . . It is terrible to behold. She treats us with contempt. She and her brother do not speak . . .'

'How is he faring, by the way?' Bless asked, completely fascinated.

'He works for Selfridge's, the department store, in the food hall, and apart from putting on a great deal of weight he seems to be fully recovered.'

'I wouldn't want to put on weight,' Diana muttered – more to herself than the others.

'But, meanwhile, your daughter . . .?' Bless prompted, sensing that this was where the juice now lay.

'My daughter, my dear young man, gave up her teaching job the week after the terrible event, and so far as my wife and I know she now works as a courier for Club de Luxe. A package-deal holiday outfit with villas and apartments in the sun.'

'Well, it could be worse. She's in work,' Bless told him cheerfully.

'She might as well have checked into the Sodom and Gomorrah Hilton,' the vicar snapped. 'Do you know what they get up to in those places?'

'You see?' Diana wailed. 'You see? I have had the same experience . . . But mine was in no Hilton, I assure you. I didn't even have running water . . .' The wail turned into racking sobs. 'I am right! What I suspected is true! I have become possessed!'

'Oh . . . Lord!' Bless whimpered, weakly.

Suddenly, like an intervention from God Himself, the front door bell rang down in the hall. The three people in the bedroom froze, staring out on to the landing.

Then, adding to their consternation and making them start back as if they were being physically attacked, a voice called from downstairs: 'It's all right, Mr 'Udson! I'll answer it!'

'Who is that?' Andrew hissed.

'I don't know,' Bless squeaked.

'You said the house was empty . . .'

'It is. It was. I . . .'

'We have been overheard! We are lost . . .' the vicar wailed, rocking backwards and forwards on his chair and hugging his arms across his chest.

'Well – go and see!' Diana sobbed, pulling at Bless. 'Go on! You keep telling us this is your house. Go and . . .'

'Mr 'Udson,' the voice from below called out. 'There is a foreign gentleman at the door and I can't make head nor tail of 'im.'

'Hey, baby!' A second voice was now heard; a deep, throbbing voice with a thick accent. 'I'm looking for someone. You wanna come down? Or you want me up?'

'It's her!' Diana croaked. 'It's her!'

'Who?' Bless whispered.

'Carlotta! She has found me . . .' and with a final wail of terror, she slumped down on to the floor.

'Oh, shit!' Bless groaned. 'She's fainted again.'

28

Alarums And Excursions

Lavinia had insisted on her gentleman caller using one of Henry's suits. 'You cannot go to the Hall House in motorbike attire. It would cause comment and certainly not give the right impression. Besides,' she added, 'leather must feel terribly hot at this time of year.' As she spoke she was leading the way along the *Romeo and Juliet* landing. Carlotta followed, draped in a kimono kindly leant by her hostess – who had held it by an outstretched hand through a chink in the *Spartacus* doorway and had refused to enter 'until you are decently covered, signor'.

Her husband's clothes were still in his closet – a small room situated beyond *The Sleeping Beauty* suite and decorated in the style of *Le Corsaire*. The room was spartan and contained only a large wardrobe, a gentleman's chest, a cheval mirror and a single and remarkably hard truckle bed with a table and lamp beside it.

'Henry used this room for his sleeping arrangements,' Lavinia confided – making the function sound relatively unimportant. 'Ours was a cultural union. After a brief halcyon coupling, he worshipped me from afar.'

Carlotta was taller than the deceased man and considerably slimmer. But trousers were found in a good grey serge that, when tucked into her knee-high boots and with the addition of a cummerbund from a dress suit and a white shirt left open at the neck and without its accompanying stiff collar, gave her a rather dashing, Cossack look.

'Hey, baby!' she exclaimed, eyeing herself in the mirror and slapping her thigh, appreciatively. 'Is good! Yes!'

'Very good,' Lavinia admitted. 'You could almost be Le Corsaire himself.'

So, thus attired and having had a good night's rest and a full English breakfast, Carlotta had approached the Hall House with a sense of confidence and a renewed zest for living. She had suffered dreadfully when Diana's midnight flit from the commune had been discovered. For days she had shut herself away, and even when the generator had packed up and the large field (called Les Champs-Elysées by Mother, who liked to use it for picnics and training sessions) required mowing she could not be persuaded to attend to these duties. Eventually it had been decided that she should take leave of absence from the Sisters of Lysistrata and go in search of her tormentor, 'the English virgin' – as Diana had now become known to the rest of the sisterhood. (Virginity was a rare commodity at the commune, most of the others – with the possible, but by no means certain, exception of the ex-nun, Auntie – having taken refuge there in order to recover from the ravages of bastards of the male gender.)

Once it was decided that she could go, Carlotta had contacted her beloved brother, Antonio. She sent him a postcard giving her address at the commune. She needed only to add the family motto – 'Torni un po' piu tardi' – to know that he would come to her side as fast as wings or a powerful car could carry him.

Antonio arrived three days later. He took Carlotta to a good hotel, put her in a comfortable suite, saw to it that she had everything that she might require – money being no obstacle to the wishes of the family da Braganizio – and set out in his car, searching the length and breadth of France, armed with a photograph of Diana and a wallet full of francs.

But Carlotta grew restless in her Michelin-listed château, and a day or two later she herself set out in search of Antonio. Thus, as Diana's Deux Chevaux skulked under a tarpaulin in Le Puy and Antonio's Audi followed its scent like a bloodhound – so somewhere, far behind, Carlotta's powerful Harley Davidson trashed the tarmac.

Who could have thought that this game of hide and seek would lead Carlotta to the shrine of her beloved Lavinia Olganina, the dancer she had worshipped as a little girl? This goddess whose brightly spinning fouetté after fouetté after fouetté had haunted her all her life like a living gyroscope. This angel whose presence here on earth had become for her the symbol of absolute womanhood and the ideal of life itself?

'Is a miracle!' Carlotta shouted to the hanging willows as she left the gates of the Towers, bounded across the green and leapt the Belling Brook in a surge of joy and almost religious fervour.

Consequently she was in the best of humours as she waited in the hall with the little old lady staring at her suspiciously from the foot of the stairs.

'Will you come, Mr 'Udson?' Doris Day called, without taking her eyes off the man in front of her. Doris had a deep distrust of foreigners. 'I don't like the look of him one little bit,' she added.

'Yes, yes! I'm coming,' Bless called from the guest room as he and the vicar revived Diana by forcing her head between her legs and fanning her with an open copy of *Horse and Hound* – purchased by Rich in a fit of extravagance when he had first contemplated the rigours and responsibilities of being the squire of the village.

Diana actually came round surprisingly fast. Though perhaps not so surprising for a woman who seemed able to faint at the least provocation.

'Has she gone?' she gasped in a voice that carried. And she would have continued, if the vicar hadn't clamped his hand over her mouth and shaken his head frantically.

'Who've you got up there, Mr 'Udson?' Doris called. She

would have liked to climb the stairs to see for herself. But she was wary of turning her back on a foreigner.

'Go down!' the vicar mouthed at Bless.

'Get rid of her,' Diana whimpered.

'Who were you talking to?' Doris demanded, as Bless appeared on the landing.

'No one,' he replied, looking down into the hall and surprised to see what appeared to be a rather tasty-looking bald-headed man in a flamboyant costume standing beside his cleaner.

'You speak to no one?' the man cried, opening his arms in a wide gesture of welcome and grinning up at Bless. 'Is not good. Sign you go loco!'

'I was . . . rehearsing actually,' Bless said, always suspicious of too much familiarity too soon. And he hurried down the stairs, fearing that they might decide to come up instead.

'Yes!' Doris agreed in a superior voice. 'You was re'earsing weren't you, dear? This man is foreign, Mr 'Udson,' she added, her tone now turning suspicious, 'and I don't know what he's after, but it's something . . .'

'I didn't expect you to be here this morning, Mrs Day,' Bless cut in, hoping to get rid of her. Life might be a shade easier, he decided, without having to cope with both her and Carlotta at the same time.

'Ah, now that's what I wanted to tell you, Mr 'Udson. You are in the presence of a real lady.'

'What?' Bless exclaimed.

'Baby!' Carlotta beamed.

Doris Day stared from one to the other, sensing a hidden agenda. But not having a clue what it could be, she decided to persevere with her original train of thought. ''Er next door! The Brigadier's sister. She's come to stay. She has more . . . ladylikeness . . . in her little finger than I've seen in a month of Sundays . . . Oh, I want you to meet her. You'll take to her so . . .'

'Mrs Day . . .' Bless interrupted her. 'Will you . . . leave us?'

'Leave you? Certainly not!' she reassured him. 'Don't you worry about that. I'm more than happy with the arrangements.'

'No . . . I mean, just for a moment.'

'Oh! You wish to be private?'

'No need to be private, baby. Your momma can stay,' Carlotta cried, clapping an arm round Doris's frail shoulders. 'I like a family.'

Now it was Doris's turn for confusion. She blinked and wriggled herself free from the other woman's embrace. 'I'm not his mother!' she squealed.

But Carlotta had already turned back to Bless and was pursuing her own concerns, oblivious to anything else. 'I look for my brother, Antonio. You have seen him. yes?'

'No! Maybe! I'm not sure,' Bless stammered.

'Once seen, you would not forget. You would want to get in his pants.'

'What?' Bless gasped. Things were moving too fast for him.

Carlotta shrugged. 'He's built like a stone WC! Don't worry! We're all grown up!' She chucked him under the chin.

'Stop that!' Doris chided. 'We don't want none of your foreign carryings-on. Not here! Do we, Mr 'Udson?'

'Ah! I understand! Momma not know about you, huh?' Carlotta winked at Bless and tapped her nose. 'You like to keep in the wardrobe. 'Sup to you! I say nothing! So, old lady . . . Mebbe we need private talk after all. You will go, please.'

'Yes.' Bless sighed. 'Perhaps that would be best, Mrs Day.'

'Well, I'll go in the kitchen then,' Doris said, deeply disappointed. 'I don't want to stay where I'm not wanted.' And turning her back she disappeared down the passage, her shoulders rigid with umbrage.

As Carlotta watched her departure she shrugged and rocked her head from side to side. 'Is sometimes difficult for the momma and poppa. I understand. When I arrived, mine wanted a boy!' She shrugged. 'My father is a prince, is understandable. So he make me into a boy! Ten years pass. He mounts the wife

again, makes a boy, and I'm on the compost 'eap! Life! Family!'
She roared with laughter. 'I glad. I have had a much better time.
But you . . . You should tell your momma. It's important, I
think. Life in a wardrobe can be very . . . how you say?' She
gasped a few times and mimed suffocation.

'Look! Please! Can we get one thing straight today, if we do
nothing else?'

'Anything, baby! Anything. I like you. My brother, Toni, he
will be mad for you when he sees you . . .'

'PLEASE!' Bless yelled.

'What?' Carlotta said, turning and giving him oceans of
attention.

'That woman . . .' He jabbed a finger towards the back
passage down which Doris Day had just disappeared.

'Your momma? Si?'

'She is my cleaning woman!' Bless roared. Then, taking a
deep breath, he continued in a calmer voice, 'She is my housekeeper . . . my servant . . . my slave . . .'

'You keep your mother as a slave?'

'She is not my fucking mother!' Bless yelled.

There was a long silence. Carlotta looked him slowly up and
down. She walked away from him. She turned. She walked back
towards him.

'Not your mother?'

'Not my mother!'

'Your . . . slave?'

'Well . . .' Bless shrugged weakly. Slave did seem a trifle
excessive.

'She is your slave!' Carlotta said quietly. 'So old to be your
slave. But . . . your slave! Really?'

'Sort of.' Bless nodded.

Carlotta nodded.

They were nodding at each other.

Then she smiled, and crossing to him she gave him a huge
bear hug. 'What ever turns you on, baby!' she exclaimed, and
she kissed him on both cheeks.

In the ensuing silence the sound of a phone ringing could be heard in several parts of the house.

'Can you get that, Mrs Day?' Bless called, fighting himself clear of Carlotta's embrace.

'I don't do telephones,' a muffled, sulky voice was heard from the kitchen.

The telephone continued.

'In here,' Carlotta exclaimed, turning towards the open door of the study and going in. 'Hey, baby!' she cried, picking up the phone and yelling into it.

'Give me that!' Bless dragged the receiver from her hand. 'This is my house . . . Hello?' he snapped, angrily.

'Bless?' a distant voice spoke in his ear.

'Who's that?' Bless demanded, most of his attention on Carlotta, who had walked back out into the hall and was looking up the stairs.

'It's me!'

'Who?'

'What's happening?'

'I'm sorry. I can't talk now. Whoever you are – you'll have to call back.'

'It's Rich.'

'Oh! Hi, Rich!' Bless said in a weak voice. 'Call me back . . . I've got a bit of a . . . CARLOTTA!' he yelled, dropping the phone and racing back into the hall, his voice stopping the woman in her tracks as she was halfway up the stairs.

'How you know my name? Huh?' she asked, walking slowly back down towards him.

'I . . . um . . .' Bless had once, very briefly, joined a men's group. There he had been introduced to the benefits of constructive aggression. Now seemed a golden opportunity to put what he had learned into practice. 'Where were you going?' he demanded. 'You come in here and use my house as if it were your own. How dare you?'

Carlotta smiled.

'My brother will eat you for breakfast!' she said. 'You are so virile when you are angry! So beautiful. I think maybe I dress you as a girl and eat you myself!'

Bless groaned and decided to try a different tack – perhaps pleading would work? 'Look, I'm terribly sorry,' he began, 'but I'm having rather a busy day. If you could leave me a forwarding address . . .'

'Sure! No problem! I stay with the dancer. You know her?'

'What dancer?'

'*What* dancer? Only the greatest! Lavinia Olganina. Here! In this village. I come to live with her. Before I leave I will have her dancing again. Also there is a little peach up at the bar – who I have every intention of plucking before the summer is out. You know her, I hope?'

'Who?'

'They call her . . . Sandra? That is how you say it?'

'I've never heard of her.' Bless sighed. He suddenly felt incredibly weary.

'So! Your name is . . .? 'Udson? Yes?'

'No. It's . . . Oh, I shouldn't worry about that at the moment.'

'Baby! I don't worry about a thing. Not any more. I arrived here with a broken 'eart. You know the virgin, Diana? Yes. You must! She broke my 'eart. If ever I see her, I will tear her apart for what she has made me suffer. Meanwhile . . . I wait for Toni. You tell him where I am. He's bound to find you, don't you worry. He has a nose for a good lay. You tell him Carlotta is here. She stays with Lavinia Olganina! Imagine his surprise! You tell him I'm all right. Say I've found a little chicken to nurse my broken 'eart. We have good times, the four of us!'

Bless was terribly weak now. He felt his legs shaking with fatigue and stress. His heart was pounding and his head ached. 'Which four?' he sighed.

'You and Toni, me and my petti di pollo! We smoke dope, drink wine and discover all the mysteries of the universe!' And with a final wink and a cheerful salute, she opened the front door and disappeared into the bright light of day.

29

Bless – Mother Of Invention

As soon as Carlotta had gone, Bless ran back upstairs to the guest room. He found Diana and the vicar both standing in the doorway, listening.

'She's gone?' Diana gasped.

'Yes!' Bless hissed. 'But the other one hasn't.'

'You now see what we're up against?' Diana lowered her voice to a trembling whisper. Her body was shaking so much they could hear her knees knocking.

'Do calm down, dear lady,' the vicar told her in a Sunday-school voice. 'The worst is over, I'm sure . . .'

'Over? Calm down?' Diana ranted. 'You tell me to calm down? You heard what she said – she's going to tear me apart.'

'I'm sure she didn't mean it. Just a figure of speech!'

'Oh, shut up!' Diana snapped. 'You – Bless . . .'

'Me?' Bless jumped.

'No!' the vicar intervened hastily. 'I'll do the blessings – I'm authorised . . .'

'Will you shut up!' Diana yelled. 'Bless – you must hide my car. She's bound to come back, snooping around . . .'

'I'm sure she won't. She seems to have calmed down . . .'

'You men! You're so pathetic! You don't understand lust, do you?'

'Certainly not!' the vicar agreed.

'Don't we?' Bless asked. He'd always rather prided himself on his capacity for lustfulness.

'That woman is crazed!' Diana raved on. 'She will stop at nothing to have me . . .'

'Actually – I think she's found someone new. You probably know her – being a local here. I think she said the name was Sandra? Does that ring a bell?'

'Of course not! I have a degree in sociology. But it doesn't surprise me. That's typical of Carlotta's type. Insatiable lust. Can't have enough of it. I'm doomed! She'll never leave me alone . . .'

'Oh – people usually get over these things,' Bless reassured her.

'No. She'll stalk me all the days of my life,' Diana said glumly. Then she shrugged. 'Well, first things first. You must get rid of my car.'

'You mean – literally?'

'I mean hide it, idiot! And I'll thank you to be very careful with her. I'm fond of Pinky. She and I have been through some terrible times together. As for you, Vicar, you'd better start looking for the devil incarnate.'

The vicar gulped. 'Here? In Bellingford?' he said.

'Certainly. Don't you listen?'

'Who are we talking about now?'

'The brother! He claims he's the only one who knows how to handle her . . . Well, then he must deal with her. But,' she warned them, 'I cannot have anything to do with him. He mustn't even see me again. I'm afraid he's as mad for me as his sister is. I'm besieged by fornicators . . .'

Both men looked at her closely, with more than a hint of doubt in their eyes. Neither of them, if they were totally honest, could see in her rather plain face and thin, shapeless body the stuff of fantasy, the object of desire.

'This is always happening to me.' Diana shrugged, running her hands through her short, badly cut and obviously dyed hair. Perhaps she was aware of her companions' shared confusion about her fatal attractions and felt the need for some explanation. 'I used to have long, luxuriant Titian locks,' she told them. Then she shrugged. 'I couldn't walk down a street without driving men wild.'

'But this last one . . . is a woman!' the vicar cut in. 'I am right? She is . . . isn't she?'

'Of course she is! Do try to keep up! It's because of her that I had to cut off all my lovely hair. The sight of it drove her to the most unbelievable passion.'

'Heaven defend us!' the vicar muttered – or perhaps, Bless thought, it might have been a prayer.

'So? Am I to be held responsible for her . . . excesses?' Diana cried, rounding on him belligerently.

'No, of course not!' he assured her.

'Oh! Thank you very much!' she sneered. 'Well – go on! Prove yourself of some use. Find the dreadful brother and order him to take Carlotta home. Tell him . . . Tell him if they don't both leave at once, you'll report them to immigration and have them deported as undesirable aliens.'

'They come from Italy, not Jupiter,' Bless protested.

'But I don't know what he looks like,' Andrew whined.

'Bless here will help you.'

'Is your name really Bless?'

'It's what I answer to – yes.'

'You come from a religious background?' Andrew Skrimshaw looked quite cheered up. It was rare for him to acquire a ready-made congregant.

'God, no! The family call me Alan and my mother hasn't been inside a church since she was courting. She and Dad used the Bethesda chapel for their liaisons. I was conceived on a tombstone.'

'They were nonconformists?' Andrew observed, disappointed.

'They were actually both drunk at the time. God knows how he managed an erection, or how she managed . . .'

'Bless – please concentrate,' Diana admonished him.

'Sorry!'

'I shall stay here,' she continued, engrossed in her own predicament.

'Where?' Bless demanded, suddenly giving her his full attention.

'In this room . . .'

'Oh no you won't,' he declared. 'You've got a perfectly good home of your own to go to.'

'You still re'earsing, Mr 'Udson?' Doris Day called from the hall.

At the sound of her voice Diana immediately went into a gibbering panic, and the vicar started muttering silent words as though he were on a hotline to his boss.

Bless realised that it was up to him to take charge. He pushed them both back into the guest room and closed the door on them. Then he turned and went to the top of the stairs. The old woman was revealed, tottering up towards him.

'When you say re'earsing – d'you mean like in plays?' she asked, rather breathlessly. 'Like that Joan Collins and all those others what we see on the telly?'

'Sort of,' he said, hurrying down and blocking her progress.

'Acting?' she asked, looking up at him.

'Yes.'

'Oh, I can't be doing with acting, dear! I went once . . .'

'Yes. To *The Pyjama Game* – you told me.' He was now pressing on down the stairs, forcing her to descend also, walking backwards in front of him.

'No. That was the kinema. The Court Kinema, Fairlow.' As she was speaking she managed to turn round, but at the last moment she stumbled and nearly fell. Bless reached out and steadied her. She grasped his hand on her shoulder and patted it. 'Thank you, dear!' she murmured. Then she continued her slow descent, with Bless following her. 'No. I also once went to a play. It was arranged by my sister, Mrs Sugar. I should've known. Anything Bessie arranges turns out rotten. It was to celebrate her sixtieth – I think it were her sixtieth, or was it her seventieth? Anyway, we went on a bus. That I do remember. All the way to Lunnun. Just to see a play.' They had now reached the hall. There she stopped. 'Ooo!' she wailed, holding up her hands and waving them above her head like one of the Furies. 'It was 'orrible. I didn't know where to look! Grown people, behaving like that. I mean, dear! What did they think they were doing?'

'Well, I suppose it's a way of making a living' he said lamely. 'And some people enjoy it.'

'Not me, dear. I can't see the point of it. I really can't!' She led the way into the kitchen, still chuntering quietly to herself.

Old Tom was standing with his back to the sink.

'Oi've come,' he said.

'Was I expecting you?' Bless sighed.

'Oi'm never expected. Oi comes when I can.'

'As the actress said to the bishop!' Bless merrily quipped, and then he sank down exhausted on to one of the kitchen chairs and leaned on the table with his head in his hands.

'A bishop, dear? Is there a bishop?' Mrs Day asked, full of enthusiasm.

'He's not a bishop. He's just our vicar!' Old Tom declared.

'Who is?' Bless sat up, suddenly alert again.

'The man upstairs in one of your bedrooms. I saw 'im through the window.'

'The vicar's upstairs?' Mrs Day asked, looking round at the door. 'You said you was on your own.'

'Yes!' Bless agreed brightly, hoping that to agree might make it all all right.

'But that means you told a lie, Mr 'Udson.'

'Only to . . .' He searched for a quick escape. '. . . a foreigner. I lied to a foreigner.'

'Oh! That's all right, then. It don't even count. Not lying to a foreigner. I shouldn't leave 'im upstairs though, dear.' She lowered her voice and leaned towards him conspiratorially. 'They're always short of cash, vicars. And you've got some nice bits and pieces . . .'

'Yes. I . . . um . . .'

'What's he doing up there anyway?' Tom asked.

'In a play with you, is 'e?' Doris suggested.

'Yes. Maybe. I was . . . going through a few of my old favourites.'

'Favourites?'

'Favourite plays . . .'

'Why?'

'Because . . . we might do one together. For the church . . . A play . . . for the church.'

'Oh, Lor! Well, I shan't come, dear. You know my feelings in that department.'

'We really won't expect you to . . .'

A sudden noise out in the hall made them all look round.

'Front door!' Doris said dramatically. And pulling herself up she hurried out of the room.

Bless rose more slowly and followed her. He reached her as she stood on the front doorstep, looking down the drive. 'It was the vicar, dear. I just saw his back disappear. He was running.'

'You have to be very fit – for acting.'

'Fancy! Still, I do hope 'e 'asn't made off with any of your objects, dear. There's a car boot sale outside Fairlow most Sundays. They say it does a roaring trade in stolen goods.'

'But the vicar couldn't be there. Sunday is his busy day.'

''E could 'ave an accomplice though, couldn't he? That's what they do. I saw it on the telly.'

'It's a lot to assume – just because you caught him . . . I mean, saw him here. Actually, he told me he was leaving. He's a very busy man . . .'

'I daresay,' Doris said, sounding far from convinced. 'Well, I can't make you check your goods and chattels if you don't want to, can I? Anyway, I must be off as well. I want to get home and then I'm going into Fairlow. I've decided to have my 'air done, dear. Maison Beryl in the 'Igh Street. I want to look my best. I shall be calling in to see Miss Phyllis tomorrow.'

'Who?' Bless groaned, too weary to take on any further developments.

'The Brigadier's sister, dear. I told you!'

'Yes, so you did. But I thought you were due to start work here tomorrow.'

'And so I am, dear. That's just the point. I shall take you with me and introduce you myself. You will thank me for it every day of your life. You see if you don't. A lady the like of which you will never have seen before. 'Ere! I'd best be off or I shall miss that bus. You don't need to pay me now for today's visit . . .'

'Of course not. I have no intention of paying you!'

'That's right, dear. I'll tack it on to tomorrow's bill. I'll be off then, Mr 'Udson.' She was now trudging down the drive, calling out to him without looking back. 'I should think twice about that play, dear. No one'll come. We don't like that sort of be'aviour down here. Too showy! If you want to make some money for the church, you could help with the fête. We always have a fête. A fête worse than death!' She laughed cheerfully. 'Tombola, white elephant stall, guess the weight of the pig. That sort of style . . .' and she continued to call until her voice was swallowed up by the distance and Bless had reeled back into the hall like a drunken man, with his head swimming and breathless with nervous stress.

30

Two Phone Calls And An Arrangement

Later that same day, during the afternoon – which was actually horribly early in the morning for him – Rich decided to put a call through to Maggie.

'Who is it?' the voice said.

'Maggie? It's Rich.'

'Who?'

'Rich. Richard Charteris!'

'Rich!' the voice shrieked. 'Where are you?'

'In LA.'

'Why on earth are you ringing me?'

'I wanted you to do me a favour . . .'

'Surprise me! You want me to fly out pronto and screen test for Mim in *Manhattan Bohème – The Movie*! I will! I will! Anything for you, darling Rich . . .'

'Maggie!' He had to yell to get her attention. She was turning out to be quite as maddening with an ocean and a continent between them as she was face to face.

'You're shouting!' she shouted. Then she swore loudly. 'Shit! Has something bad happened? Why are you ringing *me*? You've not been doing a Hughie, have you? No? Caught *in flagrante* by the vice squad? Coke and a poke captured for posterity on the camcorder . . .?

'Maggie. Shut up!' Then, when a long silence ensued, he added, 'Are you there?'

'Of course! But you told me to shut up, and I'm very good at taking direction.'

'You . . . you haven't by any chance heard from Bless, have you?'

'Not for a day or two. Why?'

'I'm really worried about him.'

'About Bless? Why?'

Rich quickly explained about the phone call of that morning – or middle of the night, as it had been for him. He told her about the strange foreign voice that had answered the phone, and about Bless sounding as though he were in the middle of a nervous breakdown . . . and about the abrupt end to the call, with Bless screaming some unintelligible word, followed by a crash and silence.

'A crash? Silence?' Maggie gasped, giving her reactions all the drama stored in her pent-up soul. 'Then what?'

'Nothing!'

'Nothing? You mean – you've not phoned back?'

'Of course I have,' Rich snapped. 'I've been trying all night. But I can't get through.'

'Why not?'

'It's permanently engaged.'

'There's a fault on the line. Happens all the time. I shouldn't worry about it.'

'Not worry? He sounded as if he was being attacked or something.'

'Well . . . I don't like to interfere . . . but is that altogether surprising? With your other friend also there?'

'Which other friend?'

'Rich! You only have two friends. Bless is the popular one. I keep telling you that.'

'Which other friend, Maggie?'

'Darling Laurence, of course. Is it any wonder if Bless sounded a trifle tense? He and Laurence were never destined to be cell mates, were they?'

'What's Laurence got to do with it?'

'Didn't you know? I thought you would. He's down there at the moment.'

There was a pause while Rich took this in. 'Laurence? Down in Bellingford? He can't be.'

'Bless told me so himself. Something about plans being drawn up for the stable block . . .?'

Rich hadn't a clue what she was talking about. But then, knowing Maggie, she'd probably got some garbled message and totally misunderstood it. Unless . . . 'When did he go down?' Rich asked. 'This morning?'

'No. Yesterday – or the day before. I don't remember. "All the days are grey, when you're far away".' She sang the last two lines because they were from one of the songs in *Manhattan B.* – as the hit musical was known to the trade.

'I haven't a clue what you're talking about.'

'That wasn't talking, Rich, darling. That was an audition.'

'Maggie – I spoke to Laurence last night.'

'Where?'

'At home. In the flat.'

'Are you sure? How very odd. Bless definitely told me that Laurence was going down to Bellingford. He said he'd be there for some considerable time. That's why I didn't go myself. Not having been to boarding school I don't feel in constant need of masochistic stimulation. Maybe there's been a change of plan?' She hesitated. 'But if so – why didn't the rat call me? He knew I was desperate to see him.'

Rich could think of a number of reasons why he personally wouldn't have called her. But he also knew that Bless was much more fond of Maggie than he was ever likely to be. She was a bit too big, too brassy, too – well, too actressy really for his tastes. A little of Maggie Heston went a long, long way with him.

'I'm sure Laurence hasn't been anywhere near Bellingford,' he said, beginning to suspect that something was really wrong.

'Well, that's what Bless told me . . . Don't worry, Rich. There's bound to be some perfectly reasonable explanation.'

'Yes. Of course.'

'There always is.'

'You're right. All the same – will you try and reach Bless for me? Would you mind, Maggie?'

'No, of course I will,' Maggie said, brimming with generosity. The darling man sounded almost as if he were crying. 'You all right, love?' she cooed.

'Yes, I'm fine,' the disembodied voice crackled. 'I just . . .'

'I know,' Maggie interrupted him. 'He loves you too, Rich. I've been Bless's friend for centuries – and I've never seen him so in love. Well, not for so long at a stretch with the same person,' she added, rather spoiling the sentiment.

'When you reach him, tell him to call me,' Rich continued, recovering his British reserve. And he gave her the number where he was staying.

As soon as he rang off, Maggie tried to phone Bellingford. Sure enough, what Rich had said was true. The engaged tone was all that she could raise. She next phoned the operator and asked for the number to be tested. The operator did so and said there seemed to be a fault on the line – unless a phone had been left off the hook. The engineers would be informed.

Eventually curiosity and a sneaking worry got the better of Maggie and she decided to call Laurence. Although she couldn't stand the man, it rather pleased her that Rich had rung her rather than him. She knew this fact would peeve Laurence. And peeving Laurence had a certain vengeful attraction for her.

It was by now early evening and Laurence had just poured his first – indecently large – Scottish beverage. 'Hello?' he said, holding his glass in one hand and the receiver in the other.

'Is that Laurence Fielding?' the female voice enquired.

'That very much depends.'

'Upon what?'

'Upon who you are, dear lady, and upon whether I want to speak to you or not.'

'I'm almost certain that you won't want to speak to me.'

'Then I'm almost certainly not Laurence Fielding.'

'Who are you instead?'

'The Bey of Algeciras.'

'Is that a place or a person?'

'Who is this?' Laurence demanded, adopting his haughty voice. Whoever it was was far too familiar and quick with the repartee for the conversation to continue without some formal introductions.

'It's Maggie. Maggie Heston.'

'I'm so sorry. Mr Fielding is not at home. This is his butler, Legless, speaking.'

'Laurence, I've just had Rich on the phone . . .'

'Why on earth would Richard want to speak to you?' He sounded suitably peeved, which was satisfying for her.

'We're never off the phone!' she lied glibly, enjoying twisting the knife. 'I'm not sure if you're aware of this but he and I have a flourishing relationship!'

'That's not what he said to *me*, the last time your name was mentioned.'

'You talk about me! How sweet!'

'No! Not talk! We sometimes refer to you,' Laurence corrected her sternly. 'Now, if you'll excuse me . . .'

But Maggie stopped him ringing off. She recounted the gist of Rich's phone call. She then went on to tell him about her earlier conversation with Bless; the one where he claimed that Laurence was on his way down to the Hall House.

'Drawings?' Laurence demanded, when she got to that point in the story. 'For what?'

'New plans – for the stable block?'

'The first I've heard about any of this. They've already got a house that is far too big for them. Why on earth would they require more accommodation?'

'I don't know!' Maggie replied, sounding rattled. Laurence's haughty voice always seemed to imply the other person was in the wrong. 'I'm just telling you what he said.'

'Then he lied to you. I have not spoken to him since the week-end.'

'What is going on, then?' Maggie said. And suddenly she felt really worried. It was so unlike Bless not to want to see her.

'It seems perfectly obvious to me that the little tart is up to something. He couldn't wait to get Richard out of the country before he's started cheating on him . . .'

'In Bellingford?'

'He's probably filled the place with his ghastly friends – present company excepted! – and they're drinking all Richard's wine and causing mayhem in the village.'

But Maggie wasn't listening. Her mind was racing. Bless was clearly in some kind of real trouble. 'I must go down there,' she said, thinking out loud. 'I can't tonight. It's too late to cancel my dinner engagement. But tomorrow . . . I shall go.'

'Do you really think that necessary?' Laurence asked, sipping comfortably at his whisky and relishing the prospect of a bit of excitement to lighten his darkness. Laurence was a dyed-in-the-wool voyeur. Other people's troubles were the elixir of life to him.

'I'm sure of it,' Maggie was saying. 'Something is not right. Of course I must go to him.'

'Then I will drive you,' Laurence said on an impulse.

Maggie was appalled. 'That really isn't necessary,' she protested. The thought of a car ride with Laurence made her feel quite ill.

'I know it isn't necessary. But I intend to.'

'Why?'

'I am looking after dear Richard's interests. That house has cost him a great deal of money.'

'You are a bastard, Laurence.'

'Why?' he asked, sounding quite surprised.

'You don't give a toss that Bless might be in trouble.'

'Oh, my dear! I feel sure that Alan can take care of himself.

Look how successfully he has manoeuvred his way into Richard's safe keeping.'

'Richard is in love with him . . .' Maggie could feel her temper fraying.

'Yes, quite!' Laurence said, his voice coming from some lofty peak of disdain far beyond her attainment. 'Do be a good girl and listen to my instructions. I will meet you by the Whitestone pond at ten o'clock in the morning precisely. Have you got that?'

'Yes, oh lord and master!'

'Good. And I should be grateful if you would refrain from travelling with any champagne. My dress suit has had to go back to the cleaner's three times.' And, without waiting for further discussion, he slammed down the receiver and sighed contentedly.

Laurence had been feeling a trifle bored since Richard had gone to America. This little diversion would suit him admirably.

31

An Immac Morning

Doris Day had had her hair done in a short shingle. 'I like a shingle, dear,' she told Bless as she led him down the drive of the Hall House. 'It keeps nice and tidy and doesn't blow in the wind.'

'Don't you think it'd be more polite to telephone first?' Bless asked her for the umpteenth time.

'No!' Doris laughed, dismissively. 'We're all girls together!'

'If you say so.' Bless shrugged. 'Actually, some people think I'm quite butch.'

'That's what she told me, dear. And she called me Doris. "We're all girls together, dear Doris."' She quoted the words as though they were straight from the Bible.

Actually, to get Doris out of the house Bless would probably have agreed to bungee-jump off the Eiffel Tower. He had completely forgotten that she was expected, and Diana was still firmly ensconced in the guest bedroom. She'd appeared in the kitchen earlier, swathed in a sheet, yawning excessively and looking for a glass of water. When Bless had, reluctantly, offered her breakfast, she'd told him, to his relief, that she never ate anything in the morning. She'd made it sound like a religious abstention – one of those practices that proves the aspirant vastly superior to other mortals. She'd stood at the sink and drunk water from the tap as though it was being transformed into the blood of her Saviour as it passed her lips. Then, after drying her hands on a towel and bestowing on him a little smile, she'd said in a tone that suggested she was doing him a tremendous favour that perhaps she would have a little something and had proceeded to order cereal, a couple of boiled eggs, toast, marmalade and a cafetiere of fresh coffee. All this was crammed on to a tray which she carried back to her room, saying that she needed her rest and not to disturb her until lunchtime.

Later, with the sudden arrival of Doris Day, Bless had been forced to ignore these instructions. He'd found her door locked and she'd been decidedly bad-tempered when she'd finally admitted him.

At first when she heard his news she'd refused to budge. 'I'll just lie low,' she told him, 'while you deal with everything.'

But Bless was adamant. There was no way he was going to be able to prevent Mrs Day from coming upstairs again. And if she got so much as a hint of Diana's presence in the house the news would be all over Bellingford within a day. 'When that happens,' he'd added, 'Carlotta will know precisely where to come to find you.'

The name Carlotta had worked like a charm. Diana panicked at once and started running round the room in ever-decreasing circles. Finally she'd taken a grip on herself. With Diana this was a literal act entailing fast, shallow breathing while grabbing feverishly at her stomach as though in the later stages of childbirth or a severe case of beriberi. However, when Bless rushed to her aid, fearing a premature and somewhat final departure, she'd pushed him away impatiently. She'd then announced with glacial calm that she would return to the loft above the summerhouse as soon as he and Doris were out of the way and that she'd remain there until he came to tell her the coast was clear.

'And after that,' he added firmly, 'you really must think about making alternative arrangements.'

Further discussion was then prevented by Doris calling from

the hall: 'Mr 'Udson? What you doing up there, dear? You writing your will or something?'

'By the time I get back, I want you out of here,' Bless hissed as he went on to the landing.

'I thought you was never coming,' Doris complained. ''Urry up, now! We don't want to keep the lady waiting.'

'As she isn't expecting us,' Bless snapped, going down the stairs, 'we can hardly be accused of doing that.'

'No! But they're always going off on day trips, aren't they? We don't want to get there and find we've missed them, do we?' Doris explained, giving her appearance a final check in the hall mirror.

'Trouble with a shingle,' she muttered later, as she led the way passed the dank little pond beside Cockpits' front drive, 'is you have to keep having it cut. I might have to put up my prices to cover additional expenses. No, not the front, Mr 'Udson! I have the back door key.' And she conducted him along the side of the house by way of a narrow passage, overhung with ivy and damp from the lack of sun.

'I'm sure you should at least ring the bell!' Bless told her. But she gave him a knowing smile and a superior toss of the head as she turned the key in the lock.

The kitchen was tidy and sparkling.

'Bless them!' Mrs Day murmured. 'They've had a really good clean. They'll have enjoyed that. They're never happier than when they're up to their elbows in spit and polish. Now, dear! You wait here while I pass through to the living quarters and inform them that you've come visiting.'

As she spoke, she checked her hair yet again in the small square mirror on the wall beside the crowded dresser. She licked a finger and thumb and plastered a wayward curl to her forehead. Then, as an afterthought, she pinched her cheeks.

'A bit of colour!' she explained, smiling at Bless, and absent-mindedly she started to sing quietly to herself as she made her way to the hall door. 'I've just flown in with my Auntie Kitty. Now Auntie Kitty is very witty, but she can't be like I am . . .'

She disappeared out of the room just as Bless was getting involved in the lyric. He followed her to the door and looked out into the hall. Somewhere a clock was ticking. The house seemed dark and strangely silent. Only Doris's quavering voice disturbed the peace. Bless felt quite attached to Auntie Kitty and wanted to hear the end of her song when Doris's voice changed from a warble into a terrible screech of shock and animal panic.

Alarmed, Bless ran across the hall and up the stairs two at a time, shouting:

'Doris? Are you all right? What's happened?'

As he reached the landing Doris's screams were joined by another sound; a strange, anguished bellow. He turned the corner of the landing and discovered Doris, clinging to a blanket box as though she had been severely winded in the stomach.

The cause of her dismay stood in front of her. It was a terrible apparition. Even Bless was shocked. A figure in a long green candlewick dressing gown was standing in an open doorway. It was this figure that was making the strange, grunting sounds. But it was the face that was so appalling; so utterly terrible to behold. It had a skin so absolutely white that it looked like a bone-china skull. The only colour was provided by two great blobs of lurid green over the eyes. Surmounting this awful death mask was a turban of brilliant yellow towelling.

'Good Lord, woman!' this ghastly spectre cried. 'What are you doing here?'

'Is it . . . is it you, Mrs Jerrold?' Doris gasped.

'Of course it is,' the figure replied.

'I didn't recognise you . . .'

'Why are you here?'

'I've brought Mr 'Udson, madam . . . to meet Miss Phyllis,' poor Doris whimpered.

'Mr Hudson?' Rosemary exclaimed, and then, as Bless moved forward she became aware of his presence. 'God in heaven!' she shrieked. 'A stranger in the house . . .'

'I'm so sorry,' Bless stammered.

'Why are you here? What do you want? I heard no bell . . .'

'I'll . . . wait downstairs,' Bless mumbled, hurrying back round the corner, out of her sight. Reaching the banisters, he leaned against them, paralysed with embarrassment. He decided he'd throttle Doris as soon as the right moment occurred. It might not alter anything but it'd make him feel a lot better.

She, meanwhile, was adding insult to injury with a few well-chosen lies, prompted by her own dismay. 'It weren't my fault, madam. 'E would insist on coming . . .' she gasped, still staring in awe at the terrible face in front of her. 'I couldn't stop him . . . God strewth!' she cried, unable to contain herself. 'Are you ill, madam?'

'What's going on out there, Rosemary?' a low, musical voice murmured from the room behind her.

'It's the servant, Phyllis,' Rosemary Jerrold said, and she started to close the door, as if she wished to protect her sister-in-law from this invasion of her privacy.

'Is it dear Doris?' the voice asked, and a moment later a second figure appeared behind Rosemary, pulling the door open once more and stepping out on to the landing.

Phyllis was wearing a flowing négligé of the finest silk, trimmed with lace. She had on a pair of high-heeled silk mules and her hair was covered in a huge silk shower cap that billowed round her head like a meringue. The face beneath this concoction was ashen white, and again there were the big dark-green discs round each eye – the effect being strangely reminiscent of a panda in drag.

'Oh, Miss Phyllis! Madam!' Doris gasped, in obvious distress. 'What has become of you?'

'We're having an Immac and face-pack morning, dear Doris! Such fun! I love to pamper myself, don't you? Girls' games! All those naughty little unwanted hairs, those cheeky little wrinkles. Begone, I say!' She laughed, a gentle titter of mirth. 'Such a delight! Rosemary and I are having heavenly female fun! And you, Doris dear! You've had your hair done, I see!'

'You noticed, madam!' Doris chirruped, overwhelmed with gratitude.

'Of course I did. And in such a sportif style! The effect is quite racy.'

'Thank you, madam.' Doris's voice glowed with gratitude. 'Oh, thank you! I had it done special – at Maison Beryl . . .'

'Then Beryl must be congratulated.'

'But, madam . . .' Doris was getting bolder. 'I mean – your eyes, madam . . .?'

'A special cucumber essence,' Phyllis confided, in an intimate whisper. 'New in at the Body Shop! I couldn't resist it. I just have to indulge when it comes to toiletries. They are one of my vices!' She shrugged, and putting a hand on the back of her neck she moved her head a few times, as if easing a stiffness. 'Rosemary was just putting Immac on my legs when we heard your singing. And after that, dearest, I think a little aromatherapy would be in order . . .'

'Phyllis,' Rosemary hissed.

'What, dearest heart?'

'We are not alone . . .'

'Oh, I don't mind Doris seeing us like this. She's a woman who appreciates our little feminine wiles.'

'Not Mrs Day, Phyllis. The young man from next door . . .'

Phyllis turned and stared at her. Then she looked the length of the landing.

'Young man? What about him?'

'He's here.'

'Here?' A degree of alarm now sounded in Phyllis's voice.

'Yes! I am most dreadfully sorry . . .' Bless announced, appearing once more round the corner and stepping into the light that spilled in through the landing window.

'I thought you'd gone downstairs!' Rosemary Jerrold exclaimed, whisking her towelling turban off her head and stretching it in front of Phyllis, hiding her from his view. 'Go away at once! You have no right to be here. Go away!' But her outstretched arms pulled at her candlewick dressing gown and this sudden movement dislodged the belt at her waist, which started to untwine. She realised that if she didn't act quickly she'd be in danger of revealing more intimate garments. Hastily lowering her hands, she pulled at the gaping gown, rescuing her maiden modesty but in so doing once more exposing Phyllis's face.

Bless blinked and remained speechless.

Phyllis Jerrold gasped and with an involuntary movement one of her hands clutched nervously at the top of her négligé.

They stared at each other across the landing.

Rosemary Jerrold stood to one side, immobile, as if suspended in space.

Doris Day clung to the blanket box as though her very life depended upon it.

'Hello!' Bless said at last, adopting a cheerful voice to hide his nervousness. 'I'm frightfully sorry about all this. I'm one of the new owners of the Hall House . . .'

'Go away!' sobbed Rosemary.

'Mr 'Udson! Avert your gaze! The lady's in 'er nightie, for 'eaven's sake!'

'Yes, of course!' Bless stammered, overcome with embarrassment again. 'I'm so . . . I mean, I . . .' He shrugged, then abandoning any further excuses, turned and hurried away.

'Wait!' Phyllis called, stopping him in his tracks.

'Phyllis!' Rosemary sobbed.

'Don't distress yourself, Rosemary. The young today are not nearly so prim and proper as we were.'

'I really am sorry to arrive unexpectedly like this,' he said, turning back to face the women. He actually felt quite relieved. The Brigadier's sister was a surprisingly reasonable person.

The Brigadier's wife, however, continued to cross-examine him with obvious resentment. 'Why are you here?' she demanded. 'What is it that you want?'

'Nothing, I just . . . Mrs Day said we should get to know each other . . . You did, didn't you, Mrs Day?'

'I told you to wait in the kitchen, Mr 'Udson. I did not tell you to come creeping up like a peeping Tom.'

'I heard a scream. I came to your rescue.'

'Rescue indeed!' Doris crowed. 'We locals don't need incomers coming to our rescue, thank you very much!'

'You shouldn't come barging in to a person's private quarters,' Rosemary wailed. 'It's most . . . ungentlemanly . . .'

'Rosemary! Children!' Phyllis Jerrold called, holding up a calming hand. 'Don't let's fall out. The young man has caught us when we are not at our best. But I'm sure he won't hold it against us.'

'Of course not!' Bless said, a trifle too quickly. He wanted only to get away and was edging backwards as they spoke.

'So sweet and kind of you. I regret that you have called at an inconvenient moment. Perhaps, if you were to return this afternoon, my sister-in-law might offer you tea?'

'Phyllis?' Rosemary groaned. She sounded on the edge of a breakdown.

'I insist, Rosemary.'

'We have things to do this afternoon . . .' she pleaded.

'Shall we expect you at four thirty? Will that be suitable? I'm sure it will be!' Phyllis simpered, deaf to her sister-in-law's protestations. 'We'll have afternoon tea. Triangular cucumber sandwiches and dainty little scones . . .'

'We have no scones. We have no cucumber,' Rosemary asserted.

'Then, dearest sweet, we shall buy a cucumber. Doris will run and fetch us one. You will, won't you?'

'Quick as a flash, madam!' the septuagenarian trilled, straining for the off.

'And we will make the scones ourselves.'

'Please don't put yourselves out,' Bless pleaded.

'It'll be fun!' Phyllis assured him. 'How often do we have such a charming young man to cook for? And your . . . companion? He must come as well.'

'He's not here . . .'

'Phyllis, we are supposed to be going to the cinema in Fairlow,' Rosemary cut in, her voice desperate.

'Oh! Cinema! Who needs the escapism of the moving picture

when we have the wonders of reality all around us? I insist . . .'

'No! I beg you, Phyllis . . . Selwyn would be most displeased.'

At the mention of her brother's name Phyllis Jerrold's face took on a disagreeable scowl. This sudden movement of her facial muscles cracked the glazed mud that covered her skin. She pressed her hands to her cheeks in a panic, as if afraid that the mask was about to shatter and fall, like plaster from a wall.

'Now see what's happened!' she wailed.

'Selwyn would not tolerate this, Phyllis,' Rosemary warned.

'As my brother isn't here,' the other woman snapped, 'it's none of his business, is it – sweet?' She made the word sound decidedly sour. Then, as Rosemary seemed intent on continuing to contradict her, Phyllis raised her hands again. 'I insist, Rosemary. I will have my way.' And she turned and went back into the room with a swirl of silk négligé.

Rosemary watched her go. Then she glowered at Doris and Bless. 'Now look what you've both done. You've upset her.'

'Oh, I do so 'ope not,' Doris sighed.

'You have quite ruined our day. How could you?' she sobbed. 'How could you?'

'Rosemary,' Phyllis called from the depth of the room. 'The Immac awaits . . .'

'Yes. I'm coming, dear,' the Brigadier's wife called, swallowing back tears. 'Go and get a cucumber, Mrs Day. And more butter. And a few sultanas. And as for you, young man, we will expect you at four thirty.' And before Bless could protest further, she turned and went back into the room herself, slamming the door after her.

32

The Wicked Sisters

Mrs Sugar's shop was crowded. But then, being a small establishment it only took two or three to be gathered together for such an illusion to be created. Margaret Skrimshaw, the vicar's wife, was at the head of the queue and was working her way through a longish list. Behind her stood Melanie Barlow from the executive estate, and behind her Marjorie Fallon – the tall one – from Pinchings. Heather Daltry, wearing jodhpurs, was not in the queue but was riffling through the sorry display of greetings cards and consequently had her back to the other women.

'Are the eggs fresh, Mrs Sugar?' the vicar's wife enquired.

'Fresh? Of course they are, dear! Fresh as the morning dew.'

'When did you get them in?'

'They came from Martin's Farm. I always get my eggs from Martin's Farm. Farm-fresh eggs! That's what we like in lovely green Bellingford . . .'

'Yes. But when?' Margaret Skrimshaw insisted.

'When what, dear?'

'When did they come from Martin's Farm?'

'Oh – moments ago. Ecological friendly. That's my slogan. You want a dozen, dear? Or more?'

'A dozen will be more than sufficient.'

'Right, dear!' Mrs Sugar murmured, filling an egg box. 'This one here is cracked, dear. So I'd be inclined to use it first.'

'No. I don't want it,' Margaret declared.

'Not want it? Not want it? Why ever not?'

'Because it's cracked.'

'Well, it's going to have to be cracked, isn't it dear? You can't get at the goodness, without cracking it.'

'I prefer to crack my own.'

'Oh, I daresay you do, dear!' Mrs Sugar chuckled ruefully. 'And what about poor old Bessie Sugar who never lets a day go by without putting herself out for her customers? I suppose you'd leave me with a lot of cracked eggs on my 'ands and no one to sell 'em to. Is that the idea?'

'I'm sorry. I must insist upon having my eggs uncracked.'

'Insist, do you?' Mrs Sugar asked, her eyes narrowing. 'So that you and the vicar can suck them, I suppose. Well, you can suck someone else's eggs. I don't have to serve you if you're not satisfied . . .'

'Do you have any more recent birthday cards than these, Mrs Sugar?'

'I'm busy here, Mrs Daltry. I can't do two jobs at once. Now,' she continued, turning her blazing eyes once more on the vicar's wife, 'do you want these eggs or do you not, Mrs Skrimshaw?'

'Yes, please,' the poor woman sighed.

'That's better!' Mrs Sugar glared at her and then tutted. 'Very nice behaviour for a vicar's wife, I must say! Oh, very Christian!' And she gave her three cracked eggs in a row – as a sort of penance. 'And what's next, dear?' she asked, closing the egg box lid with a heavy hand.

'A large jar of Marmite,' Margaret said in a resigned, defeated voice.

'Lovely Marmite.'

'A packet of plain digestive biscuits.'

'Lovely munchie biscuits!'

'And half a pound of mint imperials.'

'What a feast! Lucky old vicar. Now, shall I get you a box or can you manage?'

'I have my basket,' Margaret replied, and she started to pack her purchases in a bad-tempered manner. She couldn't help feeling she'd just lost a battle, if not the actual war.

'Be careful with those eggs, dear,' Mrs Sugar exclaimed, rubbing salt in the wound. Then she began to add up the list of figures she had jotted down on the pad in front of her. 'Is there anything else I can tempt you with?' she asked, counting numbers on her fingers.

'No. That will be all . . .'

As Margaret spoke, Doris Day came in from the street. Leaving the door gaping behind her, she walked straight past the queue, heading for the counter. Halfway across the shop, her progress was blocked by Heather Daltry's back.

'Pardon, please!' Doris said, pushing past and taking Heather unawares, so that she staggered forward and fell against the card rack. 'Morning, Bessie!' she said, arriving at the counter and sliding the remainder of Margaret's groceries to one side, making room for her handbag.

'Don't expect to see you here this time of day, Doris,' her sister grunted, not taking her eyes off the column of figures nor her mind off the higher mathematics they entailed.

'No, well. I'm on a mission, aren't I? I'm shopping for the Brigadier's sister,' Doris announced, turning and surveying the people behind her as though the statement was as much for their benefit as for Mrs Sugar.

'Excuse me, there is a queue, you know,' Melanie Barlow exclaimed.

'Yes, dear!' Mrs Day smiled. 'But I'm family. You don't expect family to queue, do you?'

'That'll be eleven pounds and thirty-eight pence, dear,' Mrs Sugar said, sliding her pad of calculations across to the vicar's wife. 'Shall I put it on your bill for you?'

'No!' Margaret said quickly. 'I prefer to pay.'

'Ah! If you pay direct, dear, I can't give you the discount,' Mrs

Sugar explained, pulling the pad back to her side of the counter.

'That's absolute nonsense,' Miss Fallon exclaimed. 'The whole point of a discount is that you get one when you pay cash.'

'Really? Is that so? But not here, dear. Here in lovely, simple Bellingford, we have a different way of doing things. Shall we call it twelve pounds fifty, dear?' she asked, holding out her hand to Margaret.

'Daylight robbery!' Miss Fallon snorted.

'I'll thank you, Miss Bridey, to keep your comments to yourself.'

'My name is Fallon,' she hissed through pursed lips.

'Mmmh!' Mrs Sugar nodded. 'Well – if you say so.' Then her attention was distracted by the money that the vicar's wife had just placed in her outstretched hand. 'What's this?'

'Ten pounds and ninety-eight pence. I think you will find that is correct, if you just check your figures.' Margaret Skrimshaw slid the pad back across the counter and looked round avoiding Mrs Sugar's furious glare.

'I say! Well done!' Heather Daltry murmured.

'You say something, Mrs Daltry?' Mrs Sugar snapped, ringing the till and depositing the money.

'Not a word,' Heather murmured, hiding herself in the greetings cards once more.

'You didn't check the figures,' Margaret said, lifting her heavy basket off the counter.

'I haven't got time, dear. I have a business to run,' Bessie Sugar fumed. 'Yes, Doris?'

'A cucumber, half a pound of butter and a pound of sultanas dear . . .'

'Do you mind! I'm next,' Melanie interrupted, pushing forward.

''Course you are, dear!' Doris beamed at her. 'Just as soon as I've got these few purchases for the Brigadier's sister. She's such a lady . . . You never did see!' she added, speaking to them all.

'I thought you never got to meet her,' Bessie said, weighing out sultanas.

'Oh, I do now. She's quite a friend. She liked my hair,' she added, patting her head.

Her sister glanced up, took in the neat shingle and pulled rather a sour expression. 'I can't say as I do, Doris,' she said. 'Makes you look a bit masculine . . .'

'No, dear.' Doris dismissed the suggestion. 'This style is all the fashion.'

'I can't say I've 'eard it's the fashion to go about looking like a navvy on a building site,' Bessie grumbled.

'Navvy?' her sister cried. 'Fat lot you know, Bessie. You haven't had your hair styled since the days of the Toni 'ome perm.'

'It's true. I prefer a more natural look.'

'Oh, very natural!' Doris rejoined, digging Melanie Barlow with her elbow. 'I'll say it's natural, don't you think, dear? Natural straw – that's what!' and she laughed as though she'd personally invented repartee.

Melanie looked down, studying her shopping list intently. She didn't want to get drawn in to one of the sisters' periodic slanging matches – a well-known part of Bellingford village life.

Meanwhile Margaret Skrimshaw had successfully negotiated the narrow floor space and had arrived at the door.

'Oh, by the way, dear!' Doris Day called. 'I saw the vicar, only yesterday.'

'Really?' Margaret asked, looking bemused.

'Yes, dear. He were upstairs in one of the bedrooms at the Hall House – with one of my gentlemen . . .'

'He was . . . where?' Margaret asked, her bemusement changing to alarm.

At the card stand Heather Daltry turned slowly, not wanting to miss an ounce of this tasty new morsel.

'Yes, dear. Well, actually I caught him as he was running off down the drive.' Doris tittered delicately, hunching her shoulders and enjoying the consternation she was creating. 'What a speed he can reach if he's pushed, can't he, dear? Like a bat out of hell! Well . . . maybe not hell! Considering his calling!'

'I haven't the remotest idea what you are talking about,' the vicar's wife told her.

'Your 'usband. He and Mr 'Udson were upstairs together.'

'Why? Was the gentleman ill?'

'No, dear. They're going to do a play together. Or that's what I was told.' Then, turning back to the counter, she added as an aside: 'Though why they need to do their re'earsing up in a bedroom when they've got a perfectly good lounge, I do not know . . .'

'Hey, baby!' A familiar voice rang out, cutting off Doris's ruminations. She looked round quickly and saw Carlotta standing outside the shop, looking in over Margaret Skrimshaw's shoulder.

'Oh, Lord Almighty! It's the foreigner,' Doris hissed, and she bobbed her head down at the counter as though, ostrich-like, she hoped not to be seen.

'Excuse me,' Margaret said, relieved by this sudden distraction. And pushing past Carlotta, she hurried away down the street, holding her head high in the hope of a dignified exit.

'Baby!' Carlotta cried, stepping into the shop.

'I think he's talking to you, Doris,' her sister confided, her eyes out on stalks.

'Me?' Doris gasped.

'Yes, baby! You remember me, no? 'Sall right.' Carlotta winked and tapped her nose. 'Your secret is safe! I don't tell nobody. Hey!' And she clapped her hands and bellowed with laughter, reaching round to encompass all the shop. 'You English! Who would have thought it of a little old lady like this? Huh!' Then she winked at Doris again and tapped her nose.

'I don't have a single . . . inkling what he's on about,' Doris confided in her sister, speaking backwards over her shoulder and never for an instant taking her eyes off the foreigner.

'Ciao, baby!' Carlotta called, and she flicked her hand to her forehead in a neat, American-style salute. But as she turned to go back to the street, her eyes suddenly swivelled round to where

Melanie Barlow was watching her with an open mouth and startled expression.

'I know you, yes?'

'Me?' Melanie gasped. 'I don't think so.'

'Yes. You were with . . . Sandra?'

'Sandra?' Melanie gasped.

'He'll mean Sandra Green, dear!' Mrs Sugar, ever helpful, volunteered.

'You know this little chick?' Carlotta exclaimed, pushing back into the shop and making for the counter. 'Hey! You – old lady! You know where I can find Sandra?'

'Not so much of the old, if you don't very much mind,' Bessie proclaimed, giving her a severe look.

'OK, then! You young, beautiful pussycat, you!' Carlotta grinned. 'Please tell me! Where can I find Sandra?'

'Well – if you're meaning Mrs Green, she lives next door to you, doesn't she, Mrs Barlow?' Bessie Sugar volunteered. 'Up on the executive . . .'

'Shut up do, Bessie,' her sister hissed. 'We don't know nothing about him. He could be a spy or something . . .'

'What is this "executive"?' Carlotta demanded, turning to Marjorie Fallon, who was standing just behind her.

'It is the estate at the top of the village,' she replied, taken by surprise.

'Top? How top?'

'Left out of the shop, past the pub and . . . you can't miss it,' Miss Fallon explained, pointing out the directions as she spoke.

'Good! Very good! Thank you!' Carlotta turned and put an arm round Melanie's shoulders. 'You tell Sandra to expect me. OK?'

'OK!' Melanie said, with a sudden bright smile. It could be amusing, she thought. No harm really. Just a bit of fun to lighten the dreary days on the executive estate.

'So – Ciao!' Carlotta said, crossing and patting Doris Day playfully on the behind.

'You get your 'ands off me, you filthy wop!' Doris Day

screamed, grabbing her handbag from the counter and laying into Carlotta with a number of well-aimed swipes.

But this only made the Italian more delighted. She hooted with laughter and dodged the blows, feinting and shadow-boxing like a prize fighter. 'So – arrivederci, signorine!' And with a final all-embracing gesture she went out.

'Oh, Lord!' Doris Day gasped, one trembling hand covering her mouth while the other straightened her skirt.

'I think you got yourself a friend there, Doris,' her sister said.

'A friend? Don't even say the word, Bessie. Lord have mercy . . .'

'Well,' Bessie exclaimed, 'whatever has become of our lovely old sleepy Bellingford? It's a hotbed of foreigners now, and unnatural practices and the like. Where will it end?'

'Ooo! I don't like it, Bessie!' Doris moaned. And, briefly, across the counter the two wicked sisters clung to each other for support while the rest of the customers in the shop paused to consider the strangeness of life.

33

The Ride Of The Valkyrie

'Do you have any idea who they were?'

Laurence had used his most disapproving, most prune-like and withering tones from the moment he'd pulled up beside the Whitestone Pond and called: 'Miss Heston! Come along!'

Of course Maggie hadn't helped matters by taking a dramatic step backwards and yelling: 'Help! Police! A kerb-crawler!' But that was Maggie. She had the sort of personality you learned to ignore.

'Oh! Do be quiet, woman!' Laurence snapped, not knowing the rules. To react was a fatal mistake – it only encouraged her.

'OK, lover!' Maggie had purred, climbing into the car and snuggling up beside him. 'Oral, manual or full service?' And, getting overexcited by the role, she'd hitched up her skirt, pulled down her silk shirt and pouted her lips within an inch of his left ear.

No. It had not been a good beginning. They'd driven through the suburbs in a haze of animosity and monosyllabic observations:

'Look! A wedding!'

'How observant!'

'I'd love a wedding!'

'Yes. I expect you would.'

Then quarter of an hour's silence, followed by:

'Left at the roundabout!'

'Thank you. I do know the way.'

And later:

'Do you have to chew?'

'It's either that or smoke.'

'Not in my car!'

'Mmmh! Generous!'

So Maggie had chewed and Laurence had bridled and there'd been no further attempt at communication until they reached the motorway. Then Laurence, forgetting himself, had observed cheerfully that at last they'd be able to get up 'a spanking pace!' And Maggie, avoiding the obvious rejoinder, had plumped for an intellectual one instead and had likened their journey to:

'The Valkyrie. They were something butch in helmets, weren't they?' And she tum-tummed the appropriate gem, making Laurence cringe.

'Please!' He winced. 'They were actually beautiful maidens, who served Odin. They would collect the heroic dead for him and carry them off to Valhalla.'

'Sort of celestial char ladies?'

'Well, no – not exactly.'

'I think that's perfect! It's us to a T!'

'Neither one of us could be described as a beautiful maiden, Miss Heston!' Laurence assured her.

'Thank you, Mr Fielding. You really know how to make a girl feel gorgeous.'

'I certainly do my best.'

And the frost descended again. Outside the car the country-side turned increasingly bosky and the traffic thinned as the last of the metropolis slid away behind them. Maggie thought she should try again.

'I knew they had something to do with horses . . .' she said cheerfully.

'Who?'

'The Valkyrie . . .'

'Please! The subject isn't worth pursuing.'

'What I meant,' Maggie persisted, 'was . . . here are the two of us, galloping down the motorway to rescue our dear friend from unknown danger. Well – I think it's rather thrilling, that's all!'

'Oh, quite! I'm sure Wagner would have been overwhelmed by the scenario,' Laurence sneered. '"The Ride Up The M 11" would have been a real show-stopper at Bayreuth.'

'Wah! Wah! Wah!' Maggie mimicked his plummy tones. And she continued to hum her version of the Valkyries' ride. But as she could only remember the opening phrase of the music this soon became irritating, and although Laurence was determined to ignore her he eventually had to give in.

'Oh! Do please shut up!' he pleaded.

'Sorry!' She trapped her lips between finger and thumb and looked suitably contrite.

'Thank you!' Laurence murmured, a gentleman to the last.

Maggie shrugged. 'I can be annoying, I know that!'

'Quite.'

After another half-hour of moody non sequiturs Laurence glanced at a passing sign and pulled into the inside lane. As he changed gear he asked: 'You're fond of Alan, are you?'

'Bless?' Maggie corrected him, surprised by the question. 'Of course! I adore him.'

'Why is that?'

Maggie frowned and pondered for a moment. 'Because he's fun. He's also vulnerable and . . . I don't know . . . I guess mostly I love him because I think he loves me. That can be seductive.'

'Really? I wouldn't know. Love has always seemed to me a very fallible emotion. I rather endorse the idea of the arranged marriage as practised by Hindus, myself. Love, as you call it, is far too chancy. A relationship based on prudence and economy is much more sensible.'

'But not nearly so much fun!'

'Fun can land one in a lot of trouble,' he observed, sounding severe.

'Oh, goody!'

Laurence glanced at her and frowned.

'And Richard?' he continued. 'Am I to take it that your little vulnerable friend "loves" Richard? As you would put it.'

'Of course. He's mad about him.'

'Absurd delusion!' Laurence spat, grinding the gears in his irritation. The car slowed as they took the turning off the motorway and headed towards Fairlow.

'You're a real sourpuss aren't you? But I have a theory that you just put it on for effect. Underneath all that bile I believe there beats a heart of the purest gold.'

'I wouldn't bank on it.'

Silence descended again. Laurence decided on a short cut he'd discovered on one of his innumerable visits to Bellingford when he was advising Rich on alterations to the house. He rather prided himself on his skills as a track-finder and enjoyed the fact that Maggie looked surprised and obviously thought he'd taken a wrong turning. They drove along one of those distinctly English lanes that cut through rolling countryside, twisting and turning between high hedges and overhung by verdant trees. Sunlight dappled the surface of the road and the sound of birdsong drifted on the warm air.

Later still, as they were drawing close to the end of their journey, Maggie, perhaps wishing to score some points before it was too late, started the conversation up again.

'Anyway – you should be pleased that Rich has met someone he wants to share his life with.'

'Should I indeed!'

'Your trouble is you're jealous.'

'Of whom?'

'Rich and Bless . . .'

'Rot!'

'After all – Rich is your flatmate.'

'So?'

'Grown men – sharing a flat? Ho hum, Mr Fielding!'

'You are a pathetic creature, Miss Heston.'

'Probably. But it's you we're talking about.'

'How very kind. But what on earth can there be to say?'

'If you and Rich . . .'

'Richard.'

'. . . if you have shared a flat for all these years . . . well, it must mean that you at least like him?'

'Of course I do. I'm very' – he searched for the appropriate word – 'fond . . . of Richard. Consequently I'm unhappy to see him being made a fool of.'

'By Bless?'

'I think your little friend is taking him for a ride. What particularly irritates me is that Richard meanwhile is behaving like a lovesick swain. He's never been like this before.'

'And you'd rather he remained as he was?'

'There is a lot to be said for the status quo.'

'Cruising the gay bars of Europe and dragging back one-night stands?'

'Careful, Miss Heston. Your prejudice is showing!'

'Prejudice? Not at all! That's how he met Bless, after all.'

'It was actually at an audition. Alan failed to get the part.'

'He got the producer instead. Praise be to God! The casting couch still exists!'

'Not I'd have thought the best way to set off together down life's highway,' Laurence observed, with self-satisfied scorn.

'But that's how it happened – and they're still together!'

'It's only been a year,' Laurence snorted.

'A year is a long time to lovers.'

'Lovers! I'm sure you won't be able to understand this, but these little casual affairs – they're just to pass the time . . . They're not intended to be taken seriously. Good heavens! Richard has a certain standing in society, a certain respect. He should be keeping his options open and waiting for a proper relationship to come along.'

'Proper?'

'He needs someone who is his intellectual and social equal. Someone who . . . won't let him down.'

Maggie looked at the older man for a long moment. Laurence meanwhile kept his eyes on the road and ignored her.

'You are a horrendous snob!' she said at last.

'Yes.' Laurence smiled for the first time that morning and nodded enthusiastically. 'I am, aren't I? But then, you see a true snob has something to be snobbish about.' He shrugged, immensely pleased. 'It's as simple as that.'

'I can't believe that Rich ever put up with you.'

'You assume you know Richard, do you? My dear! It's taken me a lifetime to begin to understand that boy. And even now he has the capacity to dumbfound me! That's why I'm so – fond – of him!' Again he gave the word a certain surprised resonance. 'Richard is a law unto himself. I wouldn't be at all surprised to hear that he's found another little . . . trick? Isn't that your modern vulgarism for what we used to call a tart? Another little peccadillo to comfort him through the long lonely nights in America . . .'

'Supposing he has,' Maggie interrupted him, 'it'll still mean that you've lost him. Won't it?'

'Lost him? He's not mine to lose. But . . .' he added, stopping her from interrupting him again, '*but* . . . he has played the field, in his own quiet way, for as long as I have known him. And, you know something? He always comes home in the end!' And as if to emphasise this trump card, he flicked the gear stick and rounded a bend, taking the corner far too wide, as if he were racing at Le Mans.

Ahead, driving fast towards them, was a sleek Audi. There was scarcely room for both the cars on the narrow lane and certainly not with Laurence slap in the centre of it.

A collision seemed inevitable.

Maggie screamed. Laurence cursed and swung the steering wheel, pointing the VW towards the hedgerow. The driver of the Audi slammed on his brakes. As if in slow motion the two cars skidded and twisted across the surface of the road.

Laurence leaned on his horn. Perhaps he was hoping to shock the Audi into retreat. Maggie closed her eyes and muttered half a Hail Mary. (Once a Catholic . . .) There followed a gut-wrenching, sickening moment of anticipation. Then the VW reached the lane side and the slow motion went into double-quick time as the front of the car ploughed forward up the steep grass verge and headed for the trunk of an oak tree.

With a crunch and a clatter of metal on wood the car jolted to a halt. But although Maggie and Laurence were both thrown forward, their seat belts prevented any major injury.

'Shit!' Maggie exclaimed.

Laurence meanwhile was already climbing out of the VW and yelling at the driver of the Audi – who had brought his own car to a smooth and well-mannered halt a few yards down the lane.

'You absolute stinking lunatic!' Laurence shrieked. 'What sort of speed do you think you were going?'

'Speed?' A foreign voice echoed his question.

'This is an English country lane, for Christ's sake! Not some bloody foreign autobahn!'

'You are all right?' the voice asked.

'No! Of course I'm not bloody well all right . . .'

Maggie, who was still sitting in the car, now heard the apologetic voice say:

'Scusi! Mi scusi!'

Turning her head quickly and looking back over her shoulder she saw, emerging from the driving seat of the Audi, a vision of manhood that sent a shockwave through her entire body. A pair of legs that beggared description were squeezed into an excuse-me for jeans. A torso that endangered sanity strained inside a white cotton shirt. Gasping and, for safety's sake, dragging her eyes away from the body, she saw a face to launch a thousand credit cards and a smile that God himself must have lost in the last poker game of creation . . .

'Look what you've done to my car, man!' ranted Laurence – who Maggie decided must either be blind or a congenital virgin.

'But – signor! You were in the middle of the road . . .'

'Don't give me that! I suppose you're going to say it was my fault? What did you think you were doing, anyway?'

'Doing?' the angel-that-had-just-dropped-to-earth enquired. Then he shrugged. 'I go round in circles. I look for Bellingford . . .'

Maggie, who was at that moment climbing out of the VW in the hope that it might restore her equilibrium, stumbled and fell against the side of the car.

'Bellingford?' she gasped.

'Yes. Is small village. Near here . . .'

'Yes. I know.'

'You know?'

'That's where we're going!' Maggie whispered, stopping her voice from rising – fuelled by a frenzy of desire.

'I don't believe!' le plat du jour exclaimed, bathing her in a dazzling smile. Maggie gulped, nodded and simpered weakly.

'You're going in quite the wrong direction,' Laurence snorted. 'And you were driving far too fast . . .'

Meanwhile the man was inspecting the front of Laurence's car. 'Is not so bad! Just a little crunch . . .'

'Little crunch?' Laurence yelled. 'It's a sodding disaster! Hell and damnation! What about us?'

'You're hurt?' the voice sounded agitated.

'We may not be hurt,' Laurence fumed, 'but it's still a bloody inconvenience?'

'Oh, pooh! No problem! I take you to Bellingford. We find a garage. I pay for the repairs . . .'

'So you admit you were responsible, do you?'

Adonis smiled. 'I admit nothing!' He shrugged. 'But I'm very rich.'

'You . . . ponce!' Laurence spluttered, 'I'll take you to court for this. You see if I don't . . .'

'Oh, for goodness' sake. It was just a little accident!' Maggie cooed, without once taking her eyes off the man of her dreams who'd so unexpectedly turned up in front of her.

'Accident? Like hell it was! He drove me off the road!'

'You were in the middle of it, Laurence!' Maggie snapped, losing her temper. 'Is it any wonder?'

'Shut up, Miss Heston. Just SHUT UP!'

'Please – don't speak to the lady like that,' her knight in shining armour ordered Laurence. 'You aren't . . . wounded, are you?' he asked, turning to her with concern.

Maggie shook her head, unable to form words any more. As she did so the man gasped, as if seeing her for the first time. His eyes slid slowly down her body, then flicked back to the chest region. Maggie was wearing a good silk shirt. The Heston breasts heaved beneath the shining fabric.

Sir Galahad swallowed hard. 'Mamma mia!' he whispered, blinking and swallowing again. 'Torni un po' piú tardi . . .'

'You're Italian?' Maggie squeaked, forcing herself to speak in spite of her racing heart.

'Si! Italian! I'm sorry!'

'Don't be!'

'Bloody wop! I should have known,' Laurence fumed. But he needn't have bothered. The other two were by now totally oblivious to his being there.

'I say "Torni un po' piú tardi"!' the man was explaining. 'It makes no sense, I know. Is something my family say when our hearts go boom! boom!'

'Boom, boom?' Maggie's voice trembled.

'Is a silly something . . . You see – is our family motto . . .'

'Family motto?' she croaked. 'You're not . . . a count, by any chance?'

'Si! A count, si!' the man gasped. 'How did you know that?'

But Maggie only shook her head and didn't try to answer him. She'd been around long enough to know that when you come face to face with your destiny you need a very good scriptwriter. If the words aren't right . . . it's wisest to keep shtum.

34

The Luncheon Hour

There is a time, round about midday or a little after, when life in an English village almost ceases to exist. No person is seen on the streets. Front doors are closed. The drone of lawn mowers is stilled and even the dogs stop barking. This is the luncheon hour. It comprises a light repast which has little or nothing to do with its bastard sister – lunch. Lunch is an event. Lunch is for businessmen – and can sometimes be entirely liquid: lunch is for the ladies of Manhattan and Knightsbridge – all calorie-counting and gossip; lunch is for office workers – sandwiches or bar snacks; for sightseers – burgers and chips; for cricketers, for shop assistants, for train travellers and for motorists – when it is known as 'the lunch break'. But luncheon is a different affair. Luncheon is the silent pause that separates the morning from the afternoon. It is an almost religious cessation of activity and may in some rural households be followed by 'the nap'. The nap is a snooze and has nothing whatsoever to do with the continental siesta – an altogether grander and more elaborate affair, which very often may accommodate an indulgence in extramarital liaisons. There is absolutely nothing sexual about the English village nap, nor should there be anything eventful about the English village luncheon hour.

However, on this particular day in the village of Bellingford dramatic events were in the air and the first hint of their coming occurred during luncheon. They were heralded – as is so often the case since the demise of 'the messenger' – by a phone call.

Edna Bridey (the plump one) Ethel Hopkirk (the short one) and Marjorie Fallon (the tall one) had just settled at the kitchen table in Pinchings. Luncheon for them comprised a loaf of brown bread, fresh butter and some strong cheddar cheese; a bowl of tomatoes and half a cucumber were also available for those who might like a little side salad. A pot of strong tea was the chosen beverage to accompany this meal. Ethel's beloved corgis – Rag, Tag and Bobtail – had a Bonio served to them on their individual beanbags. (Each bed was covered in a different tartan: Hunting Stewart for Rag, Black Watch for Tag and Cameron Highlander for Bobtail.) The dogs' beverage was water, served in their individual water bowls (each with their name painted in black on the side) and replenished from the tap before their mistress sat down to her own frugal repast.

The three women had been friends since university days. They had all gone on to become schoolteachers. Marjorie Fallon had risen to the heights of headmistress at a girls' public school near Hindhead. Ethel Hopkirk became a mathematics teacher at a ladies' college in Exeter and Edna Bridey had taught at a girls' prep school in Hampstead, London, where she had instilled in her charges a lifetime's love of English and history – and was known to have written quantities of verse herself, some of which had over the years been published in literary magazines.

When the three women retired – all at about the same time, being of a similar age – they'd decided to share a house and spend the rest of their lives in companionable harmony. As the alternative was a lonely old age it seemed an eminently feasible solution. They all got on moderately well and respected each other's need for privacy. None of them had managed to procure a husband, though both Marjorie and Ethel had at one time been engaged. Indeed Ethel might possibly have married her beau had not the war intervened. Marjorie, on the other hand, when faced with the choice between a rather dull army officer and the challenge that her career offered, discovered that she much preferred caring for the welfare of other people's girls to the messy prospect of producing any of her own. If this *ménage de convenance* caused areas of emotional disquiet within any of them they managed to sublimate their energies – Ethel into her dogs, Edna into her poetry and Marjorie into running the affairs of the village. Marjorie Fallon would be a headmistress until the day of her death – and probably after, if the tenets of her faith were to be believed.

Luncheon had scarcely begun when the telephone was heard ringing out in the hall. The dogs started to bark excitedly. They jumped up and down and raced backwards and forwards to and from the hall door. This noise was too much for Marjorie – who only just tolerated the corgis at the best of times. She held a hand to her forehead, as if in anguish, and glared severely. At once Ethel rose from the table and made everything worse by shouting at the dogs – who ignored her. As the shouting and the barking mingled, so the noise intensified.

Meanwhile Edna, who although of a fuller figure was usually the one who ran to do any little chores in the house, went out into the hall and lifted the receiver. As soon as the bell stopped, so did the dogs. And when the dogs stopped so did Ethel. In the sudden calm that followed Edna spoke into the mouthpiece.

'Hello? Pinchings!'

She paused for a moment, then, pulling a face of distaste, she placed the receiver on the table and returned to the kitchen.

'It's for you, dear,' she said, looking at Marjorie. 'It's the Brigadier.'

Now it was Marjorie's turn to register distaste.

'How very odd,' she murmured, going out to the hall. 'Mrs Day said his sister was staying. I took it that meant he was away . . .' And, lifting the receiver, she adopted her most businesslike voice. 'Marjorie Fallon here.'

'Miss Fallon,' a curt voice said in her ear, 'you are, I believe, i/c the village hall at the moment?'

'That is correct.'

'What have you got going on there this Saturday?'

Marjorie glanced at a note-calendar pinned to the wall beside her.

'Um . . . Mr Asquith is doing his antiques road show.'

'Jolly good. That's what I thought. You'll be expecting a big crowd?'

'Mr Asquith's road shows are always popular . . .'

'I will attend myself, then,' the Brigadier announced.

'Tickets may be obtained from Mrs Daltry at the Woods,' Marjorie told him, mistaking his reason for telephoning. 'Or one may simply pay at the door. Fifty pence for a spectator; three pounds for a valuation . . .'

'Seems rather steep . . .'

'The proceeds are to go towards the roof refurbishment fund.'

'So – you're sure there'll be a good attendance?'

'People are generally drawn by the prospect of discovering their heirlooms have a value . . .'

'Yes, yes!' the Brigadier cut in testily. 'But will you get a good crowd?'

'I myself will have very little to do with it. As I say, Mrs Daltry is in charge of the tickets, and Mr Asquith's road show is always popular . . .'

'Well, I hope it is. I wouldn't want to make a wasted journey.'

'I understood that you were away from the village?' Miss Fallon ventured. There was no response from the other end of the line. 'I believe your sister is staying at Cockpits at the moment . . .'

'No reason why I shouldn't be returning, is there?' the Brigadier barked.

'None whatsoever,' Miss Fallon replied, her voice cold. It was quite impossible to have a conversation with the ghastly man. Eventually she heard him snort, and then the line went dead.

'Well, really!' she exclaimed, putting down the phone and

going back to the kitchen. 'I don't trust that man one little bit . . .' And sitting at the table once more she told her friends what had transpired.

At the Towers, Lavinia Sparton was not having any luncheon at all. She would have liked to have shared a plate of pasta with her gentleman guest but she had placed herself on the strictest of diets and a punishing work régime. Signor Braganizio was determined that she should dance again, and to do so would require arduous application. Consequently she'd been at the barre for most of the morning, and by the luncheon hour she had, quite literally, worked herself into the ground. A plié too many had caused her muscles to seize up, her knees to buckle and her body to remain stuck at floor level. A spasm of cramp had then locked her legs and she was unable even to crawl to the door. After a considerable time in this most undignified position, agitation had overcome pride and she'd started calling out for assistance. But her voice, in common with many dancers, was weak and her entreaties scarcely reached beyond the green baize door of the studio. Finally she abandoned all hope of rescue. She lay back on the floor and slipped off into a fitful, dream-filled sleep . . . Lavinia Olganina, premier danseuse, is receiving the adulation of her public. She has just danced Swanilda in *Coppelia* and Henry Sparton has arrived to take her out to a slap-up banquet . . .

Carlotta Braganizio was in the kitchen at the other end of the house. She'd prepared herself a bowl of passatelli – a simple peasant soup made from strands of cheese-flavoured home-made pasta cooked in good chicken stock. Carlotta was a great cook and really, if she hadn't been such an expert motor mechanic, she could have made a profession of this other talent. But that had always been Carlotta's dilemma: the masculine and the feminine constantly at war within her. What she needed was a companion who could appreciate her full potential; someone who would let her cook for them and do their mechanical and manual chores as well. Let's face it, Carlotta was someone's treasure waiting to be discovered. Her problem was she couldn't resist a pretty woman. It had always been her downfall. What she saw and wanted she simply had to have.

Diana Simpson, erstwhile object of Carlotta's desire, was having a stale biscuit for her luncheon. She was still stuck in the loft above the summerhouse waiting for Bless to come and release her, and the biscuit was one of the large number she had taken with her on her night flight from the Sisters of Lysistrata. The biscuit, as usual, was making her dizzy. Indeed, she had discovered while she was in hiding at Le Puy, and had relied on these biscuits for sustenance, that when she ate them they had the most peculiar effect on her. She put this down to the herb that was used in the cooking. It had a rather sweet taste and she thought perhaps it might be rosemary, which had grown in great profusion round the farmhouse near Arles.

Sandra Green, the object of Carlotta's burgeoning fantasy, was eating yoghurt straight from the carton. She also had a half-chewed apple beside her on the table. Hers was more a working lunch than a luncheon – but then she did live on the executive estate and village standards were less *de rigueur* in that haven of suburbia. Sandra had been battling all morning with the end of Chapter Three of her novel, and the work was not going well. Her hero, Grayson Manderlay, had only just arrived on the scene and she was having the utmost difficulty capturing in words the spirit, let alone the looks, of this god among men. Olive Snelling, her tutor at the creative writing class, told her the only way to be truthful as a novelist was to write about what one knew. But Sandra didn't know anyone alive on earth who could measure up to her Grayson. Here was a man who could quite simply arrive at the door of a villa on an executive estate, take one look at Samantha Betterton – the exquisitely lovely young bride who had recently moved there with her husband, Clarence – and sweep her off her feet before they'd even been introduced. This kind of behaviour was a long, long way from Sandra's experience of life. Her Simon had taken seven years to propose and had finally done so while she was riding pillion on his scooter. To be fair to him, they'd started going out together when she was fifteen, and to have been swept off her feet at that tender age could have caused anguish to her parents and comment from the neighbours. But a pillion proposal and a honeymoon in Skegness were hardly the raw material for literary passion.

Sandra looked round her executive kitchen and sighed. How could she hope to write an Aga saga sitting beside a fan-assisted oven and a microwave? Where was the grist to the creative mill in fitted cupboards from Homebase and a stainless-steel double sink with waste disposal unit? She took a bite at her Granny Smith and, as she munched thoughtfully, she picked up her biro again.

Sandra liked to work in biro. She would cover pages of an exercise book with a wobbly, schoolgirl script and then type out what she had done at the end of each working day. She believed that to use a biro and write in longhand kept her more in touch with her muse. A machine, she claimed, lacked the sensitivity of creation.

But this morning the biro wasn't helping Sandra. Her muse seemed to have strayed away from home. She felt stale and uninspired. Her Grayson refused to leap off the page. She couldn't even see him in her mind's eye. She looked again at her list of notes. Grayson was: tall, handsome, hair greying at the temples *or* hair thinning a little on the forehead? thick hair, dark and luxuriant? His body was: lithe, lean, heavy and muscular . . . slim like an Italian waiter? There had been an Italian waiter at Positano who could well fit the picture. But – a waiter? A waiter didn't exactly speak passion or machismo. Would a waiter sweep Samantha off her feet? Sandra had her doubts. Perhaps what she needed was to consider Grayson as a whole . . . Perhaps she should strip him of his clothes and start from the skin . . . Perhaps her main trouble was that Simon was the only man she had ever known in a total way. What she needed – for her art, for her creative store cupboard – was experience. But where did one find experience of that nature on an executive estate?

Like a sudden stab of pain, Sandra faced the terrifying possibility that what she required was . . . a secret affair, a romantic encounter, a heart-stopping illicit intrigue. At that moment she knew without any doubt that the only way for her to release her full imaginative potential was by embracing the thrill of something dangerous and new.

'No! Not thing,' she whispered in a paroxysm of excitement and panic, 'not something! Someone!' and she gnawed at the Granny Smith until only the stalk remained.

Melanie Barlow had taken the car into Fairlow for her weekly aerobics session and was having a snack at the health centre with a couple of the other girls from the class. Consequently it wouldn't be until later in the day that she would tell Sandra that her Italian admirer had been making enquiries about her. In fact, as Melanie munched at her baby spinach and rocket salad with lardons of crispy bacon, she was wondering how best to play this interesting little wild card. Melanie had recently been puzzled that whenever she thought about her friend Sandra her attention very quickly turned to Simon instead. What had started as a mild flirtation to while away the *longueurs* of being a wife and mother was turning into something alarmingly more substantial. Simon Green – in insurance, for heaven's sake! And hardly God's gift to romance! – had in her mind started to acquire a persona of mystery and peculiarly perverse allure. Hard though it might be to explain, the cut of his business suit with the rather loose hang of the trousers over his slim, one could say bony, bum was becoming increasingly erotic to her. Erotic in the way that some people find slumming erotic, or manual workers, or sailors . . . Erotic in a kinky way. But what was it that was Simon's kink? Melanie shuddered to admit it, even to herself. She knew that she didn't hanker after a bit of rough; she wasn't drawn to a banker's bonking, nor to a sportsman's sweat. She didn't crave a gladiator's muscles, nor did she pine for media glamour. No! What she wanted – and what Simon had to offer in spades – was that peculiar sexuality that belonged to the species . . . Essex Man.

At Cockpits, luncheon was being taken in the kitchen. After their Immac morning, Phyllis and Rosemary had changed into comfy clothes. Phyllis was in a pinafore frock from an early

Laura Ashley catalogue and Rosemary in a skirt and twinset. They were having cheese on toast with pickled onions and home-made chutney. Phyllis was, perhaps surprisingly, indulging in a can of beer – though naturally she was using a tumbler and not imbibing straight from the tin. Rosemary was having water. They seemed the happiest of couples – and so they should have been. They both particularly enjoyed what they called 'kitchen tiffin', when they could kick off their shoes and not worry too much about their make-up.

But today, sadly, there was a slight feeling of tension in the air. Rosemary knew well enough what had caused it. She should never have mentioned Selwyn's name. But she had been rattled by the cleaner suddenly turning up on the landing *and* bringing the boy from next door with her. She was alarmed by Phyllis's reaction to it all and she was appalled when her sister-in-law had suddenly issued the invitation to afternoon tea.

But Rosemary so enjoyed having Phyllis there that she would do anything to keep her happy. So the cleaner had been dispatched to the shop and, upon her return, scones had been baked and cucumber sliced. The scones were even now cooling on a wire tray and the cucumber had been salted and placed in a colander to release some of its moisture in order that the bread for the sandwiches shouldn't become soggy.

Yet Phyllis still seemed edgy and not herself. It was such a shame! Particularly as the visit had scarcely begun and they had made so many plans for outings and little treats. That very afternoon they had intended to go to the cinema in Fairlow. *Rob Roy* was showing at the Court, and both Rosemary and Phyllis were partial to Liam Neeson.

'I think he will look particularly fine in a kilt,' Phyllis had said only that morning.

But now when Rosemary tried to engage her sister-in-law in conversation she seemed distracted and unfocused.

'Oh, please don't let that ridiculous cleaner spoil things for us!' she pleaded, when she could bear the silence no longer.

'Of course you're right, dearest heart!' Phyllis had said,

obviously doing her best to rally. But her voice had a disturbingly mournful timbre.

'I've upset you!' Rosemary sighed. 'I should never have mentioned . . .'

'Dearest!' Phyllis cut in sharply, stopping her from repeating the faux pas.

'I'm sorry!' the other woman whispered, chopping nervously at a pickled onion.

'Tell the truth, I have the tiniest little migraine hovering,' Phyllis explained.

This ominous announcement sent Rosemary into a frenzy of agitation. 'I shall cancel tea at once,' she exclaimed.

'No, dearest . . .'

'Yes. I shall put you to bed and tuck you up and bring you a vinegar cloth for your brow . . .'

'No. Dearest sweet! I so want to meet . . .' Her sister-in-law smiled and shook her head. 'What does one call that type of person in polite society?'

Rosemary considered for a moment. 'I suppose they're our neighbours,' she said.

'Yes! of course they are!' Phyllis's voice was clipped. 'But I had hoped for a more descriptive phrase. In other circumstances one could have said . . . the newlyweds. "I do so want to meet . . . the newlyweds!"'

Rosemary blinked and pushed her plate away from her. Her appetite had quite deserted her. Tiffin had lost its appeal.

'Or if they were old, one could say: "I do so want to meet the dear old pensioners",' Phyllis continued. 'Or "the nice couple from Marmesbury" . . .'

'Do they come from Malmesbury? I thought it was London . . .'

'I was being hypothetical, dearest one.' There was an icy pause while Phyllis considered semantics and Rosemary regretted having started the conversation in the first place.

'Anyway!' Phyllis said at last, suddenly sounding more cheerful. 'I insist upon our afternoon tea party. And I do, most sincerely, look forward to meeting the two . . .' Her voice swooped to a high peak, then stopped as if at the edge of a precipice.

Rosemary dabbed at her upper lip with her napkin. The clock in the Hall chimed the three-quarters. The cold tap at the sink suddenly dribbled (it had needed a new washer for many months).

'The two . . . good friends.' Phyllis finished the sentence in a gentle minor key. Then she looked across at Rosemary and gave her a warm, compassionate, tender smile. 'What we must do,' she added in a low voice, 'is make them feel very, very welcome. That is why we are giving them afternoon tea. We want them to know that *we* are delighted that they have come to live next to us and that, whatever they may think to the contrary, in us they have friends and neighbours upon whom they may rely. Am I not right?'

'Yes, dear,' Rosemary Jerrold said in a far from certain voice.

'I shall wear something extravagant for the occasion. I understand that particular type of young man appreciates the extremes of *haute couture*.' She stretched and holding her hands at a distance considered her immaculate manicure. 'And you, dearest heart! I insist upon you wearing your good pearls.' She smiled again and added in a flattering purr: 'They give such lustre to your eyes!'

Rosemary's heart missed a beat. The pearls had been Selwyn's wedding present to her. Phyllis had never referred to them before. It seemed a curious and rather alarming request.

35

Quiet Flows . . . The Brook

Bless had no time for lunch, luncheon or even a snack. Mrs Day, however, thought it advisable to build up her strength and was in the kitchen frying herself some bacon.

'I always need a good tuck-in, dear, when I've been busy,' she'd explained, after ransacking the larder like a sniffer dog.

Being 'busy' for her had so far entailed the disastrous encounter at the next-door neighbours, followed by a long sojourn at the village store, to shop for the neighbours, and an equally lengthy return visit – to the same neighbours – where she had apparently '. . . made your peace, dear. I told Miss Phyllis that you'd 'eard so much about 'er you just 'ad to come round to see 'er for yourself. I told 'er I begged you to wait for an invite, but – would you listen? Miss Phyllis – bless her – she quite understood. She said to me, she said . . .' And as always when Mrs Day quoted the words of the Brigadier's sister she adopted the hushed tones of the sacrament: '"Boys will be boys, dear Doris." She always calls me dear, dear. And when she says dear – she means it.'

So by the time dear Doris had returned to the Hall House she was exhausted and it was, according to her, '. . . far too late in the morning to start work. No! I'll give everywhere a quick flick round after I've 'ad a bite to eat. You sure you don't want a bit of bacon, Mr 'Udson? And a nice fresh egg? I don't mind doing you some' she added generously. 'It'll all go in the one pan . . .'

But a cosy snack with Doris Day was the last thing this Rock Hudson had on his mind. In fact Bless had been having one hell of a morning. It started as soon as he and Doris parted company at the Hall House gates.

'I'll just dash up to the village shop, Mr 'Udson, do these few chores for Miss Phyllis, and I'll be back in a jiffy,' she'd said.

A jiffy was going to take some time, he realised, as he watched her totter up the hill with all the urgency and speed of a tree sloth. But he wasn't sorry to see her go. He wanted to be sure that Diana had left the house, and until he was, having Doris out of the way was a definite plus.

He had, however, forgotten about his other staff. Tom, the gardener, was leaning on a rake watching him as he walked up the drive.

'You're 'ere, then!' he said, accusingly.

'Yes!' Bless groaned. 'And so are you!'

'Oi've been here for an age. Oi've been waiting.'

'Oh, I am sorry,' Bless said, trying sarcasm – to no obvious avail.

'Oi likes you to be 'ere when Oi'm 'ere. So's Oi don't go doin' the wrong thing.'

'Well, I'm here now.' Bless sighed.

'Yes,' Tom said, frowning and looking disapproving. 'Come on, then!' And he turned and trudged round the house to the stable yard and on through the arched gate into the gardens, making Bless follow after him like an obedient spaniel. Once there, the old man paused and surveyed his domain. Then he nodded and spat on the palms of his hands. 'Oi'll do the edges and then Oi'll do the 'edges,' he'd announced.

'Thank you, thank you!' Bless replied, utterly bemused.

'Oi 'ave me own method!' Tom explained. 'Oi like to see an 'edge neat and tidy. Oi likes a lawn short, the edges straight and an 'edge neat and tidy. If you've done the tidying, a garden looks neat and tidy. A tidy garden is a joy to be'old. Oi likes to see . . .'

Bless didn't wait for any more, and when half an hour later he looked out of the guest bedroom window, Tom was still chuntering away – either unaware that he'd departed or not requiring anyone to be present while he aired his philosophy.

The bedroom Bless was in was the one that Diana had commandeered. He'd been relieved to discover that she'd gone. But she'd left the place looking as though Hurricane Ida had recently swept through it. The bathroom was even worse; littered with small bottles, awash with puddles and knee deep in used tissues. Clothes were scattered in every conceivable place and one or two that were not. (How for example, had a pair of tights managed to end up dangling from the curtain pole? Who in their right mind would have left a sun hat rakishly poised on a bedside lamp shade?) In a fury verging on apoplexy Bless crammed all the clothes back into the suitcase they'd presumably come from and took it up to his studio in the loft. He'd get it back to the bloody woman when his equally bloody staff had left and it was safe for the bloody woman to come out of hiding.

After that he had to give the bedroom a quick hoover. There were bits of what seemed to be biscuit scattered all over the floor and in places ground to a fine dust which covered the carpet like sand. He was lifting a curtain to get at the skirting board when, glancing out of the window again, he'd seen Tom down on the lawn heading in the direction of the summerhouse and he'd had to dash down the stairs and out through the drawing room to head him off. Having the gardener discover a strange woman in the summerhouse wasn't a particularly good idea either.

Tom was caught just as he was disappearing into the willow glade. Bless coaxed him away from the danger zone by reminding him of the grey shape of his former employer, Miss Price, that the old man swore he'd seen 'aunting the place . . .

'You're right there!' Tom exclaimed, stepping back in a melodramatic fashion. Then he lowered his voice. 'Oi'd best go an' have a jimmy-riddle behind the stables. Miss Price didn't care for me relieving myself in the garden. But then – a man's got to go somewhere when he's got to go. And she didn't like me going in her bathroom, so where did she think Oi was going to go? Oi can't hold my waters at my age. When Oi got to go, Oi got to go . . .'

Once again Bless left him in mid sentence and returned to the bedroom. He was in the middle of making the bed – leaving the used sheets on – when Doris returned from her protracted expedition and started calling for him, demanding 'a bite to eat'.

As he went wearily back down to the kitchen he was in serious danger of committing GBH. But Doris was in a cheerful mood. It was then that she'd suggested he might like to share her fry-up. He declined the offer with a calm verging on arctic frost and when Tom came in from the garden, smelling cooking like a Bisto kid, he'd hurried away for fear of genocide.

So, while his cleaner tucked into a substantial brunch and his gardener accepted 'a bit of bread and dripping to keep us going', he'd returned to the bedroom and finished making the bed.

Finally he tackled the bathroom, and after another half-hour of solid work and feeling in need of a long rest in a darkened room, he was just crossing to the door when a dazzling glint of light drew his attention to the corner of the wardrobe. Something, he now noticed, had been jammed between it and the wall. More careful examination revealed that it was the dress Diana had been wearing on the evening he'd first apprehended her in the summerhouse – the ethnic number with the bits of looking glass sewn round the hem. (It was actually the light reflecting on one of these pieces of glass that had caught his eye.) The dress had been bundled up behind the wardrobe and seemed to be trapped in some way.

'Why?' Bless sobbed, having to use a good deal of force to free it from its bizarre hiding place. 'Why did she put it there?' A sudden surge of anger helped him yank it free. 'Fucking woman!' he yelled, upgrading her from merely 'bloody'. Then, as he shook the dress out, the door shot open and Doris came suddenly and unexpectedly into the room.

'I'll start up here then, dear!' she proclaimed.

'Mrs Day!' Bless gasped, scrunching the dress in his hands and absent-mindedly rubbing the side of the wardrobe as if he were dusting.

'What you got there, dear?' Doris asked, eyeing the dress suspiciously.

'Nothing . . . Some scraps . . . We're thinking of . . . having new curtains . . .' Bless burbled, pushing past her and going out on to the landing.

'New curtings? Lord above, dear! You've only just got the present ones!' she cried, pursuing him like that sniffer dog once more on the scent.

Bless was now to discover that his geriatric cleaner had the speed of a greyhound when she needed it. As he turned desperately and headed for the studio stairs – so in a trice Doris had nipped round in front of him, blocking his way.

'You don't want to crease lovely fabric like that, Mr 'Udson!' she exclaimed, reaching to snatch the dress from his hand.

'I must . . . go and see what Tom's up to!' he gabbled, backing away and making a dash for the hall stairs.

'It's what you're up to that's more to the point,' Mrs Day panted as she hurried after him. 'Is it a secret? Is that it? You tell Doris. There's many folk round 'ere like to unburden 'emselves to me. What is it, Mr 'Udson? You can trust me, dear'

Bless turned and ran. But the terrible woman continued to follow him. He couldn't shake her off – indeed she looked likely to give him a good run for his money. He charged across the drawing room and out of the French windows with Doris in hot pursuit. When he was halfway across the lawn he still hadn't a clue what to do with the bloody dress. He decided the only possible hiding place out there was the summerhouse, but as he turned in that direction Tom appeared across the lawn to his left, coming from the stable yard . . .

'Oy, you! Oi've bin looking for you,' he shouted.

'Not now, Tom. I can't stop . . .' Bless called.

He'd reached the shelter of the willow tree and was beside the brook. In another moment he'd be within the privacy of the glade . . . But then another voice boomed out behind him:

'Alan! What the devil have you been up to?'

Skidding to a halt, Bless screwed up his face and closed his eyes. Then he gulped and hugged himself, shaking his entire body as if trying to wake up from a terrible nightmare.

'Alan!' the voice roared. 'Are you epileptic as well as effete?'

Turning very slowly Bless saw Laurence standing by the yard gate. Then Maggie appeared behind him.

'Sweetheart!' she called. 'We've been worried sick about you . . .'

And before she'd even finished speaking, like the cherry on the top of the cake, Mr Sex-on-legs himself, the one and only Hunk-from-heaven appeared in the archway behind her.

Bless looked slowly round the sea of faces that confronted him.

There was Doris Day: 'What are you up to, Mr 'Udson?'

There was Old Tom: 'Oi was trying to tell you you'd got visitors . . .'

And there were the visitors: the God-awful Laurence . . . the irrepressible Maggie . . . And, as if they weren't enough, there also was oh! oh, Antonio! – who didn't even know Laurence and Maggie, had no right to be there, and whom Bless had somehow hoped had been a figment of his imagination.

'Jesus!' Bless squeaked. 'How lovely to see you all!' And as he spoke he did a well-executed pirouette that took him briefly to the edge of the Belling Brook. There, along the bank, reeds and irises and other wild plants grew in great profusion. With a quick flick of his hands, like a magician in full throttle, he threw Diana's gypsy dress over a vast clump of broad-leaved kingcups and watched as it hit the surface of the water and billowed out like a deflated balloon.

Then, relying on a distraction technique that would not have shamed a fully paid-up member of the Magic Circle, he spun back out on to the lawn. Once there he threw his arms above his head, clapped his hands and stamped his feet with all the verve of a flamenco dancer.

'Olé!' he yelled, and he ran across the lawn towards his guests and assorted staff, wanting to get as far away as possible from the incriminating article. 'I wasn't expecting you! You should have phoned! What a lovely surprise . . . Have you all been introduced?' And burbling like a mad person he rushed them all towards the terrace and the safety of the house, while Laurence snorted his disapproval and Maggie smothered him in maternal concern. Even Tom was somehow caught up in the rush and ended up inside the house, staring at his boots on the fitted carpet.

Only Doris Day lingered for a moment on the terrace, looking back in the direction of the willow tree. Something decidedly odd was going on – and she had every intention of finding out what it was. But later . . . First she'd see to the new arrivals. And she turned and went into the drawing room, where she chose one of the comfortable armchairs that had conveniently been left vacant and would give her a good view of any further excitement.

Meanwhile Exhibit A bobbed and floated on the slowly moving current of the Belling Brook. It was soon dragged clear of the border plants, and once in midstream it gathered a little speed as it followed the waterway's winding course along the perimeter of the Hall House grounds. Reaching the subterranean tunnel that took the brook first under the stable block and then on under the dividing wall between the Hall House and Cockpits, the dress disappeared from view and only resurfaced several minutes later when it sailed into sight on the edge of Cockpits' garden. Here briefly the brook emerged as a dank and stagnant pool to one side of the drive. After that the water was channelled into another tunnel and it finally emerged back into daylight on the other side of the road, whence it continued its meandering course across the village green.

The dress, however, did not travel that far. It became firmly entwined in the roots of a holly bush that had grown too close to the bank of the dreary pond. And so it was that Diana Simpson's summer frock came to rest, wet and bedraggled, close up against the driveway leading to Brigadier Jerrold's front door.

36

A Short Interlude

Inside the drawing room everyone seemed to be talking at the same time. Laurence was demanding that the Hunk should go at once to find a garage and have the VW towed to safety, assessment and repair. Maggie was telling Bless that something terribly important had happened. Antonio was speaking volubly in Italian. Mrs Day was getting comfy and Tom was chuntering. Only Bless was silent. Perhaps he'd overtaxed himself with his performance on the lawn, or maybe he was still too confused by his sudden influx of visitors to feel ready to join in.

'I still hold you entirely responsible for everything!' Laurence was yelling, pointing an accusing finger at Antonio.

'Signor! Calm yourself. Is not good for your blood pressure. Si accommodi, prego!'

'Don't you spout your wop rubbish at me . . .!'

'Oh, Lord love us! Another perishing foreigner. The place is stiff with them . . .'

'Oi can't stop 'ere. Oi've work to do . . .'

'Bless! Sweetheart! I've got something wonderful to tell you . . .'

'Signorina . . . Bellissima! Please tell him to calm himself . . .'

'Bless, darling. Are you listening to me? I want you to meet someone very special . . .'

'What?'

'Antonio, this is my best friend, Bless . . .'

'Oh!'

'Bless . . . this is Antonio . . .'

'Oh!'

A puzzled look from Maggie, then a frown: 'You two don't already know each other, do you?'

'Yes!' from Bless and 'No!' from Antonio – in unison. Followed immediately by: 'No!' from Bless and 'Yes!' from Antonio – again in unison.

'If everyone would stop talking and listen to me,' Laurence bellowed, going to the drinks cupboard and pouring himself a battleship of sherry, 'we could get things organised.'

'I'll have one of those, dear, thank you very much,' Doris called, leaning across and waving at him but not abandoning her seat.

'Oi don't feel right in Miss Price's sitting room,' Tom muttered. 'It isn't what Oi'm used to . . .'

'So – you do know each other?'

'. . . She didn't like me to come in the 'ouse . . .'

'Depends what you mean by know, darling!' Bless quipped, deciding on a light delivery.

'What have you been up to?' Maggie demanded suspiciously. 'Have you any idea who that gorgeous creature is?' As she spoke the gorgeous creature was backing away towards the window.

'As a matter of fact I have, yes!' And turning to the Hunk, he called: 'Your sister, Carlotta, is looking for you.'

'Carlotta? Is here?' Antonio's eyes searched the room.

'She's staying across the green.'

'I must go and find her.'

'What about my car?'

'No problem! It will be seen to!'

'It'd better be bloody seen to,' Laurence said, putting down his sherry and wiping his hands on a handkerchief.

'That's right, dear! You tell him!' Doris Day encouraged him, shooting out of her chair and swiping the glass just as he turned to retrieve it. 'Cheers, dear!'

'That's mine!'

'Yes, thank you!' And with a bright smile and a comfortable shrug she returned to her seat.

'Where is Carlotta?'

'I don't know.'

'I must see her.'

'She's with some dancer . . .'

'Dancer?' The Hunk sounded appalled. 'She has interfered with this dancer?'

Bless looked perturbed. 'I don't think so,' he said.

'What dancer?'

'I don't know. A ballet dancer . . .'

'Here? In Bellingford?'

'That'll be t'old biddy at the Towers. She was a dancer. Mad as a bloomin' 'atter. Oi used to do 'er garden. But I couldn't stick it. Far too fussy! Dancin' ladies everywhere – and an itty-bitty lake with cardboard swans . . .'

'You – old gentleman!' the Hunk interrupted him. 'You will show me where this dancer is living?'

'Mebbe!' Tom eyed him suspiciously.

'Yes, of course!' the Hunk purred, putting an arm round his shoulder. 'I will make it worth your while . . .'

'Oh no you don't! None of your foreign carryings-on with me, thank you very much!' Tom said, breaking free of him and hurrying out of the window.

'You're not . . . going?' Maggie wailed, running after the Hunk as he followed Tom.

'I go but then I return,' the Hunk assured her.

'You promise?' Maggie sounded crestfallen.

'Hey, bellissima! You think, having found you, I want to lose you? I see my sister – then we do the business . . .'

'Oh!'

'No?'

'Well, yes! But . . . in English that's not a very polite way of putting it.'

'Why so? My sister and I, we have much business to discuss . . .'

'Oh! I see. You and your sister do the business . . . That's quite different.'

'Signorina, you wait for me?' the Hunk whispered, getting very close to her.

'Wait?' Maggie stammered. 'Yes, I'll wait.'

'Mmmh! Mamma mia!' the Hunk groaned. 'I'll be quick.' And he turned and hurried after Tom, who was wandering across the lawn deep in conversation with himself.

As Maggie watched Antonio depart she gasped for air. Then, feeling quite faint, she groped for support on the back of the chair in which Doris Day was sitting.

'You all right, dear? Come over giddy, have you?'

'Bless!' Maggie sobbed. 'He's an Italian count!' and she slid sideways down into the chair, crushing Doris.

'Steady, dear!' the old woman gasped, lurching forward. 'Oh, now look what you've done! You've slopped my sherry wine!'

'Maggie!' Bless protested, pulling her back on to her feet.

'Did you hear what I said?' Maggie cried. 'I can't believe it. I think I'm going to faint . . .'

'Yes, yes!' Bless waved a hand in her face. 'He has that effect on all the girls.'

'Does he?' She now sounded despondent.

'Well – I can only speak for myself, of course . . .'

'WHAT?' she yelled. 'You haven't . . .? He hasn't . . .?'

'Certainly not! You may have forgotten, but I happen to be spoken for. Mind you . . . it came horribly close, and who knows what the future might bring . . .'

'We'll see, we'll see . . .' Doris Day trilled, sipping her sherry wine contentedly.

'Oh, Bless!' Maggie shrieked. 'I could kill you!' And in her distress she took several well-aimed swings at her friend's chest with her left fist.

'Oo-er!' Doris enthused, abandoning her song and leaning

forward in her seat so as not to miss a moment of this new development.

'You promised me . . .' Maggie wailed.

'What?' Bless demanded, dodging her attack.

'You absolutely vowed that if ever an Italian count came on the scene you'd LEAVE HIM TO ME!' Her voice rose in a shattering crescendo.

'Ow!' Doris wailed, putting a hand to an ear. 'Lord save us – the racket! You'll disturb Miss Phyllis carrying on like that. Shame on you! Grown girl behaving like that.'

'Miss Heston! Pull yourself together,' Laurence commanded in his most stern and scoutmasterish voice. Maggie immediately went silent, which pleased him no end. Then he turned on Doris. 'And you – cleaning woman . . .'

'Me?' the old woman gasped.

'I recognise you. We met outside the church on Sunday. You shouldn't be in here. You should be in your quarters. Run along now. And while you're about it, see if you can rustle up something for us to eat.'

'I do not do cooking,' Doris said, indignantly.

'No! She doesn't do cooking,' Bless agreed. 'Well – not officially.'

'As for you, Alan, you should be ashamed. Have you any idea how worried Richard is about you?'

'Oh, really?' Bless snapped. If Laurence was going to start accusing him, he might live to regret it. Bless's capacity for patience and understanding had been stretched to the limit, and beyond there lurked a vicious little temper. 'Worried about *me*? That is a surprise. He hasn't even bothered to telephone me for days . . .'

'Because your phone is out of order.'

'Out of order?'

'It's permanently engaged.'

'Well – I expect that's on account of its being off the 'ook in the front study room,' Mrs Day said in a haughty voice. She didn't care for the elderly gentleman one little bit. She thought, when she met him outside the church, that he showed signs of respect. But she'd been wrong. The very idea! Calling her 'cleaning woman'! Asking her to cook for them.

'Off the hook?' both Bless and Laurence said at once.

Mrs Day glared disdainfully. If they were going to be uppity with her, they'd get more than they bargained for.

'Doris?' Bless asked her, sounding penitent. 'You say the phone is off the hook?'

''As been for some time, as a matter of fact . . .'

'Then why didn't you put it back on the hook? Don't tell me! You don't do telephones!'

'I thought – since you ask – I thought maybe you was avoiding those dirty phone calls you 'ear about.'

'Oh, God!' Bless fumed, slamming out of the room with very bad grace.

She was right, of course. The receiver in Rich's study was dangling over the side of the desk. As Bless put it back in place he had a mental picture of seeing Carlotta out in the Hall starting to go up the stairs. And as she'd done so, he'd dropped the phone and run to waylay her. When? Four million years ago. Why? Because Diana and the vicar had been hiding in the guest bedroom.

'What has been going on here?' Laurence demanded, coming into the room.

Bless looked at him. Then he shook his head and laughed weakly. 'Don't ask, Laurence!' he told him. 'You'll only get confused and end up with a terrible headache.'

37

Tea And Sympathy

Laurence insisted on going.

'Don't argue with me, Alan. This is a social occasion. You can't possibly manage on your own.'

'He's right! I'd better come as well,' Maggie said.

'You?' Laurence exclaimed.

'It's what friends are for.' She shrugged. Then she crossed and stared out of the window glumly.

It was later in the afternoon and they were all in Rich's study. Even Doris Day had somehow managed to join them – although she was supposed to be cleaning the kitchen and must have had the hearing of a cat to know what was going on. Now she lurked outside the door with a duster in her hand.

Bless had simply said that he was going to the study to phone the Brigadier's wife. He needed to cancel an invitation to afternoon tea. But as he stood at the desk, copying the Jerrolds' number from the directory on to a pad beside the phone, Laurence came in, saying that of course they must go together, it would be rude not to. Then Maggie had chimed in with her offer of support.

'I don't think it was a general invite, Mr 'Udson – like a chimpanzees' tea party,' Doris observed, spitting on the brass doorknob and polishing it industriously. 'I shall be there, of course, but that's quite different . . .'

'Miss Heston will not be going,' Laurence announced, 'and neither will you, Mrs Day.'

'Oh! Says who?' Doris demanded.

'Says I!' Laurence replied fiercely.

'I'll 'ave you know Miss Phyllis is my friend . . .'

'You are Mrs Jerrold's cleaner. One does not take afternoon tea with one's cleaner.'

In the end Laurence had his way. Mrs Day went home in a huff – 'I don't go nowhere I'm not wanted' – and Maggie mooned around the house – mainly in the study because it gave her a view of the drive and part of the green.

'I'm afraid it's a case of "But westward, look! the land is bright",' Laurence observed as he and Bless went down the drive. 'The poor drab is so desperate about being on the shelf, she obviously hopes that wop is going to carry her away to paradise on his great white charger.'

Bless was too wound up and exhausted to come to his friend's defence. Besides, there'd be no point. Laurence had a mind like Fort Knox – any uninvited idea found it impossible to gain entry. The front door was answered by Rosemary Jerrold. She was wearing a tweed frock, in which she must have felt hot – for the day was warm and sunny. Round her neck was a triple strand of small pearls that seemed out of place with the thick woollen material. She also had make-up on her face that didn't go with the rest of her – it gave her an unreal quality, as though she were about to perform in a play. She greeted them politely, however, though perhaps her manner was a little subdued.

'We will take tea in the sitting room,' she said, leading the way along the dark hall. 'My sister-in-law is suffering from a migraine and can't bear too much bright light.'

Which perhaps explained why the room they entered was in a Stygian gloom. The curtains were pulled across most of the windows, allowing only a single band of light to cut through the half-darkness.

'So good of you both to come,' a voice murmured, and only then were Bless and Laurence aware that another person was present. Phyllis, whom the Brigadier's wife now introduced, was sitting with her back to the window, in a particularly dark corner. She was wearing a full-skirted silk dress with long sleeves and a high neck. The colour was possibly a pale blue, though such detail was difficult to ascertain in the half-light. She also wore a smart boater-style hat, with a veil that obscured most of her face. High-heeled court shoes completed the ensemble – with the added touch of a glittering brooch in the shape of a lizard on one shoulder. The effect was strangely theatrical and unreal. She seemed almost like a ghost as she extended a hand and welcomed the two men.

'So tiresome of me to get a wretched migraine,' she murmured.

'You should have phoned me!' Bless said, glimpsing escape. 'We must go at once . . .'

'Sweet, caring, thoughtful child! Isn't he a dear, Rosemary?'

'Well, yes! I suppose he is,' the other woman agreed, though without much enthusiasm.

'But, no!' Phyllis continued. 'It would be too disappointing. We've been so looking forward to our get-together. And this . . .' she made a sweeping gesture towards Laurence, 'is your chum?'

'No!' both the men said at once.

'Good heavens, no!' Laurence added.

'Rich is in America,' Bless said, after a pause.

'I'm . . . sorry?'

'My boyfriend – Rich . . .'

'Oh, I see! Boyfriend! How droll!' Phyllis unclasped a small bag and produced a lace handkerchief and a bottle. 'Oil of Albas! I am a slave to alternative medicine! I'm never sure if any of it really works, but . . .' She shrugged. '. . . this sometimes clears my head.' As she talked she shook the oil on to the handkerchief.

'I'm sure it would be better if we left you . . .'

'Nonsense! I won't let a little pain spoil our tea. But, sit down! Sit down both of you. Make yourselves comfortable.

Dear child, take the stool.' As she spoke she gestured to a small wooden-framed stool, with a padded seat. Bless sat on it and found it was so low to the ground that his knees reached almost to his chin. He folded his arms round them and adopted a pose reminiscent of Puck in the *Dream*, always one of his favourite parts. Meanwhile Laurence took an armchair across the window from Phyllis, so that he was looking at her through the beam of sunlight and had to angle himself in an awkward position in order to be able to see her at all. 'That's better!' Phyllis said, radiating warm hospitality. 'We don't stand on ceremony here!'

There followed an awkward pause as they each searched for a topic of conversation. Rosemary crossed and sat on the sofa, drawing attention to the fact that there had been far more comfortable places for Bless to sit. He wondered why he'd been put where he had. It was the sort of seat one would give to a small child. He wished he could move, decided against it and, determined not to be paranoid, hugged his knees and grinned nervously. Rosemary made a strange little sound between a laugh and a clearing of the throat and returned the smile shyly.

Phyllis then turned and looked down at him, with her head on one side in a quizzical way. 'You speak of your "boyfriend" – Rich? Is that right?'

'Yes. It's short for Richard.'

'I see. And you call him your "boyfriend"?'

'Well, no, not always,' Bless answered, shrugging.

'It seems such a dated term, don't you think?' Phyllis asked, dropping the small bottle back into her bag and clicking it shut.

'I don't know. Does it? I have to call him something.'

'Yes! I can see that it's awkward . . . for people like you.'

'Well – he is a boy and he is my friend,' Bless explained, trying to be generous. He wasn't sure about the 'people like you' bit.

'Of course!' Phyllis agreed, fulsomely. 'But "boyfriend" suggests sweethearts and courting couples – doesn't it?'

'All right, then . . . lover,' Bless volunteered.

'Lover!' Phyllis sniffed at her handkerchief. 'Oh to be young! And do you have a lover, Mr . . .? I didn't catch your name.'

'Fielding. Laurence Fielding.'

'Do you have a lover?' She threw up her hands and tittered merrily. 'Gracious, Rosemary! What sophisticated conversation!'

'Yes, dear,' Rosemary mumbled.

'Well, Mr Fielding?'

'Well?'

'Do you have a lover?'

'Certainly not.'

'Oh! Poor Mr Fielding!'

'Do you, Miss Jerrold?'

'I?'

'Have a lover?'

There followed a pause so pregnant it almost reached the point of Caesarean section. Phyllis stared at Laurence across the sunbeam. Laurence stared back. Bless hugged his legs and rocked a little and Rosemary massaged her pearls nervously.

'Perhaps we should have tea?' she tentatively suggested when the silence became unbearable.

'Oh, do let's!' her sister-in-law enthused.

Rosemary got up quickly and hurried to the door and out into the hall, saying as she went: 'It won't take more than a moment. I just have a kettle to boil . . .'

'Rosemary is a very fine housekeeper,' Phyllis Jerrold confided in a low voice. 'I do so admire that. And so brave. She has a lot to put up with.'

'Why is that?' Laurence asked.

'My brother is a difficult man, I'm afraid. Heaven knows, he and I cannot happily be in the same room together!' She chuckled.

'Do you fight?' Laurence asked. As he spoke he was man-oeuvring his chair, pushing with his feet, trying to get into a more convenient position from which to observe his hostess.

'No!' The woman tittered and dabbed her nose with her hanky. 'Fight! Selwyn was a boxing champion.' She swung her attention back to Bless. 'He is a fine figure of a man, when stripped,' she announced. She lowered her voice to a whisper. 'When he was a youngster he did the Charles Atlas course. You will be too young to remember, but Charles Atlas helped to build champion bodies! Do you do any gymnastics, Mr Hudson?'

'I used to work out at a gym,' Bless replied brightly. 'But I had to give it up.'

'Why was that?'

'All those sweating bodies were doing my head in.'

'Good gracious!' Phyllis gasped and she shook her own head as if in sympathy.

Rosemary returned, pushing a trolley, and the next half-hour was spent sipping and nibbling and exchanging pleasantries. The scones were hard and the sandwiches moist and the food had to balance on ridiculously small plates while the tea was served in wide-brimmed cups that slopped in the saucers and were difficult to hold. It was a relief really when Rosemary handed round paper napkins and the crocks were gathered back on to the trolley and she wheeled it away to the kitchen.

Soon, Bless thought, we'll be able to go. But Phyllis had other delights in store for them.

'Play something for us, dear,' she said as Rosemary returned to the lounge.

'Oh no! Please, Phyllis . . .' the other woman begged, hesitating halfway across the room.

'Don't be so silly! Of course you must,' Phyllis cried. 'My sister-in-law could have been a concert pianist. Did you know that, Mr Hudson?'

'Why Hudson?' Laurence asked, looking baffled.

'Um . . . no!' Bless cut in. It seemed a bit late in the day to try to correct the mistake of his name. Besides, all he wanted was to get away.

'His name isn't Hudson,' Laurence persisted.

But Phyllis was preoccupied elsewhere.

'Play Schubert,' she said, gesturing Rosemary towards the baby grand. 'You know how you like that.'

'Please, Phyllis!' Rosemary was squirming with embarrassment.

'Little ninny! She doesn't like to draw attention to herself. But if one plays a grand piano in a room full of strangers, one is bound to be noticed! With a little less reticence and a little more backbone she could have had a quite brilliant career – couldn't you, dearest?'

'I don't suppose so.'

'But, of course, she blames my brother. Don't you, Rosemary?'

'No!' the poor woman wailed.

'No? But it's obvious. After all, Selwyn stopped you playing, didn't he? That's what you always say . . .'

'No!' Rosemary cried. 'No. I don't say that. It was the army . . .' She seemed in genuine distress.

'You mustn't play if you don't want to,' Bless intervened. 'We should be going anyway . . .'

'Of course she wants to.' Phyllis's voice had an edge of threat in it now. 'You do – don't you?'

For a moment it seemed as if Rosemary would continue to resist her sister-in-law. Then instead she smiled shyly and shrugged. 'If you would like me to, dearest,' she said. And she crossed to the piano with all the eagerness of a human sacrifice.

'There's a good girl! Such a fuss!' Phyllis laughed again and sniffed her hanky. 'She adores playing. And why not? It's a great gift! Give us something gentle yet thrilling, sweetness. Something soothing but stimulating. Something to tug at the heart-strings!'

Rosemary arranged the stool at the keyboard and then sat down.

'I rather like Gilbert and Sullivan! But I'm an old philistine, I fear. Rosemary – who was trained at a conservatoire! Imagine! – is considerably more highbrow . . .'

'I will play whatever you ask, Phyllis. You know that.'

'Schubert, dear!' her sister-in-law purred. 'That lovely Trouty thing you're so keen on!'

'Oh – no!' she pleaded.

'Go on!' her sister-in-law insisted. 'Just for me.'

The two women stared at each other for a moment. Then Rosemary sighed and nodded. 'Very well. If that is what you want.' And she started to play from memory with surprising skill and sensitivity.

As soon as the music began, Phyllis started another conversation, completely ignoring the performance and acting as if it were no more than background musak. 'My brother, her husband,' she announced, 'he so dislikes this piece that he forbids her to play it.' She tittered like a schoolgirl telling a naughty story. 'But then, Selwyn doesn't care for music . . .'

The playing stopped abruptly and Rosemary Jerrold half rose from the piano as though she were about to cry out, or possibly to run away. Laurence glanced in her direction and seemed about to go to her. But Phyllis pre-empted him.

'Go on, dearest,' she said. 'It's all right. It really is . . . all right, Rosemary.'

'Phyllis,' the other woman begged, 'I'm sure our guests wouldn't mind . . .'

'Go on!'

The two women held another look, then Rosemary sat again and continued to play.

'I'm afraid my brother is not an easy man to get along with. Have you met him, Mr Fielding?'

'No.' Laurence shook his head.

'And you, dear child? Have you met the dread Brigadier?'

'Well, not exactly . . . I mean . . . we did bump into each other in the street. I think I may have given him a bit of a shock. I was covered in flour at the time.' Phyllis gestured puzzlement. 'Don't ask!' Bless waved a dismissive hand. 'Then later I called here, but he . . . wasn't at home, I guess.' He finished the sentence with a shrug.

'That's not strictly true, is it, Alan? You told us you saw him watching from an upper window. He does quite a lot of watching, I gather!' Laurence added, including Phyllis in this observation, and he settled back comfortably in his chair.

'Watching?' She leaned forward, enquiringly.

'Spying . . .'

'Spying? How dramatic!'

'Laurence!' Bless protested.

'Oh, dear boy! I rather think Miss Jerrold has the measure of her brother. I'm right, am I not? You don't entirely approve . . .'

The music faltered as Rosemary's attention was taken by their conversation.

'Rosemary!' Phyllis said sharply. And the music continued once more. 'Mr Fielding, you seem to have formed an opinion about Selwyn?'

'That wasn't difficult. The man has made it perfectly clear that he doesn't approve of Alan and Richard living next door.'

'Ah!' the woman said. It was a sound both sympathetic and knowing. 'Why would that be, I wonder?'

'Probably because we're a couple of raging poofs!' Bless merrily quipped, deciding to go along with the old adage – if you can't beat it, jump in and join the orgy.

'Raging poofs!' Phyllis tittered again. 'Dear child!'

'Do be quiet, Alan!' Laurence snapped.

'Really, Mr Fielding! It's like having a naughty boy in the house, isn't it? Imagine! He could be our son!'

'I think that extremely far-fetched,' Laurence fumed.

'Oh, Mr Fielding! Do you find the fair sex so utterly unattractive?'

'Certainly not! I simply meant that if you and I had . . . coupled, I feel sure we would have produced a more agreeable offspring.'

'You don't approve of the child?'

'Approve?' Bless screamed. 'He can't stand the sight of me!'

'Tt-tt!' Phyllis shook her head. 'Why?'

'Behaviour like this doesn't endear him,' Laurence observed. 'Our generation,' he gestured to include Phyllis, 'were brought up to respect our elders.'

'Quite!' and looking across at Laurence she shrugged and threw her hands up. Then she laughed – a long, trilling sound.

'Isn't this fun? Dear Mr Fielding! You must visit often. I promise now – I won't try to seduce you!' And she laughed again.

Laurence was entranced. He stretched his legs and laughed as well.

'Do you like the cinema, Mr Fielding?'

'Sometimes.'

'A discriminating man! One day let's go together. We can leave Rosemary to baby-sit!'

'Oh? You mean Alan!' Laurence exclaimed. And they both laughed uproariously.

Bless – who wasn't particularly pleased to be the butt of their mirth – decided to concentrate on the music. But at once Phyllis drew him back into the conversation.

'So you think my brother doesn't approve of having you living next door, is that it?'

'You could say!'

'But what gives you that idea?'

'He wrote a piece in *The Bellingford Gazette* . . .'

'Yes. I saw the article . . .'

'Actually, in some ways I have a lot of sympathy for the poor old codger,' Laurence said.

'Codger?'

'Laurence!' Bless hissed. He was aware that Phyllis's body language was becoming more and more tense. At the word 'codger' her right leg, which had been elegantly folded across her left one, twitched and jerked.

'I said as much to Richard,' Laurence continued. 'The poor old duffer' – the leg twitched again – 'can't help it if he's a bit of a blimp.' The leg jerked so much that Phyllis had to uncross it, and plant it firmly on the ground. Laurence continued, oblivious to any of this tension he was causing. 'But there was something about his wording that stuck in my craw! That "hearts of oak" stuff!' He shuddered. 'I can't be doing with it myself. Everyone has a right to their opinions of course – but I don't think they should start ramming them down other people's throats.'

'Perhaps he worries . . . for the community?' Phyllis suggested.

'Actually,' Laurence continued, thoroughly enjoying himself, 'you very often find that sort of chap has some little skeleton of his own in the cupboard. Something he doesn't want people to find out. You know? I wouldn't be at all surprised . . .'

Rosemary Jerrold slammed both her hands down on the keys, making a hideous sound that caused them all to jump.

'Rosemary!' Phyllis cried out, pressing both her hands to her forehead.

'I'm very sorry,' she said. 'I can't play any more.'

There was a long silence, during which Laurence had the grace to look uncomfortable.

'I do apologise,' he said at last, glancing at Rosemary. 'I was quite forgetting that the Brigadier is your husband. Do forgive me . . .'

'What were you implying, Mr Fielding? Were you suggesting that my husband has . . . some guilty secret?'

'Laurence . . .' Bless stood up. 'Time we were going.'

'You don't know my husband. How can you suggest anything about someone you haven't even met?'

'Please don't get agitated.'

'Agitated? I seem agitated? You have made an allegation about . . . about my husband . . .'

'Rosemary! Shut up!' her sister-in-law snapped.

'He didn't mean anything,' Bless assured her.

'Oh, really? It sounded like something to me. Something . . . most unwarranted! He's never even spoken to my husband . . .'

'Well! Look – it's no different to your husband having a go at Rich and me. He's never met us, either. But honestly it's not important, really it isn't . . .'

'He didn't need to meet you . . . He . . . Oh! I can't speak. I'm far too distressed . . .' Mrs Jerrold said, and she began to sob loudly.

'Stop that at once, Rosemary!' Phyllis's voice rose several octaves. 'It is they who have started it, slandering my brother.'

'Oh, I say! I didn't mean to . . . Slander? No! No!' Laurence implored. 'You have taken my words too literally! Slander, for goodness' sake? No, never!'

'We'll see about that, Mr Fielding. You will be hearing from our solicitor.'

'But . . . But . . . But what have I said?' Laurence stammered.

'You have implied that my brother is . . . is . . .'

'Is what?' Laurence demanded.

'A raging poofter was I think the term this . . . child used,' Phyllis spat.

'No!' Laurence cried. 'I meant nothing of the sort. It was just idle chatter.'

'The devil it was!' Phyllis snarled, her voice rising and dangerously out of control.

'We must go!' Bless declared, turning towards the door.

Then, as if God had been looking down and had also decided the time had come to end the scene, a telephone started ringing out in the hall.

'I'll go!' Rosemary gasped, hurrying forward.

'Stop!' her sister-in-law commanded. 'I will go!' And she stood up for the first time. 'I am . . . very upset!' she wailed. And, with a quite alarmingly extravagant gesture – that would not have disgraced Lucia in the mad scene – Phyllis Jerrold covered her face with an arm, and ran sobbing from the room.

'Oh, shit!' Bless sighed.

'I didn't mean to . . . I thought . . .'

'What have you done, Mr Fielding?' Rosemary whimpered, and she sank back on to the piano stool, a picture of utter dejection. The telephone stopped ringing and there was a moment of ominous silence throughout the house.

'I thought . . . I thought your sister-in-law . . . was on our side,' Laurence muttered. He looked flummoxed and started pacing the room as he spoke. 'I really took to her. I thought . . . I thought she was enjoying a gossip . . .'

'Just leave it, for Christ's sake,' Bless hissed.

'You should never have come here. We should never have invited you. You must go . . .'

'Yes!' Bless exclaimed, with too much alacrity, and he grabbed hold of Laurence's arm and dragged him away. But before they reached the door, there was a loud slamming sound out in the hall.

'The front door!' Rosemary Jerrold gasped. Then, seeing that the two men were about to exit, she hurled herself across the room and stood in their way. 'Wait!' she ordered them.

'We must go . . .' Bless begged her. But she clamped a hand over his mouth. Her other hand she held aloft, indicating silence was required. Then she stepped nearer to the door, listening.

'Oh, no!' she gasped.

'What is it? My dear Mrs Jerrold, whatever is the matter?' Laurence beseeched her.

Again she lifted her hand, stopping him speaking. Then she pressed herself closer to the door, listening.

'He's back!' she said. A look of terrible despair covered her face. 'Oh, no! No!' and a moment later, with the utmost sadness, she added: 'No!'

'Rosemary!' a man's voice called from somewhere beyond the door.

As Bless and Laurence watched with rapt and shameless fascination – not wanting to miss the merest trace of what was happening – they saw the woman in front of them change her shape. She seemed to shrink; her shoulders twisted, her toes turned in . . .

'Yes, dear?' she called, in a drained, lifeless voice.

'I'm back!' the voice called.

Rosemary opened the door and went out into the hall, calling: 'We're in the lounge, dear . . .'

'We? Who is we?' The voice seemed to be coming from upstairs.

'I have . . . our new neighbour and . . . a friend . . . They've come for tea, dear.'

'No visitors today, Rosemary!' the Brigadier called. 'I've been travelling.'

'Very good, dear.' When Rosemary turned back to look at

them her cheeks were wet with tears and smudged with black where her mascara had run. 'My husband has returned unexpectedly. You must go at once . . .'

'Come on, Laurence!' Bless said, hurrying out into the hall.

'Dear Mrs Jerrold, I feel I've upset both you and your sister-in-law . . .'

'Rosemary!' the Brigadier called, unseen, from the top of the stairs.

'Just go!' Rosemary Jerrold hissed.

'Yes . . . I . . .'

'Laurence!' Bless grabbed his sleeve and pulled him out of the house.

38

Night In Seven Keys

Darling, Hope all went well at the Stalag. Gave me quite a turn when the Fuhrer answered!! I thought he was away? Sorry about sudden departure. Did the Fuhrer explain? – or should he be Goebels? (Spelling? – anyway, he with 'ner balls at all'). I rang the agent (You know me – ever hopeful!) And LO! An interview for something at the BEEB first thing tomorrow a.m. It'll no doubt be a cough and a spit but they ASKED for me so I must go –

Love you lots, M xxx

And a wet one for Laurence – make it really DEEP.

'She can scarcely do joined-up writing and she still manages to be obscene,' Laurence remarked, tossing the note back on to the coffee table.

'None of it makes sense!' Bless said.

'The Heston woman and sense must have parted company at birth.'

They were in the drawing room, having had a supper that Laurence claimed 'would scarcely feed a flea'. 'I wasn't expecting visitors.' 'A well-run household makes provisions for the unexpected.'

The curtains were closed, the lamps alight and Laurence was nursing his second large Scotch of the evening and in a filthy mood – which for a man who expressed pleasure with a grimace and believed a compliment should be liberally coated with prussic acid didn't presage a cosy evening in front of the telly. Besides: 'I never watch television unless I am absolutely forced,' he announced when Bless tentatively suggested it.

'What would force you, Laurence?'

'A death in the royal family, Wimbledon fortnight or the promise of erotic flesh.'

Bless scoured the *Radio Times* desperately. But, like a miracle or a number 19 bus, nothing showed up when you really needed it. The rest of the evening loomed ahead like a black cloud.

It'd started off badly. They'd returned from the Brigadier's to find the house empty and Maggie's note wedged under a jar of marmalade on the kitchen table. But now, without even supper to distract them, time was dragging appallingly.

'But how could she get to London?' Bless repeated the question for the umpteenth time for the want of something – anything – to say.

'By train!'

'How did she get to the station?'

'By taxi!'

'How did she get a taxi?'

'By phoning for one! Are we going to have this conversation for the duration?'

'Sorry!'

'Phone her again.'

'I just did – it's still on answering.'

Another moody silence followed. Laurence savoured his drink and Bless stared at his hands. Then Laurence leaned over and picked up the note again.

'One thing is odd, though,' he said thoughtfully.

'What's that?'

'She implies that the Brigadier answered the phone. I suppose that's what she's trying to say?'

'I guess!'

'But it was Phyllis who went to do so. The Brigadier arrived later. Don't you recall? The door slamming and the poor wife going into a panic attack?'

Bless nodded. 'He must've already been in the house.' He shuddered. 'God! That means he was lurking somewhere all the time you were talking about him . . .'

'It was not just me,' Laurence said, severely. 'Besides, we heard the door slam.'

Bless nodded again and pondered over this.

'Maybe that was Phyllis leaving? She said they couldn't bear to be in the same room together.'

'Leaving? You think she's gone?' Laurence sounded quite disappointed. 'You mean . . . back to Scarborough?' He thought about this possible new development. Then he shook his head. 'No! It was too quick. She'd have to pack . . . She'd want to change . . .'

'I didn't mean permanently.'

'What then?'

'She took one look at her brother – what was it she called him? "The dread Brigadier" – and ran screaming.'

'So the ladies were also unaware of his presence in the house?'

'Oh, I'm sure. The wife would never have invited us in if she'd known he was there.'

'Dear me! He does seem to exercise quite a hold over them,' Laurence mused, swilling down the last of his Scotch. 'I can never understand how people of an odious disposition are allowed to get away with it.'

Strange how we never see ourselves as others see us! Bless watched in silence as the equally odiously disposed Laurence rose and crossed to replenish his glass.

'It's a mystery to me what went wrong,' Laurence continued, shaking his head. 'One moment we were having a perfectly civilised tête-à-tête – she really did seem to enjoy talking about her brother – and the next . . .'

'You were accusing him of being a sex-crazed fiend.' Bless

finished the sentence for him. Then he giggled at the memory.

'I did nothing of the sort!' Laurence replied severely, returning to his seat. 'I merely suggested that he probably had things to hide. I must admit I'd rather forgotten about the presence of the poor wife, though. That was thoughtless of me. It was she who took umbrage, I'm afraid . . .'

'Well – she may have been the first to react,' Bless agreed, 'but it didn't take long for the sister to join in. I suppose you could say you scored a double whammy. I've always wondered what that was!'

There was another silence. Laurence sipped his drink and Bless glanced at his watch and wondered how soon he could suggest bed. Then, quite suddenly and unexpectedly, the older man let out a bray of laughter.

'I say!' he spluttered. 'It was quite a scene, wasn't it?'

'You could say!' Bless agreed, grinning. 'Her exit . . .!' and leaping up, he put an arm across his face and glided to the door.

'I wouldn't have missed it for the world!' Laurence hooted. And they both dissolved into uncontrollable laughter – together, in unison, almost like friends.

'Delicious!' Laurence chuckled, wiping his eyes with a handkerchief. 'I've always maintained that a middle-class heterosexual from a suppressed background has more to hide than any of us.'

'You think the Brigadier is a closet poof?' Bless asked, pouring himself a glass of wine.

'I don't know. But there must be something he's hiding. The closet was specially designed for men like the Brigadier. What his problem is, I wouldn't like to speculate. Some sad little perversion.' Laurence shuddered. 'Thank God I'm normal!' He paused while he considered the wilder shores of human nature, then shook his head and dismissed whatever excesses he'd discovered there. 'Actually, I found his sister far more interesting. A very handsome woman! Really most appealing. She's the sort I always go for.'

'*You* do?'

Laurence glared at him again. 'It is possible for people of our persuasion to find women attractive.'

'Sure! I regularly get the hots for Maggie.'

Laurence grimaced. 'There really is no accounting for taste!' He sipped his drink. 'Phyllis Jerrold reminds me of a woman I very nearly married.'

'You? Married?'

'Certainly. When I was your age – most of us did.'

'Who . . .? Did what?'

'Queers – got married. It wasn't usual for chaps to carry on like you and Richard are doing, you know.'

'We're not carrying on. We are trying to live together.'

'Quite!' Laurence said, with a sniff.

'And you don't approve, do you?'

Laurence stared at him with raised eyebrows. 'Of what?' he asked.

'Us living together.'

'That's entirely up to Richard.'

'Would you approve . . . if it wasn't me?' Bless adjusted the question. 'It is me you don't approve of, isn't it, Laurence?'

'I scarcely know you, child.'

Bless shrugged. 'I'm not that complicated.'

Laurence glared at him again over the rim of his glass. Bless held the stare, then shrugged again and smiled. He felt embarrassed and ridiculously nervous. 'I do really love him, Laurence. Surely that must please you?'

There was a pause as the older man seemed to consider this statement. Then he sniffed and shook his head. 'I don't think it'll last, dear boy. That's all. And I should hate to see Richard hurt.'

'So you'd rather we didn't even give it a try?'

'It's not up to me . . .'

'Well, in a way it is,' Bless said, irritation making him bolder. 'Why? Neither of you gives a damn what I think.'

'That's not true. Rich really likes you.' He couldn't bring himself to say love, though that was the word that presented itself.

'And,' he continued, 'he'd do anything to avoid hurting you.'

'Hurting me? Absurd sentimentality!' Laurence took a swig of his whisky and sniffed again.

'That's why we're living here . . .'

'What on earth are you talking about, child?'

'So that you can go on living in the flat in London.'

'The flat in London happens to be my home . . . Well, ours. Richard's and mine.'

'Yes. So we couldn't have one, could we?'

'Why not? He's rich enough.'

'Yes. But as things stand now he can use your flat as his base in town – and . . . avoid upsetting you.'

Laurence looked at Bless thoughtfully. For a moment it seemed that he was going to continue the conversation, then something changed his mind. 'Perhaps we should watch the news,' he said instead, returning to his haughty distant voice. 'Who knows, there might be some important announcement . . .' And without waiting for an answer, he got up and crossed to switch on the television.

Maggie phoned at about ten. 'Sorry, darling! I didn't realise I'd left the machine on.'

Bless had gone into the study to take the call. 'How did you get to the station?' he asked.

'Antonio took me.'

'Oh, yes?'

Maggie heard his mocking tone and immediately bridled and was on her guard. 'Meaning?' she asked in a chilly voice.

'He just happened to call round?'

'Yes, as a matter of fact. He came to tell Laurence that the car is at the garage and there isn't nearly as much damage as we thought.'

'So where is Antonio now?'

'How would I know?' she asked – her voice now innocent and attempting a sort of bored disinterest. 'I expect he's in bed.' Then she added, with a touch too much concern for reality, 'I didn't wake you, did I, sweetheart?'

'Wake me? It's only ten o'clock, Mags!'

'Is it?' – all innocence again. Then a higher register for a swift change of subject. 'Did the Brigadier give you my message?'

'No. We've had rather a disastrous time, actually . . .'

'You are all right? You sound . . .'

'Spending an evening with Laurence Fielding isn't my idea of bliss.'

'I'm sorry, darling. I really had to come back.'

'Don't worry. I expect it's good for my karma. I think maybe he wants to talk about Rich . . .'

'He's heaven, Bless,' Maggie cut in – unable to contain herself a moment longer and not listening to a word he'd said.

'Who is?'

'Antonio!' She made the name sound very Italian.

'Why are we talking about him?'

'Why? Are you mad? You know, I used to fantasise about him. But never for one moment did I think I'd actually get to *meet* him . . .'

'Who?'

'Antonio!' Now she was Juliet on her balcony – all young love and midnight yearning.

Bless sighed and decided straight talking was required. 'Don't be silly Maggie – he's gay,' he said, going for a full-frontal attack.

'I mean, I knew that out there somewhere there was an Antonio.' She was practically singing the name now. 'But – was I going to meet him . . .?'

'He's gay, Maggie.'

'. . . Was I hell! Me? With my luck?'

'G. A. Y.' He tried spelling it – really just to ring the changes.

'I mean – how often do you get to meet Mr Fantasy and actually find you not only lust after him . . . but you like him . . .'

'MAGGIE!' Bless yelled. 'MAGGIE! MAGGIE!'

'You're deafening me!'

'Great! Do I have your attention for one second?'

'Oh, what?' she asked, petulantly.

'He's gay. Antonio . . . Your pizza pie . . . If not gay – then he certainly swings.'

'What are you talking about?'

'Darling Antonio . . . I've seen the way he looks at me.'

'What would you know?'

'Trust me. I've had years of training. Besides, his sister says he is.'

There was a dangerous pause while Maggie took in his words. Then: 'You're so evil when you're jealous, Bless,' she hissed.

'Jealous? Me?'

'Me?' Maggie mimicked.

'I promise you . . . I don't even want him. Well – yes, of course I fancy him. Who wouldn't? I admit his looks might be the answer to a maiden's prayer . . .'

'Not only his looks, believe *me*!'

'Actually,' Bless continued, determined not to be distracted, 'the way I feel right now, if he came back to the door I'd probably strip him in the hall. But . . .'

'Oh, really, Bless? Really?' Maggie said, now sounding extremely mean. 'So what happened to Marianne?'

'Who?'

'Miss Faithful? You were never going to look at another man . . . You'd found your Mr Wonderbra . . . Your cup floweth over . . . Remember, sweety?' The 'sweety' had an ominous ring.

'Don't attack me, Mags. I can't help it if he's gay.' Bless enunciated the word with crystal clarity.

'And Princess Diana is a lesbian!' she yelled, and the line went dead before Bless could utter another word on the subject.

'Bless says you're gay,' she said, returning to the bedroom and slamming the door with a neat kick.

Antonio, hunk extraordinaire, turned on his back and smiled at her through sleepy eyes. 'Hey, bambina! Who's counting?'

'Are you?' she asked, walking over to the window and looking out into the lamplit street.

'Please! Do me a favour! What you think? We just been playing hokey-pokey?'

Maggie sighed and shrugged. 'OK,' she said quietly. 'You know what I mean. You're . . . bisexual?'

'This some kind of exam?'

'I need to know,' she said in a small voice.

'Baby! Come here,' he growled.

'Fuck off!'

'Don't spoil the evening. What does it matter?'

'It matters to me,' and she turned her back, not wanting him to see the tears that had started to run down her cheeks.

'Maggie!' As he spoke, Antonio climbed out of bed and padded across the room. He put his arms round her and pulled her towards his naked body.

'I don't think I can cope with a bisexual,' she said quietly.

'Why not?'

'I'd worry all the time that while you were with me you were really wanting Bless's dick.'

'Hey, listen!' he whispered in her ear. 'I got enough dick for both of us.'

She felt the rough hair on his chest rubbing against her back, and the now famous dick was prodding her impatiently.

'You have, haven't you?' she whispered. 'You've made a pass at him.'

'Who?'

'Bless. He's my best friend, Antonio.'

'Listen – Bless . . . Is that really his name?'

'Sort of,' she murmured, leaning back into the warmth of his body and smelling the oil and vinegar scent of his skin.

'He's a nice boy,' he whispered in her ear. 'But . . .' She felt him shrug. Then his hands moved up to squeeze her breasts.

'Is that all I am to you?' she snapped, pushing away from him. 'A body?'

'You want to talk philosophy? I talk philosophy.' And pulling her round, he held her face in his hands.

'It's true!' she said after a moment.

'What is?'

'You do have enough dick for both of us.'

'Hey, baby!' He laughed quietly, and picking her up in his arms, he carried her back to the bed.

Back at the Towers the dick's sister was having her own problems.

Lavinia Olganina had spent the evening trying on tutus and ballet frocks. Although, since the arrival of Antonio earlier that day, she now realised that the Italian in the *Spartacus* bedroom was one of the fair sex and not, as she'd fondly supposed, a gentleman, Lavinia still insisted on trying the clothes on in privacy.

'No, no, Carlotta!' she'd exclaimed when her new friend offered to help, 'you may not see me in my dishabille!'

Lavinia had been right to insist on privacy. Not one of the dresses came anywhere near fitting her, and the discovery had reduced her to the depths of depression.

Carlotta had originally intended spending the evening in the pub, hopefully in the company of her petti di pollo from the executive estate, but her good heart could not abandon Lavinia in her hour of need. So instead they sat together in the kitchen — Lavinia still wearing her Giselle dress, gaping at the back and with the straps constantly slipping off her plump shoulders — and were working their way through their second bottle of red wine.

'You want to go out,' Lavinia said mournfully and for the twentieth time that evening. 'You don't want to spend your time with a fat old woman.'

'Hey, baby!' Carlotta sighed. 'What's fat!'

'This is fat!' Lavinia sobbed, grabbing a handful of bulging waist.

'Ah!' Carlotta waved her hands dismissively. 'We buy girdle. I see to it tomorrow.'

'I cannot dance in a girdle!'

'Before I finish with you, you will dance in the nude.'

'Never!' Lavinia shuddered at the thought and helped herself to another tumbler of red wine. 'I shouldn't care for that at all! I was never of the Martha Graham school of dance. Mine was a classical education.'

'You tell me?' Carlotta roared, as she lit the joint she'd just rolled and passed it to her friend. 'I saw you and I know you were the BEST! Hey! Just take a little drag, it'll relax you.'

'I do not care for tobacco.'

'Not tobacco – it's herbal. Very good for you. No! Suck it . . . Like this . . .'

Sandra and Simon were preparing for bed. Sandra had been in to see that Gary was sleeping soundly, and Simon was cleaning his teeth in the en suite when she returned to the master bedroom. Seeing his thin frame through the open door as he leaned over the basin, spitting peppermint into the stream of water, she wondered again if she should tell him the alarming news that Melanie Barlow had delivered that evening. But how could she explain to her Simon that an Italian lesbian was combing the lanes of Bellingford, searching for her with lust in her heart? He simply wouldn't begin to understand.

She sighed as she slipped under the floral duvet and switched off her bedside light. A lesbian lover, she murmured in her mind, what a bizarre twist of fate! Just when she'd decided that an affair would help her creative process . . . a *lesbian* had arrived on the scene? And not just any lesbian – but one with designs on her . . . With a jolt, her heart missed a beat, making her gasp for breath. She opened her eyes and was suddenly very much awake. A lesbian lover? Was that perhaps the very shock she required to help her through her writer's block? She put her index finger to her pursed lips – always a sign that she was deep in thought. Why not? It would certainly be different. It could add a new dimension to the novel; a more modern touch; and it would be particularly strong if it was written from experience. She turned on her side, staring across the semi-dark room. What would it entail – a lesbian affair? She'd have to do it in the afternoon before Gary came home from school, and not in the house because Melanie would guess at once if she saw the Harley Davidson parked outside the door . . . Oh, it was fraught with difficulties! But all the same . . . it was certainly an intriguing proposition. She closed her eyes, then opened them again with a start. With a lesbian, she realised, she wouldn't really be being unfaithful to Simon – which was the aspect of the extramarital relationship that had most worried her ever since the idea of having one had first come to her. After all, she thought, one could hardly be accused of being unfaithful with a member of one's own sex . . . could one?

By the time Simon climbed into bed beside her, smelling of toothpaste and soap, her mind was miles away. She was in a forest glade where Carlotta and she were meeting for their first secret tryst. The Italian was unzipping her leather jerkin and smiling at her in that seductive way that she had done when they first saw each other at the Hart at Rest.

'Sandra,' Simon whispered, switching off his lamp and pulling her towards him.

'What, darling?' she said, sounding normal and feeling remote.

'I've got something really weird that's worrying me,' Simon said, speaking too fast because he was nervous.

'What, angel?' Sandra asked, as she watched Carlotta dropping her leathers on the grass and saw for the first time her naked breasts with the surprisingly large brown nipples.

'I think Melanie's got a thing about me.'

'Yes, angel,' Sandra murmured, her heart beating a little too fast as Carlotta reached across and started slowly to unbutton the silk blouse with the low neck Sandra had chosen specially for the occasion.

'You knew?' Simon gasped, sitting up and switching on the lamp again.

'What?' Sandra gasped, pulling the covers round her as if he'd just caught her in the act.

'About Melanie fancying me?'

'What? What you talking about, Si?'

'I just said, didn't I? I think Melanie Barlow fancies me.'

'Melanie?'

'Yes, Melanie. I keep saying – Melanie Barlow.'

'Fancies *you*?'

'Yes.'

'Why?'

'She keeps . . . you know . . . Looking and . . . saying things.'

'Oh, Simon!' Sandra put her arms round him and cradled him like a small child. 'Melanie wouldn't fancy you. I think you're having a mid-life crisis.'

'What?'

'Darling. Melanie wouldn't fancy you.'

'You're sure?'

'Of course I am. I'm very strong on characters. Melanie and you will never be an item.' And she kissed him on the cheek.

'Well, that's all right then,' he said, switching off the lamp again and putting his arms round her.

'Oh, not tonight, Si,' Sandra whispered. 'I'm all strung up about my writing . . .'

And Simon rolled over on to his side of the bed and lay on his back, staring up into the dark and wishing – not for the first time – that she'd never started her creative writing classes.

'But what do you intend living on?' Laurence asked as he and Bless parted company on the landing. They'd been having variations of this deeply disturbing conversation for the last hour, and as the hall clock chimed midnight Bless had no intention of letting it continue a moment longer.

'Rich by name and Rich by nature!' he answered with a bright smile and a well-executed time step.

'You'll sponge off him for the rest of your life?'

'I don't happen to have much option at the moment, Laurence.'

'Doesn't that worry you?'

'Horribly, if you must know. But I don't want to talk about it now . . .'

'I suppose it's the dilemma of every young bride,' Laurence said gloomily.

'Would you mind not casting me in a role, please? We are a modern affair! We are new men! We are each of us at peace with our masculine/feminine psyche. Like organic gardening we will fuck on the rotation system . . .'

'Charming!' Laurence said, determined not to get ruffled. 'Only Richard has the money and you don't.'

'I intend to make a career out of knitting,' Bless announced, going towards his room with a swish of his shoulders and his head held high.

'Like Farrah Fawcett, I suppose?'

'Go to bed, Laurence!' Bless giggled. 'You're pissed.'

'Yes, I rather think I am,' the older man agreed, and he went into his own room without any more hesitation.

But as Bless crossed to draw the curtains he felt gloomy. Laurence had a peculiar knack of finding the weak spot in the armour and twisting the knife.

'Oh, shit!' he said out loud.

How *was* he going to make a living? He certainly didn't want to ask Rich for every penny for the rest of his life. Was Laurence right? Was the whole thing doomed? Doomed by poverty? It smacked a little too much of the Cratchit family. Was he really being asked to play Tiny Tim again? Now, so late in his career? Here he was – stranded in the country, living in someone else's house and spending someone else's money. Meanwhile the someone else was three thousand miles away, getting up to God knew what, with God knew who. Bless suddenly felt horribly lonely and strangely unloved.

'Bed!' he said, stamping on a huge wave of all too familiar angst. As he started to undress, he noticed that a light was on in the upper room of the Tower – that strange folly over the wall in Brigadier Jerrold's garden, that was just visible from the bedroom window. But Bless was too tired and too depressed and he sank into bed without giving it, or anything else, another thought.

In the Tower, Brigadier Selwyn Jerrold sorted through his

wardrobe of army uniforms. He wanted to cut just the right figure on Saturday. He must look like a leader, of course, but he didn't want to appear too dominant or daunting. After all, the assembly would be made up entirely of civilians and would lack the discipline of trained men. Perhaps battle dress would be a little too sombre? Yet at the same time would not a dress uniform seem too formal? In the end he decided on the tropical shorts. The slightly casual look would make him seem like one of the people – and the khaki knee socks showed off his calves to advantage.

As he shook out the chosen ensemble, ready for Rosemary – for want of his beloved batman, Jonesy – to give it a good pressing, he happened to glance up and caught sight of his reflection in the mirror on the wardrobe door. Slowly he leaned towards the glass, staring at the reflected image. To his horror he could detect a trace of ladies' make-up on his cheek, where his appalling sister had brushed against him earlier in the day. He shuddered and, taking a handkerchief from his pocket, rubbed energetically at the skin.

'We don't want any of *that*,' he hissed through clenched teeth. 'No bloody thank you! That won't do at all, sir.' And he continued to spit and polish the cheek until it was quite raw with rubbing.

Such is the confusing nature of the universe that at that very moment a brilliant sun was shining on the deck of a sleek yacht as it cut through a sea the colour of sapphires.

Lying supine on a comfortable double hammock under a stretched awning of green and white stripes were two extremely tanned men. One of them was in his early twenties and he was also extremely naked. The other was wearing the briefest of bathing slips and dark glasses. He was older – in his forties – and sad to relate, he was snoring.

The younger swain, who had only recently arrived on deck, hoping no doubt to find the other man there, seemed disenchanted by the rhythmic buzz of his heavy breathing. He allowed the tilt of the hammock to slide him gently in the direction of the older man until, by chance and inevitably, their bodies collided. But even this movement failed to waken the sleeper. Eventually the youth resorted to a fairly vicious nudge.

The older man moved in his sleep and reaching out he put his arms round his hammock-fellow and drew him towards him.

'Bless?' he murmured, sleepily.

'No! Brad! What's with this "Bless"?' the young man said, nuzzling up to him.

Rich opened his eyes and raised his dark glasses. 'Brad? Oh shit! Now, Brad – be a good boy . . . I've told you! NO. N. O.'

'Why?'

'Because I'm in love.'

'But not with me?'

'Not with you.'

'Why not?' Brad protested, getting up and stretching. 'You can't mean you don't fancy me?' He made the very suggestion seem outlandish and quite impossible to be true.

'I think you're gorgeous.'

Brad smiled – the beautiful are so easily pleased. Then he frowned – the vain are so quickly alarmed. 'So what's so special about Bless?' he asked.

'He loves me!' Rich said after a moment. Then he sighed. 'But I'm afraid that at this moment he's probably terribly bored and hating the thought of me.'

'Why?'

'I've stuck him away in a dreary little village in the middle of the country. And when I try to call him I find the number is permanently engaged.'

'Why?'

Rich shrugged. 'He's either left it off the hook or it's out of order.' Then another possibility occurred to him. 'Unless, of course, he's talking to a lover. We haven't been together very long and I am the last of a long string of admirers. At least, I hope I'm the last . . .' Rich sat up suddenly, making the hammock swing. 'I have to go home,' he announced in a loud voice, although he was really talking to himself.

'You haven't finished your business here.'

'Screw that! I have to go home and tell him I love him.'

'Ugh!' Brad shuddered. 'That is so uncool!' He prowled away across the deck, stretching his arms above his head and showing off his perfect physique.

'Yes, it probably is,' Rich agreed, trying not to watch.

Brad turned and flashed a dazzling smile. 'Lucky Bless!' he drawled. 'I'm going inside. This sun is outrageously hot.' And he sauntered away towards the cool of the cabins.

'I'm going home to Bless,' Rich whispered. 'I'm going home to Bless. I'm going home to Bless.' And he continued this mantra as he followed Brad in out of the sun.

Meanwhile, back in the dreary little village, an owl hooted out in the dark night, and just as Bless was sliding into sleep a tiny worry niggled at his fading consciousness. What was it that he should have done? There was some task, some favour, some promise he had made. There was some little service that he'd failed to fulfil. What the hell was it?

Diana Simpson, the unremembered source of his concern, pulled a blanket closer round her and settled down for another night in her hiding place above the summerhouse. Bless had failed to bring her the all-clear. But really she was getting quite attached to the loft and had arranged her few belongings around her to form a cosy little nest. Creature comforts had never been high on her agenda, and so long as she was warm and safe, she felt she could happily live the life of a hermit, a recluse or – why not? – a nun. Her only problem was lack of food – and the biscuits she had brought with her had nearly run out.

Such strange, sweet, herby biscuits. They made her dream of peacocks, of minarets, of spinning star galaxies and of far-away places beyond the mind's imagining.

She adjusted her rolled-up cardigan into a more comfortable pillow and curled into the foetal position. She couldn't even remember why she was in hiding any more. Tomorrow, she thought, I really must go home. Though there was a lot to be said for living a life unfettered by possessions, unhindered by the stereotypical concepts of hearth and home. And as she sank into a deep, dream-filled sleep she listened with pleasure to the night sounds out in the garden and the distant chiming of the church clock.

39

Another Dinner With Delia

The Daltrys were giving a dinner party. Well, to be honest, it was more of a duty party. The vicar and his wife, the three old girls from Pinchings and Lavinia Sparton from the Towers could scarcely be deemed the cream of society. But Pinchings and the Towers were the Daltrys' immediate neighbours, and the poor vicar's wife rarely was invited anywhere.

So Heather was being charitable. Every so often she felt it necessary to play the role of the hostess. When she'd first moved to the village she'd imagined herself giving summer luncheons, winter dinners, cocktails with small eats and other festive gatherings for the chosen. But she soon discovered that although her spirit might be willing, the available flesh was none too appealing. Bellingford society did not prove the richest of pickings. The locals were insular and the incomers, for the most part, boring. There were probably some agreeable people living in the outlying villages, but if so she had, over the years, failed to come across them. She had friends on committees – the cottage hospital, meals on wheels, the Preservation of Ancient Bridleways – but there were no real kindred spirits. So after a few abortive attempts to establish a circle of friends, and discovering that she was married to a man who was rarely in the house, she'd fallen back on a much more appealing love affair – with her horse, Belter – and satisfied her need to entertain by giving the odd supper for acquaintances and, as in this case, the neighbours.

This evening had been planned in advance and was mainly a way of giving the vicar's wife a night out. Heather had come across Margaret Skrimshaw in the churchyard one day when she was riding by on her way to Belling Woods. She'd spotted Margaret skulking behind a tombstone – in what seemed to be the middle of a good cry. And although the poor woman had insisted that she had 'something in my eye' and that she was 'perfectly all right. Really!' Heather had taken pity on her and arranged there and then to have her and her husband to dinner. The women from Pinchings had been invited, to lessen the burden. They'd all been teachers and would know how to deal with a vicar. Lavinia Sparton was a late addition – the Daltrys had been meaning to have her for about fourteen years.

Friday is always a good evening for duty entertaining. It gets it over and out of the way without making too much of a mess of the weekend.

On this particular Friday, Tony had actually come home from the office in good time, which augured well for the party. He would be there to serve the pre-dinner drinks and keep the conversation going while Heather added the final touches out in the kitchen. (This was by no means always the case. The errant Mr Daltry had been known to arrive home long after his guests were seated at table, and once – in a bid, one can only suppose, for a quick divorce – he'd actually driven up as Heather was waving the last of them off, and had explained his absence from the feast by saying that he'd thought they were expected the following evening. Which did *not* explain why he was so late and anyway sounded like a horribly lame excuse.)

'We've got far too many girls!' he now joked, as he ushered the guests into the dining room and they gathered round the table. 'You're going to have a hell of a job with the *placement*, darling.'

'Just see to the wine, Tony!' his wife ordered in a clipped voice. She did sometimes wonder if really it wouldn't be far easier not to have him there at all. She could hire a waiter to do all the things he was supposed to do – at least a hired hand wouldn't make inane remarks.

'That's me put in my place!' Tony laughed, adding to his downfall.

Heather gave him a severe look and an infinitesimal frown and shake of the head. He in turn pulled a wounded face and retired to the sideboard with his tail between his legs.

'Now!' Heather beamed at her guests. 'Vicar, if you sit here on my left. And Miss Bridey' (fat), 'you here on my right. With Miss Fallon' (tall) 'next to you, and Mrs Sparton opposite you – next to the vicar . . .'

'Here?'

'No – next to the vicar . . .'

'I so rarely come out . . .'

'Let me just finish placing people, Mrs Sparton. Now, Mrs Skrimshaw – down on the right, on the other side of Miss Fallon . . .'

'Who is that woman? She looks very odd to me,' Lavinia Sparton asked the vicar in a piercing whisper.

'She's my wife,' the vicar replied.

'Really? Our lot are still not supposed to marry. Though one does hear the strangest rumours . . .'

'And finally,' Heather cut in with a firm tone. 'Miss Hopkirk' (short), 'if you could go opposite Mrs Skrimshaw . . .'

'That was quite tricky, wasn't it, dear?' Tony remarked, try- ing yet again to be an affable host. 'We decided to make you a token man, Miss Fallon – on account of your height!'

'My height has always been an embarrassment to me.'

'Oh, I . . . Well, I didn't mean . . .'

'People think it's all right to make jokes about it – but it can be quite upsetting.'

'I like a tall woman,' Tony said, feeling he was on a losing wicket. 'After all, Heather is quite . . . statuesque herself.' Then, getting bolder, he thought he might try for a laugh. 'No! It's the little short ones that . . .' He wavered and stopped in mid sentence as Miss Hopkirk turned all her attention on him and he realised how particularly diminutive she was.

'If you'll excuse me . . .' Heather said quickly, trying to save the situation. 'I'll just . . .' and she hurried towards the kitchen door, adding: 'Unfortunately it's the maid's night off!'

'You have a maid?' Miss Hopkirk asked brightly, still looking at Tony.

'No! Heather's joke!' he explained. 'Who'd like a glass of white wine?'

'So – you don't have to be celibate, Vicar?' Lavinia asked, pursuing what she considered a far more interesting subject.

'No,' Andrew Skrimshaw replied, hoping his voice had a sufficient ring of finality.

'How does that work?'

'What?'

'Not being celibate.'

'Pretty well, really.'

'But surely . . . didn't God – or someone like that – say sex was a sin? And are you not supposed to be above sin?'

'Well, not a sin exactly . . .'

'The original sin . . .'

'I think . . . our feeling in the Anglican Church . . . is that . . .' His voice began to soar, as if from a pulpit, 'God, in his wisdom, created man and he created woman . . .'

'I converted to Catholicism as a youngster,' Lavinia cut in. The last thing she wanted was an Anglican sermon. 'It caused quite a lot of trouble with my family. The Catholic church in Dorking was not handy for the house and, of course, a Catholic, unlike an Anglican, is expected to attend on a regular basis. My father refused to drive me – so I was forced to go there on a bicycle. But I was not to be deterred. You see I didn't feel the C of E had the right passion for my personality.'

'No, I don't suppose it has,' the vicar agreed.

'A dancer is a creative soul,' Lavinia explained. 'We need

drama and suffering. Naturally my fervour didn't last. My career became my religion and . . .' she shrugged, 'I lapsed. But in the early days I found the confessional wonderfully encouraging – I liked its snug intimacy and the smell of incense was intoxicating. And of course a great many priests have a penchant for the ballet. I personally have known several who have pictures of Nijinsky or Nureyev hanging on their walls.' Sensing she was losing the vicar's attention, Lavinia beamed round at the other guests. 'I am thinking,' she announced in hushed tones, as though she were imparting classified information, 'of resuming my career. A comeback, no less! I have an Italian friend who is encouraging me . . .'

'Here we are,' Heather proclaimed, coming in carrying a large glass bowl sitting on an even bigger dish, containing mounds of cracked ice.

'My dear, how thrilling!' Miss Bridey exclaimed, clapping her hands. 'Is it a cold soup?'

'Yes, it is!' Heather said, pleased with the attention, and she started to ladle the soup into bowls.

'How delicious! We went to dinner last week at our friends in Fairlow. Frightfully good cooks! So original. We started with a sort of chilled vichyssoise flavoured with lemon grass. Imagine! It was utterly superb . . .'

'I hope you will think so again,' Heather exclaimed with a slightly too bright smile.

'Oh dear! A faux pas? Same soup?'

'I'm afraid so, yes. It's from Delia Smith.'

'Oh, she's so good!' – this from Miss Fallon. 'People swear by her.'

'And quite right too!' from Miss Bridey. 'Our friends in Fairlow use her all the time. They followed the soup with a sumptuous main course. Quite unique, I thought. Chicken cooked with sherry vinegar! Can you believe that?'

'I can, yes! We're having it tonight,' Heather exclaimed, looking round at the company, who had all turned their heads and were gazing up at her expectantly.

'I say, old thing!' Tony said, after an awkward pause. 'What's for pudding?'

'I hardly dare to tell you . . .'

'This soup is scrumptious!' Lavinia exclaimed, eating ravenously.

'Vicar,' Heather smiled encouragingly, 'would you like to say grace?' And she beamed again at Lavinia, who immediately froze with her spoon midway 'twixt plate and lip.

'For what we are about to receive, may the Lord make us truly thankful.'

'Amen,' Lavinia agreed with fervour, and popped the spoon into her mouth.

Later in the meal Miss Fallon asked Heather how the tickets had been selling for the antiques road show.

'Frightfully well! It always does well.'

They were by now on to the chicken with sherry vinegar and tarragon sauce, and Miss Bridey had slightly overdone her enthusiasm and her reassurances that 'Our friends in Fairlow didn't get it nearly as right. This has a really spiky flavour!' She had then smiled cheerfully, feeling that the word spiky was exactly how Delia herself would have described the dish if she had been present. (And who was to say that she wasn't? If not in person at the table – then certainly in spirit in the kitchen.)

It was then that Miss Fallon had decided to steer the conversation away from the tricky area of food.

'Did the Brigadier book a ticket?'

'He did, yes. He's bought two. One for a valuation – for himself, I gather – and a spectator ticket for his wife. I suggested that couples usually liked to hear the valuation together and that therefore wouldn't he prefer to have two valuation tickets? He became quite abusive! He said that the difference between three pounds fifty and six pounds might not be much to me, but was enough for a haircut to him!'

'Quite right too!' Tony chimed in. 'Heather spends my money as if it comes hot from the Almighty and not from the sweat of my brow!'

His wife glared. To mention sweat at the table was bad enough – to mention the Almighty in front of a vicar was unforgivable.

'I have an awful feeling he's up to something, you know,' Miss Fallon continued speaking thoughtfully.

'Really? How exciting!' Tony enthused. 'What had you in mind?'

'I don't know. But ever since the gentlemen arrived at the Hall House and the Brigadier put that nasty little barb in his appalling rag, I've been waiting for his next move.'

'Does anyone actually read *The Bellingford Gazette*?' Tony snorted. 'I've far more pressing things to get on with. How about you, Mrs Vicar?' He grinned at Margaret Skrimshaw, hoping to draw her into the conversation at last. She had been totally silent for the entire evening. But he had chosen the wrong way to do it. Margaret turned and glared at him.

'My name is Margaret. It's hard enough that I am expected to adopt my husband's surname; I absolutely refuse to adopt his profession as well.'

'Sorry!' Tony said with a sigh.

'Oh, I do so agree,' Miss Hopkirk, sitting opposite her, chimed in. 'Women are still treated as second-class citizens. Mrs Pankhurst would be so disappointed . . .'

'We don't often read *The Bellingford Gazette*,' Andrew Skrimshaw said hurriedly. 'What did he say about the Hall House?'

'I can't recall it all now.' Miss Fallon shrugged. 'But he was obviously having a dig at the fact that the new owners are two gentlemen . . .'

'Are they nancies?' Lavinia asked, perking up. She had had too much wine and, having been on a starvation diet for two days, she had eaten too fast. Consequently she'd gone into a bit of a trough, but the thought of nancies seemed to buck her up no end.

'We met them outside the church,' Miss Hopkirk volunteered.

'They go to church?' Lavinia seemed surprised.

'Indeed, yes,' Miss Bridey said. 'But when we met them outside the church we didn't meet them both, Ethel, if you recall. We thought we had, but we hadn't . . .' She sipped her wine greedily, though she'd already had more than enough. Then she shook her head, shrugged cheerfully and raised her glass to the vicar, in a belated toast. 'Chin chin!'

'I'm sorry?' Andrew Skrimshaw murmured, dabbing beneath his lip in a nervous manner.

'There was another one, you see!' Miss Bridey continued. 'Such a nice one – older, with an air! He looked like Douglas Fairbanks . . .'

'Another nancy?'

'Another gentleman,' Miss Fallon corrected Lavinia.

'I like a nancy boy myself. How about you, Vicar?'

'We are all God's creatures . . .'

'They don't always make the best dancers – some are inclined to glide too much. But they're such fun if you're on a long tour. They do bits of washing and ironing for you, always know where the best shops are, and quite frankly they're a lot more reliable when it comes to sanitary and medical matters . . .'

'Tony, you met one of them when that car crashed into the gatepost,' Heather said, waving her glass at him, indicating that more wine should be poured.

'Not for me!' Margaret Skrimshaw said hurriedly, putting her hand over her – still full – glass, before he'd even picked up the bottle.

'I won't say no!' Miss Bridey called out, raising her glass in his direction.

'Yes,' Tony said, hurrying to her side. 'There was a hell of a schermozzle in the middle of the night. Car pranged into the gatepost, horn blaring. I nipped over to see if I could help.' As he warmed to his story he continued round the table, topping up glasses. 'I thought, seeing they were . . . well, you know! I thought they'd be glad to have a man on the scene. The one I met seemed a nice enough lad. Bit young for a house like that, but perfectly presentable.'

'You think of houses like clothes, Mr Daltry?' Miss Bridey murmured. 'Wearing the house like a garment, a shroud or a bridal gown . . . Oh!' She quivered with creative energy. 'How wonderfully poetic!'

Tony Daltry stared across at her and smiled in a bemused way.

'Edna is a poet, did you know that?' Miss Hopkirk whispered to Lavinia.

'Who's Edna?'

'Sitting opposite.'

Lavinia peered at the fat form of Miss Bridey. Her eyes were half closed and her body swayed as she enjoyed her moment of poetic reverie.

'Is she ill?' Lavinia whispered.

Miss Hopkirk shook her head. 'She's a poet,' she repeated, feeling no other explanation was required.

'A poet!' Lavinia echoed, as though hearing the fact for the first time. 'How interesting. I say – is she published?'

'I have been,' Miss Bridey assured her, opening her eyes so as not to miss her moment of notoriety.

'Would I have read you?'

'Perhaps. If you subscribed to *The Poets' Almanac* during the early fifties,' she said, demurely looking at her hands.

'Never heard of it,' Lavinia barked, dashing Miss Bridey's moment of fame against the rocks of disinterest. 'Go on about these nancies. I rather think my guest, Carlotta Braganizio . . . Did you know I had a guest?'

'I sent her to you,' Tony said, replenishing his own glass. 'Though I must admit that, at the time, I thought she was a man.'

'An understandable error. Her brother has had dealings with the Hall House, but they spoke about it in Italian and I could not keep up with them.'

'You think the Brigadier is going to do something at the village hall tomorrow, Miss Fallon? Is that it?' Tony Daltry asked.

'I have never known him attend any village function – ever before. Why should he be so keen on this one?'

'Perhaps he has an antique he wants to know more about?'

'We shall see . . .'

Heather had done Delia's vanilla cream terrine *and* her fresh peaches in Marsala with mascarpone cream. It would have been too cruel if the friends in Fairlow had hit on precisely the same combination as well. But if they had, Miss Bridey was now too far gone to say so.

It was a bright, clear night when the guests left the house. The dark sky was crammed with stars, and a big three-quarter moon hung over the rooftops, casting a silver sheen over the silent trees and all the sleeping houses.

Only the vicar and his poor, sad wife had far to go. They said goodbye to the ladies from Pinchings in the lane and then walked with Lavinia as far as the gate to her own drive.

'Good night, sweet prince!' she trilled, stretching her arms and lowering herself into a wobbly curtsy. Then she cried out, reaching towards Andrew, 'Oh, Vicar! A hand, if you please!' He hurried forward and, grasping her by the arm, pulled her back into a standing position. 'The force of gravity was ever the curse of the dancer!' she murmured, with a gracious smile. And putting delicate fingers to her lips, she fluttered a kiss on the midnight air and turned and staggered away up the drive.

As the Skrimshaws walked across the green, heading for the farther side and the lane to the church, Andrew thought he could hear his wife crying.

'What *is* the matter, Margaret?' he sighed.

'Nothing.'

'You're crying?'

Margaret merely sobbed quietly.

'Is it my fault?'

'It's no one's fault.'

'Then what is it?' he asked, irritably.

'The night is so beautiful . . .'

'Yes?'

'I don't know why it hurts so much,' she sobbed.

Andrew sighed again – but remained silent. The mystery of

his wife's unhappiness was completely beyond him. If anything it annoyed him. He had to deal with the welfare of his flock. He found it irksome that his family should expect his attention as well. I am only human, he thought. There is a limit to my compassion. I have to use it sparingly.

And so, reaching the opposite side of the green still wrapped in a distant silence, they turned their steps in the direction of the church and of their cold and echoing vicarage beyond it.

At the gateway to Cockpits they surprised the Brigadier's wife stooping down beside the gate.

'Why, Mrs Jerrold! Are you all right?' Andrew exclaimed, alarmed by her sudden appearance, looming up at them out of the dark.

'Vicar! Mrs Skrimshaw! I'm just putting out the milk bottles. They won't deliver to the door any more. That, I suppose, is called progress!'

'A beautiful evening,' Andrew said.

Rosemary Jerrold straightened and gazed up at the silver disc of the moon and all the crowding stars. 'Yes!' she sobbed. 'A very beautiful evening!'

'Good night Mrs Jerrold,' Andrew said, hurrying away. The bloody woman was crying as well. Do all women cry? he wondered.

Rosemary walked slowly back up the drive. The moonlight shimmered palely on the surface of the brackish pond. Then, like a moment of mysterious magic, a brilliant light suddenly flickered, almost at Rosemary's feet. She crossed the narrow strip of grass and leaned down beside the holly tree that hung out over the water. The flashing light remained, winking up at her, like a divine sign.

Reaching down, Rosemary took hold of a loose fold of material. Then, slowly and strangely, she pulled Diana Simpson's ethnic dress up out of the pond, showering a cascade of twinkling drops behind it.

Rosemary shook out the dress and stared at it. Her heart lurched and her body shook with convulsive sobs. 'Phyllis!' she cried. 'Oh, Phyllis! Come home! Come home where you belong.'

And gently squeezing the water of the Belling Brook out of the dress that she was quite convinced belonged to her sister-in-law and had somehow become lost and abandoned in that remote and stagnant corner, she carefully folded it and took it back with her into the house.

40

The Road Show

The village hall was already crowded when Bless and Laurence arrived. The back rows were occupied by a lot of noisy teenagers, including a group of skinheads, who'd come out of a sense of boredom rather than any interest in antiques – though the possibility of finding out who owned what and how much it was worth in the neighbourhood was an obvious attraction to one or two of them.

It had been Laurence's idea, needless to say, that he and Bless should go. 'Nonsense! Of course we must! If one lives in a village one must take part in the social scene – however tedious it may prove to be. It's expected . . .'

They bought two tickets at the door, from a jolly woman in a knitted dress. 'Oh!' she exclaimed as she took the money from Laurence. 'You must be the chaps from the Hall House. Am I right? We were only talking about you last night. I'm Heather Daltry – the Woods. I rather think my husband came to your rescue a few nights ago . . .?'

Laurence looked blank and Bless could scarcely remember the incident himself. It seemed like a lifetime ago that the Hunk had crashed into the gate.

'It was me he met,' he explained, leaning forward. 'This is a friend who is staying for a few days.'

'But there are two of you living there?' Heather insisted.

'Yes. My . . . my partner is away at the moment.'

'Oh, that's all right then!' She laughed. 'I wouldn't like to think the jungle drums had been tapping the wrong message! Sit anywhere . . .' and she waved them into the hall.

'Partner!' Laurence snorted as they searched the rows of chairs for a suitable position. 'You make Richard sound like a business arrangement!'

'I know. But saying "lover" would have made me feel shy,' Bless whispered. 'Actually,' he continued as they squeezed along a row near the front – and as far from the noisy youths as possible, 'if Rich doesn't come home soon, you and I may have to start fucking, Laurence! Just to keep the natives satisfied.'

'Please!' Laurence protested, fiercely. 'If you're going to use that sort of language, go and join the riff-raff at the back . . .'

'Mr 'Udson! Coo-ee! Come and sit here, dear!' a voice interrupted him. It was Mrs Day. They saw her, standing up in the front row and waving to them. Mrs Sugar, sitting next to her, had also turned round and was staring eagerly. 'Come on, dear!' Doris shouted, tottering up the side of the hall. 'I saved two seats, special . . .'

'Oh, do we have to?' Bless groaned.

'I'm afraid it rather looks as though we do,' Laurence sighed, watching as Doris pushed along the row towards him, grabbed hold of his sleeve and began to drag him back after her.

'Sorry, dear! Mind your feet! Squeeze in a bit!' she told the other occupants as she beat a path to the aisle. 'There now!' she said pushing Laurence down next to Mrs Sugar and Bless next to him, so that they were sandwiched between the two sisters. 'That's better, isn't it?' she grinned.

'And how are you enjoying lovely old peaceful Bellingford?' Mrs Sugar asked Laurence. 'You've not been into my shop yet, have you, you naughty thing?' she complained, slapping his knee, before he had a chance to answer her first question. 'We all have to work to keep our dear old village shops open. It's not a charity. I'm running, you know. And we don't want to live in a dead village, now do we?'

'But I don't live here,' Laurence spluttered. Then, using his most supercilious voice, he added: 'I am a visitor from London.'

'Well, dear! That mustn't stop you coming in to make a purchase,' she insisted, undaunted by his manner. 'A nice memento of your stay in the lovely olde worlde English countryside. What could be better? I do a super-duper, top-of-the-range choice of mugs and ashtrays, with a tip-top picture – in colour – of a windmill on each and every one of them. I have known visitors buy a gross, so impressed have they been by the artwork. Then I've got a full selection of picture postcards – both local views and comic jokes. I got tea towels with wildlife pictures; tea cosies, knitted by 'and; I've even got tea pots!' She laughed cheerfully. 'You name it, Bessie's got it! "If you don't find what you want at Mrs Sugar's Shop, you won't find it anywhere in the county"! That's what people say.' She leaned forward and called across both Laurence and Bless. 'Tell 'im about my cooked 'am, Doris!'

'Oh, shut up about your cooked 'am, Bessie!' Doris Day snapped. She nudged Bless and winked. 'Cooked 'am, indeed! We can do better than that, Mr 'Udson. Can't we, dear?' And she continued to nudge him and wink as though they shared some dark and terrible habit – though he hadn't a clue to what she referred.

The Barlows and the Greens were in seats two rows back from the front. 'Those are the poofs,' Melanie announced, nodding a head in the direction of Bless, who had looked over his shoulder, hoping to curtail Doris's intimate behaviour. 'Sand says you're acquainted with a poof yourself, Si, is that right?'

Simon, who somehow had ended up sitting next to her, though he'd been determined to avoid that fate, swallowed and looked desperately along the line to where Sandra was sitting on the other side of Barry in computers.

'Am I?' he asked.

'That's what Sand said,' Melanie confided, putting a hand on his knee. 'I was quite upset at the thought!'

'Why?'

'I didn't like to think of you being tempted elsewhere!'

'Elsewhere?' Simon gasped. 'Well, I wouldn't be tempted by a . . . you know . . . not by . . . one of them!'

'Oh, I am relieved to hear that, Si!' Melanie said with a warm and caring smile. And to confirm the sentiment she slid her hand up his thigh.

'Melanie!' he exclaimed, slamming his own hand over hers and pushing it down his leg away from his thin, vulnerable crotch.

Melanie squeezed his hand and turned, so that she was facing him and with her back to her husband. 'No! Si!' she whispered. 'You mustn't! Not here! What would Barry say?'

Simon dragged his hand free of her grasp and nervously looked at his watch. 'Should be about starting,' he stammered.

Melanie smiled and tweaked the end of his nose. 'You are the most adorable thing!' she said. 'Did you bring an antique yourself, Si?' and as she spoke, she turned and drew Barry back into the conversation. 'We've brought a tankard, haven't we, Barry?'

'That's right. A silver tankard that belonged to my uncle,' Barry said, fishing under his chair and producing the object from a plastic carrier bag. 'There it is! The family heirloom!' he announced, holding up a bright metal mug with an ornate handle and a lid.

'Lovely!' Sandra said, staring at it.

'Worth a bob or two,' he told her. 'We've had it on my side of the family for years.'

'We've brought a ring of my grandmother's,' Sandra told him, 'and Simon,' she called, leaning over, 'you've brought that ink stand, haven't you, darling? I think it's ever so old. It's in the shape of a galleon. Show it to Melanie, Si. She'll be interested . . .'

'Not now!' Simon protested. 'It's all wrapped up.'

'Which are the poofs?' Barry asked, scanning the rows in front of them.

'There!' his wife said, pointing at Bless – who was so near to them, he could quite easily have been listening.

'Oh, yes!' Barry said, craning forward. 'Yes, he has the look.'

'Has he?' Sandra asked. 'How can you tell?' She had become more than a little interested in sexual alternatives herself recently.

'You just can,' Barry said with a knowledgeable air. 'It's the way they hold themselves.'

'He looks ordinary to me,' Sandra said, craning her neck to get a better view of Bless. 'I think he looks rather sweet, actually.'

'Oh, well. That's what I mean. Often they look just like blokes,' Barry said, airily. 'That's why we men have to be so careful in public places – changing rooms and so on. Like at the baths or after squash, for instance . . . Nowadays you can just never be sure.'

'Oh, Si!' Sandra nudged him. 'How can I be sure about you?'

'Would they attack you then?' Melanie asked.

'Worse. Far worse,' Barry replied darkly.

'Ladies and gentlemen!' Heather Daltry said, stepping out on to the small stage where a table and chair were positioned for the evening's entertainment. 'If I could just have your attention for a moment. Please . . . can I have a bit of hush . . . Please . . .'

Gradually the chatter in the hall quietened down.

'Thank you! Before we begin, may I just remind you of the house rules. Each of the valuation tickets has a number on it. When you hear your number called, if you would make your way to the steps here on the right – your left – that is the way up to the stage. Then after Mr Asquith has finished, if you would proceed back to your seat down the steps on the left – your right. I will have called the next number and that person will then be making their way up the steps on the right – your left . . .'

'Oh, for the Lord's sake, Mrs Daltry!' Bessie Sugar called out. 'You've got us in a complete whirl! Your left, my right . . . None of us know what you're talking about. Let's just get on and then get home!'

During this short tirade, which Heather received with a good-humoured smile which masked a far from generous spirit, a small, spidery man, wearing a large floral bow tie and a bright-yellow jacket, scurried down the side aisle from the door. He carried a heavy canvas hold-all and was obviously in some agitation, which caused him to trip on one of the right-hand (your left) steps as he scrambled up on to the stage.

'Oh, here you are at last, Mr Asquith!' Heather exclaimed, glad of this timely distraction – Mrs Sugar could be a mean fighter when provoked.

'Oh, dear!' Laurence hissed. 'He looks like a holiday camp attendant!' And he settled back, folding his arms and assuming a bored expression. 'I hope this isn't going to last too long.'

'You were the one who wanted to come, sweety!' Bless purred in his ear.

Mr Asquith had now arrived at the table and, putting down the bag, he turned and stared out front – shielding his eyes with a hand, against the far from powerful glare of the rudimentary stage lighting. 'So sorry to be a little late,' he gasped. 'I took a wrong turning . . .'

'You should know your way here by now, dear!' Doris called. 'Good Lord have mercy! You come every blooming year . . .'

'Quite! I'll just . . .' And opening the bag, he proceeded to pile reference books and other paraphernalia – magnifying glass, tape measure, even a small set of scales – on to the table.

Eventually, after a certain amount of rearrangement and a good deal of nervous apology, he pronounced himself ready and Heather declared the antique road show well and truly open. She then called the first number and the evening got under way.

Most of the items were small, and some were interesting. A man from one of the neighbouring villages brought a complete set of first editions of the Biggles books and told Mr Asquith that his valuation was 'far lower than I've already been offered by a chap in Brighton'. There was a 'lovely piece of Coleport, really quite lovely – but sadly, cracked'; a 'very fine Victorian watercolour, in a style that is becoming most collectable'. There were innumerable early pop bottles, sets of cigarette cards, and other bric-à-brac. People brought plates, jugs, cups and saucers, milk jugs and improbable cake stands from many of the best English potteries – with a high percentage from Worcester. There was 'a splendid Edwardian nursing chair. Perhaps Dralon is not quite the most sympathetic of upholstery materials – though I do see that the colour (bottle green) must go very well with yellow walls'; a Georgian silver candelabrum 'that should be insured for at least five hundred pounds' (a very satisfied customer); a piece of early embroidery that 'could quite possibly be French, or maybe Portuguese'.

Then it was Barry's turn. His silver tankard turned out to be electroplated and 'not the real thing, I'm afraid'. Barry was not pleased and was prepared to argue. 'If it had been silver, there'd have been a mark,' Mr Asquith explained, patiently. 'I know that!' Barry fumed. 'I'm not a complete ignoramus. I was given to understand that it was an Austrian country piece – and that they didn't bother with assaying.' 'Oh, dear!' Mr Asquith smiled and shook his head. 'I think you've been told a porky-pie there! No. Quite definitely electroplated. An interesting technique. The base metal is . . .' 'I don't want a lecture, thank you very much!' Barry snarled, wresting his tankard from Mr Asquith's hands and stomping off in a huff.

'Mmmh!' Melanie raised her eyes to Sandra. 'It'll be tiptoe through the tulips tonight! Barry's very proud of his silver tankard! Personally, I was never struck. What d'you think, Si?'

'I have no feeling on the subject,' Simon stammered.

When Simon and Sandra's number was called – soon after Barry had returned to his seat – they both pushed along the row and made their way to the right-hand steps.

'Hey! Baby!' a voice rang out. 'I watch you! Whatever he offers – I give you double . . .'

'Please!' Heather called, glaring up the hall.

Both Simon and Sandra stopped in their tracks and looked nervously over their shoulders. Carlotta was leaning against the side wall, near the door. This evening she was wearing a pair of Henry Sparton's silk pyjamas – in a rich purple with contrasting pale blue stripes. She'd rolled the trousers to her knees and was sporting a pair of Doc Marten boots on her feet. She also had on one of Henry's tweed caps – but with the brim to the back. The ensemble gave her a strangely oriental, mandarin look. She could have been an extra from the film *Shanghai Express*. As soon as Sandra saw her, Carlotta gave her a flick of a salute and clicked her heels.

'Who is that?' Simon whispered, peering up the darkened hall.

'Just an onlooker,' Sandra muttered, pushing him ahead of her on to the stage. But once she was by the table, she couldn't resist turning back to look at the massive bulk of her admirer. Immediately Carlotta put her fingers in her mouth and whistled enthusiastically.

'Oh, God in heaven!' Doris Day cried out, standing up in full view of the rest of the audience and then falling backwards against Bless's shoulder. 'It's that dratted foreign fella again! I swear he's following me about, Mr 'Udson . . .'

'Hey! Mr 'Udson!' Carlotta shouted as Bless now turned and looked in her direction. 'I see you take your slave with you! 'S all right! Mum!' And with a huge guffaw of cheerful laughter, she tapped the side of her nose.

'Could we please have a little hush!' Heather Daltry pleaded. 'There are still several items for Mr Asquith to value and we have to be out of the hall by ten . . .'

'Signorina Braganizio!' Lavinia called. She was sitting on a chair just across the aisle from Carlotta. 'Pray control yourself. We English are a northern race. We do not care for exuberance!'

Carlotta shrugged and bowed to her friend. Then, slipping her hands into the broad leather belt she had slung loosely round her waist, she leaned back against the wall once more and sized up her petti di pollo with a practised and appreciative eye.

Simon's inkwell was apparently 'early to mid-Victorian and could very easily have been crafted for the Great Exhibition'. Mr

Asquith was really very impressed and suggested that at a sale that attracted the right collectors it could reach as much as a hundred or even a hundred and fifty pounds. Sandra was excited, but Simon shook his head and said that he would never part with it. 'But Simon – we only have it stuck away in a cupboard.' 'I would myself be prepared to do you a deal,' Mr Asquith murmured, not wishing the audience to hear his offer. 'No!' Simon said in a loud voice. 'You see, my wife is a writer. She's writing the great English novel. And when it's published – I want this to be hers.' 'Oh, Si!' Sandra sighed, her heart melting. 'That is so sweet. Thank you, darling!'

'Hey, baby! You write a book? I buy the first copy!' Carlotta called, jealous of her loved one's divided attention.

After all that, Sandra's ring was a bit of an anticlimax. It was 'a Victorian mourning ring. See, here in the back, the hair of the dear departed . . .' 'Oh, no! How awful. I thought it was just like . . . crêpe paper or something.' 'These seed pearls and diamond chips are poor quality. But it's a nice little keepsake of a bygone age.'

'I'll never be able to wear it now,' Sandra whispered as they returned to their seats. 'Fancy having a dead person's hair on your finger. It'd make me feel like a cannibal . . .'

She was interrupted by Carlotta appearing at the end of the row, leaning across several people and calling: 'We meet later. I look at the ring for you myself. My family have many many jewels. I am quite an expert . . .'

'She *is* talking to you, Sandra!' Simon gasped. 'I thought she was . . .'

'See Sand! What did I tell you?' Melanie leaned forward and whispered.

'What? What did you tell her?' Simon demanded.

'Don't you worry about a thing, Si,' Melanie cooed, as she reached across Barry and pulled him back to his seat. 'I'll look after you.'

'Oh, Lord!' Simon moaned. 'I'm getting a splitting headache now.'

'Let me massage your temples . . .'

'Melanie. Will you please . . . stop that . . .'

'Has he gone, Mr 'Udson?' Doris asked, from her crouched position in front of her chair.

'Yes, it's all right. You're safe.'

'He's one of 'em maniacs, I think. He's after that young bit from the executive at the same time.'

'He'll 'ave you in an orgy, Doris!' her sister crowed.

'Shut yours, Bessie! And keep your head down!'

'Ah!' Mr Asquith exclaimed. 'A set of medals.'

Bless looked up, and there, just in front of him, up on the stage, stood the dread Brigadier. He was wearing a khaki uniform that included a pair of long baggy shorts, and he looked more like a boy scout than a soldier.

'This is a specialised subject . . .' Mr Asquith began.

'Not to me!' the Brigadier barked. 'Every one of these represents a memory to me.'

'I'm not sure that memories have a market value!' Mr Asquith ventured, sounding flustered. 'Nor do they strictly fall into the category of "antique"! A valuation would be difficult to come up with, without the relevant information . . .'

'Valuation? You think I would sell these?' the Brigadier barked, using his most withering, most chilling voice. Then he took the band of medals back into his own hands and turned and faced the audience. 'These, ladies and gentlemen, represent hardship and deprivation. Each one of them has the blood of comrades upon it; each one brings back a memory of fear, and tragedy. Each one represents the sunny hopes of a new tomorrow and a brave new world. These are my medals, ladies and gentlemen . . .'

'Brigadier. If you don't want a valuation . . .' Heather interrupted him. She saw trouble looming. Miss Fallon had been right. The odious little tyke was up to something.

'One moment please, madam!' the older man snapped. 'I fought a war in order that I might have the freedom to speak. Where were you at the time?'

'I hadn't been born!' Heather replied, through pursed lips.

'Quite! Exactly! Precisely! Of course! We boys fought for all of you. I fought for Bellingford . . .'

'No you didn't!' Bessie Sugar called out. 'You're an incomer.'

'I fought for this dear England, with its leafy lanes and its gentle summer meadows . . .'

'We have our own war dead, dear. We don't want you pushing your way in,' Doris Day shouted.

'Be quiet, cleaning woman!'

'Yes. Well, I might not be yours for much longer if you carry on like that . . .'

'I should listen to her, Brigadier,' Heather said in his ear 'Cleaners are at an absolute premium at the moment.'

'Oh, do bugger off, old chap!' Barry called.

'Barry!' Melanie remonstrated.

'Well, either he wants a valuation or he doesn't. It'll be closing time in half an hour.'

'Yes!' One or two other voices joined in. 'Get on with it!'

'What is it that you want, Brigadier?' Heather asked him.

'It's what I don't want that concerns me,' he replied, and to her surprise, she saw that he was actually weeping silent tears. 'I don't want perverts and deviants living next door to me. That's not what I defended these shores for. That's not why I risked death . . .'

'Selwyn – come down . . .' Rosemary Jerrold appeared at the foot of the steps as she called out.

'And you're as bad!' her husband snarled, turning and pointing an accusing finger at her. 'You are so blinded by . . . today . . . that you forget our history. There was a time when young mothers could push prams in the park in safety. When children played in meadows and came home after dark. There was a time when decent attire was the norm. When men had short haircuts and women wore skirts . . .'

Slow handclapping now started. Heather Daltry went to the side steps and peered into the hall. 'Tony!' she called. 'Vicar! I need some help here . . .'

'Yes, *Vicar*!' the Brigadier snarled. 'And what are you going to do about it?'

'About what?' Andrew Skrimshaw demanded, hurrying down the aisle and trying to fix the stud in his dog collar at the same time.

'About HIM!' the Brigadier yelled, swinging round and jabbing a finger straight down at the front row where Bless was sitting with his mouth open.

'Who?' Andrew Skrimshaw wailed, staring aghast.

'Oh, shit! He's talking about me!' Bless sighed, standing up slowly.

'Shit? You all heard him. Shit!' the Brigadier yelled.

'Gents' toilet out the back!' a skinhead at the back shouted, getting scattered laughter.

'You see?' the Brigadier raved, still pointing at Bless. 'You see how you incite people to . . . to riot and debauchery?'

'Oh, do shut up!' Bless snapped, his temper flaring. And as he spoke he jumped up on to the stage with a single movement.

This act of surprising gymnastics brought enthusiastic cat-calls and cheers from the audience. Bless, quite carried away, turned and dropped a deep curtsy. The audience loved it. They screamed for more.

'Look at him, ladies and gentlemen!' the Brigadier sneered. 'Just look at the flower of England's youth . . .!'

'Oh, thank you, dear!' Bless blew him a kiss.

'Bless, control yourself!' Laurence shouted. 'You're in public.'

'Well, honestly!' Bless snapped, his temper, that small, vicious creature that was usually kept under lock and key, finally escaping. 'If I might be allowed to say something . . .'

'No, laddie!' the Brigadier thundered. 'You haven't earned the right.'

'And you have, I suppose?'

'With these . . .' He thrust the medals into Bless's face. 'Every one of these earned me the right. They show my courage, they show my valour . . .'

'Selwyn! Stop this!' his wife implored, coming up beside him.

'Stop it? If I stop it, then my comrades died in vain.'

'Selwyn . . . You were in the catering corps . . .'

'So, woman?' her husband ranted, pushing her away viciously. 'What's so funny about that, then?' And in his fury, he ran at her again and would have knocked her off the stage, if she hadn't had the wit and the speed to dodge out of the way.

'Here, I say! Stop that!' Tony Daltry exclaimed, running up the steps and grabbing hold of the Brigadier from behind as he was about to launch into another attack.

'Army catering?' a woman in the hall yelled. 'What were you? Chief washer-up?'

Laughter rang out again, great waves of it. It was clear that many of the audience were enjoying themselves far more now than they had been during the actual road show.

'Go on, mock! All of you mock!' the Brigadier cried, swinging round and shaking himself free of Tony's restraining hands. 'You know nothing about warfare. If you did you'd know that an army marches on its stomach . . .' The laughter swelled and the youths at the back stood up, cheering, whistling and stamping their feet. 'Yes that's right . . . All of you jeer! Laugh! Deride me!' the Brigadier howled, goaded by their taunts to even greater excesses.

'Please, Selwyn!' his wife sobbed. 'Stop now. Can't you see what an exhibition you're making of yourself?'

'We must try and get him home,' Bless said to Tony Daltry, taking pity on Rosemary and wanting the whole thing to end.

But the Brigadier was too far gone to heed either his wife's entreaties or any other voice of moderation. 'A better man than I took the abuse of the crowd,' he ranted, waving his hands and stabbing the air as though he were addressing a crowd at a Nuremberg rally. 'And *he* ended up nailed to a cross . . .'

'Now look here . . .' Andrew Skrimshaw exclaimed, stepping into the fray and receiving a blinding punch from one of the Brigadier's flailing fists. As he staggered back, holding his head, the Brigadier turned his venom in his direction.

'Funny how you church wallahs don't even like to have our Lord and Saviour mentioned nowadays, isn't it? You're all too busy promoting women and protecting nasty little fairies – like this . . . this . . .' he was almost at a loss for words, so acute was his disgust, 'this . . . putrid specimen of filth . . .'

'Come away, Selwyn. Please,' Rosemary implored.

'I haven't finished . . .'

'SILENCE!' Miss Fallon bellowed – using the decibels that had once won her the position of headmistress. She strode down the hall and came up on to the stage.

'Yes! For Christ's sake!' Bless screamed. Then he bobbed apologetically. 'Sorry, Vicar . . .'

'Don't worry about it,' Andrew assured him.

'Oh, no!' the Brigadier sneered. 'The vicar won't mind if you blaspheme . . .'

'Brigadier. You have said quite enough,' Miss Fallon thundered.

'And you're a wizened old prune!' he replied.

'You . . . swine!' she gasped. And she slapped his cheek, surprisingly hard, making him step back in amazement.

'Yeah! Good on yer!' the boys at the back screamed. 'Go for his goolies!'

'This is getting silly!' Bless yelled. 'We must all calm down!'

'Let the poof have a say!' a voice called.

'Please, ladies and gentlemen!' Heather bellowed.

'I am very angry!' Miss Fallon stormed, shaking and nursing her hand, which was still smarting from contact with the Brigadier's cheek.

'You're lucky! I never strike a woman!' he fumed, still reeling from the blow.

'Just SHUT UP, all of you!' Bless screamed, stamping his feet.

'Silence for the poof!' a voice at the back shouted, and then others joined in, all chanting: 'Silence for the poof! Silence for the poof! Silence for the poof!'

A lot of shushing followed, and gradually the crowd settled down and everyone seemed to be looking at Bless. 'Look,

Brigadier . . .' he said, vamping till ready. He hadn't actually got a clue what he was going to say.

'Well?' his opponent snarled.

'What is it I'm supposed to have done? I've become your neighbour, yes. But I don't play loud music. I don't keep you awake at night or . . . break your windows . . .'

'Oh, you make yourself seem so virtuous, don't you? So reasonable . . .'

'You don't like me because I'm in love with a man,' Bless said.

'Did you hear that, ladies and gentlemen? Did you hear? He's in love with another man!'

'Well he's a poof, isn't he?' some reasonable voice shouted.

'Is that the type I fought the war for? Is that the type you really want living in our beautiful village?'

'Did he say he was in love with a *man*?' Bessie Sugar hissed to her sister.

'Oh, that's not the 'alf of it, dear. The things I know . . .'

'Fancy!' Bessie Sugar pondered. Then she grinned. 'He must be bleeding mad! Still, you rarely find people who live together still on speaking terms nowadays, do you? So, good luck to you, lovey!' she called.

'Thank you very much! Brigadier – what we do inside the house has nothing to do with you. This isn't the Third Reich!'

'Sieg heil! Sieg heil! Sieg heil!' the skinheads yelled, and then collapsed in a heap of uncontrollable laughter.

'Hey!' Carlotta bellowed, charging at them. 'No fascisti! Or you mix with ME!'

'Carlotta, dear!' Lavinia waved to her. 'Time we were going home.'

'Yes! Time we were all going,' Barry in computers said, pushing Melanie towards the aisle.

'Move, Simon!' she muttered. 'I think a quick getaway is called for. Those kids from the council estate are looking for trouble . . .'

This now seemed to be the general consensus of opinion,

and many of the audience started scrambling towards the aisle, knocking chairs in their rush and tripping over each other.

Simon was swept along in the throng but was desperately trying to turn round at the same time. 'Where's Sandra?' he shouted. 'We mustn't leave Sandra . . .'

'Just keep moving, Simon,' Melanie told him, pushing him ahead of her still. 'She'll be all right. She's behind Barry.'

But in fact Sandra was stuck behind Miss Bridey who was unable to move very fast because Miss Hopkirk was in front of her and kept being knocked sideways by the crush.

The crowd at the door was excessive as people elbowed their way clear of the entrance, and some of the youths started getting aggressive and threw a punch or two, just to show who was boss.

Mr Asquith was still on the stage – but under the table. The vicar and the Daltrys were all shouting and trying to control the hysterical crowd. Mrs Day and Mrs Sugar meanwhile had turned round and were sitting on the front of the stage, thoroughly enjoying watching the pandemonium.

'It's like VE night, Doris.'

Slowly the hall emptied and those still inside could hear the sounds of skirmish continuing in the street.

Sandra was trapped behind a pile of chairs, and as she pushed her way clear, she felt a warm hand take hold of her and pull her to the aisle. 'Hey, baby!' Carlotta whispered in her ear. 'I was searching for you.'

'I tripped and fell,' Sandra gasped. She felt quite shaky – but whether from her accident or because of the closeness of her admirer, she couldn't be sure.

'I stayed to help you,' Carlotta explained. 'I was afraid the fascisti might get you.'

'I must go!' Sandra stammered, hurrying to the door.

'Wait for me.'

'No! My husband will be worried . . .'

'You won't even say thank you?' Carlotta asked, spreading her hands in a dejected way.

'Yes, of course . . . I mean . . .' Sandra felt an uncontrollable urge to reach out and touch her saviour. 'I must go!' she panted, overwhelmed with emotions that she didn't dare to recognise, and turning, she ran for the door.

'Will I see you again?' Carlotta called, running after her.

'Yes. No. Maybe,' Sandra stammered, disappearing out of the door.

'I wait for you . . .' Carlotta called, following her.

'Your gent seems very passionate, Doris!' Bessie Sugar remarked, watching with open mouth.

'He is not my gent!' her sister protested.

'I'm going home, Rosemary,' the Brigadier announced, walking stiffly towards the steps.

'I must apologise for my husband,' Rosemary said in a strong, cold voice.

'Don't worry about it,' Bless said, feeling embarrassed and almost sorry for the man.

'I have always worried about him,' Rosemary said. 'But not any more. Not any more, Selwyn,' she shouted, as she watched him walk slowly away up the aisle. Her voice was hard and filled with a sensation that was new to her.

'Are you all right?' Bless asked her.

'Oh, I'm fine,' she replied. 'Just fine . . .'

'All this'll be forgotten in a week. You'll see.'

'Not by me. Not this time. Neither forgotten nor forgiven. I have no forgiveness left.' She smiled. 'Believe it or not – but his sister is a very nice woman!' she said, and she started to laugh. 'Oh, if people only knew! If they only knew the half of it . . .!' And still laughing she went up the aisle and out of the door.

'Well!' Tony Daltry exclaimed.

'Shall I come out now?' Mr Asquith asked.

Bless leaned over and gave the poor man a hand, pulling him up on to his feet.

'Just like VE night,' Bessie Sugar told them. 'But then it was the drink. Don't know what caused this one . . .'

'Two gentlemen, sharing, dear!' Doris said. 'It's always the way when something new comes in and disturbs the peace. Gawd! You remember when the Martins got their combine harvester! There was fighting in the street.'

'I think we should all go home,' the vicar announced.

'Yes. But first . . .' Tony Daltry said, holding up a hand, 'I think we should at least say welcome to . . . It's Mr Hudson, is it?'

'I am a person of many names!' Bless said, wearily.

'Take no notice of the Brigadier . . .'

'He's got a screw loose, dear!' Doris Day announced. 'I've always known that. But his sister – what a lady! If only she could live at Cockpits – that'd really give the village a boost.'

41

Ill Met By Moonlight . . .

Laurence would have liked a long post-mortem. But after they'd both had a drink, sitting in the drawing room with the curtains open and only a couple of lamps lit, Bless suddenly felt overwhelmingly tired.

'Yes! You're right,' Laurence said, taking pity on the boy. 'Bed! Everything will look better in the morning.'

Bless checked that the back door was locked, and by the time he returned to the hall, Laurence was already halfway up the stairs. 'I was quite impressed,' he announced.

'By what?' Bless asked, following him.

'You.'

'Steady, Laurence! Don't go out of character! It's too late and I'm too exhausted to make the adjustment.'

'I thought you stood up to him rather well.' They were both now on the landing. 'I liked what you said. What right has anyone to censure other people's behaviour? So long as they do whatever it is they're going to do in private and so long as they're both consenting . . .'

'Go to bed, Laurence.'

'Yes. I'm tired . . .'

'And anyway,' Bless added, crossing to his door, 'why should we have to do it in private? If the hets can kiss and cuddle in the park – then so can we.'

'Kiss and cuddle?' Laurence said the words with the greatest distaste. 'You are, I am afraid, a relentlessly suburban child.'

Bless grinned and waved to him. 'Thank God! I was beginning to think I'd have to start liking you.'

'Heaven forbid!' Laurence shuddered, then went into his room and closed the door.

Bless switched off the hall and landing lights and went into his own room. Moonlight filtered through the big, semicircular window, filling the place with light and shade and dark, fathomless corners. He stripped off his clothes and went to the bathroom for a pee. He cleaned his teeth in the dark and splashed cold water on his face.

He was ridiculously tired and oddly depressed. He hadn't enjoyed any of it really, though he should have done, he argued. He had, in a way, scored a few points; the Brigadier hadn't even turned out to be much of an opponent. But in the end, where was the victory? The man still loathed him and would continue to do so. Loathed him for what? For being . . . himself; for being natural to his own . . . inclinations.

He wandered back to the window and stared out into the moon-drenched garden. Why did some people always want everyone to conform to their standards? Why couldn't they allow for a world made wonderful by all its rich diversity? He had a sudden picture in his mind of Carlotta – looking rare and exotic in a pair of silk pyjamas. Thank God, he thought, for the Carlottas of this world! Eccentric? Possibly. Unusual? Certainly. But kind and fun and well intentioned. If God, sitting on his throne at the judgement day, had to choose between Carlotta and the Brigadier – there'd be no contest, surely? 'I'll take Carlotta,' the Almighty would say. 'At least with her I can look forward to a bit of laughter in Paradise. I may have created you all in my image,' He would announce, 'but I'm having a rethink about the Brigadier model. Self-righteousness and narrow-mindedness were a terrible mistake. Next time round, I shall reject them . . .'

Bless nodded at the night. 'That's what I think, anyway!' he said out loud. Then he added: 'Amen!' for good measure and, prayers over, he crossed and climbed into bed.

As he was drifting off to sleep he had a clear picture of another of God's more triumphant experiments. Antonio, the Hunk, slid into his dreaming mind. Slowly and carefully Bless stripped him of his T-shirt and then, with commendable restraint, he started on the fly buttons of the jeans, loosening them one by one. At first he thought it might be sexy to have Antonio wearing no briefs, then he dallied with a pair of black Calvin Kleins, the new ones with the pouch front – the Braganizio tackle would fill them out in an awesome way. Or a jockstrap might be rugged? A kind of instant eroticism . . . Or maybe just plain white Y-fronts? Very boyish and locker room? A pair of boring boxers? But two sizes too small . . .

'Brad?' a voice whispered.

Bless opened his eyes. He was not alone! The Hunk's swelling underwear flickered and vanished from his mind. 'Antonio?' he whispered.

'Brad?' the voice said again.

Bless reached out towards the other side of the bed and contacted firm, human muscle. Oh, Jesus! 'Antonio!' he cried, turning and grabbing the all too solid flesh on the bed beside him.

'Brad?' his sleeping companion said, waking with a start.

Bless sat up and switched on his bedside lamp.

Rich sat up a moment later, looking tousled and tanned.

'Who the hell's Antonio?' he said.

'Who the hell is Brad?'

'Where have you been?' Rich demanded.

'Who is Brad?'

'I don't know what you're talking about . . . Where have you been?'

'What are you doing here?'

'I live here.'

'You could have fooled me!' Bless spat the words and swung his legs over the side of the bed, turning his back.

'So! "Welcome home, Rich!"'

'You just . . . turn up. I haven't heard from you for days . . .'

'The phone has been permanently engaged!'

'Not for the last twenty-four hours . . .'

'Hey!' Rich said gently, putting a hand on his naked back. 'Truce?'

'Fuck off, Rich!' Bless shrugged the hand away.

'I've taken three different airlines and come in via Rome – just because I wanted to be with you.'

'Oh, really? Since when did I get the name Brad?'

'Since about the same time you gave me the name Antonio . . .'

Silence.

'Come to bed lover.'

'Hmmm!'

'Bless . . .'

'Hmmm!'

'Please . . .'

'Well . . .' He slowly turned and slid back under the sheet. 'Only because I'm tired.'

Rich slipped a hand under Bless's waist and pulled him across the bed into the warm bit where he'd been sleeping. 'That's better!' He sighed contentedly.

'So?' Bless couldn't let it go. 'Who is . . .'

'Brad?' Rich finished the sentence for him. Then he yawned. 'He's a sort of West Coast fantasy who happens to be mad for my body.'

'Oh, really? You just wait till you meet Antonio – who is demented about mine.'

'Go to sleep!' Rich murmured, and he put his head into the crook of Bless's neck and did just that.

42

The Morning After The Night Before

Bless and Rich rose late the following morning, and when they did they both carefully avoided asking each other the questions of the previous night. Putting on dressing gowns and without bothering to wash, they went down to the kitchen, where they discovered Laurence, munching through a large pile of bran flakes and looking disapproving.

'Have you any idea what time it is?' were the words with which he greeted Bless, who came in first. 'Almost midday. Those wretched bells have been silent for hours. I had thought, after last night, that we should have put in an appearance at church . . .'

'Laurence, shut up! I've got a surprise for you . . .' And at that moment the surprise walked in.

Laurence seemed less impressed by Rich's return than Rich was by his presence. 'Ah! You're back!' was his only welcome.

Whereas Rich was obviously disconcerted to see his friend sitting at the table. 'Bless! You should have told me he was here. I'm really sorry, Laurence. We could have been down ages ago . . .'

'I can't imagine what you've been doing,' Laurence fumed. Then, seeing their sideways looks, he did begin to imagine and decided to say no more.

After a brief, polite exchange – 'How are you, Laurence?' 'I am far from happy. I'm stranded here, without a car.' 'Oh really? What happened?' 'Don't even ask . . .' – Rich filled a kettle at the sink.

'Sunday!' he yawned, crossing to the Aga and waiting there for it to boil. He stretched and scratched his head. 'I can't believe it's only a week since I got that call from Sol. Seems a lifetime! New York was mad. My feet never touched the ground. Then LA!' He groaned and shook his head. 'God, I hate LA! But . . .' He paused dramatically. 'We've done a deal. Spit twice and knock on wood, there *will* be a movie of *Manhattan Bohème*! That's the good news. The bad news is it won't be starring either Alison or Justin.' He groaned again and yawned at the same time, stretching and rubbing his hands through his hair. 'God! You know what actors are like! They'll both go into a monumental sulk and I'll have their agents on the phone for hours!'

He chattered on in this vein as he made tea and searched for the bread and opened all the wrong drawers looking for cutlery and behaved like a visitor in the house. Bless sat at the table and watched him and let his talk wash over him. He felt strangely unreal. It was as if a whole lifetime had gone by since he and Rich were last together. When they woke, lying in each other's arms, they'd made love like a one-night stand – and even now they were more like strangers than lovers . . .

But who is the actual stranger? Bless thought, with increasing glumness. It was Rich's signature on the deeds of the house; Rich owned the bread knife; indirectly, he'd even bought the bread. This disturbing fact – that Rich was keeping him – had been ducked quite successfully by Bless while they were apart. But now, with Rich back in the house, it was horribly obvious that it was he who really belonged there. It was, after all, his house; it was his kettle on the Aga; his money in the bank . . .

'Bless?' he heard a voice calling, and struggling up out of the pit of misery into which he'd sunk, he discovered Rich staring at him.

'What?'

'Has it been dull for you?' Rich repeated the question for the third time.

'Dull? When? Where?'

'Here. While I've been gone.' Bless just stared at him, unable really to comprehend what he was being asked. 'What's up with you?' Rich exclaimed, irritably. 'I don't think you've listened to a word I've been saying!'

'My dear Richard!' Laurence spluttered, coming to Bless's rescue. 'You think you've been busy? Hollywood couldn't begin to compete with life in Bellingford . . .'

And, on cue, the front door bell rang.

'I'll go,' Bless said, getting up.

'It's all right,' Rich said, still sounding cross. And he strode to his door and went out into his hall as if underlining the fact that it was he who owned the place.

Or was Bless being paranoid now? He watched him go with an increasing sense of gloom. Then, turning, he discovered Laurence looking at him. He shrugged and smiled, hoping to hide his depression. 'He won't know who anyone is,' he said.

Laurence frowned. 'Just give everything time to settle down,' he advised, pouring himself tea.

Bless walked over and looked out of the window into the stable yard. Then he sighed. Behind him, Laurence glanced up, hearing the sound.

The old man sniffed uneasily. 'What you both need is a bit of time on your own,' he observed, speaking quietly.

But such luxury was not to be.

'It's a Mr and Mrs Daltry,' Rich announced, coming back into the room. 'They're asking for you, Bless . . .' Then he lowered his voice, raised his eyebrows enquiringly and whispered, 'I've put them in the drawing room – we can't ask them in here.'

'Oh, shit! What do they want?' Bless hissed.

'You!' Rich repeated. 'They were quite insistent.'

'Well – you come with me, Rich,' Bless said, going out of the room.

'You're both still in dressing gowns!' Laurence exclaimed, rising and following them with a superior air and all the confidence that a full set of clothes can bestow.

Heather Daltry was standing by the window, looking out into the garden, and Tony was hovering and looking embarrassed in the centre of the room. 'I say!' he exclaimed as they entered. 'We've come at an awkward moment . . .'

'No. Please don't worry. I only flew in from the States yesterday, and we were having a lazy morning . . .' Rich explained.

'This is a heavenly house,' Heather said, turning graciously and in full control of the situation. 'It's my fault we're here, Mr . . .?'

'Charteris. Richard Charteris.'

'I expect your little friend has told you about last night?' she said, beaming at Bless and oblivious to the cruel cut of the diminutive. 'Mr Hudson was an absolute *hero*!'

Rich looked hopelessly confused. 'Who's Mr Hudson?' he asked. Bless managed to smile weakly. Then he blushed.

'Yes! He did do pretty well, didn't he?' Laurence conceded, looking at him and feeling generous.

'Pretty well?' Heather cried. 'It was the talk of the village at morning service.'

'It wasn't that impressive!' Bless stammered.

'Not impressive! You took on Brigadier Jerrold – single-handed! Like David and Goliath!'

'What's been happening?' Rich asked.

'Later, dear boy!' Laurence murmured.

'You mean you don't know? You haven't been told?'

'We mustn't keep these good people, Heather . . .' Tony interrupted her.

'No. Of course. But you be sure, Mr Charteris, that they give you a full and detailed report. You missed quite a shindig . . .'

'Heather!' Tony said firmly.

'Yes, all right!' she snapped. Then she beamed at Bless. 'We just popped in on our way home – to say well done, and to . . . ask you – all of you – to dinner . . .?'

'Oh, thank you . . .'

'Perhaps next weekend would suit?' As she was speaking, a figure appeared outside on the terrace behind her, gesticulating wildly.

'There's a man out there!' Rich said, crossing towards the window.

'Woman, old boy!' Tony Daltry murmured. 'She's a woman.'

'She's Italian!' Heather added, turning and seeing Carlotta, as if giving her nationality explained her outlandish appearance. Today she was wearing a pair of white cricket trousers as Bermuda shorts, a charcoal-grey waistcoat with no shirt under it, and she'd tied a silk square over her head, like a pirate.

'Is me!' she announced, as soon as Rich opened the window. 'I've brought Signorina Olganina.' She turned, with a flourish, revealing Lavinia in a full-skirted dress and a battered picture hat, standing further along the terrace. She had her back to them and was surveying the garden.

'Mrs Sparton!' Heather said, ever the hostess – even when not in her own house. 'It's good to see you out and about so much!'

'This place!' Lavinia croaked, hoarse with emotion. 'The weeping willows, the glint of water from the brook. The matchless lawns . . .'

'Yes, yes!' Bless agreed, irritably. He was beginning to feel sick of this constant round of entertaining – people popping in and out of the house as if it were an emotional supermarket. He longed for a bit of time entirely on his own.

'To create a garden is a great gift,' Lavinia sighed.

'Oh, it wasn't me, dear!' Bless flapped a hand at the view. 'Tom . . . something or other . . . You've heard of Old Tom? He does the garden . . .'

Lavinia shrugged petulantly. 'He used to do mine. But he had to go. He got "ideas" . . . I do not pay staff to have ideas. But this place . . .' Her voice returned to its former rapture. 'What a setting for the Dying Swan. What boskage for *Giselle* – Act Two . . .' And lifting her arms above her head, she gradually rose up on to – well, almost on to – the tips of her toes.

'Hey!' Carlotta grinned and looked round at the others for appreciation. 'She's still . . .' she nipped her thumb and fore-finger and searched for the epigram '. . . the knees of a bee!'

'Mrs Sparton used to be a dancer,' Heather explained to Rich – whose face was expressing a confusion fast approaching breaking point.

Then the front door bell sounded again, out in the hall. Only Laurence seemed to notice it.

'But do forgive me, gentle people!' Lavinia cried, coming out of her reverie. 'We come bearing messages!' She turned now and discovered Bless and Rich standing near her. 'You, young man, did very well . . .'

Laurence, realising someone should answer the door, went himself, leaving Lavinia in full spate.

'We must never be daunted by the cruel jibes of the ignorant! Is this your chum?' she asked, suddenly changing the subject and peering at Rich. He, taken by surprise, looked aghast and backed away. He didn't like too much attention – and certainly not with an audience watching. 'I have, over the years,' Lavinia continued, pursuing him to a corner and then standing very close, 'had many good friendships with boys like you.' She shrugged. 'They were usually in the chorus. I was too big a star to risk fraternising with my partners. In our profession intimacy can seriously endanger one's work. If one is having a relationship which leads to a quarrel – as all relationship invari-ably do – one's partner is not to be trusted. For a dancer not to trust her partner is to risk being dropped from a great height.' She threw her hands in the air and let them fall, slapping against her thighs. 'Catastrophe!' She smiled and grasped Rich's hand. 'I trust we are going to be the greatest of friends. You have a charming face. So virile! I will invite you to my comeback.'

'Thank you very much,' Rich muttered.

Lavinia patted his hand and turned and looked once more across the lawn. 'Yes! Indeed I will!' she said, thoughtfully.

'The Brigadier's wife has arrived,' Laurence announced,

coming back into the room, and as he spoke, Rosemary Jerrold appeared behind him in the doorway.

'Oh!' she exclaimed, looking distraught. 'You have visitors. You didn't say . . .'

'We're just going, Mrs Jerrold,' Tony Daltry said. 'Come on, Heather . . .'

'How are you this morning, Mrs Jerrold?' Heather asked, holding her ground and refusing to budge, even though Tony was pulling her by the hand.

'I am quite well, thank you.'

'And the Brigadier?'

'Heather!'

'We're bound to ask! We can't all go around pretending last evening didn't take place.'

'I utterly agree, Mrs Daltry!' Lavinia announced, looking haughty. 'A regrettable event has occurred. We must confront it.'

'Hello!' a voice called from the hall. 'Hello there!'

'Not more people?' Rich groaned.

'It's Miss Fallon,' Heather said. Then she called: 'We're in the drawing room, Miss Fallon.'

'Not disturbing you, are we?' Miss Fallon, the tall one, asked, coming in, followed by the short one and then the fat one. 'Your front door was wide open and we could hear voices . . .'

'Oh, Mrs Jerrold!' Edna Bridey exclaimed. Then she covered her mouth with a hand and looked away.

'How is your sister-in-law?' Laurence asked, turning to Rosemary and trying to distract her from all the embarrassed, staring eyes that surrounded her.

'My sister-in-law?' Rosemary gasped, nervously.

'She still with you?'

'No. No.' The poor woman seemed in great distress. 'No,' she repeated for a third time.

'Ah!' Laurence sighed, obviously running out of conversation.

'Would anyone like a . . . coffee?' Rich asked, knotting the cord more firmly round his dressing gown. 'Or a drink, perhaps?'

'No,' Miss Hopkirk assured him. 'We simply called to see that Mr Hudson was all right.'

'Yes, I'm fine. Really I am,' Bless blurted nervously.

'Who is Mr Hudson?' Rich asked, not for the first time. One or two of the others looked at him and smiled, almost pityingly, he thought.

'We . . . we decided to come to . . . to give you our support,' Miss Hopkirk hurried on. 'We did, didn't we, Marjorie?'

'Absolutely,' Miss Fallon barked.

'Of course, we didn't expect . . .'

Again they were all looking at Rosemary.

'Why are you here, Mrs Jerrold?' Heather Daltry asked her.

'Perhaps you have a message from your husband?' Miss Fallon suggested.

'No. I have no message from Selwyn,' Rosemary told them. She looked in anguish.

'It's all right, honestly it is,' Bless said quietly, and he took hold of her hand.

Rosemary Jerrold shook her head. 'It isn't all right,' she said. 'It really isn't . . . I came to apologise . . .'

'You have nothing to apologise for,' Bless told her, still holding her hand. Then he looked round at the others. 'Mrs Jerrold was going to be a concert pianist,' he said, speaking too fast because he was embarrassed for her. 'Did any of you know that? Laurence and I have been lucky enough to hear her play . . .'

'Please don't . . .' the poor woman whispered. 'You're embarrassing me . . .'

'You play piano?' Carlotta cut in.

'Only a little . . .'

'You want money?'

'I beg your pardon?'

'I pay good money for a pianist. We will discuss this . . .'

'I'll come back when you're less busy,' Rosemary murmured to Bless.

'Don't worry! We're going now,' Tony Daltry said, literally dragging his wife towards the door.

'Yes! So are we!' Miss Fallon agreed hurriedly.

There was now a nervous exodus as they all felt they should make themselves scarce. Laurence got caught in the surge and ended up seeing everyone to the front door.

'I must go as well,' Rosemary said. Then she hesitated and turned to Bless. 'Mr Hudson, I wanted you to know that I don't . . . I do not . . . share my husband's sentiments . . . Oh, this is useless!' she cried, and she went out of the window and hurried across the lawn.

'Where are you going?' Bless called after her.

'There is a back gate,' she answered, without looking round. 'I could not face the street . . .' and she darted away into the trees at the back of the lawn.

'Goodbye, lovely boys!' Lavinia was saying. 'You will be at my comeback, won't you? It will only be very small. Not many people will be there and it won't be a long programme . . .'

'Small is beautiful!' Carlotta told her, helping her towards the hall door. 'Hey, baby!' she called, looking back at Bless. 'You see anything of Antonio?'

'Antonio?' Rich asked, his eyes swivelling round to Bless.

'No!' he replied, weakly, and he shrugged. 'I haven't seen him for ages.'

'People keep disappearing,' Carlotta grumbled, as she and Lavinia went out into the hall. 'I never did find Diana! Still, there are other kippers in the sea . . .'

'My God!' Bless shrieked as soon as she was out of earshot. 'Diana!' And turning, he ran out of the room and across the grass in the direction of the summerhouse.

When Laurence returned he discovered Rich sitting on the arm of one of the sofas, looking utterly crushed. 'What has been going on, Laurence?' he groaned.

'Well now,' Laurence replied, with a grim smile. 'If you've got several hours to spare I'll tell you as much as I know . . .'

Then Bless returned, ashen-faced.

'She's gone!' he gibbered, his hands flapping in his agitation. 'She's just . . . disappeared into thin air. Oh, this is entirely my fault. I just forgot about her . . .'

'Who has?' Rich asked, trying not to catch his hysteria.

'Diana – from the summerhouse loft. She could have starved to death by now . . .'

'Look, please! Bless!' Rich snapped, losing control and holding up both his hands. 'Just begin at the beginning . . .'

'The beginning? Oh, Christ! I can scarcely recall the beginning. You see . . . Diana was upstairs, with the vicar – she was being exorcised – and then Carlotta arrived . . .'

'What?' Rich gasped. 'Exorcised?'

'Yes. It's too complicated to go into now. She thought she'd been raped by the devil . . .'

'What?' Rich yelled. 'Bless! What the fuck are you talking about?'

'I told you it was complicated. You see – Diana joined a commune in the south of France . . .'

'I should sit down, old chap!' Laurence advised Rich. 'And I'll pour you a stiff drink. In fact I'll have one too. I only know a fraction of all this myself . . .'

43

Invitations

The Contessa Carlotta da Braganizio
cordially invites you
to
THE HALL HOUSE
BELLINGFORD

for an evening of Italian hospitality
to mark the triumphant return

of

LAVINIA OLGANINA
prima ballerina assoluta

Sunday, August 2nd
7.00 for 7.30 p.m.
the performance will commence promptly at 7.45 p.m.
carriages at 9.00

RSVP
Contessa da Braganizio
The Towers
Bellingford

'It's that blessed foreigner,' Bessie Sugar said, staring at the invitation. As she spoke she scooped jelly from one of her special cooked hams into the crook of her finger and sucked it thoughtfully.

'I shall be there, of course, on account of being part of the 'ousehold,' Doris Day told her. She'd called in at the shop early, expressly to show off her own invitation, and was a bit miffed to discover that her sister had also received one.

'What does it mean "Eyetalian 'ospitality"?' Bessie asked, looking suspicious.

'Oh, I can tell you precisely!' Doris replied, with a superior toss of her hair. (The shingle was growing out. Without Miss Phyllis at Cockpits there didn't seem any cause to go to the expense of keeping it styled.) 'I was there in the house when it was being discussed with Mr 'Udson.'

'And you listened in, did you, Doris?'

'I couldn't 'elp over'earing,' she corrected in a lofty tone.

'Go on then,' her sister prompted her, glowering. She hated it when her sister had cause to be superior.

'Well, I'm not so sure as I should divulge a confidence . . .'

'Oh, bleedin' 'ell, Doris!' Bessie snapped. 'It's 'ardly national security, is it?'

'Wine and biscuits.' Doris mouthed the words, looking towards the door for fear of eavesdroppers.

'Pardon?'

'That's what's to be served – wine and biscuits. 'Parently its the done thing in Eyetaly.'

'Wine and biscuits?' Bessie spluttered. 'They call that 'ospitality? What's wrong with sausages on sticks and vol-au-vents, then? Foreigners! Taking over our lovely olde Englishe ways. We don't go serving wine and biscuits . . .' She squeezed the last drop of scorn from the words. 'Not at a *function*. That's not how we behave . . .'

'I 'ave to say, I'm surprised you're invited, Bessie.'

'That fella of yours – the Ey-tiddly-Eytie – he brought the invite in 'imself . . .'

'So who's this Contessa, then?'

'Well, if you're in the know,' her sister said spitefully, 'I'm surprised you haven't found that out by now.'

'Matter of fact, Bessie, I find the whole thing . . . beyond me,' Doris confided. 'I haven't a clue what's going on.'

'Oo-er! Sand! Have you seen?'

Melanie had rushed straight round with her invitation, the minute she'd found it sticking through the letter box. She discovered Sandra sitting in the kitchen, with her creative writing spread out on the table in front of her.

'What?' Sandra asked, coming out of an artistic trance.

'This!' Melanie exclaimed, waving the invitation in her face.

'Oh, yes!' Sandra replied, with wide-eyed innocence. 'Simon and I received our invitation this morning.'

'Will you be going?'

'We haven't had time to discuss it yet.'

'I doubt it'll be Barry's slice of pie!' Melanie joked, surprised by Sandra's apparent lack of interest. 'Imagine that! Your dyke – she only turns out to be a Contessa . . .'

'Don't call her that, Melanie!' Sandra protested.

'Why?'

'Well – it isn't kind, is it?'

'So what should I call her, then?'

'She's a woman, Melanie,' Sandra told her, emotion trembling on her voice. 'A woman – just like any of us.'

'But she isn't, is she? For start-off, she's not going to get her kit off with Barry is she? She's going to get it off with *you*.'

'Keep your voice down,' Sandra hissed, looking instinctively over her shoulder.

'Well! Honestly! I do know what a woman is . . . as it happens! I am a full-blooded woman myself – in case you failed to notice, Sandra! – with all a woman's urges. And women don't dress up in dungarees and go roaring round the country on a bike.'

'You are so stereotypical, Melanie!'

'Oh really? And what the hell does that mean?'

'You put people into categories . . .'

'Ooh! Sand! You make me spit sometimes. For God's sake – speak English.'

'I just mean . . . There are all sorts in the world. I mean – you said yourself you quite like the . . . you know. The chap who had a go at the Brigadier . . .'

'The poof, yes?'

'Melanie!'

'Look, Miss High-and-mighty-writer! If I call them poof and dyke it's no different to calling that . . . that . . . that fridge-freezer a fridge-freezer. Is it?'

'A fridge-freezer doesn't have feelings, Melanie.'

'But it's what it is, for pete's sake!' Melanie's voice rose to a shriek of exasperation. 'It's what they are . . .'

Sandra flinched at the volume of her friend's voice, but she stayed very calm. 'All right, then. How would you like it if I went about calling you "that thirty-seven-year-old housewife"? How would that feel, Melanie?'

There was a long pause

'I'm not thirty-seven.'

'Very nearly.'

'Not kind, Sand!'

'No! Not kind at all, Mel!'

'Are you gone on her, is that it? The dyke, are you?'

'Melanie! Stop it!' Sandra sounded quite cross at the thought. 'Of course I'm not!' But as she spoke she carefully covered the open notebook in front of her with a sheet of blotting paper. There on the page, her hero Grayson Manderlay had only that morning been transformed into Gloria Manderlay. And Samantha Betterton, her heroine, was wrestling with terrible doubts as she contemplated the enormity of the emotions that were stirring in her heart.

'No one will expect you to go,' Rosemary Jerrold said, speaking over her shoulder as she collected her handbag from the hall stand.

In the kitchen her husband, the Brigadier, held up the invitation like evidence in court. 'This envelope is addressed to me. Well, to both of us – but principally to me. See, here!' He read out in a clipped voice: '"Brigadier and Mrs S. Jerrold". That seems clear enough to me . . .'

'It's only out of politeness, Selwyn. No one will actually want you there. In fact your presence would undoubtedly spoil the occasion.'

'I am invited!' the man raved.

'You are held in contempt, Selwyn,' his wife said, speaking with a slow, clear delivery, almost as though she were dictating to him. 'You always have been. But since your behaviour at the road show you have also become the laughing stock of this village. I assure you that there is no one who would want you anywhere near a gathering they were arranging.'

'Very well then!' the Brigadier fumed, losing his temper. 'Neither of us shall go.'

Rosemary turned and looked at him. 'Oh, I will be there,' she said, a note of triumph creeping into her voice. 'I have already told you that. I will not only be there, I will be performing . . .'

'I want this nonsense to STOP!' the Brigadier shouted.

His wife stared coldly and smiled. 'I am not in the slightest bit interested in what you want, Selwyn. I thought you knew that. I'm going to the Towers now. I will be gone all day . . .'

'Playing piano for a geriatric freak!'

'Your cold ham is in the larder . . .'

'Rosemary! I forbid you to leave this house!'

His wife turned and stared at him again. There was contempt in her eyes and not the fear that he was accustomed to seeing there. With a roar, he launched himself across the room towards her, raising his hand. But Rosemary stood her ground and did not flinch, and at the last moment he pulled back, breathing in short gasps and shaking.

'If you strike me,' she said, speaking with chilling calm, 'I will go to the police. If you kill me, my friends will have you put away for life . . .'

The Brigadier lowered his hand and went back into the kitchen. 'We can't go on like this,' he said, speaking morosely.

'Then let Phyllis come back . . .'

'Rosemary!' he cried out, as though the very suggestion caused him pain.

'It is the only possible solution,' she continued. 'Phyllis and I get on very well . . .'

'I forbid you to mention that woman in this house . . .'

'Oh, Selwyn! All that fuss and fume! It doesn't mean a thing. Just go away. Let Phyllis come here to live. And you . . . go away.' She repeated the words with greater emphasis. Then she added, 'When that happens, you and I need never meet again,' and without saying another word, she went out of the front door and walked away down the drive with her back to him, so that he couldn't see how much she was shaking.

'She's not coming back!' the Brigadier shouted, appearing at the door. 'You hear me? However much you plead – you'll never see her again. Not ever!' he screamed. 'Never, never, never . . .'

Rosemary Jerrold started to run, and she didn't stop until she was halfway across the Green and his voice had faded into the distance behind her. Then, taking a handkerchief from her pocket, she dabbed at her brow and pulled her skirt down over her buttocks. Straightening her back, she continued to walk resolutely and her steps grew ever more confident as she welcomed the rest of the day with increasing enthusiasm. Playing Saint-Saëns as accompaniment to an elderly dancer might present problems – it caused havoc with the tempo – but at least it took her mind off her own affairs.

'Will it be suitable for a vicar?' Margaret Skrimshaw asked as she handed the invitation back to her husband.

'As far as I can gather, it will only be a little ballet and light refreshments. That can hardly be described as an orgy, Margaret!'

'Then go, dear.'

'If you will come?'

'Of course!'

'If you will come – gladly.'

'Ah!'

'It might even be fun.'

'I don't trust "fun", Andrew.'

Her husband sighed and looked down at his hands, unable any longer to meet her accusing eyes.

'Why?' he asked eventually, when he couldn't bear the silence any longer. 'What *is* your problem? Please, just tell me.'

She saw him sitting opposite her across the table. He seemed so distressed that for a moment she wanted to reach out and comfort him. Then he bit his lip and smoothed his hands and assumed his air of studied control, and the moment passed.

'What is my problem?' she said. She smiled. 'Are you sure you have time to hear my answer, Andrew? I know how booked up you get.'

The vicar glanced at his watch. 'Yes, of course. I'm not expected at the PCC until this evening, and although I have my sermon to prepare for Sunday . . .' He hesitated, seeing her smile harden into an expression approaching a scowl. 'Please, Margaret,' he begged. 'Just . . . speak to me . . .'

She stared for a moment longer. Was her expression disbelief? Or could it have been . . . dislike? Loathing, even? He didn't know. He was almost past caring. Then, as he watched, she rose and walked over to the sink.

'I must . . . wash up,' she said, wearily.

'Margaret!' he pleaded, the name coming out as a sob.

'What is my problem?' she spoke quietly, with her back to him. 'I have two children who are strangers to me. I have to remind myself that they even exist. And I have a husband who converses with an old gentleman in the sky, who quite clearly isn't there. And you ask what my problem is?'

'I happen to believe in the old gentleman,' Andrew said quietly.

His wife turned and looked at him. Then she shook her head. 'Believe? On what evidence?'

'On the evidence of my heart,' he replied.

'I had hoped there was a place there for me.'

'There is,' he gasped, scrambling up and hurrying towards her. 'But – you shut me out, Margaret.'

She looked at him for a moment longer, a thoughtful, questioning look, then turning her back once more she continued: 'And this belief, your belief, Andrew, requires of me that should clean brass and arrange flowers for an archaic institution that offends my reason and should, in my opinion, have died out with the dinosaurs? I have no legitimate personality of my own. I am an appendage. I am 'the vicar's wife' – or 'Mrs Vicar' even,' she added with contempt. 'I have a two-one in history. I was considered one of the bright hopes of my year. I was going to be someone. But instead I married you . . . and I ceased to exist. Can you really seriously ask me what is wrong?'

In the strained silence that followed, the church clock chimed the hour – so near to the house that it seemed a part of it – and distantly a lorry was heard out on the lane as it changed gear at the top of the hill.

'I must go to the study,' Andrew said sadly. 'The sermon . . . And the invitation? We will have to reply . . .'

'Yes, of course we must go to . . . the ballet party!' Margaret said brightly, and she started to wash up. 'Oh, by the way, dear,' she called, stopping his departure, 'that woman phoned again . . .'

'Which woman?'

'Oh, I don't know, Andrew! One of your endless women . . . Another one of your flock . . .'

'Yes.' He now sounded irritable. 'But which one?'

'Simpson? I think that was her name. She used the feminist "Ms". I used to think that was an affectation – I rather like it now. Anyway, she left a number. She said you will know who she is.'

'What did she want?'

'Oh, something about the devil . . . You know what they're like! I never bother to listen. I tell them that's your department. As nobody ever phones to speak to me, I've rather lost the knack of attending to them . . .'

'So, Signor Bless. Is arranged? The piano we carry from Brigadier's house . . .'

'How carry, Carlotta? A grand piano weighs a ton.'

'Pooh! We manage. No problem. Chairs from village hall – the tall thin woman will see to that. You will get your man to see the garden is looking at its best?'

'Where is she actually going to perform?' Rich asked.

'Please don't interrupt,' Carlotta told him.

Bless and Rich were sitting on the terrace having the first drink of the evening. This was Rich's idea – and smacked of middle age to Bless. 'You'll be wanting your slippers and a pipe next,' he'd complained. 'So what would you rather we did?' Rich demanded, as he uncorked a bottle of wine. 'Oh, I don't know.' Bless had shrugged. 'You could have ravished me in the hall or been obscene in the bath . . .' 'Please! I've had a very long and tiring week . . .'

He was just back from London and hadn't been in the house more than half an hour when Carlotta appeared. She came through the arched gate from the stable yard and surveyed the garden as if she owned the place and had every right to be there. She was wearing plus fours and a loose, baggy cardigan. She was at her most masterful and didn't bother to ask if she might be disturbing them as she fired off instructions from a list on a clipboard and ticked each item after she had covered it.

'You will get your slave and her sister to serve . . .'

'Who?' Rich looked towards Bless for enlightenment.

'Do you have to be here?' Carlotta snapped.

'I live here!' Rich protested.

'It seems very odd to me. Where were you when we needed you? By the way, Signor Bless, I have had telephone call from

Antonio. He is at our house on Ischia. He will be back in time for the performance.'

'Did he say if he was alone?' Bless asked. He had been trying to reach Maggie for over a week, to no avail, and had mounting suspicions – an oddly suitable expression where Maggie was concerned.

'Antonio is never alone,' Carlotta replied with a shrug. 'If you are built like a marble lavatory you have no problem finding sex. Antonio lives for sex . . .'

'I'm really looking forward to meeting him,' Rich said grimly.

'I am in charge of cucina, and so . . .' Carlotta continued, ignoring him completely. 'My family has a small palazzo in Venice. We will serve wine from a little-known vineyard in the Veneto. It belongs to a friend and is stocked by Harrods. The bussolai I will make myself. I have adapted a family recipe and it works very well.'

'Are you sure that just biscuits will be enough?'

'Enough? Pooh! You English! There is no need to complicate the palate. Serve only the best and keep it simple. I wondered about making the guests dress incognito – uno ballo in maschera. But . . .' She shrugged. 'Where would they get the costumes? A person needs a certain style, otherwise it becomes nothing more than . . . fancy dress. Look what happened to carnivale! Typists masquerading as nobles; shop assistants dressed as gods. No. We will keep it simple.' She glanced back at the clipboard. 'Signora Jerrold plays quite beautifully – but her pig of a husband must not be allowed to come. In a moment of compassion I invite him. Is a mistake. His presence will intimidate her. If you see him – boot him out.' She made another tick on the list. 'So . . . I will make a speech. I thank you for letting us have use of your . . .' She waved at the garden. 'Your . . . plot. I explain that Lavinia Olganina is a great dancer . . . and so and so . . .' She lowered her voice, confidentially. 'She will, I am afraid, not be sur les pointes. The machine is rusty! Oh, I won't say this to the audience. But for you . . . Lavinia Olganina these days is more Isadora Duncan than Pavlova.' She sighed and spat. 'Ugh! Stamping and jumping and long, flowing scarves! Please!' She shook her head. 'If only I'd got here sooner. I hate to see talent go to waste . . .'

That same night, as they were getting ready for bed, Rich remarked that they hadn't themselves been sent an invitation.

'I think we're expected,' Bless told him. 'We live here!'

'You may! I certainly don't feel as though I do,' Rich said. And he stumped into the bathroom, looking sulky.

'That's because you spend so much time away. If it isn't London with Laurence it's America with Brad . . .'

'I have a business to run!'

Bless bit back a sharp reply about Brad no doubt being the stenographer – 'Sit on this, dear, and take a letter.' But he wisely decided to keep the peace. Since Rich had returned from the States there'd been a lot of reference to 'the business', and he'd been in London most of the time. Bless felt more and more like the little wife – waiting at home and keeping her lord and master in clean undies and proper food. He was seriously considering changing his name to Dorothy and joining the WI with Heather Daltry . . .

'The contessa hasn't a clue who I am,' Rich called, with his mouth full of toothbrush. 'But then none of them do . . .'

Bless wasn't really listening. He was standing by the window, preoccupied with his own problems. Rich would have to sort his out for himself. Bless's main problem, he realised, was that he'd got used to having the house to himself . . . And Rich coming back and behaving as if he owned the place was a serious inconvenience. He was invading his space and . . .

'How did we ever get into this?' Rich complained, coming back into the room and climbing into bed.

'What?'

'Giving a party – that isn't even our party . . . for people we don't even know!'

'It's all part of the rich patina of Bellingford life,' Bless assured him. 'You'll get used to it.'

'It's going to be a disaster . . .'

'Almost certainly!' Bless agreed, crossing to the bed. 'You'll discover – if you stick around – that life in Bellingford is based on the unexpected.' He switched off the light, adding: 'It can be quite stimulating!'

44

Selwyn Or Phyllis

The house was quiet now, though earlier in the day it had been all pandemonium, with people coming and going, disturbing his peace. The Brigadier had passed the time in the Tower. None of what was going on had anything to do with him. But then, he spent most of his time in the Tower now. He and Rosemary had ceased to communicate and he felt increasingly like a stranger in his own home.

That morning he'd watched as a group of men – none of whom he recognised – had manhandled the piano out of the French windows and on to the lawn. Rosemary had been with them. It was she who had . . . officiated. She'd been very . . . in command; almost bossy. These days she didn't seem like the Rosemary he had grown to know. It was all change in his world now.

So the Brigadier had skulked in the Tower and watched the whole proceedings in secrecy from the top room. The men had brought a trailer with them. On to it they'd hoisted the piano – with Rosemary fussing round them – and then they'd hauled it, laughing and cursing and calling out, all the way through the garden. They'd gone right below the Tower window, from where he silently watched – pulling back into the shadows of the room, so as not to be seen. They'd disappeared over the rough ground at the rear of the garden and out through the back gate.

Later he'd heard them at the other side of the wall, in the Hall House grounds. He'd climbed on to his chair to get a better view. He saw the gardener cutting the grass and the men lounging about on the terrace steps drinking beer from bottles. Then the loud, strange Italian creature came – the one he'd seen at the road show – and supervised them, pointing out where the piano should stand and actually helping them to lift it into position, out on the lawn. Finally the men were all given money from a thick wad out of the Italian's back pocket and they'd gone away, still laughing and talking.

Much later, when he was down in the lower room reading at his desk, the sound of the piano being played had forced him to retrace his steps to the top floor once more. With the binoculars he'd been able to watch Rosemary's face as she sat at the piano, in full view of anyone who might happen to be around, playing . . . tunes.

'Awful, mimsy, God-awful tunes,' he grunted, squeezing the focus until his wife's face was so clear that he felt he could reach out and slap it. She looked, he realised, at peace. It was an expression with which he was not familiar. 'Not on her face,' he murmured.

Then the boy, the terrible poofter, came out and spoke to her. He couldn't hear the words but after a moment Rosemary laughed. The odious creature had said something that so amused her that she threw back her head, like a young girl, and laughed. The Brigadier jumped down off the chair and opened the window. In doing so he lost the view but instead he gained the actual sound of that laughter. A merry, happy . . . unfamiliar sound.

'I'm getting broody,' he muttered, and he lowered himself down until he was sitting on the chair, facing the open window.

The piano started to play again. The music was not familiar. But then he had never in the past listened to his wife playing. Indeed, he forbade her to do so unless he was out of the house.

He considered music, like art, to be degenerate; a sign of weakness. But now, as he heard the sounds wafting over the high brick wall, he felt a strange shiver of — what? What was the emotion that thrilled down his spine, making him actually gasp and an unaccustomed tear sting his eye?

The Brigadier rose quickly and slammed the window closed. 'We don't want any of that!' he said. By 'that' he meant . . . weakness: by 'that' he meant . . . feelings.

But now the room seemed stuffy and confining. He strode about taking deep breaths and swinging his arms as though he feared some gradual creeping paralysis. His route took him between the two wardrobes that occupied the side walls, facing each other across the tiny space. The mirrors on their doors reflected a gradually curving infinity. Pausing to turn, he glimpsed himself in the reflection. He hesitated, drawn to look closer at his face in one mirror and able to see his stooping back reflected from the opposite one at the same time.

'Oh no you don't!' he said, staring at his face in the glass.

'Oh, Selwyn!' the face replied, his voice now warm and rich and thrilling.

'No, Phyllis!' the Brigadier snarled. 'We're finished with that.'

'Nonsense!' Phyllis exclaimed, and she tittered, throwing back her head. He saw the back of his head in the mirror's reflection behind him with its balding crown gleaming in the half-light.

'Go away!' the man howled, scowling at his face in the glass.

'No! You go away, you naughty, rude man!' Phyllis Jerrold mocked back at him. And again she laughed – a similar, girlish, tinkling sound to the one he'd heard coming from his wife.

'What do you want?' Selwyn whispered to himself.

'I want to go to the party,' Phyllis replied.

'Rosemary says I'm not wanted there.'

'Of course you're not, Selwyn – but they'll all be pleased to see me!' the woman replied.

'I can't go there,' he gasped. 'There will be people who know me.' He shook his head and trembled. His distress was appalling to see.

'Oh, get along with you, Selwyn!' the woman murmured, and she tittered again. Then, as she continued speaking, a new, excited note came into her voice. 'Do a really special make-up. Choose a stunning gown. Make me into a ravishing beauty . . .'

As she whispered to him, the Brigadier felt all his resolve ebbing away. Gradually, almost reluctantly, he started to peel off his clothes, folding each garment neatly and forming them into a pile. When he was down to his vest and underpants he turned and went to Phyllis's wardrobe. He took the key from its secret hook on the wall behind the big cupboard, and with it he unlocked the door. 'Are you sure about this?' he murmured, as the doors swung open, revealing lines of garments in dust covers.

'It'll be such fun!' she replied.

Taking a square wooden chest from the bottom of the wardrobe, the Brigadier carried it across and put it on the ground beside the table in the window. From the chest he first produced a round mirror on a stand. He put the mirror on the table. Then, bending and rising, he continued to bring out a multitude of boxes and jars and tubes from the chest. There were different powders in round containers. There were jars of day cream and night cream, moisturisers and toners, cleansers and exfoliators. There was a special concoction for open pores. There were wrinkle creams and little triangular patches to ease away frown marks. There were sheafs of false eyelashes, each with their own gum in a tiny tube. There was a whole palette of eye shadow in every possible hue. Eyeliners, mascara, eyebrow pencils, eye drops; lipsticks, lipliners, lip gloss, lip creams; blushers of the subtlest tones and little phials of glittering dust to add drama. There were brushes in a special glass vase and thick, soft pads of cotton wool in a decorative drum. He found a bottle of Diorissimo perfume, and as he lifted it from the box, so Selwyn couldn't resist leaning in towards it and sniffing delightedly, before giving himself the merest hint of a spray on the side of the neck.

The table now was crowded with this *batterie de maquillage*. The Brigadier sat back and surveyed the scene like a general surveying his troops and the lie of the land before planning the campaign for the battle to come.

Crossing to the wardrobe once more, he delved into its depths and produced a big round hat box. He returned with it and sat down on the chair at the table. Holding the hat box on his knees, he lifted off the lid. Inside there were wigs of every colour. Some were in short, smart, snappy styles. Others were longer; shoulder-length hair in soft waves or done up in a French pleat or other elaborate coiffures. Fishing a wig stand out of the wooden chest, he set it on the table in front of him.

Then rising again, quickly this time as the creative juices started to flow through his body, he skipped back to the wardrobe. His hands ran along the hangers on the rail, flicking the garments past his searching eyes, looking for one particular dress. His hand seized at a hanger, dragging the garment clear of the others. He shook it out, pulled down the zip of the plastic cover and revealed his chosen costume.

Lifting the dress from the hanger he held it against his wizened, sparsely haired chest and smoothed it against his body as he appraised himself in the long mirror. It was a dress he had never so far worn. A dress he hadn't bought himself. He had found it neatly pressed and folded on the bed in Phyllis's room not many weeks before. It was something Rosemary must have bought for her.

Under normal circumstances it wouldn't have done at all – it was far too girlish, too ethnic, too frivolous for Phyllis's tastes. But this evening was rather different. It was a party, after all; a dancing party. The dress had a gypsy look, with its little bits of glass round the skirt and its scooped neckline. It was the kind of dress in which Phyllis might be persuaded to dance herself; a tarantella, perhaps.

Pleased as punch, he returned the dress to its hanger and hooked it over the side of the wardrobe.

'To work!' he cried, pulling open the drawer at the bottom of the wardrobe and running his hands through the piles of rich silk lingerie that were stored within. 'It may be an ethnic garment,' he tittered, bringing out pale-cream gossamer-light knickers and a brassière with gathered rosebuds at the cleavage, 'but if I am run over by a bus this evening they will discover at the hospital what riches I am wearing beneath it! A lady of quality, in an amusing little frock!' And laughing gaily, Brigadier Selwyn Jerrold, OBE, pulled off his dull, flapping army surplus underpants, and Phyllis, his sister, slipped, instead, the thrill of whispered silk up over her sagging balls.

45

The Bussolai

Rich was in a filthy humour. His home had been taken over. There were complete strangers in the drawing room, and the terrace looked like picnic time at Glyndebourne. Carlotta da Braganizio was ordering people about in the kitchen, and even Laurence had been roped in to help with collecting tickets at the front door and directing the audience – audience? It was a private-fucking-house, for Christ's sake – round to the gardens by way of the stable yard.

But what had sealed Rich's misery had been the totally unexpected arrival of Alison Parnell and Justin Peters – the stars of *Manhattan Bohème*. They had turned up, out of the blue, at tea time, looking flushed and excited and demanding to see him.

'We wanted you to be the first to know!' Alison told him almost before they'd set foot in the house.

'Alison! Justin! What the hell are you doing here?'

'As soon as we knew ourselves – we decided to tell you . . .' Alison gushed. But then she'd been interrupted by the phone ringing.

It was Rich's general manager, Steve Grey. 'I thought I should tell you,' he said. 'Tomorrow's *Mail* is running a story saying Alison and Justin are getting married . . .'

So much for thespian honesty. Everyone in London probably knew and their agents would have advised them to tell Rich before he heard it on the grapevine or read it in the press.

'Congratulations!' he cried, opening champagne and trying to work out what it would do to business. They both had a lot of adoring fans who liked the fantasy of availability. Did married stars perhaps lack a certain sex appeal? Would it be bad for the box office?

Meanwhile Bless wanted them to go at once. 'If they stay they'll steal Lavinia's limelight,' he complained.

'No we won't!' Justin exclaimed. 'We'll stay in the background and clap like mad.'

This same humble leading man was even now standing in the 'background' slap in the middle of the terrace, with an arc light just happening to show off his gorgeous profile, available to sign autographs if only someone would come and ask him. And Alison – who had packed a glittering sequinned dress, so brief that many a girl would have called it no more than a collar ('Why did she pack anything,' Bless had demanded, 'if she didn't intend to stay?') – was leaning against the piano, in the centre of the lawn, idly posing for all the men of the audience, and apparently in deep contemplation about the wonders of the universe, and nature and . . . all those other spiritual matters that so preoccupy an artist's mind.

Actually, to be honest, the good people of Bellingford were not sure who either of them was. Nor were they particularly impressed by their London fashions and their condescending, guarded behaviour. So having them there made not a scrap of difference and they might just as well have both driven back to London for all the good it was doing to their egos.

Doris Day and Bessie Sugar weaved through the crowd, carrying trays on which dishes of biscuits were placed. Tony Daltry and Bless were dispensing wine into eagerly proffered glasses.

'You dunk the biscuit in the wine, dear. Like we used to do with digestives in a mug of cocoa. It's an Eyetalian habit,' Doris instructed Edna Bridey. She'd already had several of the biscuits herself in the kitchen and was quite partial to them.

'They're called bussolai,' the foreigner chappy had explained to her. 'Is a recipe from my family. My father was acquainted with Gertrude Stein, you know?' Doris had to admit that she didn't. 'She was very famous for doing not much.' 'We have that type round here as well, dear.' Doris nodded, knowingly. She was getting to quite like her foreign gentleman. 'So,' Carlotta continued, 'Gertrude's chum, Alice, was a great cook. These . . .' she proffered another biscuit, which Doris took gladly, '. . . are an adaptation of one of Alice's recipes . . .'

'Fancy!' Bessie Sugar had exclaimed, pushing past Doris and helping herself. It rather narked her the way her sister was hogging not only all the biscuits but all the attention as well.

'I warn you,' Doris was now telling Edna Bridey, 'there's something very potent in it all. You want to watch yourself, dear. I feel quite giddy myself.'

The Barlows and the Greens arrived when many people were already seated.

'Let's have a jar or two first,' Barry said, crossing to a table spread with bottles and glasses and piles of the ubiquitous biscuits.

'What are they?' Simon asked, cramming one into his mouth. 'Some sort of crisp, is it?'

Sandra was standing beside him but her attention was else-where as she watched the crowd, searching for her admirer. She was wearing a short summer dress and white sandals. She'd chosen the dress, she knew, with care. It was she who had insisted on Simon coming to the party. In fact she'd persuaded the Barlows as well. But now that she was actually here she felt nervous and wished she'd worn something less revealing; with a longer skirt at least – or trousers maybe, like Melanie.

Melanie, meanwhile was feeding biscuits to Simon: 'A bite for you, and a bite for me. A bite for you, and a bite for me . . . What d'you think of them, Si? Like them?'

'I do, quite,' he said nervously. And he took a swig of wine and then filled his glass again. He felt peculiarly light-headed and leaned towards Sandra for support.

'You all right, darling?' she asked, looking over his shoulder and catching sight of Carlotta, who had just come out on to the terrace from the drawing room.

Carlotta was wearing one of Henry Sparton's evening suits. The trousers reached to just below her knees. She had on Doc Marten boots – but with white knee socks that gave her the look of a chic urchin. The suit jacket, which was too big in the body and too short in the sleeve, she had buttoned loosely over a white dress shirt. A black tie completed the ensemble. She saw Sandra looking at her and waved enthusiastically.

'Hey, baby! I go now to collect the star. Later we talk. You look . . . as a dream!'

'Oh, Lor, Sandra!' Simon exclaimed, with slurred speech. 'It's that funny person again.'

'You shouldn't have too much more booze, Si!' Melanie said, then she slipped sideways and almost fell over. 'Cor! Something's got a bit of a kick!' And, seeing Simon's bottom within easy reach, she put a hand on one of the thin cheeks and squeezed it lovingly.

'Don't!' Simon said. But then he smiled. 'You're ever so rude, Melanie!'

'D'you mind?' she asked.

He shrugged, feeling surprisingly carefree. He rather liked the hand on his bottom. It made him feel manly. He reached out and lifted one of her breasts, as a sort of return gesture.

'I say, old man!' Barry Barlow said. 'That's my wife's tit.'

'Oh, I'm so sorry!' Simon said, dropping it at once.

Barry nodded at him and got very close. 'I should hope you are fucking sorry. Don't know what's got into you, Simon . . .'

'We'd better get seats,' Melanie said, hurriedly, 'before they're all taken. I didn't think there'd be so many people . . . Bring a bottle or two, Barry. And a dish of the biccies. I'm starving . . .' and linking an arm through Simon's, she staggered away to where chairs from the village hall had been arranged facing out from the terrace to the lawn.

'Oh, there's a piano!' Sandra said, following Barry.

'I suppose that's your writer's observation coming into play, is it, Sandra?' Barry said, his voice loaded with sarcasm.

'Yes, I suppose it must be,' Sandra agreed.

Margaret Skrimshaw had had only one biscuit and it had given her a blinding headache. She did not drink alcohol because it went straight to her head and she didn't care to be out of control. Andrew sometimes had a glass of wine, and indeed, this evening, had already had several. They were sitting to the side of the audience, with Mr Asquith, the antique dealer, and his big wife just in front of them. The three women from Pinchings were in the row behind. Miss Fallon, the tall one, was nibbling at a biscuit and pondering: 'The flavour reminds me of something . . .' Miss Bridey (plump) was slumped over in her seat and seemed to have fallen asleep. Miss Hopkirk (thin) was sitting on the end of the row and, as she watched, Margaret saw her lean over and feed biscuits to three corgis that were leaping up beside her chair, to which they appeared to be tethered by short leads.

'Good heavens! Miss Hopkirk has brought her dogs!' she exclaimed.

'Well,' Andrew remarked. 'It's an open-air event.'

'They bark so when they're excited! You wouldn't like it if she brought them to church.'

'This isn't church, Margaret! Even if they are only serving wine and wafers.'

Laurence was sitting in the hall, with the door open. He was on to his third large Scotch and had had no food apart from a plate of biscuits that the cleaner had thoughtfully brought for him. He glanced at his watch and decided that as soon as Carlotta returned with Lavinia he'd call it a day and any late-comers would have to find the way for themselves.

Just then a car turned off the lane and purred up the drive. It was the Audi, and Antonio was at the wheel. 'Ciao!' he called, seeing Laurence.

'Ciao!' Maggie Heston called, seated beside him.

'That's all we need!' Laurence murmured as the car drove round to the yard to park. Then Maggie reappeared, carrying a suitcase and looking remarkably brown, and moments later Antonio joined her, taking the case and kissing her cheek.

'Behave!' she told him, pushing him away. 'I told you! You've got to be good while you're here. We don't want to upset Bless. Why are you sitting in the hall, Mr Fielding? Have you been sent out for being naughty?'

'Areyouexpected?' he asked, noticing that the words bumped into each other in his mouth and came out as one long sound.

'Are you drunk, Mr Fielding?' Maggie took up the theme as she swept past him, followed by Antonio.

'You do know there is a function on,' Laurence said, speaking very carefully, being aware that he did sound as though he were drunk.

'A function?' Maggie asked, looking bemused.

'Cara, I told you. Carlotta – she arranges some charity . . .'

'Oh, I'd quite forgotten,' Maggie said with the broadest of smiles. 'We've just flown Air Italia from Rome, Mr Fielding. We've been at the villa on Ischia . . .' She managed to make it sound as if the villa and indeed the airline belonged exclusively to her.

'Have you indeed?' Laurence said, and catching sight of Antonio, he smiled sympathetically. The boy certainly had what they used to call 'bags of oomph'. Laurence winked at him – and was gratified to note that he got a wink in return.

'We'll go up and change,' Maggie said, firmly taking hold of her lover's arm and manoeuvring him away. 'If you see Bless, could you tell him we're back, please. Mmmh! These are the most delicious biscuits,' she added, taking one off the plate on the hall table and popping it into her mouth. 'Try one, Toni!' And as she spoke she pressed one between his lips and let her finger linger longer than was strictly necessary inside his warm, moist mouth.

'How strange!' Antonio remarked, tasting the biscuit and

then taking another to make doubly sure of his observation. 'This is the same biscuit poor Diana was living on when I found her in the hovel in Le Puy. Where did this come from, old man?' he asked, turning back to Laurence, who was actually helping himself to another at the time.

'Not so much of the "old", sonny!' Laurence growled, speaking with his mouth full.

'HAH!' Antonio cried, striking his forehead with a hand.

'What's the matter?' Maggie shrieked, alarmed by his sudden behaviour.

'I am a fool – that is what is the matter! My sister! She is up to her old tricks!' He clapped his hands. 'Hash cookies! Her speciality!' He laughed delightedly. 'She's a great girl – didn't I tell you?' He now picked up the plate of biscuits and carried them and Maggie's suitcase towards the bottom of the stairs. 'Let's find your room, cara . . . Carlotta's cookies are guaranteed. They take you straight to Paradise!'

'I've already been,' Maggie said breathlessly. She turned and smiled at Laurence. 'I thoroughly recommend the trip!' And she hurried after Antonio, who was already up on the landing.

Laurence reached out to them and tried to speak, but his tongue seemed stuck to the roof of his mouth. 'Oh mugger!' he mumbled, and he went off to the drawing room in search of more whisky and consequently missed the arrival of the star attraction, sitting pillion on the back of the Harley Davidson and clinging to Carlotta as though her life depended upon it – which of course it did.

Lavinia was swathed in a huge coat that was too warm for the summer evening. She also wore a veil over her face.

'They must not see the make-up before the performance,' she'd explained. 'It isn't professional to be seen in the street in one's make-up.'

In fact she seemed more worried about people seeing her before she started her performance than she was about the performance itself.

'Is OK,' Carlotta assured her. 'I fix everything.'

'Oh, dear Contessa!' Lavinia had sobbed. 'I do so hope that I don't let you down . . .'

'Please! Baby!'

Once they were in the stable yard it was easy for Carlotta to hurry her round the side of the lawn and into the willow glade beside the brook. There in the summerhouse she had prepared a makeshift dressing room for the star; with lights, a basin of water to wash in, a mirror to check her make-up . . . and a few biscuits – in case she got peckish.

When they arrived there Lavinia's good friend Rosemary Jerrold was already ensconced, having been home to Cockpits to change and having returned via the back gate.

Rosemary was wearing a pale-blue frock with a long skirt that she had bought during a happy shopping spree with Phyllis the previous year. Little did she think, when at the time she had protested at the extravagance, that she would wear it at such an auspicious moment in her life. With the dress she wore her pearls, the only present that she could remember Selwyn having given to her. She felt nervous and strangely calm at the same time.

'You all right, baby?' Carlotta asked her.

'Oh, yes, thank you, Countess. I have waited most of my life for this moment.'

'Yes?' Carlotta asked, not understanding.

'I was going to be . . . a performer, you see.'

'Hey!' Carlotta grinned and wiped a tear away from her own cheek. It was good sometimes to make people's dreams come true. 'Tonight – they will see! Two artists . . . at work!'

'Contessa da Braganizio,' Lavinia said in a small, terrified voice. 'Would you help me?'

'Anything,' Carlotta exclaimed, hurrying to her side.

'I am afraid . . . that is to say I think . . . the zip has gone on the back of my dress . . .'

'Hey!' Carlotta cried, saved from emotional collapse by the need to be practical. 'I fix! I have safety pin!'

46

The Comeback

Rosemary was playing her beloved Schubert. Her fingers travelled across the keys as if they belonged to another being: she felt so detached, so unreal. It was certainly her piano – but what was it doing out in a garden? Why was she sitting there playing, with the evening shadows gathering around her and a bird singing somewhere high in a tree? Had she perhaps died and gone to heaven? It could well be so – for she felt so utterly, deliriously . . . free. Looking up from the keys, she could vaguely make out people sitting facing her away across the lawn. They seemed to be listening. She was playing for herself and yet she was playing for an audience as well. It was the most exquisite, thrilling . . . gratifying experience. She felt, for the first time in so many years it seemed like for ever, exactly right. She was doing what she had been born to do. Making the sound of divine music spill out from her soul through the piano, on to the still, tranquil air.

On the terrace her audience was mercifully in a half-light so she did not see that many people were asleep, that others were in hysterical conversation and that one or two were indulging in pursuits more suited to the cinema than a concert hall. Carlotta had employed an electrician from Fairlow to fix up spotlights that bathed the centre of the lawn where the piano stood, and where Lavinia would soon perform, in a brilliant light while leaving old Tom's neatly perfect edges, his 'edges, and all the deep recesses of the garden – and, more importantly of the terrace itself – in a mysteriously shaded darkness.

The sky above held still a limpid blueness but the sun was sinking into the west and the last rays were tipping the treetops with honey and gold and staining a thin trail of cloud to a dark mauve-purple.

Sandra Green was standing at the corner of the terrace behind the rows of seats. Simon and Melanie had both dozed off, with their legs strangely entwined, like two teenagers in the back row. Barry was sitting in a morose stupor, finishing a bottle of wine. He'd tell Melanie later. He couldn't quite remember what he'd tell her, but he'd fucking well tell her . . . As they were all lost in their own dream worlds it had been easy, too easy, for Sandra to get up and move away. She'd been sitting on the end of the row and none of them even noticed her go. She'd done it while Carlotta was making her introductory speech and she'd seen the Italian glance in her direction and knew that she understood. Now, as she waited for the object of her desire, she felt her blood streaming through her veins and her heart pounding beneath her breasts. She leaned back against the warm bricks of the house and let the last of the sun's rays play on her lovely face. No longer was she Sandra Green, wife of Simon in insurance, mother of Gary. She had become her own creation; the living and breathing heroine of her book. She was Samantha Betterton and she was waiting for Gloria Manderlay to come and sweep her off her feet.

Bless was sitting on a step of the terrace. He was probably one of the few people in the audience who was actually listening to Rosemary playing. He was also one of the few who wasn't absolutely stoned out of his mind. Except perhaps for the vicar and his wife, though something seemed to have moved even them. They sat hand in hand listening to the music, and Margaret occasionally took a little nibble at a biscuit. She was getting to quite like the taste, and really, with the music playing, with Andrew sitting beside her, with the sky turning such a glorious, lustrous pink and the night air soft and warm on her cheek, she was half persuaded that she'd seen the old gentleman looking down on them after all. 'I think I saw Him smile, Andrew,' she whispered. But Andrew didn't hear her. He was trying to remember how many glasses of wine he'd drunk, and he giggled as he wondered what the vintage would have been at the marriage at Cana. '"An amusing little nose," saith the Lord, "rounded, with an oakey bouquet."' 'What, dear?' his wife whispered, drawing closer to him. 'Nothing,' he told her, and leaning over he kissed her on the cheek and wondered why it couldn't be like this more often.

Nearer to Bless, Heather Daltry, wearing a brightly flowered frock, was chain-smoking cigarettes – which she'd found in a box in the drawing room, with a lighter beside it. She hadn't smoked for donkey's years; since she was a girl, really. Gosh! It was such fun at school; more fun then than it ever was after. One really could have fun with the girls: swapping stories, telling things. Mainly about boys. We were all boy-mad! She laughed out loud! Then clamped a hand over her mouth and continued to giggle. She was having the most super conversation. But no one was listening; no one was even there. Tony, her husband, had fallen fast asleep; Tony always was asleep when she needed him. If he wasn't asleep, then he was in London. Poor Tony, who worked so hard. He was no substitute for the girls in the dorm, bless him!

Miss Fallon was sitting bolt upright in her chair. The full power of her attention was tuned to the pianist. But she wasn't in the Hall House garden. She was in London at the Queen's Hall at a concert being given by Myra Hess. She'd brought a group of her most favoured girls with her. She had told them that to hear Dame Myra play would be a privilege, and so it was proving to be. Miss Hopkirk was fighting with Tag. Bobtail was sleeping peacefully and Rag, always the most obedient of her boys, was sitting quietly. But Tag wanted to play – and worse, Tag wanted to bark. Miss Hopkirk had a hand round the dog's snout and would take him home if he didn't behave. Miss Bridey was fast asleep and, unfortunately, snoring. Unfortunate because Miss Bridey was a poet and she would have been the first to acknowledge that there is very little poetry to be found in a fat woman, with her chin on her chest, snoring.

Doris Day had her feet up and was stretched out on one of the sofas in the drawing room, admiring her Alec's plasterwork on the ceiling. She was really comfy. She'd got a glass of wine and a bottle on the floor beside her. She'd eaten enough biscuits to make her burst and she felt as cheery as a buttercup.

'The Dagwood bus comes trundling over the hills . . .' she crooned in a sleepy, warbling voice. 'With the people waving and the conductor ringing his bell. Heavenly day . . .'

'. . . a beautiful sky!' Laurence joined in, singing lazily, with his eyes closed and getting as confused with the lyric as Doris was. He was lying full length on the other sofa with his own bottle of wine.

'Why, dear!' Doris cried, lifting her head to look at him, then dropping it back on to the comfort of the cushion. 'I didn't know you knew the songs, Mr What-ever-your-name-is.'

'Indeed I do, Mrs Day,' Laurence replied in a slurred voice. He was flat on his back and felt heavily inert, almost how a dead body would feel if a dead body had feeling – and who was to say that it hadn't?

'Isn't that nice!' Doris sighed. She closed her eyes and could feel the warm glow of human friendship coursing through her old body.

'When I was younger,' Laurence confided. 'I used to be the life and soul of any party. I wasn't a chorus boy, you understand! Nothing like that. But . . . popular! I played the piano at cocktails . . .'

'Just fancy that,' Mrs Day murmured and she continued to sing, quietly: 'Pass down the bus!'

'Pass down the bus!' Laurence endorsed, generously.

'Pass down the bus!' they both concluded.

Bessie Sugar was in the kitchen going through the cupboards. She was looking for something, she couldn't remember what, and she was in a stinking temper. 'Supermarket?' she spat, staring at a bag of flour and dropping it on the floor, where it broke with a silent *puff*. 'London!' she cried, dropping a jar of sundried tomatoes. 'Supermarket! Supermarket! Supermarket!' she snarled, dropping the offending articles – a bag of sugar, a packet of pasta and a bottle of olive oil. The floor was beginning to look like a battlefield. She opened another cupboard, found a packet of cornflakes, turned in her rage – discovering a Safeway sticker on the side of it – and as she hurled it across the room, yelling, 'Supermarket!' she slipped on the greasy surface where the olive oil had spilled. Her feet went from under her and she fell backwards, dragging a chair over beside her and ending up in a heaving heap not far from the Aga. 'Supermarket!' she sobbed.

Rich was in the study. He knew he should be with his guests but he didn't know any of them, and besides, he had several phone calls to make, including one to Sol Fienstein in New York, to whom he was now speaking. The details of a contract had just been finalised for a new show they would co-present – a musical version of *Born Yesterday*. The key role – played in the film by Judy Holliday – required a gutsy singer with a strong voice and, according to Sol (who was New York, Jewish and heterosexual), 'the sex appeal of a rattlesnake'. (Which left Rich wondering what New York heterosexual Jews got up to and whether it might be fun to try it.) 'Who do we get for that?' Sol yelled. (Sol always yelled when he was excited). 'We need the voice of Garland, the body of Monroe and the acting talent of Dame Judith frigging Anderson. You tell me, Richie baby. Where do we get all that in one little broad?' Then, before Rich could get a word in, he continued, his voice getting even louder, 'This is the show to make a star, not to remake one. Someone new, someone vibrant . . . Where are these girls?' 'We'll find one, Sol. We'll find one,' Rich assured him.

Maggie, a star-in-waiting, was plighting her troth for the four thousandth time with the Hunk from heaven on one of the guest

room beds just above Rich's head. They'd enjoyed a few of
Carlotta's hash cookies and then thrown discretion to the wind.
They had been intimate, to put it mildly, with increasingly boring regularity on Ischia and had been relieved to do a little
shopping instead in Rome on the way home. They'd started to
get used to each other. There are not that many ways of screwing, whatever the *Kama Sutra* may try to tell you – and sucks
boo to *The Joy of Sex* they'd picked up at the airport. Now, as
they did it in a new bedroom, which was a kind of variation,
and as Maggie rode Antonio towards the winning post – with
her fingers gripping his hair, while he slapped her, indecently
hard, on the rump (which was not at all what you expected the
horse to be doing) – she heard herself shouting, 'YES! YES!
YES!' And later, when she sank on to his heaving chest and felt
his hair tickling her breasts, she wondered what exactly it was
that she had so noisily affirmed.

Finally, and as Rosemary neared the end of her solo spot in
the garden in Bellingford, what of the self-appointed stars of the
evening? What had become of Alison Parnell and Justin Peters,
the toast of the West End and the darlings of the gossip
columns? They had simply slipped quietly away some time
before. Their departure had been as unremarked as had been
their presence there. For two such glittering personalities it had
been a depressingly muted exit, and they were now hurrying
back to the safety of London in Justin's VW Golf (with the
pram roof). 'If you visit the sticks,' Alison observed drily, dabbing scent behind her ears, 'you can't expect much in the way of
sophistication!' and she settled back in her seat and wiped the
unpleasant experience from her mind. They might be in time to
get a table at Joe's, she suggested, glancing at her watch. Joe
Allen was a restaurant in which they felt comfortable. People
knew them there. They knew people. Their kind of people. 'It's
Sunday!' Justin reminded her. No wonder she was depressed.
Sunday was always the dullest of days. 'How weird,' Justin said
later and not for the first time. 'What?' Alison enquired.
'Richard Charteris – with his millions. Dumping himself down

in that dreary village . . .' 'It's the boyfriend, darling. Apparently he's got some hold over Rich. And Rich thought it wisest to buy him off by hiding him away in the country.' 'Who is the boyfriend?' 'Someone Maggie Heston found years ago – in rep!' 'God! Did Maggie Heston do *rep*?' Justin made the idea sound as outlandish as a theatrical engagement on Uranus. 'Yes, darling!' Alison said, feeling deliciously bitchy. 'Maggie has always been big in the provinces.' And they both laughed cosily, enjoying the safety of being in work and forgetting that no job lasts for ever. 'I love Maggie,' Alison added, with a twinge of guilt. 'I wish something wonderful could happen for her.'

In the summerhouse Lavinia Olganina, prima ballerina assoluta, listened to Rosemary playing the final Schubert impromptu. It had been agreed that she should not be announced. Rosemary would pause. She would strike three chords. That would be Lavinia's final cue. Then, with the first notes of the Saint-Saëns, Lavinia would appear, floating like thistledown and trailing great lengths of white gossamer behind her (the curtains from the *Sylphides* bedroom specially washed for the occasion). The night air would catch in the folds of her dress and in the clouds of net, enveloping her in an ethereal mist. It would seem as if a phantom or a dream was floating down to earth – a swan, caught at her moment of supreme poetic beauty, trembling with longing for this world and expectation for the world to come, before finally bowing to the inevitable and sinking gracefully into the unspeakable tragedy of death . . .

She would dance as she had never danced before; for Lavinia knew that she would never dance again. Indeed, that she was to do so now was an indulgence and a travesty. 'I am an old woman,' she said, speaking tearfully and out loud, and she nibbled one of Carlotta's biscuits for comfort. 'I can't do it,' she sobbed. 'Why did I let myself be seduced? Why didn't I stop her? I can't do it!'

With a sudden rush of recognition she realised the stupidity of the situation. It was all right for Rosemary Jerrold. Old women could still play the piano. But dancing? A dancer had to be fit. A dancer had to be in training. A dancer was a grey-hound or a race horse – not a pug dog or fit only for a brewer's dray.

'I can't do it!' she screamed. And running towards the summerhouse door, she determined to make her getaway.

'Steady!' a voice cried out, and the next moment Lavinia ran slap into the arms of a strange woman whom she had never seen before. A woman in a gypsy dress, with her red hair caught up in a gypsy kerchief. A woman with the most beautiful smile and gorgeous make-up. 'What's the matter?' this angelic creature murmured, holding Lavinia in a warm embrace. 'You mustn't cry. You are the star of our show.'

'But I can't . . . I mustn't go on,' Lavinia sobbed.

'Oh, but you must,' the woman told her. 'Faint heart ne'er won fair lady! Come, I'll help you . . .' and still tenderly holding her, Phyllis Jerrold led Lavinia Olganina towards her awaiting public.

Carlotta was standing next to Sandra. She felt incredibly, unbelievably shy. She didn't know why. Perhaps she'd had too much dope. She felt like a silly teenager. She felt sad. 'Bad trip, baby!' she murmured. As she spoke she sensed the woman beside her go tense. The poor girl was so rigid she was ready to snap. 'Loosen up, cara,' she whispered. 'What's the matter, huh? Tell me. What's wrong?'

'I don't usually do this,' Sandra stammered. Just finding the words was impossible enough; expressing her true feelings was beyond hope.

'Do what?'

'This,' Sandra sobbed. She suddenly wished she was sitting next to Simon. She wanted to feel safe.

The Italian shrugged. 'I will not force you. I forced a woman in France. A stupid virgin woman . . . She made me want her.' A tear trickled down Carlotta's cheek. 'All my life I search for the right person . . .'

'But – maybe you should . . . try it with a man?' Sandra whispered, knowing that Samantha Betterton was pushing Gloria

Manderlay away. That if she did not dare now then she would lose her chance. But chance of what? Her chance to be different, to feel . . . new and exciting and brave. 'Honestly,' she gasped, stamping on those desires, 'you should . . . go after a man, Contessa!'

'Pah!' Carlotta snorted. 'Why? I do not even like men. Men . . . possess you. I not like that. I possess! That's why Diana was so wicked . . .' Why was her mind still on that girl? Why could she never be free of her?

'Diana?' Sandra asked, feeling a twinge of jealousy.

'The girl in France. I told you, cara! A bad girl. She took my heart and she broke it into little pieces . . .' Carlotta let another tear trickle down her cheek.

'Don't cry,' Samantha Betterton, the heroine, told Gloria Manderlay. But it was definitely Sandra Green who turned towards Carlotta da Braganizio and, after smoothing the tears from her cheek, kissed her full on the lips.

'Why did you do that?' Carlotta gasped, staring into her eyes.

'I don't know.' Sandra's voice trembled as she spoke. 'I felt sorry for you. I wanted to . . . comfort you. I don't know . . .' And she kissed her again.

'Please, Sandra. Don't do it unless you mean it . . .' Carlotta said, pushing her away. 'Do you mean it, my petti di pollo?'

'I don't know,' Sandra wailed. 'I don't even understand half of what you say to me. I'm a married woman, with a dear little boy who wants to go to Disney World. I don't know what I mean . . .'

'I am too vulnerable to be toyed with, cara. I warn you! If you ask for my heart then I must first get it back from that wicked girl who stole it . . .'

And at that moment, as Carlotta sobbed uncontrollably and Sandra began to worry that people might be watching them, Rosemary struck the three, thrilling chords that warned Lavinia of her entrance.

After the briefest of creative pauses, during which Rosemary placed the new music in front of her on the piano, she started to play the first bars of Saint-Saëns' tragic eulogy to the dying swan.

Through the willow branches at the back of the lawn a figure in a white ballet dress trembled into view.

'Hey!' Carlotta roared, remembering her better self and putting her own misery behind her. 'Bravo!' she roared. 'Lavinia Olganina! Lavinia Olganina, prima ballerina assoluta!' and clapping wildly, she placed fingers in her mouth and whistled.

'I can't!' Lavinia wailed.

Many members of the audience were roused from their slumbers by Carlotta's cat calls and whistling. 'What . . .?' What's happened . . .?' 'Si! You've got my leg in your crotch . . .' 'Bravo! Bravo! Bravo!'

'I can't!' Lavinia shrieked, turning to flee back into the welcome obscurity of the willow tree.

'Oh yes you can, my girl!' Phyllis declared. 'We can. Let's dance, my dear!' And taking the old woman by the hand, she swung her out into the bright lights of her stage.

Rosemary faltered in her playing, seeing a second figure emerging from the trees. Then she gasped.

'Phyllis!' she exclaimed.

'Keep playing, Rosemary!' her darling sister-in-law hissed. And as Rosemary continued to do as she was told, so Phyllis stretched out her arms and stood back from the pale and trembling figure of the Dying Swan, and she lifted her hands and clapped and swayed in time to the music. Lavinia raised her eyes and looked into the wild face of her saviour. She smiled, nodded once, and then, fluttering her arms like the wings of a swan, she launched into a *grande jeté* and crashed in a heap on the grass.

Phyllis, distressed for her new friend, ran to her aid. As she did so the full glare of the lights caught the little glass squares on her dress and the brilliant red of the material and threw it into such startling relief that it was if an exotic bird had flown on to the lawn from some secret other world.

Carlotta stared for one stunned, heart-stopping moment.

'Diana?' she gasped. Then she yelled, 'DIANA!' Her voice

rang out, an agonised clarion of grief. Using the wall of the house as a springboard, she launched herself off the terrace and out into the centre of the lawn.

One or two people stood up, feeling that something was required of them. Bless stared in disbelief.

'Carlotta!' he shouted.

'I kill you, Diana!' Carlotta screamed, paying no heed to anything or anyone.

Phyllis looked round, seeing this terrible apparition bearing down on her.

'DIANA!' the voice rang out as Carlotta reached out to grab at her.

Selwyn, or Phyllis – either or both of them at once – took fright. They were staring death in the face. Turning, they started to run back towards the willow. But Carlotta already had a head start. She reached out, grabbing at the scooped neckline of the dress. There was a terrible ripping sound and, as if joined together, the two figures disappeared amid the branches of the tree.

'No! Contessa!' Rosemary wailed, abandoning the piano and running in pursuit. 'You mustn't! That isn't who you think it is . . . Oh, Phyllis!' she sobbed as she followed them out of sight into the willow glade.

Bless was halfway across the grass when a terrible chilling scream rent the air. He stopped, feeling panic surging through him. There was a moment of utter stillness, then everyone on the terrace began running about and shouting. Miss Hopkirk's corgis all started barking and tugging at their leads. Miss Hopkirk stood up, releasing her weight from the chair. The dogs bounded free. Being corgis they at once started snapping at the heels of any passing human. Their sharp, gnashing teeth inflicting wounds on vulnerable flesh caused further screams and indignant cries. As the chair was pulled from under her, Miss Hopkirk toppled backwards, bumping into the sleeping mound of Miss Bridey and knocking her flying. Miss Fallon reached out to help Miss Bridey and was knocked over by

Heather Daltry, who had just been bitten by Bobtail and was hopping about on one leg. 'Gosh! Sorry!' she exclaimed and tripped over Tony, who was still asleep.

Into the middle of all this chaos, Rich emerged from the drawing room. He'd been confused to find Maggie Heston wandering along the landing upstairs, looking for the bathroom and wearing nothing but a sheet. He had been bemused to find Mrs Day and Laurence both fast asleep on the drawing room sofas. He was absolutely gobsmacked by the mayhem on the terrace.

'Good evening, Vicar!' he said, recognising the face of the man who was busy snogging a woman in the chair next to him. 'Has there been an accident?'

'Don't worry about a thing!' Andrew Skrimshaw advised him, looking up. Then he laughed cheerfully and continued to devour his wife.

'AAAAGH!' Another chilling scream filled the air.

'God!' Rich said to no one in particular. 'It's like the Hammer House of Horror.' And as he hurried out on to the lawn to see if Bless, who he'd just spotted, could fill him in on what was going on, so Carlotta came flying out of the willow grove, waving her arms and wailing like a banshee.

She was clearly in the most awful state. It seemed as if she would die of fright. Bless caught hold of her, but she was too strong for him. Rich tried to grab her, but she tossed him aside like a broken reed. Then Antonio appeared on the terrace, wearing nothing but a pair of jeans.

'Carlotta!' he yelled, pushing his way through the crowd and standing on the top step, looking down on to the lawn. 'Torni un po' piu tardi!' He spoke the words of the motto with all the authority and all the dignity of his ancient family. It did the trick. His sister ran into his arms, sobbing and gasping.

'Cara! What is it?' he asked in Italian.

'A woman,' she sobbed, answering in the same language. 'A woman with . . .' She shook her head and was unable to continue. Her eyes stared, her breath was fast and shallow. Out of her clenched fist she let fall a ripped and tattered pair of lady's silk knickers.

'Oh, Christ, Carlotta!' Antonio sighed. 'Now what have you done?'

'A woman – with men's parts . . .' she sobbed.

'What?' her brother exclaimed.

'A woman . . . with all the . . . full male accoutrement!' Carlotta sobbed. And taking a huge breath, she fainted into his arms, making him stagger back against an empty chair.

47

A Promise

Bless, Rich and Antonio between them carried Carlotta into the drawing room. Laurence had woken with a start, hearing the sound of battle from beyond the windows and trying to remember where he was and why he was there. As he stood up, the three men pushed past him and deposited their burden on the sofa.

'I say! Bit of a problem?' he asked, blinking and rubbing his aching head.

'Don't make so much noise, dears!' Doris Day called from the other sofa and she turned on her side and put her thumb in her mouth, sleeping like a baby.

'She's coming round,' Rich said, leaning over Carlotta as she started to move and feeling her brow.

'Thank God!' Antonio exclaimed, and he looked up into Rich's eyes and gave him a warm, inviting smile.

'I don't think we've been introduced,' Rich stammered, feeling the blood rushing to his head.

'Allow me!' Bless said, squeezing in between them both. 'Rich, this is Antonio da Braganizio. Antonio, this is my lover . . .' he said the word with a triple underline '. . . Rich.'

'Hello, Rich!' Antonio said, leaning across Bless and extending a hand.

'Antonio!' Rich said, taking the hand and shaking it. 'I've heard so much about you!'

'You're lucky boys,' the Hunk said, embracing them both.

'Antonio!' his sister whispered, and he leaned down and put his ear to her lips.

'Cara!' he murmured, his voice brimming with sympathy. Then he looked up again as Bless and Rich moved away, sensing that he required privacy. 'My sister has had a bad trip, I'm afraid . . .'

'What happened to her?' Bless asked.

'She thinks Diana was a man!'

'But it wasn't Diana,' Bless said.

'Yes, Diana!' Carlotta wailed. Then she gasped as the full enormity of what she had seen came back to her. 'My Diana . . . with a *man*'s paraphernalia?'

'Cara,' Antonio comforted her. 'You had too many cookies.'

'A man?' Bless said. 'She thought she was . . .?' And slowly he turned his head, looking out into the garden, in the direction of the Jerrolds' house. His mind was racing. The memories and ideas that were forming seemed quite bizarre.

'Was a terrible experience,' Carlotta sobbed. Antonio folded her in his arms and hugged her to his bare chest. 'Take me home!' his sister pleaded. 'Antonio, caro. Take me home to Italy . . .'

Lavinia Olganina limped in from the terrace, still trailing her nets and looking dishevelled. 'What has happened?' she whimpered.

'Oh, Signorina Olganina,' Carlotta sobbed, struggling up off the sofa and running to her friend. 'You are all right?'

'I think so,' Lavinia replied.

Then Maggie appeared from the hall, carrying Antonio's T-shirt and his shoes. She was dressed now and looked quiet and subdued. 'Seems like we missed quite a party,' she said, handing him his clothes.

'I suppose coffee might be a good idea,' Rich said, and he looked down at Mrs Day. 'No point waking her, is there?'

'Absolutely none,' Bless assured him. 'She doesn't do food. Actually . . . there's something I need to see to . . . I'll be back in a minute, Rich,' he called, and he hurried out through the French windows and across the terrace, where many of the guests were still lingering and talking and where Miss Hopkirk, having rounded up Rag and Bobtail, was pursuing Tag in ever-decreasing circles and knocking into people in her agitation. But Bless didn't hesitate. He hurried away across the lawn towards the back gate. The guests, he decided, were perfectly capable of looking after themselves.

'Time we were off,' Barry in computers was saying. 'What did you think of the dancing, then?'

'I quite liked it,' Melanie replied. 'Did you Si?'

Simon looked sheepish. He wasn't very good at lying. He crossed to where Sandra was sitting on a chair alone. 'You all right, Sand?' he asked.

'Yes. I'm fine, Si,' she whispered.

'That Italian chappy . . . Bit of a nutter, if you ask me.'

'Oh, Si!' Sandra sobbed, and she started to cry.

'What's the matter?' her husband asked, a note of panic creeping into his voice. He was wondering if she'd seen him doing whatever it was that he'd been doing – which he couldn't quite remember, but which he knew had been seriously out of order – with Melanie Barlow.

'I love you,' she told him.

'I love you too,' he said. And Sandra got up and put her arms round him, holding him close. Over his shoulder she could see Carlotta in the drawing room, and the sight of her made the tears well up into her eyes and her body shake. Silently sobbing, she clung to Simon, almost as if she was afraid she'd drown in her grief.

'Oh, Sandra. I'm sorry,' Simon said, totally misunderstanding her. 'I'm sorry, Sandra. I'm so . . . sorry.'

'Let's go home,' she said, taking his hand. And they followed their friends the Barlows out through the stable yard.

Bless reached the farm track that skirted the back of the

estate and followed it until he came to the gate into Cockpits' garden. He walked across the rough, unkempt grass and approached the Tower from behind it. Night had come and with it a pale moonlight. Across the lawn the main house was in darkness, but both floors of the Tower were illuminated. Bless paused, looking at each of the windows in turn. 'Hello!' he called hopefully. 'Mrs Jerrold?'

'I'm here!' a voice said behind him, and turning he saw Rosemary standing in the shadow of a yew.

'I'm so sorry . . . about everything,' Bless said.

'Yes! But not your fault,' she replied.

'Aren't you cold?'

'No.'

'You should go in,' Bless said, holding out a hand to her.

Rosemary Jerrold shook her head. 'I don't want to leave . . .' She nodded towards the Tower.

'Is the Brigadier there?' Bless asked.

'Yes . . . I think so. I never go in.'

'And . . .' Bless hesitated as he saw her turn and look at him. 'Phyllis?' he said, his voice rising nervously.

'Oh, yes. She will be there as well.'

'She . . . wasn't hurt, was she? By Carlotta?'

'Shocked, I think. My husband believed the Contessa was a man attacking him . . . That is to say . . . I mean . . .' and Rosemary put a hand to her mouth, realising her mistake.

Bless stared at her and blinked. He couldn't think of anything helpful to add. 'You played beautifully,' he said at last.

'I wish you hadn't come here,' Rosemary said, walking slowly and wearily towards the Tower.

'Now, you mean?'

'Ever,' she corrected him.

'Why?'

'You've changed everything,' she said. 'I used to so look forward to Phyllis's visits. She was a very nice woman. We had such . . . sisterly feelings.'

'She'll come again,' he told her. As he spoke, a movement

attracted him to the window of the upper room. Bless pulled back into the shadows, away from the light spilling from the windows. He saw Phyllis Jerrold looking down at him. She had removed her kerchief and her long hair was falling across her face. She stared down, but Bless couldn't be sure whether she saw him or not. Then he realised that Rosemary was talking again.

'. . . won't come back. Not any more. You see . . . when you arrived, my husband was appalled . . .'

'I know. He didn't exactly hide the fact!' Bless told her, still staring up at the figure above him.

'But . . . Phyllis wanted to meet you. Phyllis wanted to be your friend. Phyllis . . .' The poor woman was sobbing now. She stood bolt upright, clasping her hands almost as though in prayer, and stared away into a distance somewhere beyond this world. 'She had such a . . . longing for enjoyment; such a questioning mind. She loved . . . clothes and outings and . . . We did things together.' She paused and shook her head, remembering. 'We did things! We went to the flicks; to country houses; shopping in Debenhams . . . Sometimes in the evening she would sit in the sitting room and listen to my playing. Even that! She would allow me to play! We had so many happy times . . .'

While her voice continued to recreate this simple, companionable life, Bless watched as, up in the window, Phyllis slowly unpinned her hair. Each pin she dropped from a height on to an unseen table beside her. Then, with infinite care, she removed the red wig and revealed the Brigadier's thinning hair beneath it. Next, with finger and thumb, she peeled off each false eyelash, making her eyes seem small and somehow naked. Then, picking up a jar from the table, she covered her face with a thick layer of cream that smudged all the colour of her make-up into a grey sludge.

So, as his wife mourned the passing of the sister he never had, the Brigadier slowly and reluctantly obliterated her; wiped her out; banished her back into the wardrobe of his fantasies.

'Why couldn't Phyllis stay here?' Bless suggested, speaking with sudden urgency, as though wanting to turn back the clock before it was too late.

'No! That would never do,' Rosemary said.

'Why not?' Bless asked.

'You cannot live with pleasure all the time, Mr Hudson. It has to be something one longs for, something one snatches at . . .'

'I don't agree,' Bless protested. 'If you are both happy together, then – get rid of the Brigadier. Let him go away and let Phyllis stay.'

'But everyone knows us here,' Rosemary protested, looking towards him. It seemed almost as though she wanted to believe in his suggestion. 'We couldn't . . . risk being found out.' And she smiled at him wistfully and shrugged. 'But we are found out, aren't we?' she sighed. 'Because you know, don't you?'

Up in the window, the Brigadier leaned forward, listening.

'Whatever I know,' Bless said, 'I won't tell anyone.'

'Oh, Mr Hudson!' Rosemary mocked. 'You'll not be able to resist it. It will make so many good stories for the dinner table!'

'I promise you,' Bless said.

The woman looked at him closely, and at the same moment, up in the window, the Brigadier moved away and disappeared from view.

'I'm someone who always keeps my promises if I possibly can,' Bless said.

'That is very rare, my dear,' Rosemary murmured.

'Rosemary,' the Brigadier called from the upper room, 'we mustn't be too late. Phyllis has a long journey in the morning . . .'

'Go away,' Bless whispered. 'Sell up here. Start again somewhere new.' He shrugged and shook his head. 'Have your happiness. Why not? What possible harm does it do to anyone?'

Rosemary stared for a moment longer, then she moved her head in an almost imperceptible nod. 'Yes, dear,' she called. 'Mr Hudson is just going.'

'Tell him goodbye from me,' Phyllis called from the upper room. 'Tell him . . . I enjoyed our tea together.'

'Yes, dear,' Rosemary called, and she took Bless's hands in hers and patted them. 'Good night!' she said.

48

A Key Change

When he returned, most of the guests had departed. Mrs Day was sitting on a chair on the terrace with her head in her hands. 'Cor, dear!' she said when she saw him. 'I feel as though I've been through an 'edge backwards.'

The vicar and his wife were just leaving, but paused when they saw him and came back towards him. They were walking with their arms round each other – Andrew holding Margaret's shoulders and she with an arm round his waist. They both looked surprisingly, remarkably, blissfully happy.

Margaret called out, 'It was such a lovely party, Mr . . .'

'Maynard,' Bless told her firmly, determined that at least the vicar and his wife would know him by his correct name – if not, then one day there could be terrible confusion on his gravestone.

Rich appeared, coming out of the drawing room and looking flustered. 'I wouldn't go in the kitchen if I were you,' he said as he approached.

'Oh, God!' Bless groaned, then he snapped his fingers. 'Sorry, Vicar!'

'Oh, God!' Andrew Skrimshaw laughed. 'He doesn't mind!

That's what he's there for – to cry out to! What has happened in the kitchen? Anything we can help with?'

'I'm not quite sure,' Rich said. 'It looks as if we've had vandals in.'

'It's my sister, dear,' Doris Day called. 'She never could hold her drink.'

'But what was she doing in our cupboards?' Rich asked.

'Ah! She's a rum one, dear,' Doris told him, lowering her voice. 'She 'as some very funny 'abits. Not to worry. I'll be in in the morning. Make everything lovely and shipshape.'

'I just wanted to say,' the vicar cut in, 'it couldn't have been Diana Simpson . . . The lass that the Contessa mistook, she couldn't have been Ms Simpson . . .'

'No,' Bless said, not wanting to pick over the details.

'I've spoken to her, you see. She's gone into a retreat up in Scotland – with some Buddhist nuns. I rather think she may be going to join the order – but of course it's early days.' He shook his head. 'Pity, really! I had thought she was one of ours.'

'Come along, Andrew,' his wife said, tugging at his arm. 'Time for bed!' and she smiled shyly. She couldn't remember the last time she'd been in a hurry for bed. 'A really lovely party. It went with quite a swing!'

'Yes! You could say that!' Rich said wryly, looking round at the fallen chairs, the scattered glasses and the empty bottles.

'Oh!' the vicar called from halfway across the lawn. 'Ms Simpson said would you look after Pinky and she'll get in touch later. Good night.' He waved cheerfully. 'Good night, everyone!' And he and his wife fairly ran away through the stable yard, heading for their double bed.

'Oh, shit!' Rich groaned. 'Who's Pinky?'

'I haven't a clue,' Bless admitted thoughtfully.

'Another stranger?' Rich moaned, and he started to stack the village hall chairs into some sort of order.

Laurence came out from the drawing room. He was carrying a mug of something hot. 'There's the most terrible mess in your kitchen,' he said, as he sauntered over to the piano, holding the mug gingerly, trying not to spill the contents. He closed the lid of the piano and put a pile of Rosemary's music on top. Then he set the hot mug down on the music, so as not to mark the wood. He sat down, adjusted the stool and ran his fingers lightly up the keys. 'Not bad!' he said, and he started to play quietly. His opening piece was 'Poor Little Rich Girl' – in a surprisingly jazzy version. 'Just warming up!' he called.

'Good!' Rich answered, taking the empty cigarette box and lighter that Heather Daltry had commandeered back into the drawing room.

Bless was collecting empty bottles and putting them under the trestle table. 'I don't know where all these things came from,' he called. 'The table. The chairs. How do we get the piano back? Carlotta was supposed to have arranged it all.' No one answered him, so he went on collecting glasses and bottles and stacking them on the table anyway. 'I don't think it'll rain,' he said to himself. 'It can all wait till tomorrow.'

Maggie came out of the house. She was holding a glass of red wine. She walked over to the piano, where Laurence was now playing 'The Party's Over' – the Coward song, not the one from *Bells Are Ringing*. She joined in, singing the words for a few bars and then asked: 'Do you speak Italian, Mr Fielding?'

'A little, but I'm frightfully rusty.'

'I thought you might. You have the look of an educated man!'

'Thank you!'

'What does "Torni un po' piú tardi" mean? I didn't like to ask Antonio. Being his family motto,' she gave the words a grand ring, 'it seemed rather personal!'

'You were worried about being too personal?' Laurence asked with incredulity. 'After all you'd been doing together?'

Maggie shrugged. 'I'm just a quaint, old-fashioned girl.'

'Now let me see. "Torni un po' piú tardi" . . . Something "a little later".' He puzzled and frowned. 'I think it means: "Come back later".'

Maggie thought about this for a moment, then laughed. 'I think it an entirely suitable motto for the Braganizio family. I can tell you first hand – the second son kept coming with admirable regularity!'

'Mmmh!' Laurence mused, running his fingers over the piano keys. 'I'll have to think about that!'

'D'you know "Secret Love", dear?' Mrs Day asked, staggering across and sitting on the stool beside him. And she started to sing a distant approximation of the words as Laurence vamped in an appropriate key.

After a moment Maggie joined in, singing the standard version of the lyrics.

'Oh, lovely!' Doris said, full of bonhomie. And putting her head on Laurence's shoulder, she nodded off to sleep again.

'It's her car!' Bless called, seeing Rich come out on to the terrace.

'What is?'

'Pinky! I suddenly remembered. It's Diana Simpson's car – and it's in one of our stables.'

Rich looked gloomy. 'D'you think I'll ever catch up on all that's been going on here?' he asked.

'I doubt it!' Bless told him. Laurence was now playing Cole Porter and Bless stopped clearing glasses and crossed to his lover. 'Are yer dancin'?' he asked.

'Are yer askin'?'

'I'm askin'!'

'Then I'm dancin'!' Rich told him, and he put his arms round him and the two men slowly moved across the lamp-lit lawn, holding each other close and forgetting that anyone else was there.

'Do you ever feel lonely, Mr Fielding?' Maggie asked, watching them.

'Most of the time,' Laurence replied.

'I am so sorry,' she said, with genuine sympathy.

'I've grown used to it. Besides, it has been of my own making. I never had . . . the courage, you see.'

'You and me both,' Maggie agreed.

'Are you and the delicious Italian not destined for life's highway, then?'

'No!' Maggie laughed quietly. 'You don't settle down with people like that – they're too . . . fantastical. Can you imagine having spots, or an upset stomach . . . can you imagine sitting down to breakfast with someone like that?'

'Is breakfast so important?' Laurence asked, changing to another tune.

'Sometimes you have to be ordinary. Sometimes you have to be fat and flabby. I couldn't be! Not with Antonio!' And hearing Laurence playing 'Ev'ry Time We Say Goodbye', she started to sing the words quietly.

Rich and Bless moved slowly in time to the music, their cheeks close together, their arms encircling each other. Rich put his fingers up into Bless's thick hair and slipped off the elastic band, so that the ponytail fell free.

'Oh, look!' Mrs Day said, opening her bleary eyes. 'Don't they make a lovely couple?'

'Yes!' Maggie said, and she nodded and started to cry.

'Don't cry, lovey!' the old woman told her, reaching up and massaging her shoulder. 'There's always someone for everyone. You'll see. Don't rush in . . .'

Maggie drew a steadying breath and continued singing.

'Excellent, Miss Heston,' Laurence told her, sounding genuinely impressed. 'You really are . . . very good!'

'That's lovely, dear,' Mrs Day said, and standing up she put her arm round Maggie and they both leaned back against the side of the piano. 'Play it again, Mr What-ever-your-name is. Play it again, dear.' And, as Laurence did so, both Maggie and Mrs Day continued the song together, more or less in unison.

'Why, Doris!' Bless called. 'I didn't know that was one of your songs!'

'I know a lot of different tunes, Mr 'Udson,' she called.

'Who is Mr Hudson?' Rich asked.

'Don't ask!' Bless told him, and kissed him long and deep, with both his hands holding Rich's face, as their bodies slowly moved and turned with the music.

'I love you so much!' Rich told him when their mouths finally parted.

'I love you too!' Bless said, and with a sudden surge of emotion he clung to Rich with both his arms.

'You go on, dear,' Doris said to Maggie. 'It's a young girl's song.' And she stood back listening as Maggie continued to sing.

'Hit it, Heston!' Bless called from across the lawn.

Rich looked over Bless's shoulder at Maggie leaning against the piano, poised, elegant and in complete control.

'That really is quite a voice,' he said.

'What happened tonight,' Bless whispered. 'There's something I can't tell you. But I don't want to have any secrets from you. What do I do about that?'

'There is a difference between privacy and deceit,' Rich told him, still listening to Maggie and holding his lover gratefully in his arms. 'Is it about the Brigadier?'

'How did you guess?'

'I saw where you went. I saw how you looked when you came back . . .'

'I promised not to say anything . . .'

'Then don't!'

Behind them Maggie's voice broke gently from the major to the minor key as she sang her heart out with effortless ease.

'God, Bless!' Rich whispered. 'She's fabulous!'

'I told you!' Bless told him, brimming with pride. And, as if to confirm something, Rich kissed him hard on the lips.

'Oo-er, look at 'em now, dears!' Mrs Day gasped. 'Did you ever see the like! Cor! Whatever would Miss Price think if she knew? Well, there you are! Just like I said. Two gentlemen, sharing!'

And so they were; two gentlemen sharing – at last.